THE TEMPLE BUILDERS

By Loyst R. Streeter

There are three types of people in the world:
The Builders, the Users, and the Destroyers.

This is a story of the builders

The Temple Builders

Published by Sharron Press Publishers, LLC
P.O. Box 594
Sublimity, OR 97385

Library of Congress Control Number

2007901728

ISBN-13: 978-0-9718130-2-1

Printed in the United States

To Sharron

With Love

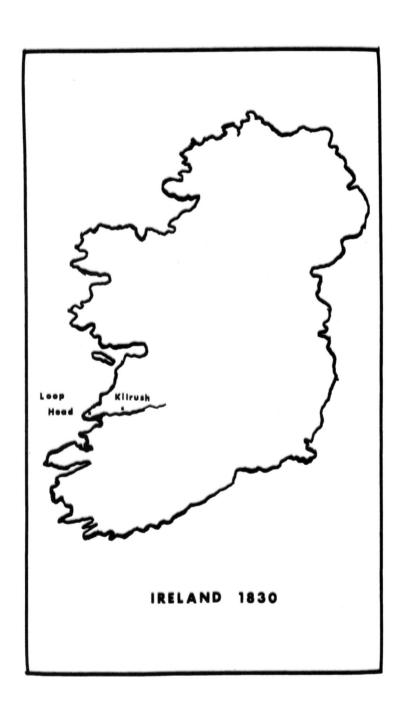

Loop Head   Kilrush

IRELAND 1830

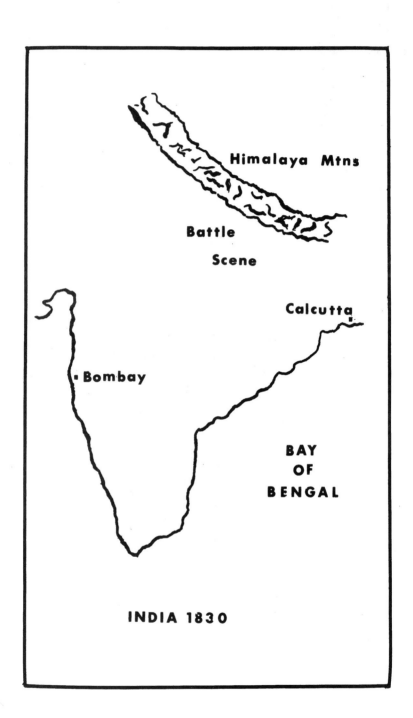

Forward

This book is a work of fiction.

The Reader should note that while actual historical events; political actions; important legislation; buildings; geographical features; and the names of key political leaders have been incorporated into this novel; all of the remaining characters are purely fictitious. Any resemblance between them and persons living or dead is purely coincidental.

The dialog attributed between historical and fictional characters has been created to further the story, and is not intended to imply or suggest that such discussions ever took place. However, the subject of these imaginary conversations, corresponds to recorded historical events.

Preface

The history of Ireland has been intrinsically bound and interwoven with that of England and Scotland for over a thousand years. For centuries, both Ireland and Scotland independently waged intermittent wars with England in an attempt to free themselves from British rule. But although there was political animosity between the three nations, they were united by a single religious faith, Roman Catholicism. In the early sixteenth century however, a series of great historical events transpired, which forever changed that common bond, and resulted in the escalation of enmity between them.

Simultaneously throughout Europe, the sixteenth century witnessed the sweeping transformations precipitated by Reformation and the Renaissance. As never before in history, the power of the Roman Catholic Church was being challenged and threatened on both the theological and political fronts. In 1534, the English King Henry VIII, requested the Pope to grant him a divorce from Catherine of Aragon who had failed to give him a son. When his request was denied, the King seized upon the Pope's refusal as an excuse to break England's religious and political ties with Rome. Parliament quickly passed the Act of Supremacy, which renounced all papal authority, and established the Church of England with Henry VIII as its titular authority.

No sooner had England had become a protestant nation, than Scotland followed suit. The Presbyterian Church founded by John Calvin, the French theologian and reformer, sent missionaries to Scotland. In the space of a few years, almost all of Scotland's Catholics were converted to Protestantism, and the Church of Scotland was established. Now flanked by two protestant nations; Scotland to the east and England on the south; Ireland alone remained faithful to the Roman Catholic Church. As a consequence, it became the nexus of religious political intrigue and papal plots to over throw the kings and queens of England. In retribution, the Irish Catholics found themselves continually being targeted by the English Parliament, which enacted numerous repressive anti-Catholic measures. In addition, Parliament sought to further weaken Ireland by opening its borders to English and Scottish immigrants.

In the years that followed, Northern Ireland became a Protestant bastion and eventually wrested political power from the Catholic south. In 1690, James II attempted to regain the throne of England and introduce a policy of religious toleration toward Roman Catholicism; although many believed he intended to make it the state religion. His army, composed of Irish Catholics; was defeated by William of Orange at the battle of Boyne. Thus with each succeeding generation the hatred between the Protestants and Catholics grew, and with it the burning desire of the Irish to free themselves from the growing English tyranny and oppression.

The Irish chance of independence came again in 1798 while England was fighting for its life against France. With the aid of French troops and money; Ireland seized upon the conflict to break the shackles of six centuries of English rule.   The rebellion was short lived, and was savagely crushed three weeks later at the cost of the lives of 30,000 Irish men and women. Fearing future uprisings; England increased its army in Ireland to over 100,000 men and tightened its grip - with more hope than belief - that any future rebellion would be impossible.

On January 1, 1801; to further secure its hold on Ireland; the Act of Union between England and Ireland was signed into law, joining the two Countries both politically and economically. The Irish Parliament, which previously had met in Dublin, Ireland was dissolved; and the Parliament at Westminster England became the governing body for both nations. Public pronouncements before the historic vote proclaimed that this union would greatly benefit Ireland. Passage of the Act, it was claimed; would put an end to centuries of discrimination; greatly increase free trade; result in more capital investments in Ireland; the emancipation of the Catholics; and provide Ireland with a new voice in her political affairs. In reality however, England intentions were not to aid Ireland, but to further bring her into subjection. There had been several Irish leaders who clearly saw the proposed Act of Union for the deceitful subterfuge that it was. Tragically, their attempts to stop the legislation's passage was doomed by massive bribery; including the granting of English titles that were later to be known as Union titles.

In the years that followed, the promised reform was forgotten. There was neither increased investment nor free trade; with the result that the Irish industry which had previously existed; mostly mining, fishing, and woolen goods; collapsed and unemployment escalated. The Catholics, who comprised seventy-five percent of the population, were not emancipated; and were still denied the right to hold public office; vote; or purchase land; and the men barred from military service. The Irish Catholics could neither send their children to local schools, or send them to other countries for their education. Upon the death of a Catholic landowner, the estate was broken up and divided among the sons to dissipate the wealth and potential political power. If however, the eldest son became a Protestant, he inherited the entire estate. If anything, the Act of Union served to increase discrimination.

With the demise of Irish industry, workers were forced to turn to the land to survive. The great estates, most of which were owned by absentee English landlords, were turned over to their agents and overseers who divided up the land into small parcels and rented them at exorbitant rates to the desperate families who now subsisted on what they could grow on their little patch of land. In times past, a family would typically work three to five acres. In good years, a family of five could survive on the potatoes harvested from an acre and a half, and the excess crop provided a source of income for paying the land rental fee and other necessities.

As the demand for land increased however, due to the unemployed workers, greedy agents reduced the size of the parcels to as little as a quarter of an acre, while at the same time increasing the rental fees. Furthermore, land leases, which previously had been signed for a period of years, were replaced by a Contract to Occupy, which limited the rental of the land to grow only one crop. Under the new system, the occupants even lost whatever tenants rights had existed under the leases. Families unable to pay the rent were driven off the land. Barring help from relatives or friends, the majority of whom themselves were struggling to survive, the landless were left to wander and starve.

Poverty increased rapidly. The homes and neat little cottages which were common before the Union Act; were soon replaced by one room windowless mud huts in which over half the population lived. Furniture became a luxury few could afford. Less than one person in a thousand had a bed. There were thousands upon thousands for whom even the mud hut was beyond reach; and who lived in ditches over which they placed a few branches for shelter. Thousands more lived in holes dug into the ground. The need for medical services, which greatly increased as a result of growing unsanitary living conditions, were all but forgotten. Major cities and towns might have one clinic for 6,000 to 20,000 people. In the rural areas, an entire county with a population in excess of 250,000 would be served by a single clinic, which, more often than not did not have supplies sufficient for a small town, let alone a county.

Reason would suggest that such grinding poverty and lack of hope would reduce the dream of marriage and raising children, but the oppression had the opposite effect. With little hope of a better future, young people married for what little joy they could squeeze from life. The attitude became that of, 'why wait, nothing is going to get better.' Further, they reasoned that as long as the earth produced a good crop of potatoes, there was always enough food to feed them, their children, and livestock. While their reasoning was correct regarding the scant hope of the political situation improving; their belief that the fertile Irish soil would always supply them with an abundance of potatoes was to prove fatally wrong.

Potatoes, because they could not be stored for long periods of time such as grains, quickly become the source of widespread calamity. The most dangerous times were the summer months when the last of the old crop was consumed, and before the new crop could be harvested. During these weeks, if the old potatoes ran out, the families were forced to buy grain at outrageous prices. And if the new crop should fail, complete disaster could ensue.

Tragically, potatoes which had literally become the life blood of the Irish, proved particularly susceptible to failure. There had been over twenty crop failures during the previous century, but those in the early part of the 1800's were localized to particular districts. Thus while the potato was well known to be unreliable, no effort was made to find a replacement crop. One reason was that potatoes were cheap and easy to grow, required no special tools or farm equipment, and unlike grain, they needed no processing before consumption. Anyone with a plot of ground and a stick to dig a planting hole could raise them. The common potato was at one and the same time, the source of salvation to the Irish; and also the means of plunging them into horrible famine; unimaginable misery; and death. On this single unstable crop, the entire economy and very survival of the Irish population precariously balanced on a razors edge from year to year, and generation after generation.

Ireland 1830

Kilrush was a small village in southwest Ireland on the north side of the River Shannon, approximately twenty miles east of Loop Head where the river empties into the North Atlantic Ocean. The land is gently rolling grass lands that very slowly rise from sea level to no more than 250'; it is very stony ground. Large stones, small stones, middle sized stones, tiny stones, scattered over the land as if a giant hand had sprinkled salt on a sea of green. Generation after generation had gathered the stones from the land, and built low walls around their fields. They used millions upon millions of stones to build roads; byres for the cattle; tens of thousands of homes and cottages; hundreds of churches; great castles; scores of elegant manor houses; and still the hills and the fields overflowed with stones.

This story is about the people who were born; grew-up; lived; worked; married; raised their families; struggled; wept; laughed; died; and were buried in and around these stony green hills.

Chapter 1

Colin Cunningham, at age 17 was unusually large. At 6' 2" weighing over 200 pounds of lean muscle and crowned by a shock of reddish brown hair, he was a young man who had become something of a local legend. What was remarkable about his reputation as a street fighter, was that beneath that brawling veneer was the quiet soul of a poet. By the time he was twelve he weighed 160 pounds and had learned that his overgrown frame made him a target of every would-be bully. To survive and avoid fighting, he began creating an image and reputation of being a brawling kid always ready to punch out anyone who chanced to get in his way. By the time he was fourteen he had added another twenty pounds and there were no more local boys willing to challenge him.

Despite the fact that no one could ever say with certainty that they had ever seen him fight with anyone, the general conscientious was to keep well clear of him. Only once when he was sixteen did Sean Egan, the town bully in Kilrush, challenge him.

Sean, who was twenty-seven at the time, was the eldest son of Kevin Egan, a decent hard working fisherman who had been swept overboard during a sudden storm and drowned off the mouth of the River Shannon when Sean was nine years old. Like many of the widows of the time with no source of income to raise seven children, Carrie Egan set up a Still and began brewing poteen, an illegal white, mountain type brew. Sean, who early on had shown signs of rebellion, quickly seized upon his father's death as an opportunity to bully his younger brothers and sisters.

By the age of fourteen, he was regularly stealing poteen from his mother's Still and becoming more violent. When neighbors would ask his mother about the bruises on her arms or face, she would reply that they were the result of a fall. She fooled no one.

At sixteen, Sean, tired of having to do what little work he did at home, set out on his own. He was a hansom lad who looked older than his age and possessed natural charm; two qualities that in time proved to be his undoing. When he was sober, which became less and less as he grew older, his good looks and easy way with girls and women quickly proved to be the ticket to live a life of idleness.

He drifted from town to town, worked occasional odd jobs, but mostly lived off the money given to him by lonely foolish women whose husbands worked twelve to fourteen hours a day; and who returned home too tired to do anything more than eat and fall into bed asleep. If Sean had used even the slightest amount of common sense, he would have moved to London where young men with half his wit and charm lived lives of comfort and ease; paid for by silly older women of independent means.

But Kilrush was not London, and the few sparsely populated towns and surrounding area was too small to hide his growing reputation. By the time he reached his twenty-fifth birthday, there were very few women who had not heard of him. Whispers had long since turned to open talk of how he had abused any number of women and girls. Now when they saw him coming, they crossed to the other side of the street. Fortunately, the girls and women who had fallen victim to his charms were spared the added tragedy of pregnancy. After their brief affair, each would confess their transgressions to the local priest, and bless Mother Mary for saving them from the ultimate humiliation of a having a bastard child. In fact, Mother Mary had nothing to do with their good fortune. Sean had become sterile at fifteen; the result of a kick in the groin by a sick cow he was attempting to milk.

His reputation; having spread throughout the region, ended the easy life. His once good looks had been chipped away by countless brawls in which he generally emerged the victor, but at the cost of another scar or lost tooth. There were still a few men who would hire him for the occasional odd job providing it was nowhere near their homes, wives, and daughters. His time between jobs which increasingly grew longer, was spent in the local pubs spending the few shillings he earned. Unable to afford a place to live, he cleaned the local stable in exchange for a place to sleep in the back room.

At age twenty-seven, Sean had become a mean drunk and a bully. An angry man who looked out upon a world which, he had convinced himself, had treated him badly and never gave him a chance. And since the chance for wealth and a life of ease had eluded him; he seized upon whatever opportunities that came his way to bash and humiliate anyone whom he imagined to be more fortunate than his self. On this particular day, fate decreed it would be Colin Cunningham.

It happened one morning as Colin walked to town to pick up a hoe the blacksmith had repaired for his father. As he was leaving the blacksmith's shop, Sean chanced to step out of the Pub just in time to see him pass by. Feeling very superior at the moment, a belief strengthened by a couple of pints of beer, he called out to Colin and challenged him to a fight to see which was the better man. Colin glanced at him leaning against the porch rail. He had no desire to get in a fight with a man several years his senior and well known as a dirty street fighter. Sean hurled several insulting taunts as Colin turned away and continued walking, smiling to himself as he recalled his mother's words to him when he was a small child, '...Sticks and stones may break your bones, but names will never hurt you.' Somehow, that simple little phrase had taken root and become a part of his character to the point that it was almost impossible to rile him with insults or profanity. Colin simply refused to be challenged by insults that would have enraged most other men. Insults which invariably led titled gentlemen to resort to swords, or guns, and the rules of the infamous Code Duello.

Colin and Sean were vaguely familiar with the basic terms of the Code Duello; the unofficial Code that set forth the fine points of preserving ones personal honor. Technically speaking; the Code, and its 36 rules which had been adopted in Ireland in 1777; dealt with issuing and answering a challenge and had been intended only for gentlemen. Copies however, had drifted down into the lower classes of society, and were discussed and argued far into the night at local pubs. Few books had ever provided so much entertainment as did the Code Duello.

Following a couple of pints of beer, any tiny bump or nudge at the bar was sufficient reason to challenge the offender. Great care was taken to lay down the challenge as they imagined a gentleman would, and equal care was given in accepting it. Seconds were chosen as the other patrons moved the tables back to make room. Bare knuckles were the weapons of choice, and each man was allowed only one punch. Since both men were tipsy more often than not, it was seldom that anyone got hurt. The sole function of the seconds was to hold the combatants mugs of beer. After the mock duel, the occasion called for another round of drinks regardless of who won. Mean drunks and bullies however, were something else. Their taunts and jeers were not made in jest, but were purely intended to draw the selected victim into a fight.

Sean, seeing that his insults did not have the desired effect, redirected his sharp tongue not against Colin, but his mother Kathleen.

Colin was perhaps a half block away with his back to Sean when he heard him yell out in a loud voice that his mother was a whore. He stopped and turned to see Sean laughing, yelling, and making crude gestures to people in the street as to what Colin's mother did best. In truth, Sean knew very well she was well known and respected, but the vicious slander did its work.

"I'm sorry Mum", Colin muttered to himself as he turned and headed back toward the tavern. While he seriously doubted that anyone would consider Sean's taunts to be true, the mere possibility of such a slander against his mother being repeated, or left unchallenged was too much to bear. "The name's they call me don't trouble me none, but I canna abide the likes of that drunk talking about ye that way."

"Well, well", Sean called out as he watched Colin turn. "If it ain't the whore's son himself coming back ta get his ass kicked."

Anticipating a fight, a small crowd of men had begun to gather. "I feel sorry for the Lad," one remarked to the man standing next to him.

"Aye. Before he knows what's happnin that dirty drunkard will kick him in the jewels, and then kick him in the head when he's down." He took a puff on his pipe and added, "Blessed Mary, we've seen it too many times before have we not?" Several of the men nodded in agreement.

"But maybe this time it'll be different, Aye?"

"Ah, it would be a glorious day ta see the Lad whip him. He's big enough, but he's no match fer Sean. Still, t'would be Glorious indeed", he said crossing himself and glancing skyward. "Mother Mary, let this be the day,"

Colin handed the hoe to one of the men nearby who whispered, "watch out Lad, he'll try and kick ye first, or throw dirt in yer eyes." Colin nodded a thank you, and walked over to where Sean was still casually leaning against the rail, laughing.

Colin was trembling so much that he was afraid to speak, but he was resolved to defend his mother's honor even if it meant taking a beating. Sean jumped off the porch to the street and they began circling each other looking for an opening, while trying to avoid the small puddles of water left over from the rain the day before. Sean continued to taunt Colin as they jockeyed for position. He had learned long ago that the easiest man to defeat, was one who became blind with rage. He could see from Colin's white knuckles that he was mad; but his eyes were steady and cool...too cool. Something within him told him that maybe he had made a mistake; but there was no turning back now. Besides he told himself, a slight grin curling his lips; Colin was only a big overgrown kid.

Suddenly, Sean's left foot shot out in the expected kick to the groin. The attempt was clumsy, and Colin easily avoided it as he stepped back into a small puddle. He countered with a right swing. As his arm swept forward, his right foot accidentally slipped forward in the mud throwing his entire body weight forward behind the punch. By a stroke more of luck than skill - or divine providence depending upon who later told the story - his first blow caught his opponent alongside the head just forward of his left ear. There was a crunch of bone as Colin's huge clenched fist powered by 200 pounds of muscle connected with Sean's jaw. The tremendous force of the blow sent Sean staggering backward. He stumbled, tripping over his own feet, and crashed down on his right elbow, shattering his upper arm on impact.

For a few seconds, unaware of the severity of Sean's injuries, Colin stood poised waiting for him to get up. Encouraged by having knocked his opponent down, he yelled out, " Apologize for what ye said about my Mum." "Ye heard me, apologize for what ye ...." his voice stopped suddenly as he saw the blood began squirting from the broken bone protruding from Sean's arm above his elbow.

"He can na answer ye Lad," a bystander called out. "His jaw is busted up good."

Colin turned his eyes away from the mangled arm and looked into Sean's eyes. A few seconds ago, he had expected this bully to beat him. Now Sean was lying in the street, his eyes wild with pain, blood dripping from his arm, and his face contorted by the smashed jawbone. Lowering his arms and unclenching his fists, Colin turned and looked for the man holding his hoe.

"He should na have said those bad things about my Mum," he said to the man holding the hoe. Taking back the hoe, he quietly headed down the street toward home, wondering to himself if this fight would lead to other fights. Maybe a bully in another town would now decide to take him on; would he have to fight him? and maybe others after him? What should he tell his mother about the fight? These and other thoughts troubled him all the way home.

In reality, as for future fights he had no need to worry. Once word about Sean's severe injuries became known, any lad or man who had given thought to fighting Colin quickly departed; especially when the story tellers, and there were very many; demonstrated the amazing feat exclaiming, "with one glorious punch mind ye."

For several minutes the men who had gathered around to watch the fight, stood silently still looking down at Sean lying in the dirt. For years they had waited for someone to come along and give the bully a real beating. Now it had happened, and Sean lay there in agony. As if breaking out of a trance one man called out, "we better get 'em inside, is anybody here who can tend his wounds?"

"The Doc's up County, will na be back for a week," a voice from the back of the crowd called.

"Well somebody's got ta tend to him now or he'll be dead before the Doc gets back."

Two men stepped forward and tried to pick up Sean as gently as possible, and carry him into the back room of the Pub where he lived. Twenty minutes ago, they would have loved to bash Sean themselves, now they were doing everything possible not to cause him any more pain. Perhaps it was because they could see that Sean would never bother anyone again, not physically anyway.

"Do ye reckon that Kathleen would fix him up?" a man in a tattered sweater asked.

"Kathleen?" one of the carriers replied. "Are ye daft man, she's Colin's mother."

"Aye, Colin's mother she is," the man replied glancing around, "I guess I wasn't thinkin."

"And even if'n she weren't," another exclaimed, "not twenty minutes ago, Sean here was standin in the street callin her a whore."

"Well, with the doc gone, looks like Sean ..."

At that moment Bridgit, a woman who had been in a store across the street when she heard about the fight and Sean's injuries, walked in. She glanced quickly at Sean and was shocked, nothing had been done except to carry him inside and lay him on his cot. "I can na believe how worthless ye are leaving him like this." Seeing that none of the men were doing anything to help, she added in jest, "as usual men are only good for talkin, drinkin, and fightin." She then hastily asked the men to step aside and let a woman get to work.

"One of ye lads bring me some hot water and clean rags," she said to no one in particular. "We kin at least clean the mud off, and try ta stop some of the bleedin. With the bunch of ye standin about gabbin, it's surprizin that he ain't bled ta death already."

"Ah, Brigit my love," one of the men chided, "we were waitin for yer own sweet self. Ain't it so boys?"

"True enough," another replied.

"And don't ye be callin me yer love, Johnny," she said as she gave his hand a squeeze , "or I'll be tellin yer Martha ye been flirtin with me agin."

Bridgit was twenty-five years old, and a spinster by choice. When she was fifteen, Tom, the boy whom she had been in love with and planned to marry, was killed by a crazed bull that had broken loose and was about to attack his little sister. Without hesitation he ran up and whacked the bull with a scrap of lumber that was lying on the ground hoping to drive him off. Unexpectedly, the bull turned suddenly and caught him on one of his horns. In seconds, Tom was lying on the ground dying with a tragic bewildered look on his face. Bridgit held his head in her lap as his life ebbed with the blood flowing from the terrible wound in his side. Unseen by the onlookers; Bridgit's love which had been at flood, also ebbed and died. Not love of life, but the deep love that bonds and unites a boy and girl, a man and woman.

During Tom's wake, she quietly stood along side the coffin looking at his still body; his big toes tied together so that he would not return as a ghost. She didn't believe that superstition, but it was done to calm the fears of her aged grandmother who still believed in many of the old superstitions; including opening all the windows and doors to let the spirits out of the building; and fairies, and the little folk; especially the fairies who could steal a person's soul. Later that evening when the grieving was past and the wake became festive; she quietly remained by his side, her hand on his.

The following day as his body was laid to rest, she quietly vowed that never again would she love so intently, or completely, and would remain unmarried. A vow the townsfolk and Priests believed to be that of a grief stricken young girl, which would pass with time.

Time however, did not diminish the strength of her decision. With long raven black hair, deep blue eyes, and a peaches and cream complexion, she had been very pretty as a young girl. The years had brought her maturity and beauty rarely seen; she was unquestionably one of the most beautiful women in Clare County, perhaps even in all of Ireland. When she was still a young girl, numerous village boys tried to date her; and for many years later various men, some good and honest, others sly and conning, tried to woo her to no avail. But while she would never consent to being courted, she did enjoy public dancing and kidding with the men, and they with her. Over the years, her remarkable stainless reputation was such, that there wasn't a wife or sweetheart of any man who considered her anything but a friend. However, they still kept a close eye on their husbands, and prayed daily to the Blessed Mother that the right man would come along and marry her.

Well, that wasn't entirely quite true. There were several women her age who had married and now had five, six, and in one case, seven children. When they looked at themselves in the mirror, they saw bodies half worn out; their once firm perky breasts were now sagging, almost flat, the result of nursing numerous children. The cares and anxieties of raising a family had plowed deep furrows into their once youthful faces; and their hands had become callused and sinewy, rubbed raw from constant washing and gardening. When they looked at Bridgit, they saw what they had once been, and might still be but for marriage and their children.

Only two things kept the natural resentment from erupting: their love for their children; and the fact that Bridgit was the first to help anyone in time of need. When a baby was born, she was there to help care for the other children; if there was sickness, she was there with the pot of hot soup, or the cooked chicken. It was hard to hate an angel. As for the men, in fairness it must also be reported that there were any number of men who looked at Bridgit and wished their wives were half as attractive and sweet.

In the years that followed; she became the finest seamstress in the County, and most of her work was commissioned by the wives of the wealthy landowners. She developed a great love for nature and began the habit of taking long walks early in the morning. Only a severe rain storm or the rare winter blizzard would keep her indoors. After her parents passed away, she continued to live alone in the little cottage she was born and grew up in; and as long as the weather permitted she worked in a little side porch her father had built for her.

It had been on one of her walks several years ago that she encountered Kathleen, Colin's mother, who was on her way to treat a woman who had broken her arm in a bad fall. Bridgit asked if she could come along and perhaps help. As they walked and talked, they soon discovered that there was something in their natures, a kindred spirit, which almost immediately bonded the women together. Thereafter whenever she had the time, Bridgit began to assist Kathleen. Consequently, when a neighbor saw her in a local store that morning and told her about the fight and its outcome, she immediately left the store and headed for the Pub. She never doubted for a moment that when Kathleen learned of the fight she would come.

As he topped the rise and started down the path toward home, Colin could see his mother working in the field; she looked up saw him, waived, and returned to her work. As he got closer she called without looking up,

"You're late. Wasn't the hoe ready?" When he didn't reply she stopped and glanced at him. With a mother's intuition, she sensed something was amiss. She could see now that he was carrying the hoe, and as he approached her she saw the blood on his shirt. "You're hurt," she yelled dropping the rake and running toward him.

"Na, Mother I'm not hurt. Tis Sean's blood."

"Sean! Did ye have a fight with him? Oh Colin, I've told ye a thousand times ta stay away from him, she said has she pulled him into her arms and ran her hands over the blood splattered shirt. "He could've killed ye."

"Aye, maybe so. But he won't be hurtin anyone anymore."

She pulled away, "what do ye mean by that? Is he dead?"

"No, but he's hurt, real bad. His arm and jaw are broken. He was still lying in the dirt in front of the Pub when I left."

"And what about yer self, do ye have any broken bones, cuts, bruises? Who started the fight? What was the fight about?"

"Mum, I'm ok, not even a scratch," he said turning around for her inspection. He reached down and took her hands in his. "Sean started it, and I could na walk away this time."

He told her the story as they walked toward the house, and she felt a warm rush of pride hearing how her son had fought to protect her honor. Standing slightly over six feet, Kathleen was a solid big boned woman, and stronger than most men. Her father, who in his prime had been 6'5" and 280 pounds, had been a giant among his contemporaries.

Much to the dismay of her mother, she inherited her father's genes, including his large hands, ruddy complexion, and unruly brown hair – now streaked with gray -. Whatever good looks she may have had as a very young girl, had vanished as moonlight with the rising sun as she advanced into middle age. But the gods were kind to her, for whatever they took in beauty, they replaced with an abundance of patience, grace, and love for those around her.

"My own Sir Galahad," she said squeezing his hand. "We need ta clean yer shirt before the stains set and ..."she stopped, "what about Sean, who's taking care of him?, was anyone there ta help him?"

"I do na know Mum. He was still layin in the dirt when I left."

She was now busy gathering up what medical supplies she had, and talking over her shoulder. "Doctor Cain's up north, away for several days. From what ye said, Sean's not likely ta last till he gets back. Walk back ta town with me, I'll need yer help"

Colin watched his mother with admiration. It was from her side of the family that Colin inherited his size, strength and gentleness. As he watched her scurrying about packing her medical bag, he thought of what a remarkable person she was. Other mothers, most he suspected, would be thankful their son had survived, happy the other chap had been smashed up and let it go at that; but not her. Most of her life had been devoted to helping others at all hours of the day and night, hot summers, bitter winters, drought, or flood. If she could get to the one who needed help, she would go.

Her husband Tom and the children, had long ago learned that helping others was to her a calling from God himself. In her mind, it no longer mattered that Sean would have severely beaten Colin had things gone his way. Nor did she give a second thought about the terrible things he had said about her. Only one thought now occupied her mind, get to Sean as quickly as she could and do whatever she could to tend his injuries.

As for the medical supplies, she probably had more than the County clinic. Over the years she had unofficially become Doctor Cain's right hand assistant. And although she lacked any formal medical training, doctor Cain had taught her more than many nurses would ever know, including some minor surgery. She dropped a roll of clean cloth into her bag wondering how severe the arm fracture was. If the bones were broken and through the flesh as Colin said, she doubted it could be saved. She recalled that two years ago, one of the wealthy landowners had been thrown from his horse and broken his arm in a similar manner, and despite the efforts of the best London doctors he lost the arm. "But a life with one arm 'tis better than no life at all," she mumbled to herself as she closed the bag and set it on the table. She grabbed her sweater and called to Colin, "Up with ye and pick up that bag, it's haste we better be makin now."

Unaware that Kathleen was on her way to help, Bridgit was in the back of the Pub struggling to cope with Sean's injuries, which were far beyond her medical capabilities. She had done her best to clean off the mud and dried blood as best she could. A tourniquet had been wrapped above the break in his arm to stop the bleeding. Because she assumed that the arm would be lost, neither she nor the few men in the room made any effort to periodically loosen it.

Lacking any drugs to control pain, the men had tied Sean down to prevent him thrashing around causing any more injuries to himself, and then given him several shots of poteen which eventually put him in a semi-conscious stupor. Every now and then he would roll his eyes and pull at the restraints, but these efforts grew less and less as the alcohol took full effect. Fortunately for all concerned, Sean was the type of drinker that initially became belligerent and even violent, but a few drinks more put him under the table. He was at the point of completely passing out when Kathleen and Colin walked in to the room.

"Oh Mary Mother of Jesus", Bridgit exclaimed seeing them come through the door. "I was afeared that ye would na get here in time. He's bad, very bad. I do na know if ye can even keep him alive till Doctor Cain returns." She stepped aside to let Kathleen approach the cot. The men present removed their caps and also expressed their gratitude for her coming.

"Yer a true saint, ye are," one exclaimed.

"Ain't it so," another added looking around at the other men.

"Aye, that she is. Only a saint would come to help a devil like Sean. May the Blessed Mary bless ye Kathleen."

Quickly assessing the situation, she thanked Bridgit and the men for doing what they could. "Somebody loosen the tourniquet for a few seconds and then re-tighten it," she called while she rummaged through her bag, "though I'm doubtful the arm can be saved." She looked Sean over again, "first, let's see if we can fix that jaw."

"Don't see that much can be done. Fairly well smashed up," one volunteered. The others mumbled in agreement.

Kathleen paid them no heed and began by carefully probing along the jaw line. After determining that there was severe dislocation but no actual break, she started to gently move Sean's lower jaw. Pain shot through Sean's jaw and he regained consciousness just long enough to open his eyes and see Kathleen and Colin standing next to her. His eyes popped opened until the whites encircled the iris and then he passed out and his body went limp.

"Quickly," Kathleen called to Colin," I think I can get the jawbone back in the socket while he's unconscious. Ye hold his head very firmly like this," she demonstrated, "and I'll pull his jaw back into position."

"Mother of God!" one of the men exclaimed, ye cannot do that, that's the doctor's work. Besides, the jaw is broken. If'n ye pull on it, 'twill make it worse."

"'Tisn't broken, only dislocated," she replied. "And if we wait fer the doctor, it'll be too late to fix it. Colin, are ye ready?" He nodded, and tightly held Sean's head in a vise grip. She carefully wrapped her left hand with a thick cloth to protect her fingers in the event Sean's jaw snapped shut. Then placing her fingers inside his lower jaw she pulled it down and twisted it to the right. There was a faint but audible snap as the upper end of the jaw bone popped back into place. Bridgit and the men stared in silent amazement at the miracle they had just witnessed.

Kathleen stood back and carefully looked at Sean's face. Satisfied that the jawbone was ok, she turned to the others. "His face is swollen, but that'll start comin down. We'll still need ta tape his jaw ta keep it in place. Bridgit, did ye see any other cuts or injuries when ye cleaned him up?" "Aye, right his ankle is all puffy."

Kathleen examined it carefully. "Musta twisted it when he fell. Bridgit, make a plaster, pour in some liniment and bind it up. I'll see what I can do with his arm."

With fields over-flowing with rocks for folks to trip, stumble, and fall over; adults and children being kicked by horses and cows; and children falling out of trees, broken bones were common place. She had set many arms and legs over the years. But Sean's was not a simple common fracture. The bone had almost snapped in- two, and to complicate the injury, dirt had gotten into the wound. She was certain that if Doctor Cain had been there, he would have amputated the arm then and there, but she was not prepared to do that. She knew all to well that almost half of those who had an arm or leg amputated died within a few weeks. Suddenly, a remarkable thought entered her mind,

"Ye can all start prayin, and someone get me lots of hot water" she called out, "I'm gonna try ta save his arm." To everyone's amazement, she pulled a scalpel from her bag and everyone gasped as she cut Sean's arm open. A moment later one of the men returned with a kettle of hot water. First, she carefully cleaned away the dirt and carefully pushed the bones back inside. Then she did something even more remarkable. "I need a bottle of whisky," she said.

"Holy Mother of Jesus," one of the men replied, "she gonna start drinkin."

"Not in yer lifetime Willy," she replied. "I need it for him."

One of the men handed her a bottle, and they all watched as she poured some of the whisky into the open wound.

"Mother of God, what are ye doin?" several men called out.

"I do na really know. I jes felt Mother Mary telling me to do it. Bridgit, now we need ta bind his arm up with a splint ta hold it in place." She turned to the men, who were almost speechless from what they had just witnessed. Although she was very confident that she had done what she could do, she was not a doctor. "Now we'll just have ta hope that the doctor gets back early."

"He's gonna need tendin," she said to no one in particular, "an when the poteen wears off he's gonna have some terrible pain." She reached into her bag and pulled out a small bottle. "Who'll stay with him tonight?"

After some discussion, one of the men said he would stay until sun-up, but then he had to get back home.

"Here's a little opium," she said handing him the bottle. "When he wakes up give him something to eat and more poteen. Don't use this unless he gets really bad and starts thrashin around. That bottle's all I have, and his pain's gonna get worse before the doctor gets back. I'll be back tomarre after breakfast." Turning to Colin, "let's go home son."

Colin picked up her bag and they left through a side door and stepped outside. As they walked out into the street, she told Colin that even if the doctor got back in a day or two Sean's chances of survival were not good. And if gangrene took hold the infection could spread to the rest of his body before the Doctor could amputate his arm. She stopped and turned to Colin, "But for the Blessed Virgin watchin over ye, that coulda been yer self."

"I know Mum, I know."

They walked the rest of the way home in silence, each pondering in their mind all that had happened, and what good could come from it. Kathleen thought of her decision to pour that whisky into the wound. Had that really been the Blessed Virgin Mary that had whispered in her ear? and if so, why?

Word of the fight had quickly spread. First through Kilrush, then Kilkee, as far east as Clare, and west to Loop Head at the mouth of the River Shannon. Sean had been well known and a feared bully and hooligan having beaten up many men, and according to some rumors he even hit even a few women and children. First, came the news that he had been beaten very badly. Throughout the County many a pint was raised and downed to celebrate the occasion. Several days' later a rumor followed that gangrene had set in and the doctor had amputated his right arm. More pints were downed at the news that Sean would never fight again.

The news also made Colin something of a local hero, and also someone to be feared. Whether his punch was one of luck or skill was debated for months in the pubs. The few bye-standers who had actually witnessed the fight, were quick to capitalize on that fact. Wherever they went, they were offered a pint or two to relate the details of the now famous battle. With each telling the fight grew until Colin himself would have difficulty recognizing it as the one he had with Sean. As for how dangerous Colin might be, the general consensus was that it was better to err on the side of caution. No one challenged him again.

The following week Colin returned to town to have his boots repaired. Ryan, the blacksmith, waved his arm and called to him as he passed by the shop.

"Colin, might I be havin a word with ye." Colin walked over and stood in the open doorway watching crimson sparks fly as Ryan's heavy hammer begin flattening a red-hot piece of iron.

"How would ye like ta come and work fer me?" he said as he plunged the iron back into the white-hot coals. "Tis sure enough that ye have the strength," he said laughing. "And I need a good strong lad ta help me."

Colin said nothing as he watched the iron begin to glow red then white.

"Of course if your folks need ye at home..."

"Oh no", he blurted out. "Matter of fact, tomarree I was headin down to the docks to see if I could get some work on a fishing boat. Mum and Dad need money more than another pair of hands in the fields." He fell silent again he watched as Ryan pulled the white-hot iron from the coals and laid it on the anvil. His eyes followed the hammer as it arched up and down again and again, and as he watched the piece of iron began to form into the shape of a gate hinge.

Ryan rested the hammer on the anvil and looked up. "Can ya be startin in the mornin? There's a lot more ta being a Smithy than swinging a hammer", he said as he turned the now cherry-red hinge over and raised the hammer again.

"Aye," Colin answered, "there's magic in it."

"Magic?" The words took Ryan by surprise. He glanced up and saw the look in Colin's eye. The look he recognized as the one he himself had had some fifteen years before. His instincts had been right, the Almighty had never meant Colin for a farmer. He was created to forge hot iron. He was not about to let the Lad slip away.

"Would ya like ta try your hand and take a swing or two?"

"Ta be sure I would," Colin said stepping inside the shop as Ryan handed him the hammer and tongs.

As Ryan stepped back, Colin took a stance along side the anvil as if he had worked there for years. He gripped the tongs placing the hot iron hinge against the anvil, balanced the hammer in his hand and began the swing. There was poetry of motion, a fusion of power, heat, and thought, that worked together to create something that was needed and practical; and at the same time a piece of art. With that first blow and the ring of iron on iron he knew he had a great deal to learn. But he also knew that he had found his calling in life.

Ryan watched as Colin awkwardly tried to manipulate the tongs holding the hinge. His grip loosened for just a split second and the red hot hinge dropped to the dirt floor

'Aye, the Lad needs teaching sure enough,' Ryan muttered to himself. But he had what was far more important than knowing how to hammer metal. He could sense that Colin had a feeling for iron without which no one could become an artist; and the finest smiths were all artists' first, blacksmiths second.

"Sorry about that," Colin said handing the hammer and tongs back to Ryan.

"Nothin ta be sorry fer Lad," he laughed. "After twenty years I still have one get away every now and then. That's why blacksmith shops always have dirt floors. If we didn't," he laughed as he picked up the hinge, "we'd always be building new shops."

"Aye," Colin said laughing. "Be seein ye in the mornin then." As he walked out of the shop; it was hard to tell who was more pleased, Ryan or Colin.

"Tomarra mornin it is," Ryan called through the open door as he plunged the now dark hinge back into the forge. "Tomarra mornin things are gonna start ta change around here," he said to himself and started whistling.

Chapter 2

Saint Patrick's was the oldest church in Kilrush, dating back several hundred years. As the decades and centuries passed the congregation grew; the main sanctuary was enlarged, and rooms were added on for various needs such as quarters for the additional priests needed for the growing parish. As a consequence, the building had been remodeled and repaired so many times it was almost impossible to visualize what the original church had been like. At one point, Rome had considered building a second church in Kilrush. However, after determining that the feelings of loyalty to Saint Patrick's and to Father Carmichael were so strong, they questioned if anyone would attend the new church and the plan was dropped.

While it was true that Carmichael was almost seventy - some members joked he was there when the original church was built - his vigor was that of a man in his mid-fifties. Many a new young priest had been sent to Saint Patrick's expecting a doddering old man and an easy schedule. They quickly discovered that his twelve to fourteen hour days, six days a week, left them worn out and eagerly looking forward to Sunday, or a transfer. It was doubtful that any young priest in Ireland so embraced the biblical injunction against working on the Sabbath, as did Carmichael's boys as they were called. But his discipline proved itself over the years. Rome learned that if an Irish parish needed help, dedication and solid leadership, send a Carmichael boy.

Father Samuel Patrick Carmichael had first come to Saint Patrick's in Kilrush in 1793 at age 30, to assist the aging Parish Priest, Father Timothy O'Connor. He was young and ambitious, and came with the belief this was but a stepping stone to more lofty positions. He had a very quick mind, a calm clear-headed presence, and a charismatic personality. It came as little surprise that as Father O'Connor gradually slipped into senility, Carmichael had within a few years, assumed many of the affairs of the parish. Although he was well liked by the members of the church who knew him, to others he appeared somewhat aloof and distant in his mannerisms. Consequently, many locals continued to view him as an outsider, a temporary priest until a permanent replacement was sent for Father O'Connor. All of that changed dramatically with the Insurrection of 1798 when the Irish aided by the French, attempted to defeat the English and regain control of Ireland.

The Irish had a long list of grievances against the British government and English landlords, the most recent being the latter switching their land to grazing, which deprived tenants of desperately needed land for crops. In 1797, the hostility between the British Protestants and the Irish Catholics intensified. County Clare, in which Kilrush is situated, was considered critical because it was here the French planned an invasion to aid the Irish. Accordingly, the United Irishmen were actively recruiting in Clare County.

Simultaneously, the English Landlords and Planters formed the Yeomanry to counteract what they viewed as sedition. Even before the major battles took place, the Yeomanry scoured the countryside looking for anyone who was sympathetic to the Irish rebels. Beatings, hangings, and being shipped off to fight in some foreign war awaited those who were caught. The Irish tenants retaliated violently by attacking the estates of the English Landlords, killing their livestock, and cutting down thousands of their trees.

Tragically for the Irish, the French invasion planned for the River Shannon, never took place for a variety of reasons including bad weather and poor seamanship. Despite this major setback, the Irish proceeded with their plans for revolution. Unfortunately, the ruling classes of the Catholic Church, having witnessed the Revolution in the American Colonies and France, believed that the rebellion would lead to atheism; and thus betrayed their own members by supporting the British, thereby helping to maintain the status quo.

In the spring and summer of 1798, Lord Cornwallis, the British General, commanded approximately 76,000 government troops and crushed the armies of the Irish and the French. Over 30,000 Irish fighters and civilians were killed in three weeks. The inhabitants of Kilrush and the surrounding area witnessed horrible acts of violence. Homes and businesses burned to the ground; scores killed; others beaten; livestock slaughtered; widespread looting.

Upon being told of the atrocities taking place, Father O'Conner who had been at Saint Peter's Door for several months, suffered a heart attack and died. Without waiting for instructions from the regional Bishop, Carmichael jumped into the void and assumed full control. He was everywhere throughout the parish; organizing and directing help programs; caring for the wounded; comforting the widows and their children; organizing groups to help repair and rebuild homes and businesses. Saint Patrick's quickly became the local rallying point and storehouse for food and clothing, the doors were never closed. It did not matter if the individual was a Roman Catholic, protestant, non-believer, or avowed atheist. All that mattered was that the person needed help, and was willing to lend a hand when they were able. Within a few weeks, Carmichael had become the guiding beacon, the local hero to those around Kilrush.

When he learned of everything that had happed; the Bishop, who had previously picked a successor for O'Conner, withdrew the name and appointed Carmichael as

Parish Priest, head of Saint Patrick's. Under his leadership, the membership grew, and he became more involved in the affairs of the town. Local businessmen and landowners, including many who had not darkened a church door in many years, returned to the church and became his personal friends. He was invited to sit on the town council. Most startling of all to many staunch Catholics, he became a close friend of Reverend Swagart, the struggling Pastor of the Methodist Church and his family. During the week, they were often seen walking down the street together talking, joking and laughing as if they were brothers. His remarkable gifts and skills, all of which were faithfully reported by his Bishop to Rome, did not go unnoticed. When the Bishop was accidentally killed in a carriage mishap, Carmichael was offered the position, which he declined. Ten years later, when the succeeding Bishop was elevated to Archbishop, he was again offered the position, and again he declined.

The first time he refused the promotion, Pope Leo XII sent him a personal letter asking him to reconsider. That was almost twenty-five years ago. Had he accepted then, he might be an Archbishop, perhaps even a Cardinal by now. But he sent the following letter back to the Pope thanking him, but declining the post.

Your Holiness:

It is with a profound sense of gratitude that you have honored me by the offer for the office of Bishop, but I must decline. I know my strengths and also my weaknesses. My strength comes from serving the people in this Parish, they are to me what Samson's hair was to him. If I were to be shorn from them, what I am would be lost.

As for my weakness, it may surprise you to learn that it has always been a lust for power. That is why as a very young lad I decided to become a priest, because I saw that as the first step to gain power. Oh, I was smart enough to realize that being Irish rather that Italian had its disadvantages, but if I played my hand right I might become a Bishop, a very heady idea for a young ambitious young man. Those were my thoughts and plans. And now once again, unwittingly of course, you have placed my original goal within my grasp.

But God works in mysterious ways, does He not. On celebrating my very first Mass many, many, years ago, an old woman took hold of my sleeve, pulled me aside and whispered, 'Beware of the sin of pride. Remember, Our Lord said that he was the servant of all.' That was all she said. She let go of my sleeve, turned and walked out of the church. But her message stayed in my mind and did its work.

What the woman said to me didn't make much sense to me at the time, but what she told me has never left me. Beware of the sin of pride. Beware of the sin of pride. Since that day I have prayerfully sought and taken whatever measures I could to avoid the temptation. You see, I fear that becoming a Bishop could lead to my undoing.

I respectfully request therefore, that I be permitted to remain here at Saint Patrick's. Here I shall tend the flock God has entrusted to my care; and do all that I can to teach the lads coming out of the seminaries what being a Priest truly means.

Your humble servant,
Father Samuel Carmichael

A month later, a letter from the Pope arrived telling Father Carmichael that he was very sorry his offer had been declined; and wishing him the best in his continued service of the Church. Realizing that not every priest received a personal letter from the Pope, he read, and re-read the letter several times. 'I had my chance', he smiled as he thought to himself, 'I had my chance.' He then carefully folded the letter and placed it with his few treasured personal effects.

About ten years later, he was asked again to reconsider his previous decision, and take the office of Bishop for southern Ireland. Once again he respectfully declined, stating that all the reasons he had cited in his original letter still held true. In truth, while he did not say so, he had become even more attached to Saint Patrick and the local people. He could not walk down the street, or say a Mass without seeing the faces of couples he had married; those he had known since childhood; men who had once been Alter Boys; the widows and widowers of those he had buried. They had become his family many, many, years ago. There was no office so grand as to leave them after almost forty years.

In the passing years the letters were all but forgotten, until out of the blue yet another letter came from Rome. This time it stated that the Pope was sending a personal emissary to Kilrush to meet with Father Carmichael on an important matter. The sisters flew into a dither scrubbing and cleaning until Father Carmichael ordered them to stop before they rubbed the paint, varnish, and gild off everything in the church. Since the emissaries name was Ciaccia, they immediately began practicing cooking Italian dishes. Father Carmichael suggested that the emissary might enjoy a good hot bowl of Mulligan stew.

Sister Agnes the cook, looked him in the eye, threw her arms into the air and replied, " No doubt that if the Holy Mother Mary herself came, you would want to serve her Mulligan stew."

"Ah Sister Agnes," he said taking her hands in his, "I have it on good authority," he lifted his head and looked up," that you will be asked to fix some of your marvelous stew for the great feast in Heaven."

"And were it not for the fine work you do here," she replied clutching his hand, "blarney such as that would keep you out of heaven and tasting it if I did." She smiled, gently pulled her hands away and headed back to the kitchen. On the way, his words repeated in her mind. She smiled and a soft chuckle escaped her lips, "And why not a fine Mulligan stew in heaven?"

The weeks passed, the church was ready, and the daily business of the Parish went on. Then, on one particularly bright June morning without any notice, a carriage pulled up in front of Saint Patrick's, and out stepped Cardinal Ciaccia, the Pope's emissary in his bright crimson robes and hat. A Sister who happened to be working near the front of the church, saw him step out of the carriage and went running calling, "Father Carmichael, Father Carmichael, he's here, he's here." Running to see what all the commotion was about, Father Carmichael and several other priests and sisters were stunned speechless to see a Cardinal walking up the front steps.

They stood staring at each other in silence for a few seconds, and then Father Carmichael walked down the steps to greet their distinguished visitor. "As you can see your Grace, you've taken us by surprise and left us at a loss for words, a terrible, terrible thing for the Irish. We were expecting a young priest, an assistant to the Holy Father, perhaps even a Bishop, but never in our wildest dreams a Cardinal."

The Cardinal grasp Carmichaels' hand and let out a hearty laugh. "Father Carmichael, His Holiness would have come himself if it had been possible. Now let me say right here and now," he said laughing, "I'm not here to offer you another position as Bishop. "No, no. The Holy Father understands what your wishes are, and I was not sent here with the intent of persuading you to change your mind a third time."

He leaned closer , "Do you know that you're the talk of Rome these days?" he did not wait for an answer. "As a matter of fact, half the Cardinals in Rome wanted to come here to meet the famous Father Carmichael, the Irish Priest who said 'No' to the Holy Father not once, but twice. I was honored to be chosen."

"Saints be praised," Sister Agnes exclaimed.

"And so they are," he replied reaching out to shake the hands of the other young priests and sisters. "This is a very special day for all of us. For the next few days, I want you to forget that I'm a Cardinal and consider me as one of your family. That is, as soon as I can get out of these robes," he chuckled. "Now which of you is Sister Agnes?"

She slowly raised her hand, uncertain as to what he wanted.

He walked over to her and whispered something close to her ear.

"Oh Holy Mother of Jesus," she blurted out, quickly putting her fingers to her lips. "Oh forgive my language your Grace, but ye cannot be serious?"

"But indeed I am. The word in Rome is that you make the best Mulligan stew in the world, and His Holiness would never speak to me again if I returned without trying it....his very words."

"One step closer to the great feast I'd say, wouldn't you Sister Agnes?" Carmichael laughed softly. "I little inside joke," he said turning to the Cardinal. They excused themselves and walked inside. After changing his clothes, he and Carmichael went outside for a walk around the church.

The Cardinal looked up at the weathered stone face of Saint Patrick's Church, and put his arm around Carmichael's shoulders. "I was very serious in there when I said I wanted to be one of you. Every young priest we have sent here has returned to Rome a changed man, more dedicated, even inspired. I, we, want to know why. Show me your world, the one you love so very much that you turned down two promotions, one that could have lead to a position in Rome itself."

Before Carmichael could answer, he continued. "There's something else; I'm curious about the old woman who told you to beware of the sin of pride so many years ago." He waved his hand, "oh yes, we've all heard the story. Who was she?"

Carmichael smiled. "No one knows."

"But surely you questioned her."

"Never had the chance. As soon as she finished speaking she turned and I watched her leave the church. I later inquired as to her name and where she lived. Strangely enough, no one else recalled seeing her in church that morning, and several folks who had lived in the village all their lives told me that they knew of no one fitting her description. Sister Martha claimed she was an Angel in disguise, but in the months that followed I discovered that wonderful old Martha considered anyone she didn't know on sight as a potential Angel. But, perhaps she was right. Sister Martha went to be with the Saints and Angels two years ago. It was a wonderful day for Heaven, but a sad day for our church and community. She is still very much missed here." He fell silent for a moment, turned and looked toward the cemetery. "That's her stone over there," he said pointing to the one with an angel carved into it. "One of our members donated it because Martha had been such a blessing during his wife's illness."

For the next hour they toured the old church. "Tell me", the Cardinal asked, "where is the broken window,"

"You know about that?"

"Everyone in the Vatican knows about it. It made such an impression on the priests we've sent here, the Holy Father has even talked about breaking one himself, not in the Sistine Chapel of course," he laughed.

"I had no idea how far my sins have traveled. Come around here to the front of the church. Up there," Carmichael pointed out the now apparently famous broken window.

The Cardinal craned his neck and saw the small broken glass pane. Before he could say anything, Carmichael pointed upward. "I use it as a lesson that if you take care of the little things, you can avoid bigger problems later on. You cannot see it from here, but we put some oiled paper behind the pane to keep in the heat and the cold out."

"You're amazing. When I get back, perhaps I should recommend that we bring you to Rome to handle our maintenance," he smiled as he placed his hand on Carmichael's shoulder. They turned and headed toward the garden.

"I envy you Father, I truly do." The Cardinal stopped and turned to face him. "We, that is those of us in Rome, sometimes tend to lose sight of what the real mission of the church is. We get so caught up in arguing- yes arguing, about budgets; scheduling endless meetings; deciding who will be appointed to this parish, or that one; should we build a new convent in Africa, or South America; and what to do about America; so many of our people are immigrating there now..... it's endless."

He turned and started walking again. "But you haven't forgotten. Perhaps I would be a happier man today, had an old woman pulled on my sleeve." He pulled on a red sweater, "Oh yes, I have the robe, but you've truly found the kingdom of God, and an inner peace I do not possess." He turned his face toward heaven, "Lord, forgive me the sin of envy."

As the days passed, Cardinal Ciaccia, discovered what it really meant 'to be one of them.' He was continually being interrupted with questions everywhere he went; by everyone in the church from priests, nuns, and even parishioners helping clean up the grounds. Then one morning, he announced sadly that he had to leave the next day. Later that afternoon in Father Carmichael's study, the Cardinal reached into a beautiful tooled leather carrying case and pulled out a letter. "This is for you," he said handing the letter to Carmichael, "the Holy Father wrote it himself." He wished to thank you again for your letters, and he agrees that your mission is here. Saint Patrick's will be your parish as long as you wish. His Holiness also wanted you to ...."

His words were suddenly cut short by knock at the door. Carmichael opened the door and spoke to a young priest. He turned to the Cardinal and explained that a small matter had come up, could he please be excused for a moment? The Cardinal nodded and the two priests left. A few minutes latter, Carmichael returned and apologized for the interruption.

The Cardinal laughed, "Please don't apologize. It has truly been wonderful, having you consider me as one of you. How very refreshing to literally be taken at your word. I will miss all of this, even the interruptions." He paused for a moment and looked out the window toward the garden inwardly thinking about what he had just said... 'as one of you.' The moment passed, and he turned to Carmichael, "Now' before we get interrupted again," he laughed reaching out his hand with the box, "the Holy Father wants you to have this as a token of his appreciation." He handed Father Carmichael a beautiful silver box containing a magnificent engraved communion goblet of solid gold. "Understand Father, this is a gift to you personally." He smiled as he carefully handed it over.

Carmichael tenderly held the goblet in his hands and read the inscription, "To my friend, Father Carmichael, who refused me the privilege of making him a Bishop...twice." It was inscribed with the name of the Holy Father himself, Gregory XVI.

"All this and heaven too," the Cardinal whispered as he touched Carmichael's shoulder.

"Amen," Carmichael replied holding the box close to his breast. "Amen."

Chapter 3

Two months had passed since Cardinal Ciaccia had returned to Rome, and life at Saint Patricks had returned to normal, or more correctly, what they considered normal. There was however, one notable exception, Sister Agnes seemed to be serving a good deal more Mulligan stew, and a revolt was beginning to take shape among the young priests, sisters, and workers. Father Carmichael was on his way to the kitchen to head-off the growing crisis, when a young sister ran up to him and handed him another letter from Rome.

"My, my," he exclaimed as he opened and read the letter," we certainly seem to be popular these days." A few moments later, he folded the paper and turned to the sister, "Rome is sending us another priest," and continued on toward the kitchen. "Doesn't tell us much about him," he called back, "except that he is an older man who had once served in the military.

It was a rainy afternoon three weeks later when a middle aged priest entered the church, told a sister who was cleaning windows that he was Father Gordon Grant, and said that he was there to see Father Carmichael. She ran down the aisle and disappeared through a doorway. Twenty minutes later, Carmichael appeared and introduced himself. "Father Grant, I'm sorry to have kept you waiting so long. I was in the garden shed fixing a hoe, Sister Mary couldn't find me."

Grant quickly realized that what he had been told about Carmichael was true. He was a very practical man, who despite his age and senior position, was ready to roll-up his sleeves to get the job done. He could also see that Carmichael's hands were partially crippled with arthritis.

"It is a privilege to meet you Father Carmichael. From what Cardinal Ciaccia told me about you, I'm not surprised that you were busy fixing something." Pointing to Carmichael's hands, "Must be kind of hard on them isn't it, working on that hoe?"

Carmichael glanced at his hands, "It would be harder if I didn't keep using them. They'd set-up and I'd never be able to do anything. Now let's go to my study and get acquainted," he motioned to Grant to follow him.

From long experience, Father Carmichael had developed a little system that helped him learn something about newcomers; he walked along side them on the way to his study, observing their walk and mannerisms.

Grant was in his mid-40's, medium height and stocky, with graying hair. When he walked, he carried himself with the assuredness that came from many years in the Army. Even before their lengthy conversation began, Carmichael knew that this man was very different from the typical young men just out of the Seminary. While he didn't want to get ahead of himself, he began to hope this could be the man he had been praying for: a mature priest who could begin to handle the growing burdens of the Parish. Like it or not, he was well aware that the years were beginning to take their toll on his body.

Carmichael opened the door to his study and motioned for Grant to go in ahead of him. Upon entering, Grant immediately scanned his eyes over the room, noting every detail. His eyes fell upon the goblet on the book shelf and he walked over to examine it.

"May I?" he asked.

"Certainly," Carmichael replied, "pick it up."

"A remarkable piece....and from the Pope himself. You must treasure it very much." He placed it back on the shelf.

"Indeed I do. But I never let myself forget it's just a cup. Special to me of course, but still a cup." He motioned for Grant to sit down. "Now tell me something about yourself."

Grant considered what he had just heard. Ciaccia had been right, Carmichael was a very humble practical man who was not enamored by the trappings of position or special recognition. He glanced around the room again and walked over to the window over-looking the garden. "I'm 45 years old, served almost eighteen years in the British Army as an officer. For twelve years I was stationed in India; have been in numerous battles; and saw more than my share of tragedy and death among my men, and also among the people in the cities and slums of India," hr paused.

"Four years ago, while stationed in Bombay; I received word that my wife, and all three of our children died in London from Cholera." He hesitated, and Carmichael could see that even after six years, relating this tragedy still moved him close to tears.

"You must have loved them very much."

"They were everything to me, everything that mattered. All those years in the service, far from home…." his voice started to falter. "It was all for them. In a few more years, I could have retired, and we had planned to buy a little farm over-looking the ocean. Mary, that was my wife's name, loved the sea. Every time I came home on leave, we would spend it in some little Inn by the sea where we could take the children, let them run and play on the beach." He turned from the window and sank down into the chair. "My world ended when that letter came, a world I could never bring back. It was four months before I could get back to England and visit their graves."

He paused for a moment, straightened up in the chair, then continued. "I went back to India for a few months, but it wasn't the same. Mary had sent me letters every week, of course she had written them several weeks earlier, and so they came in batches. I lived for those letters. I don't think I could have endured all those years without them." He paused, "Now there were no letters. It was all gone: my wife, children... the reason for everything."

Carmichael said nothing. This was a time of catharsis, or perhaps the end of that period.

Grant got up and went to the window again. "So I determined to begin a new life. A life where I would never again risk losing a wife, or children. I resigned my commission, returned to England, and entered the Seminary. I was done with the killing; dying; death." He turned and faced Carmichael, " now I want to spend whatever years I have left helping others to live."

They both remained silent for a few moments, then Carmichael asked.

"But why the Catholic Church? You were not raised as a Catholic."

"No. I was brought up in the Lutheran Church," he paused as if thinking back. "But it always left me cold. I never felt the message was reaching anyone. I'm sure that it was just me, maybe it wasn't my time."

"Timing is everything," Carmichael replied. "The Apostle Paul was not too far from your age, when he began preaching the gospel. The Holy Spirit knows when it is time to quicken the soul."

"Yes, I re-read the story of Paul many times when I was in Seminary. It gave me hope that perhaps it wasn't too late, that I could do some good somewhere. As for why the Catholic Church, there was a Catholic priest in our Regiment, Father Harness. He was a man who truly lived his faith, and was a wonderful inspiration to the men - not all of them of course - but to those who cared about religion. At the time, I really didn't care much about it myself; but I did see the effect he had on the men. In the most terrible of times he could lift their spirits, and give them a glimpse of something greater than themselves. I'm certain that not all the priests are like that, in fact I've heard that some are little more than reprobates in priests clothes. But Father Harness was the one I knew and respected."

"So what brings you to Saint Patrick's?" Carmichael already knew, the reason was in the letter he had received, but he wanted to hear what Grant had to say.

"Well, it was something of a coincidence. After I finished Seminary, they weren't quite sure where to send me. The Bishop suggested that I go to Rome to meet an old friend of his, Cardinal Ciaccia. As it turned out, he had just returned from visiting you." Grant leaned forward, "I met with him and after talking with him for half an hour, he jumped up waved his arms and said, "You're going to Saint Patricks." So here I am.

"Ah yes," Cardinal Ciaccia. "We had a wonderful time while he was here. Quite a remarkable man for a Cardinal. What I mean by that," he quickly added, "is that he's unaffected by his high position. Very much the common man."

"That's what impressed me," Grant replied. "When the Bishop told me that his friend was a Cardinal, I had expected all the pomp and circumstance. Especially since I was a nobody right out of school."

"Well, they're...." Carmichael carefully searched for the right words, " the Cardinals that is, are not all like that. Ciaccia is a very remarkable individual. So what did he tell you?"

"He told me he was sending me to the one man who could guide me to what I should be doing. You."

"Did he now?" Carmichael got up and walked to the window.

"Yes. I had been told he was a very busy man and that he could only see me for half an hour. When I started to leave, he asked me if I had some free time. He wanted me to meet some other people." Imagine asking me if I had any free time, like I was someone of importance." He shook his head, "I still have a hard time believing it. After our lunch which lasted almost two hours, we spent the rest of the day together. He took me to meet over a dozen people in the Vatican; other Cardinals; Archbishops; the Pope's secretary. It was incredible. I've probably met more of the hierarchy of the Church than most priests meet in a lifetime of service."

Carmichael gazed out the window and then turned to Grant. "It's evident that he saw something in you he doesn't often see, a mature leader of men." He walked back to his chair. "Oh don't get me wrong we have some wonderful leaders, but virtually all the men coming out of the seminaries these days are very young men with very little real life experience. There are a few older ones as well, but for the most part they are men who had seldom ventured more than a few miles from where they were born; and certainly had never commanded much more than the cow they used to plow with."

"I was told that's why they send a number of the young priests to you, to help them develop into responsible priests."

"So I have been told," he chuckled. "But I don't think that's what the Cardinal had in mind for you. No, you already have the maturity. What you and I will need to work on; is where you can best use your many skills for the church." Carmichael pulled his chair closer to Grant's. "Don't misunderstand, the Mass is very important; but living your life with the people and becoming part of their everyday lives is far more important. That's what Saint Patrick's is all about; family. When something happens here, some crisis, we all pitch in together to solve it. If a man's cow falls into the ditch, you jump right in there with him to get it out. When a man, or woman, is dying, you take the whole family into your arms and weep with them.

It's not just their family that is suffering loss, but ours as well.   As I mentioned earlier, the Sunday Mass is important, but the other six days are even more important. God worked for six days, and on the seventh He rested. That's what we try to do here; take one more step toward Zion everyday."

"...Everyman is a piece of the Continent, a part of the maine," Grant said quietly.

"So you're familiar with the works of John Donne?"

"My wife loved poetry - almost everything in print - and was always sending me books on various subjects.   She never went to school; but taught herself to read when she was a child and read everything she could get her hands on. She had an amazing knowledge of many subjects.   In truth, much of what I know was because of her.   She was always prodding me, and the children of course, to read, listen, and ...," he put his head in his hands.   "I will never understand why God took her and my children."

"Never is a long time."   Carmichael replied.   "Perhaps someday, the reason will be revealed to you."   He paused for a moment, and continued.   "You've been telling me about yourself; now there's something I must tell you."   He sat back in his chair and folded his arms across his chest.

"Shortly after you began talking this afternoon, I began to feel a quickening in my spirit.   Do you know what a kindred spirit is?"

"My wife told me it was when two people have a special relationship, a spiritual bond."

"I'm certain that I would have loved to have known your wife," Carmichael said.   "She was very rare, and she was right about kindred spirits.   Even though we have just met, I believe that you and I are such people; and such a relationship brings with it a deep sense of trust.   Therefore, I need to tell you things you must know if you are going to stay here at Saint Patrick's."

"I'm not certain I understand?"

"You will," Carmichael said, "you will. First, this is Ireland, and Ireland has been at war with England for hundreds of years; it's critical that you understand that fact. Not for twenty years, or fifty years, even a hundred years; but for hundreds of years. The distrust and hatred of the English had started long before of course; but it intensified when England and Scotland converted to Protestantism, and Ireland remained Catholic. Thereafter, Ireland became a magnet for all the political intrigue and schemes between England and Rome. Hundreds of battles, the Spanish were involved, the French were involved. The most recent major battles were fought right here in this area a little over thirty years ago when you were a boy. We still have a number of people in this Parish, even members of Saint Patrick's who were personally involved. They've not forgotten." He got up from his chair and walked around for a moment.

"In January of 1801, shortly after the Insurrection of '98 in which 30,000 Irish men and women were killed in a few weeks; the English Parliament passed the Act of Union between Ireland and England which politically tied the two nations together. It was ballyhooed and hailed as the great solution that would bring an end to the hostility and grant new freedoms to the people of Ireland. Many grand promises were made: There would be free trade; our small Irish industries would get vital new capital investments from England; Catholics would be emancipated, and would be assured of English justice; Catholics would even be permitted to become judges and members of Parliament. The promises were mostly lies."

He sat down and leaned forward in his chair. "What actually happened was that England was afraid that the Irish would rise up again. The way to stop that from happening was to destroy Ireland by deceit. They passed the Act of Union with little or no intention of honoring it. Proof you ask? Here it is. Soon afterward, they sent an additional hundred thousand solders here, does that sound like and end of hostility and new freedoms? They dissolved the Irish Parliament in Dublin, and shifted all political decisions to Parliament in London." He intertwined his fingers and rested is chin on his hands for a moment, and then continued.

"There's more. The English made no investments in Irish business, unemployment became widespread. And the much touted Catholic emancipation, which they said was to happen immediately, was almost forgotten. In fact, it finally happened almost thirty years later in 1829, but only after many, many, bitter struggles in Parliament.

"What did happen was that the oppression increased. Catholics were not allowed to have schools, so we held classes in secret places in the hills. We created secret codes by which we could communicate our faith to our children. Land owned by the Irish, could no longer be inherited unless the heir renounced Catholicism and became a Protestant. Many of the English landowners became even more hostile and ruthless, cruelty became the norm. The absentee owners leased their land to Agents for so much an acre. They in turn sublet the land for even more money. On and on it went until the local folks could not afford the rent and were ruthlessly evicted. For others, their cattle and pigs were killed, girls were raped. Nothing was ever done to those who committed the crimes, even when their identity was known. Long ago the people gave up on any hope of justice from the English magistrates. The result was inevitable; secret organizations of Irish men - and even women - sprang up, who began taking matters into their own hands."

"Let me ask you a question," Carmichael said. "Did you ever hear anything about Ireland when you were a boy?"

"No. My father died of pneumonia when I was five. I had three brothers and a sister, the oldest was twelve. After my Father died, my mother did laundry twelve-fourteen hours a day. She was too exhausted to really talk about anything, let alone history and politics. When I reached fifteen, I joined the Army. It was a very hard life."

"You see, that's the difference. All this history that I'm telling you about, is mother's milk to the children here. By the time they're age ten, they've heard the stories a hundred times. Now here you are an Englishman, the avowed enemy of Ireland. Before you even start you have one strike against you. Strike two, you were a protestant before coming a priest. Why should anyone here trust you?"

Carmichael reached over and placed his hand on Grant's arm. "I believe in you, but it's going to take a while before the people here do.... some of them may never trust you. You're going to have to work very hard to prove yourself to them," he patted Grants arm and sat back.

"I'm very grateful you told me this," Grand replied, "and that you trust me. As for the people, I'll do everything I can to earn their trust." He shifted in his chair, "the scripture states that a good man's steps are ordered of the Lord. I certainly don't claim to be a good man, but too many things have happened to bring me here to be considered mere coincidence. How many priests just finishing their training are invited to Rome, and are invited to have long lunches with a Cardinal? How many get to meet other Cardinals and Archbishops in the Vatican itself? What are the chances that Cardinal Ciaccia just happened to visit you a few months ago? No, I don't think they were coincidences, I believe that God's plan was for me to come here."

"So do I," Carmichael replied with a big smile, "so do I."

At that moment there was a knock on the door, it opened and Sister Ruth announced that dinner would be served in about fifteen minutes." She turned to leave, then stuck her head back inside, "surprise! It's Mulligan Stew."

"Mulligan stew!" Grant exclaimed. "Why, Cardinal Ciaccia told me to be sure to have some of that. He raved about it. In fact, he has one of the cooks in the Vatican trying to make some. He told me they just can't seem to get it right."

"Imagine that Sister Ruth," Carnichael said winking at the sister. "Perhaps we could give Sister Agnes a little leave to go to Rome and teach them."

"I'm certain everyone here will say Amen to that idea," the she replied with a soft.
laugh.

"Am I missing something?" Grant asked.

"Sister Ruth, shall we tell him, or let him discover this for him self?"

"Oh, discover it on his own," she quipped and was gone.

Grant watched and listened to this bit of very casual banter between Carmichael and Sister Ruth. He smiled, these people were going to be his family. He hadn't even unpacked his bags, and he was beginning to feel at home already.

The days quickly turned to weeks, and the weeks into months. Grant, under the guidance of Carmichael had traveled every road, lane, and bike path in Saint Patrick's parish. He had repaired roofs; walls; helped lay-up stone hedge-rows; dug ditches; pulled cows out of ditches; and a dozen other jobs. In the course of his work, he had met well over a hundred people, and had now learned to recognize a good many people on site. It was now quite common to for him to hear his name being called out as he walked down the street. More important, when a problem arose, the members increasingly asked for Father Grant. They had nothing against the other new young priests, and when the occasion presented itself they were happy to have one of them help with their problem. But when it was a more serious matter, it was the maturity and wisdom Grant possessed they sought.

It was now late November. Carmichael stood by the garden window watching Grant heading down the street on another mission. He smiled to himself. It had worked out even better than he had dared hoped. Grant was now handling at least half of the situations that Carmichael had previously been required to do himself. Now he was free to handle important administrative duties, which had often been neglected; and he was also able to spend more time with the young priests. These two things in themselves had been an answer to prayer; but the icing on the cake, was that Grant was finding his strengths and place in the Church and among the local people.

He looked across the church cemetery at Sister Martha's monument and raised his hand, "You would have liked him Martha," he whispered. He started to turn away and then looked at her grave again. It must have been caused by the tears in his eyes, but he was sure he had seen the Angel's wings move.

Chapter 4

Lord John Bligh had inherited the vast family estate at age twenty-two, from his father who had been killed in a duel by a man who had accused him of cheating and ruining him in a business deal.   Under his father's guidance, he had grown into a hard driving taskmaster who had zero tolerance for mistakes in the management of his business affairs and estates.   Tall and lean with deep-set dark brown eyes, razor thin lips, and a sober expression as rigid as marble, he conveyed the warmth of an undertaker.

"It's all about power Jack," his father had drummed into him day after day. "And power comes from money, never forget that. With enough money, you can get - or take - what you want. With money and power you get to do it your way," an attitude that had worked until he crossed a man who was so distraught he resorted to pistols.   His father's business Partners, and servants all clearly understood this. John's father did not believe in giving anyone an even break, or a second chance. "Never show any sign of weakness, or compassion, it'll make you soft." The latter was true even if the error was caused by an unforeseen event. One mistake and the individual, guilty or not, was out on the street.

After taking over the reins of the estate he issued his first order, he was never to be called Jack again, the nickname his father had given him. Secondly, he announced that he intended to control and run everything just as his father had done. Love and understanding were two words that were not in his vocabulary.   Not surprisingly, he quickly developed a reputation for being rigid and ruthless. Those who entered into a business deal with him were advised to think long and hard before doing so. More than one businessman had been destroyed by making the mistake that he was dealing with a man of honor; a person who would do the right thing. John quickly proved to be as ruthless as his father had been.

Two years later, he married Elizabeth Browning, the eldest daughter of a very wealthy family from Southampton, a marriage that surprised everyone because they were as different as black and white. Very plain and petite, it was her soft brown laughing eyes that mirrored her love of life, and her effervescent spirit that captivated all who met her. When their wedding announcement was published, the matrons of London society gasp, "Elizabeth and John! John Bligh? The marriage will never last."

At first, their marriage was nothing more than a typical aristocratic arrangement, more of a social-business contract between two powerful families than a marriage. John continued to take care of managing his estate; and Elizabeth, typical of her social status and the culture in which they lived, became involved in various social events. Aside from having dinner together, they seldom had much contact with each other.

In the years that followed, they would attend various social functions, and take occasional trips to the seaside together at which time he would begin to show some signs of a softer, more tolerant side of his nature. It was as if deep within him, there was another John who had been imprisoned at an early age. Elizabeth had seen this in him when he visited her at her parent's estate even before they were married. After their marriage, she began looking for ways to free the *inner John* as she called him.

A year later, the initial platonic relationship began to change, and gradually a genuine feeling of affection developed between them. It was not yet love, but there were hints and signs that the seeds were there. Elizabeth felt that what their relationship needed, was a common unifying factor in their otherwise separate lives. Something, perhaps an event which could be used to unlock the tower in which the inner John had been imprisoned.

When she became pregnant; she felt that this would be what she had been waiting for. Sadly, their first son Robert proved to be a problem child. Rather than bringing them closer together, he became a divisive force. Fortunately Lawrence, who was born a year later, was a happy child who brought joy back to the household, and helped heal the wedge that Robert had created between John and Elizabeth.

The next few years were very busy and went by quickly. John was involved in managing his business enterprises and the estate; Elizabeth's days were busy caring for the boys, plus an increasing demanding social calendar. It wasn't until several years later after the boys had been enrolled in private schools that they really began to have time to spend together. Throughout all these years, Elizabeth had continued to pray that the inner John would someday be set free, and awaken to the joys of life.

The opportunity came unexpectedly one morning when John read an advertisement in the London Times for an estate being offered for sale in Ireland. The idea of buying land in Ireland intrigued him because after all the years following his Father's death, he was still trying to break away from simply following in his footsteps. Buying land in Ireland was something his Father would never have done. When he mentioned the idea to Elizabeth, at first she was surprised because this didn't fit the pattern she had come to understand. Elizabeth however, was very intuitive and quick to recognize an opportunity. The Irish estate could provide a unique opportunity to bring them closer together.

"I think it's a wonderful idea," she replied, "how soon can we go up there to inspect the property?"

John was completely taken by surprise by her answer. First, by her interest in the idea itself; and secondly, by her desire to go there. "Elizabeth," he said laying down the paper, "did you understand that I said the property is in Ireland? It could be dangerous up there."

"I heard you very clearly," she said walking over and putting her arms around his neck, something she had never done before at the breakfast table. "I can be ready to leave tomorrow, how long do you think we will be gone?"

"Tomorrow?" he exclaimed being hit with another surprise. But as he thought about it, why not tomorrow? the timing was right. The boys were in school for the next four months, and they didn't have anything else requiring their attention at home. He repeated her question, "How long would we be gone? Well there's the trip over and back; plus inspecting the land; the newspaper advertisement states over three thousand acres; the buildings; checking on the town - oh, by the way, it's in southwest Ireland near a town called Kilrush. I think we should allow at least a month, maybe more. Do you really want to be away from London and your friends that long?"

"My friends are my friends, and will still be my friends no matter how long I am gone."

That was true, she had wonderful friends. Most of his friends on the other hand could care less if he came back. In fact there were many who would prefer that he never came back.

"It's settled then," he said folding the paper and placing his hands on hers. He felt a strange sense of elation, excitement, and his heart began beating faster. Not only was he breaking away from his father regarding the possible purchase of land in Ireland, but because Elizabeth was going with him. He could never remember a single instance in which his father had ever consulted his mother about anything, let alone have her accompany him on a business trip.

"You're certain you want to do this?" he asked, afraid that she might have been kidding with him.

"Absolutely."

He stood up and she put her arms around him and gave him a long passionate kiss in front of one of the servants, something else that had never happened before and it slightly embarrassed him.

"Oh John, I'm so happy that you asked me about your idea. This is going to be a wonderful adventure for us." She let go of him and ran out of the room calling back, "I'm going to start packing right now."

"I'll tell Albert [their Butler] to let the servants know," he called after her. Suddenly he realized that he had several other matters to attend to if they were going to leave tomorrow. He could now feel the blood coursing through his veins in a way he had never felt before. She was right, this was going to be different than anything he had done before. It could be an adventure.

The trip from London to Bristol where they would board a ship to Ireland was uneventful, and even pleasant. The weather was warm and dry, and the road was in good condition so that the carriage was not jolted and bounced by ruts and pot holes. After a good days travel, John and Elizabeth spent the night in a warm roadside Inn that catered to wealthy travelers, and were on their way again early the next morning. Twice during the journey, Elizabeth had Grove, their coachman stop and wait while she got out and picked roadside flowers.

"Isn't this exciting," she would say climbing back into the carriage, "just look at how beautiful these flowers are."

"Yes they're very pretty, but you have several flower gardens at home."

"True," she smiled, "but these are wild. They grew here by themselves with no one to water and tend them except God."

John was amused at how exciting she found the trip to Bristol to be. Too tell the truth, he found it a bit exciting because of her presence.

———————————

Bristol, England had been a seaport for hundreds of years, and everything and everyone there appeared to be connected to the sea in one way or another. For several blocks around the wharf, the streets and alleys were lined with dozens of warehouses; ships chandleries; sail lofts; rope and chain dealers; block manufactures, iron and brass foundries, dry-docks, lumber and timber yards dedicated to out-fitting and rigging ships of all sizes. In every direction, were taverns, pubs, and Inns of every description. Elegant hotels with Doorman attired in red and green livery awaited wealthy travelers coming from and going to distant lands; America, South America; the Gold Coast of Africa; India; China. Inns of varying lesser degree stood waiting to welcome less affluent travelers and seamen. Last, but by no means least, were the common taverns and brothels liberally sprinkled along the waterfront.

John had been here several times, but each time he came he found the atmosphere exhilarating. The first time he had been here was long, long ago when he was a boy. One of his father businesses had been in the import-export trade. They had come to Bristol on their way to Ireland, a place his father hated, to arrange for a shipment of Spanish goods. Bristol had grown since then, but many of the businesses along the waterfront bore the same names as when he was a lad of twelve. He recalled seeing what appeared to him as a boy, to be hundreds of tall masted ships tied up along the dock while others were anchored off shore waiting their turn to load and unload their cargos.

Unlike many other boys his age however, he never imagined himself going to sea. Perhaps this was in part because had read the old newspaper articles his father had saved about the mutiny on HMS Bounty. Although the event had taken place just months before he was born, it was almost three years before Captain Bligh returned to England and the Admiralty trials began. In fact the famous incident was recent enough that stories were still being told.

Even though Captain Bligh was exonerated by the Court, the public continued to read articles in the press, and heard repeated tales of brutal ships masters, thereby becoming much more aware of how cruel life for ordinary seamen could be. Consequently, the thought of being confined to a ship at sea for months, let alone years, held no appeal for him, even if one were fortunate enough to get a kindly Captain.

This time however, Bristol would be much different because Elizabeth would be with him. She was full of energy and a sense of exploration, as if Bristol was a remote village in India. She held on to his coat sleeve and pulled him from street to street, shop to shop. Not just shops filled with china, jewelry and finery, but hardware stores, and dark cavernous warehouses filled with ships tackle. And in every place she stepped foot, she talked with shop keepers, clerks, patrons, the workers splicing lines, carpenters making masts, spars, sheaves and blocks.

Nor did her curiosity and love of adventure end there. Once, a couple of days later during a heavy downpour, she signaled Grove to stop the carriage, grabbed John's hand and bolted out of the carriage. "Hurry she yelled," crossing the street in the direction of a brothel, laughing and teasing him, flipping her skirt as she had seen the local tarts do, and getting them both soaked and muddy in the process. A couple of the women watching out the brothel window pointed and laughed at the sight. Upon seeing them, Elizabeth joined in their laughter. Then she did the unthinkable. She asked John for some money, went over to the house and handed it to the women as she talked with them, turned and pointed back to John. The women began laughing, waved at him, blew him a kiss, and then disappeared into the house.

Astonished as to what he had just witnessed, he asked her what she had said. "I told them you said that all pretty girls need a day off," she answered.

"You told them I said that," he exclaimed in surprise.

"Why yes, surely you agree don't you," she laughed as she grabbed his arm. "Mind you now John," she winked at him, I don't want you coming back here by yourself."

He turned and looked back for a moment. "Well, it was my money," he said squeezing her arm, "maybe I could...."

"Don't even finish the thought," she said pulling him down the street. "Besides, I'm more than you can handle now."

He watched and envied her enthusiasm and passion for life, which he was just beginning to understand and experience after sixteen years of marriage. Her great talent was the ability to relish every moment of life, wherever they happened to be, and to accept others as they were. The afternoon before they were scheduled to board the ship to Kilrush, she purchased a dozen or more gingham dresses and had Grove take them to a poor area of town. There, she got out of the carriage and walked down the street, passing them out to women whom it was evident had not had a new piece of clothing in many years. The women were so startled by the gifts, they were speechless. On seeing the puzzled look on her husband's face, she remarked, "We have been wonderfully blessed. But for God's grace, you could be that man over there," she pointed to a shabbily dressed man poking through a trash bin. "Or I could have been one of these women." She looked directly into his eyes, "Jesus said, to whom much has been given, much is required."

The following morning they boarded the ship that would take them to Kilrush on the Shannon River, a two day voyage in good weather. Once again, Elizabeth quickly made friends with everyone from the Captain to the deck hands. Since some of these men were Irish, this was her first real experience to meet and speak with those who many of her friends referred to as despicable people, although she suspected few had ever met an Irish person outside of London.

Two days later as the ship entered the Shannon River, John called her over to the rail. "I need to caution you again," he said, "Ireland is not England, it can be dangerous here."

Her response was, "So what's an adventure without a little danger."

Kilrush was a very neat, clean town of about 10,000 people, with a main street lined with numerous shops, taverns, two hotels, and several churches. On the side streets were more dry good dealers, stables, and blacksmith shops. They booked into the best hotel there, modest but suitable; and decided to walk about the town while Grove took care of unloading the carriage, horses, and luggage.

The next morning as they left to meet the land Broker, they quickly discovered that once outside the town, Irish roads were poorly kept; and having been accustomed to the finest Inns, many of the road side Inns resembled stables more than accommodations for humans. They had been warned that the danger to English travelers increased in relationship to the distance from the port. True, there were scattered detachments of English soldiers stationed to protect travelers against thieves and discontent Irish terrorists, but they could not be everywhere. More than one English Lord had been murdered on his way to inspect his land: land that more often than not, had been confiscated by the English government under one pretext or another, and sold or given to an English family with the right political and social connections.

It was not without cause therefore, that the Irish hated the English, who in turn hated them. The English landowners were fearful of the Irish and only reluctantly visited their estates there. In fact, some absentee landlords never personally inspected their property. That dangerous task was left to hired overseers and managers. Many of the latter, given free reign and with the owner's hundreds of miles away, abused the Irish tenant farmers financially, physically, and emotionally. Under such harsh conditions, the farmers were not inclined to do their best, and the Overseers and managers sent reports that the declining income was due to the lazy, dirty Irish. Thus a vicious circle was perpetuated year after year. It was thoughts such as these that occupied John's thoughts as he watched the countryside from their carriage window. As for Elizabeth, she was not in the least troubled by such dark thoughts, she was simply fascinated by everything she saw.

"Fortunately," John said breaking the silence, "the estate we're going to inspect is only ten miles from Kilrush. I was told that this area had been relatively free of violence."

"That's nice," was all she said.

When they arrived at the estate, the Land Agent who worked for the Owner's Solicitor, was waiting for them at the gate. Not a beautiful wrought iron gate, but a simple wooden frame with wire to keep out livestock. When they drove up the drive and approached the manor, their first impression was one of disappointment. The advertised Manor House was really little more than a large farm house obviously in need of repairs. A short time later, they observed that the barns and other outbuildings were in similar condition. John felt that if the buildings had been neglected, it was probable that the land had been as well. Tomorrow they would begin touring the fields. The Agent told them that the reason the property was being offered for sale, was because the previous Owner had been accidentally killed by a horse over a year ago. Having left no sons to inherit the estate, and a young widow with two small girls, the property had to be sold.

Having heard many horrendous stories of how estates could be quickly ruined by corrupt English managers; John said that he wanted to meet the present manager who was Irish. Further, if they purchased the property, would he consider staying on until someone else could be found? The Agent said that he had discussed that with Neil McLeod, the manager, who said that he would consider staying. They would meet him tomorrow morning, and McLeod would show them the property and answer any questions they might have. Meanwhile, the tenant farmers upon hearing that the property might be sold to an English Lord, feared for the worst. But when they later learned that Neil might be kept on, they began to feel a bit better.

Neil McLeod was as Irish as Irish could be, a stocky five foot-eight in height, with a ruddy complexion and more freckles than stars in a clear night sky. He had managed the property for the previous Irish owner for almost five years. "It was a great tragedy, M'Lord, M'Lady," he said in perfect English, "when Mr. McGillicutty died, he left a fine widow and two wonderful little girls. We will all be very sorry to see them go." Having expected a disgruntled manager who spoke broken English with a strong Irish accent, both John and Elizabeth were pleasantly surprised; it was a good sign.

The next morning when the Bligh's came to inspect the property, Lord Bligh was exactly what the tenants expected. Mounted on a beautiful chestnut mare, he acted every bit the cold indifferent, arrogant, English aristocrat, and he spoke to no one except his wife and McLeod. Lady Elizabeth however, stopped and talked to everyone. Several times, to the tenant's delight and John's dismay, she dismounted to inspect small flower gardens planted by the cottages. She laughed, picked up small children, let a young girl with long raven tresses ride on her horse while she walked along side. Once, she was invited by a farmer's wife into their tiny cottage. The Irish farmers and their families had never witnessed anything like it before, and talked about it for weeks, long after the Bligh's returned to England.

"And I'm tellin ya, she's got ta have some Irish blood in 'er or she's Catholic," Tommy McGuigan exclaimed as he lifted his pint off the bar.

"Na, I do na think so, but thanks be ta Mother Mary, she's not like her husband," came a reply.

"That's so," several voices chimed in.

"Do ye suppose that they might come ta stay?...here in Kilrush I mean? Now she could make a difference."

"Live here?... in our fair land?" another voice exclaimed. "Ye must be daft man, the English only want our land, they do na want ta live with us."

"Aye", came the reply. An we do na want the dirty land-stealin English livin here!. Right lads?"

The response was a rousing chorus as every man in the tavern raised his glass, "To Ireland."

The room was quiet for a few seconds and then Tommy spoke up.

"Nay lads, the Bligh's will not be stayin. McLeod told me they would be leavin in a coople of weeks, soon as they look over the land. Till then, no one knows if'n they'll buy it."

The days passed as the Bligh's carefully inspected all of the estate. Every field; barn; cottage; stable; the creeks; stone hedgerows.... everything. Neil McLeod rode at their side pointing out this and that, and answering questions. After the first day, it was apparent to McLeod that the Bligh's knew very little about Ireland, and even less about farming. Still, although stern and rigid, John Bligh did seem to be a man interested in learning. The best days of course were when Lady Elizabeth rode with them. Not only was she open and lively, but her presence softened her husband. It was evident to everyone who saw them together that they meant a great deal each other, and that she would play an important part in the decision to either buy or walk away.

Neil McLeod carefully observed and listened. He wanted to know what made Lord and Lady Bligh tick, why they were considering buying Arden, especially since they had no farming experience or background. If they hired him, how long would they keep him on? How much authority would they give him to manage the estate? Would they be returning for inspections? and if so how often? Or would they buy the property and never return, as did many of the English landowners.

Over the next two weeks, he and Lord Bligh spent almost every day from sunrise to sunset covering every aspect of managing the property. McLeod was happy to learn that if they bought the estate they were not going to replace him for at least a year, which was to be a trial period. Furthermore, they were willing to grant almost full authority to someone they had confidence in. As the days passed, it was also becoming apparent that Lord Bligh would be very serious about developing Arden to its full capacity. Not simply to exploit the land to maximize quick profits, but to carefully develop Arden into a showcase estate as well as a profitable business. While McLeod had harbored serious reservations when he first met Lord Bligh, by the end of their first two weeks together, he was actually beginning to like the Englishman. For their part, John and Elizabeth felt that McLeod was an exceptional manager and would be crucial in running the estate for the first couple of years. After that, time would tell.

Had McLeod been born in England under the right circumstances, he would have risen and gone far in business and politics. Born in Kilrush and with only a few years of formal schooling, he had done very well thus far. Even as a young boy he quickly grasped the reality that the

English were in Ireland to stay, and that learning to speak properly would be crucial if he was going to rise above the poverty and ignorance he saw all around him. Starting as a young boy, he made every effort to become friendly with the owners of the local estates regardless of whether they were Irish or English. By the time he was twelve, he got a job working with the hired English manager of an English estate. When other boys were playing, he was learning how to properly read and write English. When the owner of the estate observed his zeal for learning, he offered to lend him books from his own library on agriculture, animal husbandry, biology, and history. Within four years having read every available book on these subjects several times, he turned to the financial and management aspect of running a large estate. By the time he was twenty-five, it was generally acknowledged that he knew more about agriculture and estate management than anyone within fifty miles of Kilrush.

None of this was lost on Lord Bligh, who had done a little investigating of McLeod. His original plan had been to keep McLeod on temporarily until he could find an English Manager to replace him the following year. The past four weeks however, had completely changed his thinking. In McLeod, he saw the chance to get more than a manager who would simply keep things running. McLeod had the knowledge and skill to develop Arden in ways that had never even occurred to him. Furthermore, because McLeod was Irish, he had the loyalty and support of all the tenant farmers and workers on the estate, to a degree an English manager could never hope to achieve, a value that could not be over estimated.

What impressed John most however, was McLeod's understanding of business economics. Not the daily rise and fall of the business and stock market, such as he was involved with. But a fundamental grasp of supply and demand as they related to agriculture. One afternoon they were   riding past one of the larger fields planted in potatoes.   John, who was beginning to recognize good healthy plants, commented on them.

"Fine looking field."

"Aye, that it is", McLeod replied.   "But too many potato fields."

"Too many?   John pulled up on the reigns and looked at McLeod.   "I don't understand."

"It's all in potatoes, M'Lord." He swung his arms around gesturing toward all the fields.   "Potatoes and nothing else."

"True McLeod, but there is a growing market for them. They are one of the surest money crops there is."

"Aye, that's true today.   But it may not be next year, or the next.   What if there's a crop failure like twenty years ago, or another terrible frost like in 1807?   Everything could be lost in a year." He remained silent for a few seconds to let that sink in

"I remember that frost, horrible time even in England." John said softly.   "Lady Elizabeth and I had been married for three years when it happened.   Several businessmen I knew lost fortunes; one killed himself when he discovered he was ruined."

McLeod noted the look of sadness on Bligh's face, "it could happen again M'Lord. I tried for several years to get the former owner to put in some grain in a few fields. The ones that were not fairin so well, but he would not do it."

John nudged his horse and started moving again.   "He must have had a reason"

"Oh that he did.   He did not believe there would be another frost or failure like that again for many years. And he believed that a small profit was better than the risk of no profit." McLeod stopped his horse, dismounted, and pulled up a potato plant.   "See this", he said holding it up for Bligh to inspect.   "Now this here field is a good one, and these will continue to grow. But over there in that field," he pointed a distance away, "they will not develop as well because the soil is different. But grain would do well there." He carefully replanted the young plant and climbed back on his horse.

"Do you think there would be a market for grain here?"

"Aye, I do." "For one thing, there's always a shortage of oats for the horses through the winter." He turned to watch Bligh. "And for another, the town is growing fast and the women need flour for baking. It's not like it was ten-twenty year ago. Back then most everyone was livin on their own patch of land and grew things for themselves. Now, the town folk need to buy everything." He could see the expression on Bligh's face change as the slightest hint of a smile formed.

"Is there a mill in town?" Bligh asked.

"Aye. It's old, but still running." A grin crept across McLeod's face as their pace slackened.

John stopped again. "So what would you plant, wheat, oats, barley? And how many fields would you start with?"

"We have... excuse me M' Lord. There are five small fields, about twenty acres in all that could be planted with wheat and oats. This fall, I'd put winter wheat in the two larger fields," he turned in the saddle and pointed, "about 12 acres, and oats in the other fields come spring."

"What about potential profit?" John started moving again.

"The fields we would change made little profit last year. The first year will need some extra work fitting out the fields, so I figure the first year profit will be a little less than the potatoes, maybe even a small loss. After that it should go up."

John thought about this for a few moments. He had done very well in other business ventures because he was not afraid to take risks. McLeod's proposal was very modest and even if there was a loss it would be minimal, so he had no objection to giving him the approval to get started.

What he was more interested in, was how far they could extend the crop changing idea."

"Understand McLeod, Lady Elizabeth and I have not yet decided to purchase the property. However, for the sake of discussion, say I gave my approval to get started. Where do you see this going in.... say five years?"

McLeod was taken back by the question. He had tried and failed for so many years with an Irish owner, he had almost decided not to even ask the new English owner. Bligh's quick acceptance, followed by what he took to be a much broader openness to major change surprised him.

"Can I speak freely M'Lord?"

"I would not have you manage my property if you do not," John replied looking directly at him.

"Thank you M'Lord. You'll always get the truth from me." McLeod turned his horse so that he directly faced Bligh. "Fact is, I'm worried about the potatoes. I hear reports from some of the lads in other counties about partial failures, blights and the like. They seem to be increasing. All the land around here is in potatoes. If a bad frost or blight struck here, it would be terrible for you, for everybody. The folk here live on potatoes, it could be devastating." He leaned forward and stroked the neck of his horse, and whispered in her ear. He straightened up in the saddle and noticed that Bligh had a puzzled expression on his face. "They're no different then we are M'Lord, animals like to be loved too."

John watched this little demonstration with interest. Except for a dog he was fond of, he had never really cared for animals. To him, a horse was simply an animal to do his bidding. The idea of caressing and talking to a horse had never occurred to him. "I'm curious, what did you whisper in her ear?"

"Just that she's a good girl and I'll give her some extra oats when we get back to the barn."

"And you really think she understood you?" John asked in astonishment.

"Aye. That she did. Isn't that right Daisy," he said to the horse at which point Daisy shook her head as if to say yes.

"McLeod," John said laughing, you're an interesting man. I must tell Lady Elizabeth about this tonight." They nudged their horses and started toward the manor. "And I'm certain that you are right about the potential for disaster here. Everything in potatoes is a very high risk."

As they rode back toward the manor, John had already made up his made to buy the property. Tonight over dinner he would discuss it with Elizabeth. His concern was that although she had not said anything, she was very disappointed in the manor house, and may not see the potential in the land. At that instant he realized that for the past four weeks, he had never given a moments thought to what his father might have done or said; what mattered now was what Elizabeth thought, how she felt about this idea. Riding up to the house, he found her standing on the porch waiting for him.

"John," she called excitedly running down the steps and over to his horse. "I think we should buy Arden. I've got a good feeling about this land."

Completely surprised at her remark, "but what about this old place?" he said pointing to the house. "Of course we could tear it down and build a larger home."

"No. While you have been inspecting the fields, I've inspected every nook and cranny of this old house. I love it. All it needs are repairs and a few modifications; it's perfect for here, for us. A huge manor like the one in London is fine for there, but it wouldn't belong here."

He dismounted and looked at her with a wonderful smile. Once again, she was ahead of him.

Chapter 5

It had all happened so very suddenly. They had been scheduled to make their fourth trip to Arden to check on the completion of the renovation work on the old manor, which they had transformed into a beautiful country home. Just before leaving for Ireland, Elizabeth received word that her sister had become ill, and decided to pay her a brief visit in Southampton. A week later, John was looking forward to her return when he received an urgent message that she had been stricken with Scarlet fever.

They had been married for almost eighteen years, but tragically, it had only been in the past two years that they had begun to spend most of their time traveling and in Arden together. In those last few days being alone with her by her sick bed, all the cares of business and politics were swept away as the morning sun dispels the fog. How clearly he could see now that what truly mattered was the time they had spent together, and how important she was in his life. Now, despite the finest medical help available, those wonderful days were drawing to a close.

"Promise me", she had whispered, her body burning up with fever, "that you will continue to go to church." She reached out to him and he leaned forward grasping her hand. "I know that you have only attended because of me; but it's very important that you go. You may not understand why now, but in time you will."

"I promise Elizabeth. I promise because I love you and...." his voice faltered, "and because I will feel very close to you there."

A warm smile crossed her lips. "I'll see you in the morning," she said and closed her eyes. When she opened them she was in another world. He was left in his; still holding her hand.

For months after her funeral, he never left their estate near London, except to visit her grave and to keep his promise by attending the Sunday morning church service. On her grave he placed a huge marble angel with wings curving forward and the face looking down as if in prayer. The inscription read,

> Do not say goodbye to me here, but one day,
> Bid me good morning in a far brighter land.

Two or three days a week he would sit at the base of the angel and spend hours talking quietly to her, telling her everything that had occurred since he had last visited her. He related stories about what was happening at their home; he read the newspaper to her about the social events; the parties and balls; about business matters; even politics about which she had never cared. He never spoke about Arden, it was too painful to bear. At first, the local Vicar would stop by and ask if everything was alright, did he need any help? But he soon determined that he was so broken in heart and spirit, only God and time could mend such a stoic and harsh nature as John Bligh possessed.

Each Sunday, he would attend the morning service because of his promise. But his mind was never focused on the service. Out of habit he would rise for the prayers, but never hear them; from rote he would mouth the words of the hymns, but never comprehend them. As for the sermons, if losing his fortune depended upon his recalling the sermon text, he would have soon become penniless.

The months passed by. Summer faded to fall, then winter. Christmas and New Years came and went, and he was absent from all the gala holiday parties Elizabeth had loved so much. He was now 41 years old, a very wealthy widower who could have become very popular with the ladies at all the social gatherings. But despite the numerous invitations and pleas from his friends, he never attended any of them. Aside from his business dealings, his only contact with society was at church, and even that was minimal.

Then one Sunday morning in late March, as he sat alone in the family pew, he slowly became conscious of words the minister was saying.

" ... To everything there is a season, and a time to every purpose under the heaven: there is a time to be born, and a time to die; a time to plant, and a time to pluck up that which is planted; a time to kill, and a time to heal; a time to break down, and a time to build up; a time to weep, and a time to laugh; a time to mourn, and a time to dance; a time to...." the minister's words faded away. His mind returned to his wife's grave, and the emptiness of his life. Moments later, the minister's voice again interrupted his melancholy thoughts. ".... and so the daughter born to David by Bathsheba, the wife of Uriah, died. And David, who had lain on the earth fasting and praying for her recovery, arose from the earth, washed, anointed himself, got dressed, went to the house of the Lord and worshiped."

The words repeated again and again in his mind, "...he arose from the earth, washed, anointed himself, got dressed, went to the house of the Lord and worshiped." It was as if a switch had been turned on in his mind. The gray twilight of the past months that had enveloped his mind dissolved into the clearest daylight, and he was able to see clearly what he must do. Elizabeth had been right in demanding that he promise her to attend church. She had known what he did not, that his recovery would only come from hearing God's word. In that moment, to the great shock of those around him, he humbly knelt down in his pew as tears flooded down his cheeks. Salvation came to John Bligh.

That very afternoon after arriving home from the service, he began preparation to leave London and go to Ireland.

The times they had spent there had been a happy times, and he recalled their plans for Arden; but with her death, that had all changed. Now he would go to the estate, evaluate his holdings, and sell everything. While the sale would result in a considerable loss of income, he calculated that by reinvesting the sale proceeds in another business in England closer to London, in time he could make up the loss. A messenger was dispatched to McLeod, his manager, stating that he would arrive in about a fortnight.

For the next two days, he conferred with his bankers and business partners in London, and had the staff of his estate near London close down the main living quarters. Since he was expected to be gone for several months, Albert, the Butler who managed the house, said he would let some of the staff go to save expenses, something Lord Bligh had always harped upon. To Albert's surprise he said no, and told him that the full staff was to remain. He then further shocked the him by commenting that these were not the best of times, and he did not want to further add to anyone's misery by putting them out of work. When later that afternoon, Albert repeated this to the rest of the staff during dinner, the head cook exclaimed, "my word, but the Lord does work in mysterious ways, don't he."

In early April, the entire staff gathered in front of the manor house to say goodbye as the carriage and wagon were loaded. John would ride in the carriage along with three small trunks containing his important business records, books, and papers. The wagon that followed was packed solid with enough clothing and materials for his anticipated stay. All this was necessary, as in the past he and Elizabeth had never stayed at Arden more than two or three weeks at most, and therefore they had very few personal belongings there.

When he and Elizabeth purchased the property, his first intention had been to change the name that had been given to it by the former Irish owner. The name came from The

Forest of Arden, which adjoined Stratford-upon-Avon, in which Shakespeare set his play, "As You Like It." Arden therefore, meant a place of romance, and Elizabeth asked him not to change it. "It will represent our new life together."

He closed his eyes at the remembrance, and the sense of melancholy that started to envelope him was cut short by Albert's voice.

"M'Lord, the carriage is ready to leave."

The trip to Bristol was far from pleasant. From London to Bristol on the west coast of England, the roads were generally in fairly good condition, but the heavy April rains had turned some sections into muddy quagmires, causing numerous lost wheels and breakdowns. These mishaps in turn quickly filled the numerous Inns and taverns with travelers and merchants waiting for their carriages and wagons to be repaired. The result was that many travelers, fearful of a breakdown late in the day and no place to stay, stopped much earlier exacerbating an already bad situation. Thus what in good weather would have been a two day trip, took three.

He was looking through some papers when suddenly without any warning he was jolted from his seat as the front wheel of the carriage hit a large rock hidden under the mud, pitching the carriage sideways. John was thrown from one side to the other, and he could hear Grove calling 'Whoa, whoa,' to the horses. When the carriage stopped, he opened the door and stepped down into the mud as Grove climbed down to inspect the wheel.

"The wheel's not broken M'Lord", he said running his hand along the outer rim, "but the blow loosened the iron rim. If we take it slow, it should hold till we can get it fixed in Newbury, the next village."

John glanced at the dim disk of the sun starting its downward path toward the horizon. "How far is that?"

"Bout eight mile."

John quickly calculated that he was going to loose a half days travel. Even assuming the wheel could be quickly repaired - which was very unlikely given how busy the wheelwrights were at this time of year - he would be spending the night in the village. "Is there a good Inn

"I do na know M'Lord."

John placed one foot on the step, and taking hold of the boarding handle, pulled himself up. He then carefully turned around so that he was sitting on the edge of the seat. Grove pulled a rag and brush from a small box and cleaned the mud off his boots. "Well Grove," he said, 'lets get on to the village and see what we find there."

"Aye Sir." Returning the rag and brush to the box, he climbed back up to his seat. John tapped the side of the carriage door, Grove snapped the reigns, and the carriage lurched forward.

Bligh's thoughts were no longer in the past; they were on a carriage wheel that he and his driver both hoped would stay together until they got to Newbury.

As they entered the town, Grove noticed a blacksmith shop and pulled up in front. The Smith, seeing the expensive carriage out front, stopped what he was doing and went out to see what the problem was. John stepped out and pointed to the wheel.

"We hit a rock, the rims loose. How long before you can repair it?"

The Smith thought about the horse he was supposed to shoe for very little money, and exclaimed, "I kin start on it now, M'Lord."

"Excellent. Can you direct me to a good Inn or hotel?"

The rest of the afternoon was frustrating. The wheel repair was completed within an hour, but because it was now late afternoon, the rest of the day was lost. He told Grove to be ready to leave in the morning at first light.

This time, Bristol held no magic for him, and he was anxious to sail to Kilrush as soon as possible. When Grove pulled up in front of Bleakman Manor, the hotel where he and Elizabeth had always stayed, the Doorman opened the door and John started to get out, then changed his mind. "Another time," he said. "Grove, lets find a small Inn down closer to the docks." He looked back at the hotel as they pulled away. "Too many memories," he whispered to himself, "too many memories."

They passed several small rundown hotels and Inns that John questioned whether he would survive the night if he stayed in any of them. A few blocks later, he noticed what had once been a beautiful private home, and now had a small sign advertising, 'The Captain's Lodge.' There was no doorman standing outside. He tapped on the carriage ceiling, "Stop here," he called. Grove turned the carriage toward the curb and stopped. "Don't get down Grove," he called as he opened the carriage door himself, "I'm going to step inside for a moment."

"Aye, M'Lord, " he answered.

Grove leaned forward and whispered to the horses, "I do'na know what's happenin to the Master. Sometimes, he loads the travel cases on the carriage his-self; now he tells me not to get down an open the door. One of these days, he may decide ta drive this carriage and tell me ta ride inside." He shook his head in bewilderment, and the horses nodded as if in agreement.

The entrance door was painted a bright red, and a ships spar projected out above it flying the Union Jack. A polished brass plaque along side the door said to knock and walk in. Inside, there was a small foyer with oak settees, coat racks, umbrella stands, and a pair of open French doors leading to the entry hall. On the left through a set of double sliding pocket doors, was a reading room, which had been converted into an informal office. On the opposite side of the hall, a matched set of doors led to the Parlor. The fireplace mantle was constructed in cherry, and inset with small beveled glass mirrors. Various pieces of ships equipment were placed on the mantle: a beautiful brass sextant, pocket compass, and telescope. He stepped closer to look at the small framed portraits. "Most likely the retired Captain who now runs the Inn," he thought to himself. He glanced around the room. The silk upholstered furnishings; numerous lamps; books scattered around; and the daily newspaper neatly folded on the leather drum-top table. It was all very warm and inviting, and he immediately felt at ease.

"May I help you Sir?" The woman's voice started him for a moment, and he turned to see a slender attractive woman standing in the doorway. At first glance it appeared she had cut her hair very short, but on closer examination he could see it was red with very tight curls. She had a perky look about her that made it difficult to determine her age, but he guessed that she was in her late thirties, the Captain's daughter perhaps.

"Forgive me," he replied, "your Inn is so inviting, I almost felt like I was at home. I sincerely apologize for walking in unannounced." He took a step toward her. "My name is John Bligh," he continued, "...and no, no relation to Captain William Bligh," he added anticipating her question.

"Well I'm happy to hear that - that you're not related that is," she replied. "My late husband, that's his portrait you were looking at; served with Bligh for two years. But that was long before the Bounty incident. My name is Catherine Smyth - that's Catherine with a "C" she added - but everyone calls me Cassie"

He looked at her and then at the picture again.

Seeing the puzzled look on his face, she explained, "My husband was considerably older than I when we were married. It was love at first sight. His ship had just returned from taking some troops to India, and he attended a party at the home of one of my friends. We saw each other across the room; he introduced himself; we danced; became engaged a week later; and married the following weekend. Many of our friends thought it was all rather scandalous. Somehow, the twenty-three years difference in our ages never mattered to either of us." Suddenly she stopped talking. "But forgive me, I can't imagine why I'm telling you all of this."

John smiled, "Oh it is quite obvious. You still love him, but he's no longer here to talk to. Therefore, you talk about him to anyone who will listen, and that eases the pain of your loss."

She looked at him, "You understand this because you have suffered a similar loss. Am I correct?"

"My wife Elizabeth. She died of Scarlet Fever over a year ago. We were very close, and spent many enjoyable times here in Bristol."

"I'm sorry for your loss. So to even things up for talking about my husband," she smiled warmly, "what do you want to tell me about Elizabeth?"

"Well, that could take some time," he laughed. Then almost as if being compelled by some inner force, he heard himself asking, "Would you have dinner with me tonight?"

She was startled by this sudden invitation from a stranger, and surprised herself by answering, "On one condition."

"And that is?" he asked.

"You call me Cassie, and we both promise not to spend the entire evening talking about the spouses we loved, but who are gone."

"I accept your conditions. How about 7:30 PM. I know a wonderful restaurant with excellent food. By the way, Elizabeth and I never ate there."

She then showed him the accommodations, and he chose the small suite of rooms on the second floor over looking the harbor. Grove stayed in the servants quarters on the fourth floor. Bad weather delayed their departure for three days, during which he and Cassie had time to get to know each other. That was the beginning of what gradually developed into a wonderful friendship.

Several times a year, whenever he passed through Bristol, he stayed at the Lodge and reserved the same suite. He and Cassie would spend time together exploring the city; trying out different restaurants; shopping – he loved buying her new clothes - or something for the Lodge; hiking in the nearby hills; or just sitting quietly in the evening talking and reading. It was a warm, comfortable, undemanding purely platonic relationship. He also felt it was something Elizabeth would have approved of.

One morning as he came down for breakfast, he passed by Cassie's office and overheard her talking to a young couple.

"I'm very sorry, but that suite is not available. However, I do have a smaller but very lovely two room suite in the back over looking the garden."

The young couple talked to each other, obviously very disappointed. "We're getting married in two days, and we wanted that suite for our honeymoon, so we could look out at the harbor. We've been saving our money for months."

John knocked softly on the door casing, "Excuse me for interrupting," he said to the couple, "Cassie, can I speak to you a moment." She excused herself and stepped out into the hall. "I couldn't help but over hear the conversation. Is it the suite I'm in they wanted?"

"Yes."

"Well let them have it," he said with a big smile, "they're getting married. I don't need all that space, I'll move to the suite in the back."

"Are you serious?"

"Yes, and when they check out mark their bill paid. It will be my wedding present."

Cassie went back into her office and told the couple that there was a sudden cancellation and the suite would be available. They were elated; thanked her again, and again, and literally skipped out the door together.

After they left, he walked into her office beaming. "I can't remember when I felt so good about doing something nice for someone. I have a suggestion; you set up a program to provide a free honeymoon suite for a nice couple, say – once a month. I'll pay for it. Anonymous of course"

She looked closely at him and into his eyes and began to see something that she hadn't noticed before, or perhaps it was there but had remained dormant. She also began to feel stirrings deep within her that she assumed long dead. "That's a wonderful thing to do. Whatever prompted you to suggest something like that?"

"Something Elizabeth said to me many years ago, "too whom much is given, much is required. It's time I began to do more, much more."

"You realize that sometimes you may have to stay in the back again," she laughed.

"The front, the back, it makes no difference. I'm here with you, that's all that matters." He took hold of her hand and they walked to the dinning room.

This last visit had been more pleasant than he could have imagined, and for the first time they began taking long walks together hand-in-hand. All too soon it was time to return to Arden, and their joyful days together came to an end. As he climbed into his carriage and Grove snapped the reigns, she was standing in the doorway waving goodbye. Listening to the clatter of the carriage wheels on the cobblestone street, he smiled, wondering if he should invite her to Arden. She might not like Ireland, he thought to himself. Bristol was a bustling city, the quietness of the country might not suit her; perhaps his home in London would be better. Something to think about. Yes, definitely something to think about.

Chapter 6

Lawrence Bligh, youngest son of John and Elizabeth Bligh, Captain in a British Regiment; lay on his stomach behind a hilltop ridge in northeastern India. Binoculars to his eyes, he slowly scanned the valley below. Somewhere down there along the tree lined river, a fanatical Indian group that hated the British was reported to be on the move. Their objective was unknown, but presumed to be the East India Company's trading station thirty-five miles to the south.

Begun in 1600 AD with a Charter from Queen Elizabeth I, the East India Company had begun with a single trading station in Machlipatanam.   Protected by the British military, it expanded its trade areas and initiated a clever policy with the Mughals, a promise to maintain the peace in return for annual tribute. The result was that over the past two hundred years, the Company had systematically gained control over much of India. Most recently, Nepal had been defeated in 1816, and the Marathas in south central India were on the edge of defeat. As is often the case, unbridled power without responsibility, such as the East India Company enjoyed, leads to outright oppression and cruelty. The British now had many enemies in India.

It was August, and even at this higher elevation the intense Indian sun burned through Lawrence's clothing. He tried to console himself by thinking how much hotter it would be back in Calcutta where he had spent over a year before being re-assigned here, but it did not work.

"See any of the brown buggers Sir?" the corporal lying next to him asked.

"Nothing moving down there." He took the glasses from his eyes and rolled over on his back.

"Maybe we should be startin back to camp Sir. It'll be gettin dark soon."

"Not yet. If the report was right, we need to locate the bloody bastards as soon as possible. They might be under that heavy tree cover next to the river. If so and they're moving, eventually they've got to cross one of those open savannas."

Sitting up, he took the cap off of his canteen and tipped it to his lips taking just a swallow of water. He looked out over the rolling green hills. To the north east beyond his vision he could imagine the majestic snow clad Himalayas their white peaks disappearing into the clouds. For a moment his mind drifted to the lowlands, the dark green forests, the dense humid jungles, the lush grasslands, and of course the Indian people themselves. In spite of the heat; almost unimaginable monsoons; and the oppressive humidity; he loved India and its people. He felt alive here in a way that he had never experienced back in England. How very far this ridge top was from his ancestral home and his father.

"Sorry Father," he mumbled to himself, "this was the right thing for me to do."

"Did ye say something to me?" the corporal asked.

"No, just thinking to myself," he replied.

He could still vividly recall his father's anger when he had first told him he was joining the Army, a few months after his mother had died.

"That's a bloody stupid thing to do. You're my son, the only one I can trust. All this will be yours someday," he said waving his arm indicating his vast property holdings. "What if you get yourself killed?" He turned and gazed out a window. "What then? The whole bloody lot will go to your worthless drunken brother, who will turn this place into a whore house filled with those drunken leaches he calls his friends."

It was true that his older brother Robert had become a scandal to the family. At first his drinking problem was confined to the men's clubs where it was kept rather quiet; but after numerous complaints by other members, he had been permanently refused entry to any gentlemen's club. He then began frequenting the pubs in the red light districts. Because of his good looks, and more importantly the inheritance from his mother, he quickly gained a large following of moochers. Soon there was hardly a month that went by but that his father received a letter from one solicitor or another demanding damages resulting from a barroom brawl, or a young woman alleging Robert to be the father of her child. Whether or not he was, was never contested. It was simply more practical to pay them off and have them sign documents precluding any further claims against the family. The cost was considerable, but Bligh's wealth was such that it was a mere trifle.

Lawrence could recall numerous times seeing his father standing by a window in his study, a crumpled letter in his hand. All the disappointment and anger had long since drained from him. He could not even bring himself to say his son's name aloud anymore, now all he would ever say was, "I'm glad that your mother never lived to see what has become of our eldest son."

His Father's grief following his mother's death, greatly added to the difficult decision he had made about joining the Army. There had been a lot of talks and heated arguments between them about family responsibility, doing ones duty, but in the end his Father respected him for having the courage to stand up for what he believed best for his own life.

"Do your patriotic duty Lawrence," he had said as they made their goodbyes standing on the dock waiting to board the ship for India. "Get it out of your system Son and come home." He shook Lawrence's hand and bid him farewell.

But even as he uttered the words, "…get it out of your system and come home," he inwardly knew that Lawrence appeared destined for a military career. He recalled his own youth when he wanted to join the Army, but then he did not have the emotional strength to stand up to his father. Years later he did, but by then it was too late; his Father had been killed in a duel, and everything fell on his shoulders.

He watched his son board the ship and waved a final farewell. Turning away he thought of how quickly life hands out terrible surprises; first Elizabeth and now Lawrence, both gone. Perhaps however, India would do what he had been unable to do, get his son out of the service and back home. It was a hope that sustained him, and held at bay the horrifying thought that Lawrence might never come home alive.

That dockside goodbye had been almost eight years ago. Life had not granted his Father's hope, not yet anyway. The Army and getting stationed in India had changed Lawrence's life to the point he could no longer picture himself as a civilian; or spending a lifetime in England confined to an office managing the family's business enterprises. Nor could he imagine being bored to tears by tedious obligatory social events and silly porcelain skinned women. Not when all of India, beautiful dark raven-haired women, adventure, and danger was before him.

He knew that one day he would have to return home, marry, and have a family. Even now the letters from his Father reminded him of his responsibility to the family heritage. Perhaps in a year or two he would go home and the dreaded events would begin. The Balls and Parties at which the over anxious, and sometimes desperate mothers, of eligible young daughters would parade them before the potential heir to one of England's richest families. The carefully practiced courtesies, the twittering mothers, the carefully mannered ball room dances that had all the excitement of a funeral march. The very thought of such a life sent a shiver down his spine. He glanced over at the Corporal who was still watching the valley.

"See anything?"

"Nothin movin Sir."

The corporal scooted down the side of the hill on his belly just enough so that he could sit up. Unlike the Captain, he hated India; the heat; filth; the food, especially curry; the people; he hated everything about it. He had enlisted believing that he would be stationed in Ireland, just a short distance from his home in Scotland. Instead, he had been shipped out to India. Now all he dreamed about was completing his tour and going home.

"It's a bonnie time of year in Scotland. If I was there now, I'd be salmon fishin. Have ye ever caught a salmon Sir?"

"No," Lawrence replied as he turned back over and resumed his observation of the valley. "Maybe one day I'll take a trip to Scotland and see if the fishing is as great as you claim it to be."

"Ah, tis better than ye can imagine." He crawled back up to the ridge just in time to see a flash of something at the edge of the trees. "Did ye see that Sir?"

"Aye, that I did Corporal," he said in his best imitation of a Scottish brogue as he carefully glassed the area.

They had been serving together almost three years now, and had developed a close bond between them. In some ways, the Corporal seemed like a younger brother. To the Corporal, Captain Lawrence wasn't like the other officers he knew. He could talk, joke freely, and be himself. Captain Lawrence would be the only thing he would miss when he left India.

"It's them; no doubt about that," Lawrence said as he carefully jotted down notes as to their numbers; wagons;

equipment; and tried to determine how many officers there were. The latter was difficult because these roving quasi-military groups seldom wore any type of uniform or insignia. It was only by watching to see which men appeared to move freely along the column and be giving orders, that he could estimate the number of officers. After half an hour of observation, satisfied that he had the information he wanted, they slid down the hill to their horses hidden in a small grove of trees. As they started back to camp, he turned to the Corporal,

"So how big do your Scottish salmon get?"

"Huge Sir. I once saw one that went aboot five stone. T"was almost as long as I am tall."

"Well right now," he said mopping the sweat from his brow, " I'd settle for a swim in one of your cool rivers."

"My Father has fished there, up near ...," he paused searching for the name of the town. "Oh well, doesn't matter. When he came back he said he caught several, but none as big as five stone."

"Does your family have an estate there Sir?"

"No, my Father was a guest of Lord Peel. Our family does have an estate in Ireland, on the west coast by the River Shannon. I've never been there."

They rode on in silence. The Captain, trying to imagine what fishing for salmon in Scotland must be like; and the Corporal wondering what it would be like to be so very wealthy, like the Captain. Like many other enlisted men, he also wondered why so many of the officers, many of them from very rich families, were risking their lives in such a god-forsaken place as India.

The sun was a blazing fireball slipping below the hills to the west when they arrived back at the garrison. The Corporal headed for the mess hall, and Captain Lawrence toward headquarters to make his report. It had been a good day; a very good day.

Two days later, at 7:15 in the morning, British troops under the command of Major Howard Wilkins waited for the enemy near the east end of a long valley, Scouts having reported the column less than two miles away. The Major took these last few minutes to confer with his staff officers and commanders regarding the placement of artillery, the infantry, and cavalry. Satisfied that everything was in position he mounted his horse, "Remember, hold your fire until they're past the first battery unless they see you. They're marching into the morning sun, but stay hidden as much as you can. We want to trap and hold them between the first and second batteries as long as we can." He then ordered the commanders to their posts. Carefully hidden from view, the British officers silently watched the enemy column draw closer to them.

At this point, the valley is less than a half-mile wide with the river running closer to the southern side of the valley floor. Because the southern side received less sunlight and direct heat, the trees were much denser making troop movement difficult. Consequently, the enemy column was moving along the more open northern side of the river. To further complicate the very bad position the enemy was in, the valley floor dropped quite rapidly at this point, causing the river to turn into a series of long heavy rapids dotted by massive jagged rocks. This combination of geographic features had not been over-looked when Major Wilkin's drew up his battle plan. He had the enemy exactly where he wanted them.

Completely unaware of what lay ahead; and having marched over seventy miles without encountering the British; the enemy officers had grown lax, failing even to send scouts ahead. Consequently, they marched past the first battery hidden in the trees on the south side of the river, unaware it was there until it opened fire. With cannon fire coming from behind them, they began running forward. Approximately five minutes later the second battery, hidden by a slight rise of ground directly in front of them, opened fire. Caught suddenly by a second barrage of cannon, one of the officer's horses reared, throwing him to the ground where he was instantly killed by a severe kick in the head by his horse. Before the panicked men could break ranks the commander yelled, ordering them to get down and hold their position.

The officers now realized that there were two separate artillery batteries, and they were caught between them. The valley was filled with the thunder of booming of cannon; heavy shot whistling overhead; and exploding shells; which echoed and re-echoed until the ranks of the enemy imagined that there must be hundreds of cannon, when in fact there were only ten in the first battery and another ten in the second. Taken completely by surprise, it was remarkable that the ranks did not immediately begin breaking apart, as the frightened men frantically looked around for a way of escape. Meanwhile, their officers raced back and forth among the column which threatened to disintegrate at any moment into a pell-mell flight.

With their men trapped between two cannon batteries, steep hills on the north side and raging rapids on the south, the Indian officers had to decide on a course of action quickly: attack or retreat. What British forces lay beyond the artillery in front of them was unknown, but most likely the infantry and perhaps Cavalry. The orders went out: retreat, and have their own canon begin firing on the British artillery across the river. If they could retreat quickly enough, and with a good deal of luck, they might be able to get out of range before it was too late.

Major Wilkin's watched them through his binoculars from his observation point slightly above the battlefield. The speed at which they re-assembled and brought their few cannon to bear on his first battery impressed him. They were certainly no match for his regulars, but even so credit was due. He thought of how much more dangerous they would become if they ever had proper military training and good equipment. The task of the British military was to stop them before that happened.

Unlike the disciplined British Regulars with their carefully prescribed battle tactics, the Indian form of fighting was more of a wild melee. Fanatical charges by screaming wild men could overwhelm even the best troops if they became unnerved. At this point the battle could still go either way despite his superior position. Wilkins had taken a gamble by placing half of his artillery on the other side of the river. If the Indians decided to courageously attack the battery in front of them, they could quickly overrun his troops. Long previous experience however, told him there was a far greater chance that they would not attack. Typically, these groups were not daring unless they had the advantage of surprise. Even so, he was greatly relieved to see their officers galloping back and forth directing a retreat.

Wilkins turned to his aide, "they just made a fatal mistake Mr. Burke. Signal the second battery to stop firing, and order the cavalry and infantry to commence their attack".

Seconds later, Captain Bligh and the cavalry bolted out from the small grove of trees just beyond the second battery where they had been hiding. The cannon were still smoking as they swept past the now silent guns and cheering artillerymen. With the sun at their backs, they had a clear view of the backs of the enemy troops now less than a half mile away.

Now in retreat, the Indian officers became aware that the cannon behind them had stopped firing, and turned around to see why. Because they were looking up the valley and the sun was in their eyes it took a few seconds before they saw the cavalry quickly bearing down on them, and following the cavalry, ranks of infantry on a run. The officers knew that what they needed now was their cannon to stop the charging cavalry. But their guns were at the far end of their column, and were being loaded and firing at the first British battery across the river. Even before they began shouting orders to the men to turn about and face the charging cavalry, dozens of men who also saw the oncoming cavalry broke ranks and began running. Some made a dash toward the river, others headed for higher ground to the north.

The British artillery men in the first battery - hidden in the trees on the south side of the river - watched with joy as the enemy column disintegrated. They saw the first puff of smoke as one of the Indian cannons fired in their direction, the ball falling far short splashing into the river. Upon spotting the racing cavalry, the British artillery re-directed their fire from what had been the front of the column to the rear and the enemy cannon. Disciplined and fast, within a minute they could see the billows of dust and smoke as their shot tore into the mass of confused officers and troops. Just before the cavalry reached the main body of the enemy, the order came to redirect their fire towards the men fleeing toward the hills.

Bligh and his men were riding hard. He could feel the pounding of the horse's hooves under him and hear the cheering of his men as their sabers flashed in the morning sun. Less than two hundred yards in front of him he could see the enemy officers trying frantically to rally their men to face the on-coming attack. He watched as an Indian officer shot one man who started running toward the river and then another, but even that failed to stop panic. In seconds, scores of men were dropping their rifles running in every direction. The officers, seeing that the situation was hopeless, turned their horses and raced toward their last hope, the few cannon they had.

Not all the enemy troops panicked and fled. About a dozen men stood in a cluster, calmly raised their rifles and began firing at the on-rushing cavalry. Bligh could see the puffs of smoke coming from the barrels of their guns but heard no sound. Suddenly he became aware that all sound had ceased for him, as if the battle was in pantomime. He turned to see the rider to his right get hit, saw his mouth open in a scream as he fell from his horse, all without a sound. An instant later, a bullet tore through the sleeve of his left arm, barely grazing the skin; with the burning sting, the full din of battle came crashing on his ears.

The small group of men that had stood their ground had no time to reload their ancient muzzleloaders before the cavalry swept over them. Some turned their rifles around attempting to use them as clubs, others were still attempting to reload as the horses' hooves and slashing sabers cut them down. As they raced on, Bligh looked back and saw scattered twisted bodies on the ground where just seconds before a group of very brave men had stood. He wondered if he had that kind of courage. To calmly face a hundred charging horses, flashing sabers....and almost certain death.

Across the river, the first artillery battery continued firing over the heads of the cavalry at the men fleeing toward the hills, and Bligh could hear the sound of the shot as it whistled overhead. To his right he could see the fleeing men and the explosions that were throwing clouds of dirt, rock, and bodies into the air. Ahead, through the smoke and billowing dust, the Indian officers were racing toward their cannon and he could imagine them screaming and yelling at the top of their voices to turn the cannon toward the onrushing British cavalry behind them. One crew frantically pulled their gun around to face them, but fired in such haste that the blast killed several of their own officers and horses. Upon seeing what they had just done, the gunners fled, starting a general rout that quickly abandoned all of the cannon.

Onward the cavalry raced slashing left and right, their well trained horses jumping over the bodies of the wounded and dead. Here and there an individual or small group fired their muskets in a vain attempt to stop the on-coming wave of Redcoats. Bligh saw one fanatic less than fifty feet away raise and point his rifle directly at him and fire. He felt the shot tear through his tunic, missing his body, but smashing into the chest of the rider behind him. On his left a horse took a direct hit to the head and went down tumbling end over end, hurtling the rider into the path of the following rider. In minutes, they were past the last enemy troops and into clear sunlight. They rode on for another fifty yards slowing their horses, stopped, and turned around. Glancing around at his men, he could count four vacant saddles, and another horse with a rider slumped over in his saddle. He couldn't tell at this point how many of his men and horses might be lying wounded or dead in the battlefield, but he doubted there were more than half a dozen at most.

"Lieutenant Moore," Bligh said loudly to the officer next to him, "try to take a roll call and see who's missing. Sergeant Dunn, check and see who else is wounded besides Lieutenant Rogers," he pointed to the rider slumped in the saddle.

"I'm alright Captain," Rogers called straightening up in the saddle. As he did, they could see his left arm was dangling and covered with blood. "It was that last cannon blast Sir, it cut the Indian officer in two and then hit my shoulder."

"Get him off his horse and bind up that arm before he bleeds to death," Bligh yelled. But his order was unnecessary; two men had already dismounted and were running to Roger's aid.

The Infantry which had been following the cavalry at a run, had now reached the tattered and broken remains of what was left of the main body of enemy troops. All order had collapsed, and there was no organized resistance. The order went out to round up prisoners. Meanwhile, all along the river scores of the enemy soldiers hoping to escape were frantically searching for a tree branch or anything that would help keep them afloat in the raging river. Dozens of others simply leapt into the river and were instantly swept away by the powerful current. Major Wilkins ordered his men not to fire on them. It was doubtful that very many would survive the two miles of heavy rapids and rocks. Of those who were lucky enough to survive, it was very likely that they would have broken ribs, arms, and legs. It would be a long time before any would be fit enough to fight again....if ever.

Bligh was giving orders to his men to form up for a possible second charge, when his aide called his attention to an Indian Officer in the distance waving a white flag of surrender. Major Wilkins also saw the white flag through his field glasses and gave the order to cease-fire. For the next few minutes there was sporadic shooting, followed by the strange silence that descends on a battlefield when the fighting is over. At first, after the deafening sounds of cannon, gunfire, hundreds of horses and yelling men, one hears nothing as their ears take a few moments to adjust to the sudden cessation of loud noise. Then gradually, little by little one becomes aware of the moans and cries of the wounded, the dying; and the calls of survivors walking among the dead and fallen looking for their comrades.

Captain Bligh ordered his men forward toward the Indian officer with the white flag. Scattered around them were scores of wounded sitting or lying on the ground. Most of the wounds appeared to be serious, but not life threatening if treated properly. The terrible injuries, the missing arms and legs, were mostly the result of cannon fire. He doubted many of those men would live to see the next sunrise.

As he approached the young Indian officer, he could see that his right arm was missing below the elbow and a piece of rag had been bound on the upper arm as tourniquet. The entire right side of his clothing was covered in blood. He was barely able to stand upright and a young soldier - more boy than man - helped support him. Bligh dismounted and walked toward him. From the anguished look on his face it was evident he was barely conscious and in terrible pain. The officer awkwardly withdrew his sword with his left hand, and offered it to Bligh.

"I studied medicine at Oxford Captain," he said in perfect English. "You have a wonderful Country, why don't you let us have ours?"

Bligh reached out to accept the sword, but before he could take hold of it or reply, the sword fell from the officer's hand as he pitched forward and fell dead. Bligh knelt down and carefully slid the sword back in the officer's scabbard.

Standing up, he looked at the young man," do you speak English?"

"Yes Cap-a-tan, some words only."

"Then please go home and tell your friends not to fight the English, you cannot win. The Officer here," he pointed to the ground, "...why did he waste his life?" He turned and walked back to his horse.

"He wanted India to be free Cap-a-tan," the boy called after him, "like in your country."

The British had won another battle and went back to their compound. Throughout the early evening, and until late at night, there were the hurrahs and cheers of the victors. But that night as Bligh lay awake in his cot; and for many, many, more nights the Indian Officer's last words played over and over in his mind. "You have a wonderful Country, why don't you let us have ours?" Why indeed he pondered.

Chapter 7

When the ship docked at Kilrush, Fathers Carmichael and Grant were there to meet Lord Bligh. After expressing their condolences, they reminded him of how they had all loved Elizabeth, and were broken hearted when news of her untimely death arrived. Now they wanted to know what his plans were.

"I came here to place Arden up for sale, it was to be our special place. Now with Elizabeth gone, I see no reason to keep it."

Carmichael started to say something, but Grant interrupted. "I know what it is to lose a wife, someone you dearly loved. I've told you about how after I lost my family I left the army. The priesthood became my new life, and from it I gained a new family. I'm certain that I speak for both Father Carmichael and myself when I ask you to wait for a while. Maybe God has something else in mind for you, maybe even here. You can always sell Arden."

"That's true," John replied, "but first, I want to thank you both for your letters of condolence, they meant a great deal to me. That was a terrible time in my life, and only now," he said grasping Grant's hand, "can I begin to understand what you must have gone through at the loss of your wife and children. You were both very special to Elizabeth, and even though we are not Catholic, Saint Patrick's became a part of our lives here. As for keeping Arden, I made up my mind to sell it before I came here. But I'll make you this promise; I won't do anything for at least a couple of months. It will take me that long to take care of other business matters."

"We ask one for one more promise," Father Carmichael asked placing his hand on John's shoulder, "pray about this matter. God will give you direction."

McLeod and several of the tenants were waiting for him in front of the manor when he arrived at Arden. He had not been there since Elizabeth's death, and the sight of the completed house was bitter-sweet.

"We're all sorry for your loss, M'Lord. Sorry for our loss as well," McLeod began. "Lady Elizabeth was as precious to us as one of our own."

"Aye, that she was," several other voices called out.

"T'was a terrible blow ta all of us. When we got the news, we couldna believe it, she bein in the prime of life."

John was moved by this genuine outpouring of sorrow from McLeod and these people who were his tenants. "It was so sudden," he said. "She was so excited about coming here to see you all again, and to see the house." He paused to control his emotions. "She never lived to see it finished."

"Oh sure it is that Mother Mary brought her here to see it," someone called out. "We've all felt her presence here M'Lord."

"Aye, she's here," one of the women called out. "Jes look out back at the flower garden she planted. We've never seen anythin like it."

John followed them around to the back of the manor. There before him was a garden of hundreds of wild flowers of all sizes, shapes, and colors.

"Tis like God his self planted it," a voice said.

"That's exactly what she wanted," John replied, "completely natural. I brought with me a small bronze plaque she had made to place in the garden: it reads, God's

Garden." Placing the plaque at the front of the garden, he turned and thanked everyone for coming. To keep his emotions from completely overwhelming him he called to McLeod, "there are a lot of things we need to discuss. I'll meet you after lunch, right now I need to get settled in."

"Yes M'Lord. And before I forget, welcome home to Arden."

John was startled by McLeod's statement, "welcome home." He said nothing about it, but thought it odd that McLeod would say that knowing that his home was in London. "I'll meet you at the stable, say 1:00 o'clock," he called back."

"I'll be there."

That afternoon they began a very thorough investigation of the entire estate. John had been gone for over year, and McLeod, having been given full authority had made numerous changes. The buildings, barns, stable, and numerous tool sheds, had all been repaired and painted. In addition, he had built a storage silo for grain.

Pointing it out to John he said, "this will give you more leverage at harvest time. If prices are down, you can store the grain, rather than being forced to sell it." He had also added an area in the barn for cattle. "Since we had the room, I thought that we could try raising a few head of dairy cattle. We could graze them in the summer months on the steeper hillsides that aren't being used, and in winter feed them with hay and grain. This way, we could supply all of the tenants here with milk and butter so they wouldn't have to keep their own cow - unless they wanted to. If this works out, in a year or two I think we could increase the herd and start selling milk and butter to the town folk, if you're interested that is.

John was pleased beyond words. If only Elizabeth could have been here to see this.

The next days and weeks were spent touring all of the fields, McLeod showing him the ones that he had switched to grain. The past year, while John was away, he had planted an additional two-hundred acres in wheat and barley, plus an additional fifty in oats.

"We do have a problem M'Lord," he said as they looked out over one of the larger grain fields. "The old mill in Kilrush will not be able to handle much more than this. Last fall it broke down twice. If Colin hadn't been able to make the parts to repair it, it would have taken several weeks to get them shipped here. We could have lost part of the crop."

John looked at McLeod. With everyday he was getting to know him better, not just because of what he said, but by what he didn't say. "Let me guess Neil, you're thinking I should buy the mill in town and enlarge it. Am I right?"

"Well now that you mention it," he smiled leaning forward and scratching his horses neck, "I think that would be a very good idea." He looked at John, "by increasing the mill's capacity, I think other folks might consider planting some grain and fewer potatoes."

"I can see," he said with a chuckle, "that if I adopt all of your suggestions, within a matter of years Arden would become the largest producer of grain and dairy products in Clair County, to say nothing about milling operations."

"I wouldn't have a problem with that, would you?"

"But you well know I came up here to sell Arden, not enlarge it."

"I did hear something about that plan from Father Grant, but he said you wouldn't make any decision for a couple of months. During that time, I'll do everything I can to show you why selling would be a mistake. Oh, I'm sorry M'Lord, I overstepped my position when I said that."

"No apology necessary, "John laughed, "do your best to convince me not to sell, I want to hear all of your arguments. In the meanwhile, when we're working together please call me John. I get enough M'Lords in London. Secondly, I want you to be free to say what you think and feel. When you think I'm wrong say so, no apology necessary. You're critical to the success or failure of Arden. Lady Elizabeth and I both agreed on that shortly after we first met you. She had every confidence in you being able to manage Arden, so do I."

"Thank you very much for your confidence in me, and I'll do my best not to disappoint you M'Lord... I mean John. Calling you John is going to take a while to get used to."

John nudged his horse, "Tomorrow morning I have to go to town and see Father Carmichael, I'll even make an inquiry on buying the mill while I'm there – just in case you're able to convince me not to sell. Now, what else is going on in that Irish head of yours? Oh yes, the cattle, and the dairy, and...." he burst out laughing. "Tell me, do you ever stop to sleep?"

John followed Neil as they worked their way toward another field as he talked about another idea, damming up a creek. He had grown even fonder of Neil, his honesty, and forthrightness. He tried to think of any of his business partners in London that he could trust as much: he couldn't think of one.

Time has a way of slipping by almost unnoticed, so it was at Arden. The weeks turned into months, two months went by, and then another, and another. At the end of the harvest, John told Neil he had to go back to London and take care of other business, but that he would return as soon as he could. "Maybe while I'm gone, you could take a little time off and find a pretty Lass to marry. I can see that until that happens, I'll never get much rest around here."

"I just might do that M'Lord, The winter nights can get cold and damp here," he gave a mock shiver. He smiled; although John never told him in so many words, it was evident he was not going to sell Arden.

Two months later John returned from England, and the months turned into years as together they turned Arden into a very profitable agriculture business shipping grain, flour, and dairy products to several ports in England. In addition to the tenant farmers and their families who lived at Arden; they now employed over a hundred people. Along the way, Arden became the showplace John and Elizabeth had one day hoped for. There was seldom a month that went by that they had visitors from other parts of Ireland, Scotland, and England to see how they operated. Neil did get married and started a family. And day-by-day, month-by-month, something else also happened; Lord John Bligh changed.

In the years following the purchase of Arden, John Bligh had become the largest landholder in the vicinity of Kilrush, owning approximately 5,900 acres. At age 52 he was a very neat trim man, slight of build, but wiry and much stronger than he appeared. He had grown very fond of walking; and where other men of his social class rode their horses to inspect the land, he generally walked. Also unlike his peers, he would spend hours talking to his tenants and inquiring as to their health and their families well being. The result was that he personally knew every inch of his estate; the names of all of his tenants; and their children's names as well. On occasion, he was even known to step into the Pub and have a pint of dark stout with some of the local men. Had all the English landowners been like John, the history of Ireland would have been vastly different. Unfortunately for both the Irish and the English, they were not.

For the first couple of years, there had been a persistent rumor in Kilrush that William Bligh, the infamous Captain of HMS Bounty, had been his uncle, but no amount of disclaimers on his part could stop it. In truth, with the exception of an exceptionally remarkable memory for details, which both Captain Bligh and Lord Bligh possessed, he was quite different. Where Captain Bligh's temperament was overbearing and rigid to the point of cruelty; over the years John's had become flexible and mild. Where the former never hesitated to inflict punishment for the slightest infraction; John was never known to even raise his voice to an individual regardless of the damage he or she may have caused. The only weapon he ever used, if it could be called that, was his voice. The effect of hearing John quietly say to the guilty person, "...well mistakes sometimes happen. You won't let it happen again will you?" was profound. Not only did the person take great care to not make that mistake again, they went out of their way to correct other things even when they were not part of their duties. Further, many of his employees carried the idea to their own homes. Many a lad and lass expecting a sound whipping after some transgression, was shocked to hear their father or mother utter virtually the same words as John. The parents in turn rejoiced at the more often than not positive outcome.

There was of course the occasional lackey who even repeated beatings would not have corrected. John, so far as anyone could recall, had never raised a cane to anyone. After determining that the individual was uncorrectable, he simply let them go. As for future employment, once it was learned that Lord Bligh had let the person go, it became almost impossible for them to find work anywhere around Kilrush.

"If Lord Bligh let 'em go, the Blessed Mother Mary herself wouldna hire 'em", was the generally accepted belief.

John also differed from his English counterparts in another notable way. At a time when the majority of the English Landowners detested not only the Irish people but Ireland itself, and spent as little time there as possible, it now required a crisis of considerable importance to get John to leave Arden. Even then, he lost little time in

London taking care of the business at hand, and then heading back to his home.

These qualities did not escape the notice of his Irish neighbors, nor his English countrymen. As the years passed, another rumor took root that he was in fact of Irish decent. To the Irish it was as plain as a buttonhook in rainwater that no Englishman could possibly be as kind and friendly as the Irish. To the English, it was as equally plain that only an Irishmen could live among, let alone love the dirty Irish. In truth, John was as English as English could be on both sides of the family tree. He simply possessed a very rare quality; he saw individuals as they were regardless of nationality, education, religion, or color. Elizabeth had been right; the tower had been unlocked; the inner John was now free.

Chapter 8

It had been raining for five days straight. Not that this was all that unusual for the Kilrush area; but this had been a hard, steady rain, and judging from the look of the sky to the west, it was not going to stop soon.

In the hills, the tiny little rivelets which had been mere trickles gurgling over the stones, were now little brooklets several inches wide. The larger creeks and streams, being fed by thousands of these little brooklets, were becoming cascading volumes of water which were beginning to wash out stream banks, and uproot brush and small trees. Land owners, and local farmers, who well recalled the flood twelve years ago which had destroyed many bridges around the area; quickly sent out men to clear away the growing amount of debris from the dozens of small bridges around town.

In the meanwhile, the cottiers, the people who had built their small cottages near these brooks and streams, were becoming increasingly concerned and alarmed at how quickly the water was rising. At the present rate, the water would be lapping at the doorsills of their houses within the next twenty-four hours. In fact, some folks who had foolishly built next to a stream in low lying areas, had already gathered up their belongings and evacuated their homes.

About twelve miles to the east of Kilrush, was a place known as Holy Jim's Canyon, jokingly named after the recluse who had built his cabin there many years ago, and who was notorious for habitually using language that would make even hardened sailors wince. The canyon was, in fact, not a true canyon but a very narrow valley. However, the hillsides were steep enough to create a potentially deadly channel for floodwaters. In this canyon, a Clachan, a small cluster of tiny ancestral homes - some better described as huts - were now facing an impending disaster.

Shortly after the flood twelve years before, the local landowners had built an earthen dam upstream from their homes, which they believed would help control the flooding in the area. For several years it had been carefully maintained, and provided the safety factor it was intended for. But after the first eight years during which nothing happened, the landowners and local people became lax. Cattle and sheep were allowed to graze on the dam; the small brush and trees that had been planted to help stabilize the ground were eaten by the goats. In one place, the cattle and sheep had actually worn a deep path down the face of the dam as they made their way to the stream to drink.

Until the heavy rain started, no one had really paid attention to what had been gradually happening over the years. It was when Tommy came running home and told his father that water was leaking through the dam, that they awakened to the impending disaster. As word quickly spread, the men and boys from every home ran to the dam to see what could be done. No one needed to be told what would happen to their homes and fields if the dam gave way. For hour upon hour, every effort was made to shore up the dam. Wagonloads of dirt and rock were dug and hauled in the pouring rain and dumped on the dam. As the hours passed however, it became obvious that the lake above the dam was growing at a rate beyond their capacity to control. Even if the dam held, the water cresting the top would be sufficient to flood the homes and land downstream. And if the dam failed…. Well, most people did not want to think about that. There were however, a few men and women who did think about it, and began to organize an evacuation.

Meanwhile, the day before in Kilrush, Kathleen and Bridget had been talking about the steady rain, which lead to a discussion about the dam at Holy Jim's Canyon. "Has anyone asked Father Carmichael or Father Grant about the what the situation is up there?" Kathleen asked.

"I'm not sure," Bridget answered, "but I'm goin ta the church now. Ifin they don't know, I think we should plan on goin up there ta see if everythin is alright."

"While you're at the church, see if we can get a wagon and horses," Kathleen replied. "If we go, I think we should take some tools and supplies... just in case."

Father Grant, who happened to be watching the rain from just inside the front door of the church, saw Bridget running toward him, a cape pulled up over her head. Concentrating on her footing on the slick cobblestones, and not looking ahead, she dashed up the stairs and ran directly into Father Grant almost knocking him down, and drenching him with the rain that had collected in her cape.

"So Bridget," he said laughing brushing the water from his face and clothes, "have you come to baptize me?"

Without wasting any words on an apology, she replied, "No Father, I've come ta get yer help. Kathleen and I been talking, and we're thinkin there may be trouble with the dam at Holy Jim's Canyon. Have ye been there lately?"

"Two months ago," he replied, "I went up to visit with Jim, and while I was there I took a look at the dam. It's in bad shape, and I told the people they needed to get started repairing it. I even offered to get some men from town to help. They were supposed to let me know when would be a good time." He shook his head, "with all this rain, it might be too late for that now."

"Ye went up there ta see Jim," she asked with surprise, "the old recluse?

"Why sure. He's not a bad sort once you get to know him. His language takes a bit of getting used to when you first meet him."

"Well I'll be," she replied. "I had no idea anyone from here ever went ta see him. When did ye start that?"

"Not long after I came here. Father Carmichael had been visiting him for years, and suggested that I go up and introduce myself, so I did."

"So how did yer meetin go."

"A real jolt to my ears," he said laughing. "I hadn't heard that kind of language since I left the Army. Not sure I even heard that much profanity even when I was in it."

"Ye need na tell me the details," she said putting her hands over her ears. "I'm here because me an Kathleen want ta go up there today, right-a-way. We'll be needin a wagon and team, ta carry supplies. Can ye help?"

"Certainly, and I'm going with you. Who knows what the situation is there now. I also need to check on Jim. He's farther up stream above the lake so he's probably ok, but I still want to see for myself."

"So ye'll help us. Will ye get the wagon and horses?"

"I'll take care of all of that, and I'll get Father Timothy to come along. He's the new young priest that came here last month."

"Don't think I've met him."

"Very shy young man. Not a real sociable type. This will be a good chance for him to get involved and meet some folks outside the church." He turned to leave, "you get back to Kathleen and tell her to be ready to leave in half an hour. We'll pick you up at your house." He started to walk away and then called back, "be sure to bring some wool blankets, extra clothing, and good boots. It's going to be a very wet trip."

As he walked back to find Father Timothy, his mind went back to the day he first met Jim. It had been a warm summer morning in early June. He had taken a horse and cart, and was taking a few supplies to the people that lived up the canyon. The thought occurred to him that now was a good a time to meet Jim as any other. After dropping off the supplies, he continued up past he dam and the lake behind it. About a quarter mile past the lake, he pulled up to the small cottage and getting down from the cart called out. "Anyone home?" Not hearing anything, he called out again, "Anyone here?"

A moment later a short, stocky, clean shaven man in his mid-sixties came from around the corner of the cabin wearing short knee breeches and stockings; not at all the thin, ragged clothed, unshaved, bearded recluse he had expected.

"Who in hell are you?" the man yelled at him.

Grant was startled. It had been a long time since anyone had spoken to him like that, not since his Army days. "I'm Father Grant. Are you Jim?"

"And just who the hell do you think would be living here, Saint Patrick?" He walked up to Grant sizing him up. "So, another god damned priest coming up here to try and save my soul, is it?"

"No. As a matter of fact, Father Carmichael told me you didn't need saving."

"Oh now, did he really?"

"Indeed he did." Grant replied. "He also told me he didn't know another soul that used God's name more often than you, including himself."

"Carmichael. Is that old son-of-a bitch still alive? I haven't seen him since late last Fall. Figured at his age, he probably croaked. Went with the leaves as they say."

"He's very much alive, and sent me up here to check on you"

"Check on me?" He said spitting on the ground. "What gives him the god damned right to check on me? Or you for that matter."

"It's this damn crazy notion that we are to be our brothers' keeper. Comes with the collar," he said pointing to his neck. "Kind of like when I was in the Army checking on my men." Looking at Jim, he could see that he was shifting his weight and favoring his left leg. "What happened to your leg?"

"Old war injury....we was fightin the god damned English. I was with Fireball McNamara movin up Vinegar Hill back in 1798 when a cannon ball hit a tree. Shattered the tree and a piece of it tore through my thigh. Damned near lost my leg," he said patting his thigh. "Yer English, right? You bastards are still trying to take my Country." He laughed and didn't wait for a reply. "So you were in the god damned army, now yer a priest, well, well. First ye try and kill us, now ye come back to save my soul." He looked at Grant, "were ye stationed in Ireland?"

"Never served in Ireland, I was in India," Grant replied.

"India," he exclaimed. "I had a cousin that joined his Majesty's god damned bloody English Army and he was sent there to steal their Country. Lost his leg he did. Served the bastard right, he was a traitor to our beloved Ireland. Now he hobbles around his little patch of land on one leg and a crutch that sinks into the ground every other step. Funny as hell to watch him," he laughed. "So what in hell caused ya to leave the service and join the soul police?" He shifted his weight and tapped his bad leg. "No good for me to stand still too long. Com'on in," he said heading for the cabin door. "We'll sit a spell and have a wee bit to drink. Between the army and the church," he said turning to Grant, "I'm sure ye learned how to drink." He winked, and limped toward the door.

Once inside, Grant was in for his second surprise, a very well kept tidy house with shelves of books floor to ceiling; good books on history, literature, philosophy, and religion. One book in particular caught his eye and he pulled it from the shelf. It was William Tyndale's English translation of the New Testament. Jim watched him as he opened the bible and thumbed through the pages.

"T'was sent to me by a cousin in America. You know of course the Catholics had Tyndale burned at the stake as a heretic. Can na have the people read the bible for themselves, they might get the wrong ideas." Jim lit his pipe. "No, no, no; gotta keep 'em in the dark. Read the catholic version to the poor folks in Latin, a language they can na even understand."

Grant put the bible back, and turned to look around some more. Over the kitchen window was a carved wooden crucifix. When Jim saw Grant take notice of it he pointed to it, "a Christmas gift from Carmichael. I do-na hold to that any more, but out of respect for my friend I leave it there. Not what you had expected, right?"

"No. I'm beginning to think Carmichael played a little joke on me," he said sitting down.

Jim laughed, "have a wee spot of poteen. I get it from Carrie Egan, Sean's mother. None finer anywhere around these parts."

As the afternoon wore-on, they exchanged stories of how they had both arrived at this point in time and place. He also learned that Jim and Carmichael had been very close friends for many years, and spent many hours debating church doctrine, and the future of Ireland. Jim told him that he turned against the Catholic church when the Vatican sided with the British in the Insurrection of 1798.

" Do ye know that the church owns about two-thirds of the land in Ireland – most of everythin except for what that the British landlords own." He drew a puff from his pipe. "The church was afeared that if the Irish won the war, they might lose their land. They were far more interested in keepin the property than freedom for their members. Oh, not the local priests like yerself and Carmichael who really care about the people. It's those hoiti-toiti Cardinals and the Pope. A bunch of greedy liars in fancy robes."

As for his foul language, he said that was outside talk. He used it as a defense against unwanted snoopy visitors; especially widows with children looking for their next victim. Inside the house, not a word of profanity was uttered. In fact, Jim told him that he got a big kick when Carmichael told him that Holy Jim's canyon was named because of his profanity. "Canna tell a book by its cover." He raised his glass in a toast, "the luck that is not on us today, may it be on us tomorrow."

The sharp bang sound of a slamming door brought Grant back to the present.

"I understand you're looking for me," Father Timothy called standing in the doorway.

"Yes. We're going up to Holy Jim's canyon and check on the families and the dam. Bring extra clothing and good boots. I'm going let Father Carmichael know where we're going, and I'll meet you to help hitch up the team and get some tools."

"Meet you in the barn in a couple of minutes," Timothy said heading for his room to get more clothing. "At last," he whispered to himself, "a chance to really do something useful." He glanced out the window at the rain, totally unaware of what the next few hours held in store for them. For most of his life he had been an outsider, a loner who never felt at ease around groups of people. Part of the reason was that he was tall, gangly, and had an under nourished look about him, especially in his face. As if these were not enough strikes against him, his motor skills had almost, but never fully developed: in a word he was clumsy. Consequently, he avoided playing sports of any kind, and so far as anyone knew had never dated a girl.

His parents had previously lost four children, and his mother had promised God that if she had a son that lived, she would have him go into the priesthood. Consequently, beginning at a very early age his parents had constantly encouraged him – pushed him would be more accurate - to go into the priesthood. Dutiful son that he was, he did.

After hitching up the team and picking up Kathleen and Bridgit, they headed toward the Canyon. Because the dirt road had been almost totally washed away in some areas, it had taken them almost three hours to reach the canyon.

Three times they had been forced to get off and walk along side to lighten the wagon enough for the horses to pull it through the mud. About a quarter mile from the cottages, a woman covered in mud came running toward them yelling and screaming. "Father, Father, the dam's beginin ta come apart, we do-na know what ta do."

Father Grant had fully and mentally prepared himself for what they might find there. Father Timothy eager and fresh from London had not. He leapt out of the wagon and ran towards the woman, only to slip and fall face down in the mud. The woman stopped to help him get up, only to slip and fall herself. Grant, Kathleen, and Bridgit glanced at each other, shook their heads, and tried to keep from laughing.

"He may be more of a hindrance than help," Grant remarked as he directed the team to a piece of high ground. "Kathleen, our first priority is to get everyone - especially the women and children - away from the stream and to high ground." Meanwhile, the woman who had run towards them had gotten to her feet, and was gesturing wildly and pointing at the cottages immediately downstream from the dam.

Father Timothy, wiping the mud from his face and embarrassed by what had happened, approached the wagon asking what he could do.

Jumping down from the wagon, Grant told him to drive the wagon to the small knoll to the right side of the dam and wait for him. "If you see the dam start to give way, get the hell out of there and get the wagon as far from the dam as you can."

"Yes Sir," Timothy replied surprised at Grant's language. He snapped the reins heading toward the knoll.

Grant immediately started down the hill toward a group of men who were just standing there helplessly looking at the dam. "Follow me," he yelled motioning with his arms. "I think there is still time to save the dam, but not from here." As the men walked toward him, he told them to get shovels, pick-axes, and get to the wagon as fast as they could.

One of the men turned to the others, "I wager it's too late, but anythin beats jes standin here waitin fer it ta go."

Within five minutes there were eight men and the two priests climbing on the wagon. "Tim, we want to go up there," he pointed to a cluster of trees about a quarter of a mile above the dam.

Timothy, startled for a second by being called Tim, didn't waste any time. He stood up in the seat and slapped the end of the reins against the horses again and again, "Move it", he yelled, rain pouring over his muddy clothing. On the higher ground, the road was not as muddy; but bare rocks, the dirt having been washed from between them, protruded everywhere. Everyone had to hang on for dear life to keep from being thrown from the wildly lurching wagon.

A few minutes later, they were at the trees. Grant jumped down, "over there," he said pointing. "Get your tools and start clearing an area just below those trees. Tim, move the wagon away from here, hitch the horses to something solid, really solid. In the back of the wagon there's a large bundle wrapped in oil cloth, meet us over there," he said pointing, "and bring the bundle with you... very carefully," he added. He then headed down to where the men had started clearing away the brush.

He could see the bewildered look on the faces of the men as he approached. "This is an old creek bed. I noticed it two years ago when I was up here. Several years ago, it ran down through Lord Bligh's land. He wanted to consolidate two of his fields, so he damned the creek up here, and filled in the creek bed down below."

"So how is this going to save the dam?" one of the men asked.

"I'm gonna blast this open again, and let some of the lake empty out here. It'll take pressure off the dam."

"Lord Bligh will not be like'n us ruinin some of his crops and land," another yelled.

"I'll deal with Bligh later. Right now my concern is saving your families and homes. Are ye with me Lads?"

They all raised their picks and shovels and with a shout plunged with new vigor into clearing away the brush and trees for a blasting area as fast as they could. Meanwhile, Father Timothy had secured the horses and wagon some distance away and was carefully walking back carrying the large bundle, not knowing that it contained a keg of black gun powder.

Some of the men attended Saint Patrick's and knew Father Grant, none had met Father Timothy. While they had long known about Father Grant having served in the army, no one knew exactly what he had done. They were now about to discover he had been an engineer with considerable experience in explosives and blasting.

Working carefully, but surprisingly fast, he had soon set several charges among the rocks which had been hidden by the brush and trees, carefully covering them with pieces of oil cloth to protect them from the rain. Directing everyone to move back and get behind cover, he lit the fuses and ran.

Meanwhile down below, Kathleen and Bridget had worked frantically to get all the women, children, and elderly up to high ground. It had been a terrible ordeal, made even worse because of the torrential rain. Several of the elderly had to be physically dragged out of their cottages. Why on earth, when they were warm and dry, should they leave their homes. The Dam had held before, it would again.

"Do-na argue with 'em," Kathleen told the women. "Pick 'em up and carry 'em if ye have ta, but get 'em up on that hill."

There were of course a few who griped and complained about these outsiders coming in and taking over. Most however, were grateful that finally someone was taking charge and doing something. The children, being in almost total ignorance of the grave danger facing them, were having a wonderful time playing in the rain and mud, and for once not hearing their mothers yelling at them.

Suddenly, as the women were all standing around on the hill top talking, there was a tremendous blast that shook the ground at their feet. At first, some thought the dam had burst. But when they looked beyond the dam they could see the fire, the rocks and debris being thrown high in the air.

It would have been hard to determine whether the men with Grant at the site, or the people on the hill above the dam voiced more, "Holy Mary, Mother of God" expressions of surprise. Those on the hill didn't know what had happened. The men at the site however, were quickly struck with awe as they watched the earth and rocks give way and a torrent of water start gushing through the opening and ripping open a channel down the hill. One glance at that power sent chills through them as they imagined what would have happened to their homes and families had the dam given way.

Having opened the outlet, Grant yelled to the men over the roar of the cascading water, growing in volume by the minute, "Nothing more to do here, let's get back to the dam."

On the way back he turned to one of the men, "do you know who owns this land?"

"Do na know who he is, but he doesn't live around here. Someone told me he is from somewhere up north."

"What about your homes, the land you farm. Do you own that?"

"No, we pay rent. The landlord gave us each a contract so that we could build our homes and raise our crops. He sends someone down after the harvest to collect it. I don't think any of us have ever seen 'em." All of the other men nodded in agreement. "Whoever he is, he's been more than fair."

Grant decided that he would check into the ownership later. In the meanwhile, the present crisis was not yet over. There was still the dam to deal with.

When they arrived at the dam, Grant was surprised to find Jim there, "what brings you down here?"

"Just surveying the situation. I was on my way when I heard the explosion, so you blasted the old creek open. Good thinking. I told John Bligh four years ago it was a bad idea to block it."

"Seemed like the best and quickest way to relieve pressure on the dam. It will also drop the water level down below the top of the dam so there will be no spill-over." They walked along carefully checking the dam for serious damage. "So why are you interested, your place is way above here?"

"I'll let you in on a secret. This's the best trout lake in these parts, didn't want to lose it."

"And the fate of these folks had nothing to do with it?"

"Well…as I see it, saving the trout also saves the people, right?" he smiled.

"What I think is that you're not the old cranky recluse you pretend to be."

"Now you're not going to spread that notion around are you? I thought we was jes gittin to be friends."

Satisfied that the dam would hold, they walked over to Jim's wagon. Noting a large bundle Grant asked, "So what's under the oil-cloth?"

"Why powder of course," he laughed. "You jes beat me to the creek head."

Grant threw his arm over Jim's shoulder. "Just to save the trout."

"Why of course. Ye don't think I give a tinkers damn about these cottiers do ye?"

At that moment Kathleen, Bridget, and some of the men and women walked over to where they were talking.

Seeing them approaching, Jim immediately went into his act, "god damn rain, as if we don't have enough god damned trouble around here," he sputtered," as he walked away. At which point Grant burst out laughing, leaving everyone wondering what was going on.

A week later, the crisis past, Grant walked into Carmichael's study. "Got a question for you. I went and checked the County land records, and it shows the land around Holy Jim's canyon is owned by somebody named Percy J. Kilpatrick. I asked the folks out there if they knew him. Seems nobody has ever seen him, said he lives somewhere up north. Said he always sends someone else to collect the rents." He sat down in a chair. "Ever meet him?"

Carmichael walked over and sat down next to Grant. "Met and talked to him many times."

"Really?" he exclaimed with surprise. "So who is he."

"Well, I'll tell you on one condition. You must promise never to reveal his identity to anyone, and I mean anyone. This must remain a secret between you, and me, understood?

"You have my pledge. Now who is it?"

"Why it's Jim."

"Jim!" Grant exclaimed, "Holy Jim?"

"I thought that would surprise you. Percy always hated his first name. His middle name is James, but he goes by Jim. He owns over a thousand acres there. He's a good man, one of the best. He simply wants to live his life quietly, and that would all end in the blink of an eye if the people around here knew. That's why you never see him at any of the landowner's meetings. He's got a devoted manager to handle all the meetings, contracts, and collections. John Bligh and Neil know who he is, but they've also kept it to themselves."

"Well I'll be," Grant exclaimed. "He once remarked that you should never judge a book by its cover. What a sly old fox he is." Grant got up. "The last time I saw him, he said the lake up there was filled with trout. I've never fished for trout. Maybe its time I had Jim teach me."

"Let me warn you," Carmichael replied, "Jim only fishes with artificial flies. He makes them himself. He showed me a few once, little bugs made out of feathers and fur. So don't go walking up there with a can of worms."

"I'll tell you this," Grant said leaving the study, "he's one of the most interesting men I've ever met."

"Oh he's that to be sure," Carmichael replied, "and more, much more."

Chapter 9

It had been a quiet morning at Saint Patrick's, and Father Grant took advantage of the lull to work on clearing up some paperwork in the Study. Father Carmichael was sitting in his favorite chair reading the London Times, which had arrived that morning on the Mary Jane. The paper was four days old, but it was still 'current news' to the residents of Kilrush.

Grant was just dipping his quill into the ink well when an unexpected yell from Carmichael caused him to whirl around in his chair to see if he was having a heart attack.

"They did it!" Carmichael yelled jumping out of his chair. "That......" he fought to hold his tongue, "that arrogant, conniving, penny pinching, British Parliament has just passed the Poor Law Amendment." He threw the paper across the room, something Grant had never seen him do.

"So what is it?" Grant asked. "What's so upsetting about the Amendment?"

Grant, who paid little attention to politics, could see that whatever the Parliament had done must be very serious to get Carmichael this worked up.

"They've just placed another knife in Ireland's back, that's what they've done," he replied walking over and picking up the paper. "I'm sorry Grant, after all these years I shouldn't let their actions get me so riled up. Mother Mary," he said looking toward heaven, "give me grace."

Grant walked over to where he was standing. "I think it's time for you to let me in on what's going on."

"Yes, yes," Carmichael answered, "come over and sit down; but before I tell you about what Parliament just did, you need to understand the history behind it."

Grant pulled his chair up close to Carmichael's, "the student's ready," he smiled.

"This goes way, way, back. Before the Protestant Reformation started in 1532 - I'm sure you learned about King Henry and his numerous wives – six as I recall. Now up until that time, it was generally considered to be a religious duty for all Christians to follow the teachings of Jesus: feed the hungry; give drink to the thirsty; welcome the stranger; clothe the naked; visit the sick; visit the prisoner; and bury the dead."

"The Seven Corporal Works of Mercy," Grant replied.

"That's right. But after Henry broke with the Roman Church and established the Church of England, a lot of those old religious duties went bye-the-board as the saying goes, and many of the old morals and values gradually disappeared. As the Anglican Church took less and less interest in helping the poor, the duty of caring for the poor increasingly shifted to the government. Consequently, Parliament began passing numerous laws to register the poor; raise money for relief; and establish agencies to administer the varied governmental aid programs."

"In 1601," he continued, "to consolidate all the laws that had been issued over the years, Parliament passed the Elizabethan Poor Law. Simply put, it set up the following: A compulsory tax known as a Poor Rate to be levied on every parish; the collection of the tax from property owners; the creation and appointment of Overseers of Relief; and establishing work programs for the poor."

"Yes, I know about all those things," Grant responded. "It set up two types of relief for the poor. Outdoor Relief, allowed the poor to remain in their home and they were given a dole, or clothes and food. Indoor Relief, required the poor to be removed from their home and taken to a local almshouse; the sick to a hospital; orphans to an orphanage; and the idle poor, i.e. those persons capable of working, were sent to a workhouse and put to work."

"I'm impressed," Carmichael replied. "I thought you said you didn't care about politics?"

"I don't, but I do try to keep up on the laws."

"We need to," Carmichael said, "the folks around here depend on us to help watch out for their welfare in this world as well as the next. I don't hold to the notion of some priests who are so heavenly minded they're no earthly good."

"Anyway," he continued, "the problem with the Poor Law was that it didn't establish any uniform standards. Consequently each Parish was left to interpret the law as they wished; with the result that there were great disparities between parishes. Secondly, because the law only appraised land and buildings to determine the tax rate, and did not consider personal and/or movable wealth such as goods and securities, the tax burden fell entirely upon the landowners. The corporations and commercial groups were exempted."

"Now here's where things really start to go wrong. Approximately forty years ago, about the turn of the century, there began a major shift in thinking about life, morals, and wealth in particular. A few radical economists came up with the idea that there were no moral obligations attached to money. Just because you had it, didn't mean you had to share it. As if this wasn't bad enough, they also began promoting the idea that government aid to the poor interfered with the free market."

"So the wealthy who had previously felt a moral obligation to help the poor, were let off the hook," Grant replied.

"You got it! The former moral economy was replaced by a political economy, with the result that the historic traditional rights of the poor to claim relief were gradually worn away. Just because you're poor doesn't mean anyone as to help you, became the accepted norm."

"Time moved on. In 1832, the Royal Commission on Poor Relief began its investigation based upon the latter premise. Accordingly, it came as no surprise when the Commission issued its Report claiming that the Poor Laws were a cause of - now listen carefully." He held up a finger, "population growth, in other words the more children the poor had, the more relief they received; and" he continued holding up two fingers, "secondly, under-employment and low wages."

"So if I understand you correctly, the way they looked at it," Grant replied, "was why should any one seek to work when the government would take care of you?"

"Right again," Carmichael said. "But the Poor Laws didn't create the problems. They were the result of a bunch of economic factors; the Law had been written to address them.

"Anyway, the result of the Commissions Report was the Poor Law Amendment Act of 1834. Draconian legislation by which the poor were to be treated as criminals and could even be sent to prison. Many of the poor reacted by choosing to starve, rather than applying for relief and being sent to prison. Now here's the important part and which brings us to today, that law only applied to England. That's because the Commission determined that Ireland had an entirely different economy based on farming; and therefore the law should not be applied to Ireland."

"Seems to me the law was terrible to begin with," Grant responded.

"No argument from me on that score. But Parliament didn't like the Commissions idea of excluding Ireland. So they did what any group does when a committee hands them a report they don't like; they hired their own experts who came to the conclusion they wanted, and now they've applied the Poor Law Amendment Act to Ireland.

"But if we had a really bad year," Grant replied, "good people could possibly go to prison for something they had absolutely no control over."

"Precisely," Carmichael replied.

"Look, I've been here long enough now to know that even in the best of times, which are very few, poverty for most of these folks is never more than a few days away. Even a major storm and flooding could quickly wipe out dozens, even hundreds of tenant farmers. What if - God forbid – there was a failure of the potato crop like you had twenty years ago? Hundreds, perhaps thousands of people would be left almost destitute; and they could be sent to prison. What on earth was the Parliament thinking?

"That's easy," Carmichael replied, "use fear to keep people from applying for help. Given the choice of going hungry or going to prison, which would you choose?"

"Given a choice, I wouldn't choose either."

"Saint Patrick's has been helping folks around here for decades; look at all the work we've done since you've been here. But it's been very limited, a family here, a family there. We don't have the resources to help dozens let alone hundreds at a time."

"Then we better start thinking of what we can do to change that," Grant said.

"I've been thinking that we should begin to draft an emergency plan; something that we can use to provide temporary help. Your years in the army could be of great help; storing and distributing supplies…that sort of thing." He got up from his chair and started walking around the room. "How would we set it up? Who else might be able to help?"

"First," Grant replied, "we must begin by estimating how many people might need help: for how long; determining what will be needed; then setting up a store house. It won't be easy, mostly guess work at this point. The basic problem is that almost everyone around here grows and lives on potatoes. If for example there was a blight, how extensive would it be?" He paused for a moment, "one idea, would be for us to begin immediately trying to get some of the local families to begin planting other crops, like grain. A few of the large landowners like Lord Bligh, began switching to grain several years ago. Why haven't any of the local folks?"

"In a word," Carmichael said, "lack of tools and education. Anybody can poke a hole in the ground with a stick and plant a potato, but you need to till the land to plant grain. Then to, a potato can be eaten just as it comes from the ground; grain must be ground and processed."

"Yes, that's true. But grain can be stored for long periods, potatoes cannot. Don't the people understand that?"

"Oh they'll agree with you. But then they'll point out that for generation after generation they have planted and lived on potatoes. Why should they change now? As for Lord Bligh," Carmichael added. "We've had several discussions about planting grain. He told me it was Neil McLeod his Manager, who first made the suggestion. "

"Very interesting man; seems to have the rare ability to foresee future problems - fortunate to work for Lord Bligh. I think we should try and get Lord Bligh and McLeod to help draw up a plan."

"Excellent idea. I also think ...."

Before Carmichael could finish, Grant interrupted, "If it's alright with you, I think we should also include Reverend Swagart. If a real disaster comes, there will be a lot of non-Catholics, as well as Catholics, in need of help.

Carmichael laughed, "that's just who I was going to suggest. Fine man, he would have made a wonderful priest if the Methodists hadn't got him."

"I'm not to sure about that," Grant replied. "He has a lovely wife and three children."

"Ah yes. Some men need a wife and children, so the priesthoods not right for them." He turned to Grant, "and you; do you miss that part of your life?"

"Not unless I really think about the past. I had all that once. But now this is my life." Grant turned to Carmichael, "When I first came here, I recall telling you that the loss of my wife and children was unbearable; that I never wanted to be in that position again." He laughed, "Now here I am with dozens of children that I love. When Jimmy O'Donnal drowned last year, it was almost as hard to bear as when I lost my own."

"It's like the story of Job, Carmichael replied. "He lost his family, and God gave him another. Only now yours is much larger, which brings us back to the emergency plan."

"I'll start jotting down some ideas," Grant replied.

"Good. I have a sense that we need to start working on this right away."

Grant left the study and Carmichael walked over to the window. There was something he couldn't put his finger on; but he had a definite feeling that the Holy Spirit was sending him a warning: be prepared.

Chapter 10

On the other side of town, Colin was finishing a beautiful wrought iron gate. The past five years had been very good to him. Under Ryan's training, he had quickly learned all the basics of blacksmithing. Not satisfied with typical smith work however, he had spent hundreds of hours working late into the night developing new techniques and skills. By the middle of his fourth year, his specialty work was in increasing demand, more than doubling the shops annual income.

As he was practicing and perfecting his skills, Ryan's daughter Mary who was only thirteen when he began working there, had set her eyes on him the first time she saw him. It wasn't long before she was spending a great deal of time in the shop, talking with him as he worked. At first, Ryan and his wife were a bit concerned, she being thirteen and Colin almost eighteen, but they soon noticed that he looked upon Mary as a little sister. As the years went on Mabel, Ryan's wife, became aware of something else: Colin would make a wonderful husband for some young woman. With this discovery, it wasn't long before Ryan's wife, Mabel, began initiating future plans for her daughter Mary.

Mabel was what some individuals would have called a wise woman; others might have said clever; still others just plain shrewd and conniving. She herself would have said she was just being concerned for the welfare of her family, the same as any good wife and mother would be - especially one with four daughters.

First, she recognized that Mary, who was the eldest of her four daughters, was also the least attractive. Accordingly, finding a husband might prove to be difficult. Secondly, their only son had died in childbirth, and the complications forever ended any possibility of more children. Thus there was no one to take over the shop when Ryan could no longer work. In Colin, she saw the answer to two problems: a husband for Mary, and a son-in-law to eventually take over the blacksmith shop.

Getting Colin to work there had been her idea from the start. She had seen him in town several times, and continually asked Ryan to speak to him about a job. "He's big and strong Ryan, just the kind of man ye need ta help here in the shop."

"Yer right Mabel, I know yer right, and I will ask him one of these fine days when I get a chance."

"Don't wait fer the chance, make it!" she replied trying to keep her frustration under control. "Yer not gonna be young and strong forever; and besides, what if ye got hurt?"

Ryan hadn't been concerned about growing old, but getting hurt was always something to consider. He'd had some very close calls more than once. The day of the fight therefore, had provided the perfect chance to talk to Colin, and there was not a happier man in town than Ryan when he went home and told his wife, "Colin will be startin in the morning." Had he known how many kisses, hugs, and other treats that bit of news yielded, he would have gone to Colin's house and asked him months before.

With Colin happily working in the shop, Mabel put the second part of her plan into action. First, make sure that Mary stopped by the shop every day. They had to get to know each other. As for Mary, Mabel knew that at age thirteen, she would fall for the big hansom teddy-bear. Colin however, was another matter. She had no doubts whatsoever that there would be any number of girls, better looking girls, chasing him given the chance. Her goal was to make certain they never got that chance.

The fact that Colin quickly became totally involved in his work turned out to be a real blessing. Working from early morning until late at night eliminated most chances for him to meet other girls. To make certain that local girls wouldn't hang around the shop, she had Ryan put up a sign that read, No Loitering. Next she became concerned about him meeting girls when he was walking home for supper and then returning. Inviting Colin to have supper with them would kill two birds with one stone: Colin would be safely in their home out of the reach of competition, and it would keep him close to Mary. All she needed was time, and this arraignment would put time on her side.

Stopping by the shop one day to drop off Ryan's lunch, she called to Colin. "Colin, are ye plannin on working late tonight?" In fact, she knew he worked late everynight.

"Yes Maam. I'll come back after dinner like I usually do."

"Well, I was thinking. Why walk all the way home and back again. Stay and have supper with us? It'll save ye a lot of time."

"That's kind of ye, and I'd like ta," he replied with a smile. "But my Mum's expecting me tonight, I'd have ta let her know first." He laughed, "No difference ta her that I'm almost nineteen. If she didn't know where I was she'd start worrying."

"I'm a mother, I understand," she answered happy that he was open to the idea. "Why don't ye tell her tonight that tomorrow you'll stay here and have supper with us."

"OK, I'll tell her," he turned to the forge. "And thank ye," he called after her.

She looked over at Ryan who was opening his lunch pail, and smiled. He of course had no idea of what she was planning.

That first supper quickly turned into Colin having meals with Ryan's family almost every night. Colin loved it because it saved him a lot of time walking home and back again. Ryan enjoyed it because it gave him more time to talk to Colin about his plans for the future, something that was almost impossible during the day because of customers, and the constant noise of heavy hammers on iron. And even though Colin still thought of Mary like a little sister and really didn't pay that much attention to her, she was absolutely delighted to sit across from Colin night after night. But the person who enjoyed it most was Mabel, who smiled knowing that the second part of her plan was working.

There remained only one other major threat, the dances at Saint Patrick's. If Colin started attending them, she could lose him very quickly. She therefore devised a clever scheme. She contacted various merchants and tradesman in town and offered them special prices for custom smith work. However, there was only one special requirement: the jobs had to be done at certain times. Ryan was always surprised and amazed at these rush jobs, which he failed to notice always coincided with the dances. Colin never gave them a second thought. He was happy for the custom work, and didn't especially care about the dances anyway.

Nothing remains the same. At age fifteen, Mary's body began maturing, developing into that of a young woman; and like a bee to a flower, Colin started becoming much more aware of her. No longer did he see her as a little sister. Having been raised to be polite and not wishing to interrupt her father at the supper table, Mary seldom spoke. Even so, Ryan found it increasingly difficult to carry on a sustained conversation with Colin, when Colin's eyes repeatedly drifted back to Mary.

"Colin," Ryan would say in an attempt to break the rapturous eye contact, "about that new job yer workin on?"

Colin would glance back at Ryan, answer the question, and then the routine would repeat itself.

"Mabel of course, just smiled and hummed to herself. "Yes indeed," she thought, "Colin is going to make a fine catch, a fine catch."

Mary had just turned sixteen. She was tall and slender, and while she wasn't the prettiest girl in town, she had a sweet disposition and a smile that brought a smile to everyone she came in contact with. Colin could never determine exactly when he fell in love with her, the love just gradually evolved unrecognized, day-by-day, month-by-month, year-by-year. It was something like the metal he worked on, one day it was just a bar of wrought iron, and gradually it became a thing of beauty.

So it was with Mary; for years she had been the little girl just like a sister, then one day she walked into shop and stopped in the doorway. He looked up, saw her, and in that moment he knew. He laid down the iron frame he was working on, walked over to her and started to propose. Before he could finish, she said yes jumped up, wrapped her arms around his neck, and kissed him.

When Mary told her mother the news, Mabel blessed Mother Mary, and then reminded her that there were still three girls to go. Ryan of course just thought it was all a stroke of good luck.

The wedding was a gala event. Both families belonged to Saint Patrick's, and because many of the local people knew Ryan and Mabel, Mary's parents, and Colin's mother Kathleen, the church was filled to capacity. Because Lord Bligh had done a considerable amount of business with Ryan he was invited, although it was doubted that he would attend. Much to the surprise and delight of everyone, he came.

A modest reception was held on the church grounds, and the gifts to the bride and groom were opened. There were all the usual small items to help equip a starting household, and a small amount of money. The last gift however, was totally unexpected; a small envelope from John Bligh; the gift of a week stay at the Captain's Inn in Bristol, including round trip passage on the Mary Jane, and some fun money.

Finally, the musicians turned up their instruments and the dancing started. This time, Mabel had no objection to Colin dancing. As he danced with Mary, several of the local single young women gathered in a small group and talked. How could they have possibly overlooked such a handsome hunk as Colin? Where had he been hiding?

It had been a wonderful day in Kilrush. Colin and Mary were safely married and soon to be off on a great adventure to Bristol. They would come back with stories that would be told and retold for many years to come. Mary would come back with a few dresses she would wear out, fold and store away, and treasure for the rest of her life. Colin visited a couple of blacksmith shops while she was shopping, and learned a valuable new technique for welding iron. John and Grant had a lengthy discussion about the emergency plan they were developing. Lastly, in two chairs off to the side of the dance floor, Father Carmichael and Mabel sat talking. He very pleased that another young couple were now starting their home, and at how well everything had gone. As for Mabel, there wasn't a happier woman in all of Ireland.

Chapter 11

Unlike the good years that Colin had enjoyed, Sean Egan's had been anything but good. From the day he had been so badly injured in the fight, it had taken several months for his broken bones to mend. His jaw, which had been driven to the right by the power of Colin's punch had been badly dislocated; and although Kathleen had attempted to straighten it and wire it in place, it never healed properly. The result was that Sean's upper and lower jaws and teeth were noticeably misaligned to the extent that his speech was slurred, and he had difficulty chewing his food. The former handsome young man was disfigured to the point that women and girls now turned their gaze away from him.

The disfigurement of his face was difficult enough for him to bear, but the almost total loss of the use of his right arm was economically devastating. As fortune would have it, on the day of the fight Doctor Cain had been out of town. Kathleen and Bridgit had done what they could to align the broken bone, wrapped his arm in a splint, and placed it in a sling to support it until the Doctor returned. Miraculously, this saved his arm from amputation, but at an unexpected price.

A combination of bad weather and unforeseen complications with another patient kept the Doctor from returning for almost two weeks. By the time he returned it was too late to attempt to reset the bones which had started to fuse. What truly amazed the Doctor, when he examined Sean, was that there was no sign of gangrene which he fully expected to find. That the arm did not have to be amputated, was solely due to Kathleen and Bridgit's daily cleaning and dressing his severe wounds. Unfortunately, the bones in his elbow also fused, fixing his lower right arm in what almost amounted to a permanent horizontal sling position. He could swing his arm outward to pick something up, but was unable to raise or lower it. The result was that there were few physical jobs he could perform well, and getting steady work became almost impossible.

As the years went by, Sean became quite adept at basic tasks by using his right hand to grip an object, such as a rake handle, and his left arm for the muscle work. He continued to live in the back room of the Pub, and eked out a meager existence cleaning out stables, and general clean-up work around town. It was enough money for food and drink, mostly drink. Understandably, he had grown increasingly bitter towards life. Because of the slur in his speech he seldom spoke to anyone, and generally answered with a grunt or a nod of his head. He was seldom fully sober, and since he could no longer fight men, he had developed a habit of kicking every dog and cat that happened to get within range of his boot. Consequently, the town dogs and cats had long since learned to stay well clear of him.

One afternoon as he was sitting alone at the far end of the bar, one of the men noticed him holding his drink in his left hand. Given Sean's physical condition, no one feared him anymore and he had become the butt of many jokes.

"Hey, Lefty," he called, "been dancing with any pretty girls lately?" Most of the men at the bar laughed, but Sean remained silent. He had learned that trying to reply to the taunts only led to more. The men turned away and continued talking; but from that day on he only drank alone in his room.

Most of the people who knew him would have laid odds on him getting run over by a horse and wagon as he staggered dead drunk down the street several times a week; or perhaps freezing to death in an alley on a winter night. They had already written off Sean's life: a no-account drunk, story over. But a story doesn't end until the last chapter has been written. Sean's story still had several chapters to go.

In late July 1842 a remarkable event took place in Kilrush. Reverend Swagart, Pastor of the Methodist Church, invited a traveling evangelist to come and hold Revival Services for a week. William Cook, Billy as everyone called him, had been saved under the ministry of one of the Wesley brother's disciples. Having felt the call of God on his life, William Cook now traveled around England and Ireland proclaiming the Good News that Jesus saves sinners.

The Methodist church in Kilrush was a rather modest building compared to the huge edifice of Saint Patrick's. And unlike the latter it was not adjacent to a lovely garden and cemetery. In fact it was located on a small parcel of ground on Francis Street in the center of Kilrush only four doors away from O'Reilly's Pub. It was not unusual on a warm summer evening when all the church doors and windows were open, for the patrons of O'Reilly's to hear the singing; and if it happened to be good hymn, to join in. This particular July happened to be very hot, and the temperatures in the evening remained unusually warm. Every window in the church was wide open, and the door opening to the street as well.

The Revival Services, which began on Sunday morning, were also held every evening at 6:30 throughout the week. For the first two evening services only the regular church members attended, but the numbers quickly grew as word spread that on Wednesday evening, William Cook was going to give his personal testimony. Rumor had it that he

had been a former drunk and wife beater, and had spent
time in prison for almost killing a man in a barroom brawl.
On the second night, Sean was on his way back to
O'Reilly's from the stable where he worked, and as he
passed the church the singing caught his ear. For a brief
moment, it reminded him of his mother who always sang as
she worked around the house. He stopped and leaned
against a fence across the street to listen. Several people in
the back of the church chanced to turn around and saw him
standing there, but no one considered approaching him or
inviting him to come in for the meeting.

On the third night, after the service started, he sat down
on a stone wall just outside the church so that he could
better hear the singing. As he listened carefully to the
hymns, none that he recognized, he found the words
comforting in a way he didn't understand. He had been
raised as a Catholic, but had avoided church like the
plague.

These Revival services however, were totally different
from the Mass. He found that he liked the music, and even
the preaching in a language he could understand. Although
he was outside and still had difficulty hearing everything
that was being said, there were words that caught his ear,
and his curiosity grew. After the service ended, he quickly
left the area and went back to his room in the rear of the
Pub. There, lying on his cot he laid awake until the early
morning hours, with the music and some of the words
running through his mind.

On Wednesday, the fourth night, he waited across the
street until everyone was inside, then quietly slipped in and
sat down in the pew closest to the door. The melodies of
some of the hymns had now become familiar enough that
he hummed along, occasionally he would attempt to sing
the words he could recall, but the slur made them almost
unintelligible. He thought back to the day before the fight
and his injuries had happened, and wondered if the rest of

his life would be like this. After the last hymn was finished, Reverend Swagart made several announcements and the evangelist, William Cook (Billy), stepped to the pulpit. Tonight was the night he had promised to tell his life story.

For a moment Billy just stood there, eyes closed, softly uttering a short prayer. Then he looked out over the congregation and began speaking.

"There is a story in the scriptures about a man who was devil possessed; a terrible man that hurt anyone who came too close. Billy Cook was once such a man. My friends and fellow pilgrims, the man you see standing here tonight, is not the Billy Cook you would have seen ten years ago. You would not have wanted to meet that man; and if you saw him walking down the street, you would have crossed to the other side.

That Billy Cook was demon possessed; a falling down drunk who beat his wife, a wonderful woman who never did anything to deserve the treatment she got. Some of you here tonight may know what I'm talking about. That Billy Cook was a liar who had forgotten how to tell the truth; a thief who stole from his own wife and children. A man that would take the rent money to satisfy his unquenchable thirst for alcohol, and then beat his dear wife if she asked him for money to feed the children. An alcoholic who spent night after night, week after week, year after year, in Pubs and saloons, drinking, gambling, and whoring. I'm sorry if my language offends the ladies here, but you need to understand what that Billy Cook was like."

He paused for a moment as if reflecting on the past, then in a quiet voice he began again.

"One night, half drunk, when he believed another man had cheated him at cards, he drew a knife and lunged at the man. Had it not been for another man who jumped up and grabbed his arm, he would have become a murderer and surely would have been hanged. As it was, he spent five years in prison for attempted murder. His wife left him and took their four children. I say, 'that' Billy Cook, because he is dead. The man you see here tonight met Jesus in Revival Service just like this one, ten years ago." He stepped away from the pulpit, and in a loud voice called out, "the old Billy Cook died, praise God, and I who stand here before you tonight, was raised in newness of life. Amen!"

"Now you might ask, Billy, who were those demons that possessed you? Well, I'll tell you," he stepped from behind the pulpit, "I'll tell you their names, Whiskey; rum; beer; ale; poteen; wine.... And they have friends, lots of demon friends: lying, stealing, fighting, cheating, brutality...." He paused and took a drink of water.

"And understand this; many of those demons that possessed Billy Cook ten years ago live right here in Kilrush." He paused, "There are men and women in this town who know them, maybe some of you here tonight," he said as he swept his pointed finger around the room.

"Where are these demons you ask? They live right here," he reached under the pulpit and pulled out an empty whiskey bottle. "Right here in this bottle!" he said raising his voice as he stepped down from the platform, "and when you invite drunkenness, the first demon into your life, he soon invites his friends." He waved the bottle in the air, "how many of you men here tonight know what I'm talking about; how about some of you ladies?"

He waved the bottle again, and again, as he walked down the aisle. "Ten years ago if you had tried to take a bottle of whisky from me I would have hit and beaten you without a second thought. Not only strangers mind you, but even my own wife in front of our precious children." He had reached the end of the aisle, and looked down at Sean. "You know what I'm saying's true don't you?" He turned and headed back up the aisle, but not before Sean felt the intense heat of conviction taking hold of him. "So how did I get from the gutter to here. What happened to that Billy Cook? Did he just up and decide to change one night and give up his worthless existence? No! What happened was that an evangelist came to town one night and preached, just like I'm preaching to you here tonight. I stumbled into that meeting very drunk and mad, and I intended to teach him a lesson. I staggered up the aisle a bottle in my hand expecting him to turn and run, but he didn't. He just stood there with a smile on his face.

I became even more angry; and as I got close enough to look directly into his eyes, I raised the bottle to bring it down on his skull. At that moment, a powerful force knocked me off my feet, threw me to the ground and held me there. I looked to see who was doing this, but there was no one there but the preacher and me. Suddenly, I became terrified. I was on the ground paralyzed with this man standing over me. Then he knelt down beside me and in a quite voice asked me a question, "would you like to be free?"

"Free?" I stuttered, "What do you mean free? I'm English, I'm a free man."

"No. You're a slave. A miserable slave living a life of hell," isn't that true?"

"I started to say no, but something gripped my tongue, the words would not come out. Instead, in a moment, in the twinkling of an eye, my life flashed before me. All the terrible things I had done to others; the wonderful chances I had missed; the friends I had turned away; my wife and children who had left me. And in that instant, I saw that I was exactly what he said I was; a slave in chains. I was not in control of my life, something else was." He paused.

The preacher reached out and took the bottle from my hand. "Now let me ask you again, do you want to be free?"

"Billy Cook," he paused, "that old Billy Cook was not a crying man. Crying was a sign of weakness. But on that night he looked up at that preacher and began crying. "Yes," he cried, "I want to be free."

The preacher took my hand in his and looking toward heaven cried out, "Satan, in the name of Jesus, release this man!" He then pulled me up from the floor and said, "You're free. Jesus has set you free, the demons have gone. Now he's going to start turning your life around."

Billy walked back to the platform and stepped back on to the platform. "My life did turn around. When I woke up the next morning, I felt different. For the first time in many years, I was not angry. I got dressed and went to the shop where I had worked and asked if they had a job available. When they first seen me they said no, they were not interested in hiring drunks. I told them I had changed and didn't drink anymore. Of course they didn't believe me. They laughed and said to come back in a month... if I was still sober. I did go back, and they hired me. Three months later, I went to visit my wife for the first time and told her what had happened. I then told her I would come back again in a month, and the month after that."

"It took time, but eventually she could see that I had changed. In fact it became evident to everyone I knew; I was a new man. It took almost a year to regain my family; our old friends. Then something remarkable happened; one day as I was walking to work I felt God speaking to me, telling me to tell others about how Jesus had freed and saved me. I obeyed his voice and here I am." He picked up the whisky bottle, held it over a small barrel and smashed it. "How many here tonight want to be free?"

Sean knew he wanted to be free. Everything he had touched he had hurt and destroyed, maybe now there was a chance to start over. He raised his hand, got up and walked toward the alter; he never made it that far. Before he reached the front of the church, Billy met him, reached out his hand and touched him on the forehead. Sean staggered backwards as if he had been hit with lightning, and fell to the floor. When he woke up, Billy and the Pastor were sitting on the pew close to him, the church was empty; he had been unconscious for four hours. He told them about the strange dreams he had had about meeting new people, of having many friends, and being filled with joy.

"That was a vision of your new life Sean. Jesus has set you free. The demons are gone, I seen 'em go out yonder door," Billy said. "But remember my brother, they're still out there and they'll lie to you; try and convince you that you're still a worthless drunk. You need to tell 'em they're liars and that Jesus saved you."

As Sean walked home from the church, the words kept repeating themselves in his mind: Jesus has set you free; and remembering the dreams of a new life. Gradually he became aware of shadows walking along side of him. He stopped and looked down; there were two dogs at his feet. He reached down, patted them on the head and they began licking his hand. He smiled, then he laughed joyously for the first time in a long, long time. "So even you know that I was saved," he said. They wagged their tails, gave a little bark, and they all walked down the street together. His new life had just begun.

Chapter 12

On a bright and sunny June morning, Bridgit was busy sewing in her enclosed porch, when she glanced out the window to see Father Timothy coming down the street towards her cottage. Thinking that perhaps that a member of the church had a problem and he was coming to ask her for her help, as had happened several times before, she went to the door to meet him. Before he even knocked, she opened the door and invited him to come inside.

"So Father, who's needen help this time? she asked.

For a second, he was startled. "Why....no one," he stammered. "What made you think someone was in trouble?"

"Because when ye come here, it's ta ask fer my help."

"Yes, of course, I guess I do," he replied stepping into the house. "Not this time, I came to see you."

"Me. Why?"

"It's...." he paused and looked down at the floor, "It's complicated."

"Well, sit ye down and tell me about it. OK if I sew while ye tell me?"

"Yes....I mean no," he stammered. He looked up from the floor and directly into her eyes. "I love you," he blurted out.

Startled by what he had just said, she just looked at him.

"I love you," he said again. "Do you understand that?"

"But yer a Priest, ye can na love me."

"I know I shouldn't..... that's what makes it complicated."

"No," she said firmly, "tis not complicated. "Yer a Priest and ye have made vows ta the Church." She stepped back away from him.

"But you love me too. I've seen it in your eyes, the way you look at me."

"The way I look at ye? I do na look at ye in any special way. Tis true I like ye, yer a fine young man and a Priest, but I do na love ye in that way."

"I've seen you wink at me, and nudge me with your elbow," he exclaimed.

"Oh heavens- ta-Betsy, I wink at all the Lads. They all know it means nothin. I wink at 'em and they at me. I dance with the Lads too, and tis all in fun, nothin more."

"No!" he said, with a touch of anger rising in his voice. "I've been in torment these past eight months thinking about you." He stepped toward her. "I want to marry you. Not in a church of course, we couldn't do that. A secret marriage."

"Marry me! A secret marriage? No! The lad I loved died many years ago, and as he died in my arms I vowed never to marry. And what of yer vow ta the church? Does it mean nothing to ye?

"The vow was not to marry and have a public wife, it didn't mean I couldn't love someone and have sex with them."

"So some of them rumors we've heard about Priests and even the Pope his self havin mistresses and children are true?"

He didn't respond in words, but the look on his face answered her question.

"Well I'll have none of it. I can na change what they have done, but I will na be part of it. Now before ye goes any farther, I'm askin ye ta leave my house."

For a brief moment he stared at her, and then turned toward the door. As he reached toward the doorknob, he suddenly whirled around, reached out, grabbed her by the arm and kissed her. Partially in shock she stood still, neither pulling away, nor responding to his kiss. He held her tightly, kissing her again, and again, but still she did not respond. Completely bewildered and frustrated at what was happening, he stood there holding her uncertain as to what to do next. He was like a rider racing his horse across a meadow, at one moment holding the reins and in control, and in the next losing the reins and control. He pushed her away slightly but still gripping her arms, he pushed her backwards through the bedroom door.

"Please take your clothes off," he asked. When she shook her head no, he reached down and pulled her dress up and over her head, and pushed her down on the bed. He was startled and taken by surprise as he looked at her lying there completely naked.

He had seen his younger sister when she was about nine years old, but never a naked adult woman. He had also seen women nursing their babies, with an exposed hanging breast and large dark nipple; but Bridgit was not like that at all, her breasts were firm with small rosy nipples. Her face and hands, having been exposed to the sun were a light tan color; but the rest of her body except for her nipples, was as white as alabaster. What totally surprised him was her thick black mass of curly pubic hair. He had always assumed that because women had very little hair on their bodies, their pubic area would also be hairless like his little sister's had been.

She lay there silently with her eyes closed, not moving. He stared at her body for several seconds, over-whelmed at her beauty. Pulling off his robe and clothing, and tossing it into the corner, he climbed onto the bed and began fondling and kissing her breasts. He continued talking to her softly, running his fingers through her long hair, telling her that he loved her; but nothing he did brought any response. She lay there silent and still as if in a trance. But if she was in a trance, he was not. The sight of her spread out on the bed, and running his hands over her body had brought him to full arousal.

He had never had sex with a woman before, and because he had made the false assumptions that she loved him, she would willingly help him. He knew now that she would not help him at first, but if could get her aroused, a word he had over-heard men in a bar talking and laughing about, she would change; after all she had sex with other men; his second false assumption. He slid his hands down her thighs and pushed her legs apart.

As he made a clumsy attempt to penetrate her, she turned her face toward the window and looked out. She could see a small yellow finch sitting on a tree branch. In her mind, she went to a warm summer day when she was eight years old, and her parents had taken her on a birthday picnic. On that day, as they sat on a river bank eating their lunch, she had watched a yellow finch perched in a nearby tree, singing to its mate. She tried to recall every moment of that day and the fun they had, completely blocking out what was happening to her now.

He had heard stories about having sex and they made everything sound simple. His desperation grew as he tried to penetrate her, something was wrong, why was she so tight. Finally after several attempts, just as his penis started to enter her vagina he ejaculated prematurely shooting most of his semen on to her thighs and abdomen. Nothing had gone as he had imagined it, how he had fantasized of it night after night in his room. She was supposed to have said that she loved him; to have responded to his kisses with her own kisses; to have returned his ardent passion. Now, even when he believed he was making love to her, she had turned her face away and laid there without any response. He sat up straight on his haunches, dropped his head and looked down. That's when he noticed the blood.

"Oh my God, you're a virgin," he exclaimed. "But I thought you had…....." his voice trailed off. The enormity of what he had just done began to sink in. He had not made love to her, he had raped her. He got up from the bed and sat down on the floor in the corner, pulling his knees up tight to his chest; over and over whispering softly, "what have I done, what have I done."

For a couple of minutes, Bridgit continued looking out the window; then, realizing that he was no longer on her, she got up. She looked at him huddled and whimpering in the corner, she could see the blood on his hands, legs, and his face where he had touched it. Silently, she walked out to the kitchen, took a basin of water and began washing away the blood and semen. That done, she put on a clean dress and returned to the bedroom.

"Ye had better clean up and go," she said quietly, no trace of emotion in her voice. She gathered up the bed linens and carried them outside into the back yard, dumping them on a small pile of brush she had picked up the day before. She looked down at the blood stained quilt she and her mother had made shortly after Tom had been killed by the bull; it had been one of her most treasured possessions.

She struck a match, set the pile on fire, and stood there watching the flames and smoke curl up. Part of her was going up with the smoke; it would never be the same again. She doubted that she could ever laugh again, or dance with the Lads from the village: it had all been so innocent. She was still staring into the fire and sobbing when Father Timothy walked out the front door unnoticed.

He smoothed out his robe with hands now clean, but so recently stained with her blood. For several hours he walked through the hills uncertain as to what to do. Would she go to Saint Patrick's and tell Carmichael and Grant? Her cottage was on the edge of town and there were no next door neighbors who could have seen what happened; but what if someone had seen the smoke and came over? By eight o'clock, it was starting to get dark and he headed back to the dormitory. It was dark when he slipped in through the back door of the church unseen.

The next morning he walked down the hall for breakfast, expecting any moment to be called out, but nothing happened. At breakfast, Sister Agnes mentioned that they had missed him at supper, and he mumbled something about eating in town. He hurriedly ate his breakfast, avoiding conversation with anyone. Then he went to Father Carmichael's study and knocked on the door. He needed to quickly get away, but above all he did not want to run into Bridgit who often stopped by the church during the day.

"Father Timothy," Carmichael began as he opened the door, inviting him into the study. "I'm glad you stopped by, I need to talk to you."

"This is it," he thought to himself. "While I was out walking yesterday, Bridgit stopped by the church."

"Sit down, make yourself comfortable. What I wanted to talk to you about was this special emergency plan father Grant and I have been preparing. We need you to be a part of this."

Relieved at this news, he sat up a little straighter in his chair. "Why I'd love to help; when do you plan on meeting?" he responded hoping it wasn't in the next few days.

"Toward the end of next week. Father Grant is still collecting some information and needs a few more days."

"Oh good.... about meeting next week I mean. I've been concerned about my uncle, he's getting on in years, and lives about thirty miles from here. Would it be alright with you if I took a week off to visit him?"

"Certainly, certainly. We've been very pleased with what you have done here so far." Carmichael got up, and put his hand on Timothy's shoulder, "Be sure to say hello to your uncle for us."

Carmichaels hand on his shoulder was like a hot poker, and Carmichael noticed that he flinched ever so slightly. "Everything alright?

"Its fine," he said a little too quickly. "I've just been worried about my uncle."

Carmichael sensed there was more to this, but lacking anything specific he decided to let it go for now. When Timothy was ready, he was certain he would come to him.

"Thank you Father. I'll be back in time for the meeting." And with that, he left the study, hurried down the hall to his room, quickly packed a few personal items, and left the church. Only when he was about a mile away, did he turn and look back. The thought of spending a week away from here, far enough that it was doubtful any word would reach where he was going, began to release the tenseness in his head and shoulders, and he began to relax. He looked back at Saint Patrick's and the town. He wondered what would be here to greet him when he returned.

For the next several days Bridgit did not stop by the church, and missed Sunday Mass for the first time in almost two years. Carmichael asked everyone if they had heard from or seen Bridgit, was she sick? No one had heard or knew anything. He decided that tomorrow he would visit her.

Bridgit had not left the house or spoken to anyone since she had been raped. She stayed indoors and worked on her sewing, not even going out to work in the garden that she loved. Looking out the back window, she could see the pile of ashes and small bits of cloth that had not burned. She determined that tomorrow she would rake all of that away. In the house, she had moved all of her things into the other bedroom. It was much smaller and didn't look out into the garden, but right now she needed to block out any visual reminders of what had happened to her.

The following morning, Father Carmichael walked down the street toward her cottage. Turning the corner, he noticed that the curtains were still dawn which was unusual because Bridgit was a morning person, an early riser. As he knocked at the door, he also noted that her garden had not been tended. There was no answer, so he knocked again, perhaps she has been away he thought to himself. Just as he was about to leave the door opened.

"I'm sorry Father, I was working out back and didn't hear ye knock at first. Please come in."

Carmichael stepped in and quickly glanced about the room. He had known Bridgit since she was a little girl, an only child. Undoubtedly, she was the most meticulous person he had ever met; a place for everything, and everything in its place: something was amiss. "We've missed you at church," he began, "have you been sick?"

"A little cold," she replied, not convincingly as she went around pulling open the curtains. "How's everyone at church?"

"Oh, everyone at the church is fine. Father Grant and Sister Agnes told me to say hello. I told them I was going to stop by to see if everything was alright. Everything is alright, isn't it?"

"Yes, yes. I'm sorry I missed Mass last Sunday," she said fussing with her hair which had not been brushed. "I can na remember the last time I missed," she added. "Is anythin new? Did I miss anythin?"

"Well, we announced that we are working on an emergency plan for our Parish, Father Grant is putting together some facts for a meeting next week. I hope that you will be there, because you and Kathleen will be an important part of the plan. Oh yes, Father Timothy is gone for a week to visit his uncle." As he said that, he could see her body tense, but she said nothing. They continued talking for half an hour, then Carmichael said that he had other calls to make. "Now, can we expect to see you soon?

The church doesn't seem right without you stopping by everyday."

"I'll be there," she said smiling. "And thank ye for comin, it's been good ta see ye agin." As he left, she looked around the room and wondered how much he had noticed. She stood at the door as he walked away and then noticed her untended garden. "Time ta get ta work," she said to herself. "Nothin will ever be the same, but I mustn't let others know that." She continued watching Carmichael as he walked away.

Halfway down the block, Carmichael turned around and looked back; she was still standing in the doorway and he waved. Something was amiss. Bridgit was not her usual happy, effervescent self. Something else to add to his prayer list; as if it wasn't full enough already.

Chapter 13

When Lord Bligh opened and read the letter, he literally shouted for joy, startling the servants who were nearby. He waived the letter in the air shouting for everyone to hear, "My son Lawrence is coming home from India, he's coming home for a visit. He'll be here in two months." At that moment he suddenly remembered that he was at Arden, and Lawrence would be returning to London. No one here knew Lawrence; all of his friends were in London. He must quickly return to his Estate in London and plan for a grand welcome home party there.

This was going to be a problem because he had not been living in London for several years. Even when he went on short business trips to London, he spent most of his time in Bristol with Cassie. In addition, his disposition was not the London society type; Elizabeth had taken care of that. He would need someone to plan everything for him; and so he began thinking of the women he knew in London who might be willing to handle all of the details. He made a list and then one by one, for this or that reason, he crossed their name out; so far it was not going well. It was not until he began making up the guest list that he found the perfect person; the question was; would she be willing. He sent a letter and a week later received her reply. She said that she was both surprised and flattered, and yes she was willing on one condition: she had to find someone to run the Lodge while she was in London. He immediately wrote a very brief reply.

Dear Cassie:

Close up the Inn, I'll reimburse you for whatever income you may lose, and I'll cover whatever other costs you may have including your staff.   How soon can you come?

Sincerely John

He looked at what he had written, tore it up, and tried again.

Dearest Cassie:

Close up the Inn, I'll reimburse you for whatever income you may lose, and I'll cover any other costs you may have including your staff.   Assuming this plan will be acceptable to you, I will meet you in Bristol in a fortnight, and we can travel to London together.

Love John

"Much better," he said to himself.   It was true, he did love her, and it would be wonderful traveling together. Lawrence's homecoming had just taken on even more excitement.   He was as happy as a schoolboy on summer vacation.

The days flew by as preparations were made to leave for London.   Over the past few years, Arden had become a large working estate with over a hundred and fifty full time workers, plus over a hundred tenant farmers.   Under Neil's management, almost eighty percent of the land was now in grain production.   There were numerous meetings with Neil regarding the harvests and replanting should he not get back in time; instructions to the Head Butler; Housekeeper;

groundskeeper; etceteras. Neil was also to supervise the other department heads regarding shipping the crops to England, shipping products to over twenty countries, the collection of rents from the tenants, etceteras. They would keep in touch by mail, but his key employees needed the authority to make decisions on their own in cases of emergency when hours, not days, could make the difference between success or failure. In this regard he was confident that he had very reliable people whom he trusted implicitly. Arden was their home, they would take very good care of it.

It was raining lightly the morning he set out for the docks in Kilrush, where he and Grove, his driver, would board the ship for the voyage to Bristol. If the weather was fair, the trip would take about two days. Cassie had written and told him she had made all the necessary preparations to close the Lodge, and would be ready to leave when he arrived. From Bristol to his home in London would also take about two days. Three weeks ago a letter had been sent to the Albert, his Butler in London; and he had received a reply that the manor was ready for their arrival.

The day the ship sailed into Bristol, Cassie stood waiting on the dock to greet him. It would have been hard to say which of them was more excited. Traditional customs however, limited their public greeting to a polite touch of their hands and, "How good it is to see you again." They took a public carriage back to the Lodge, while Grove stayed by the ship and seen to the unloading of their luggage, carriage, and horses. Since it was late in the afternoon, they stayed at the Lodge and left the next morning.

"I haven't been to London in almost four years," she said. "It will be wonderful to see it again. I had planed on going last year to see the Coronation of Queen Victoria, but the Inn was so busy I couldn't get away. Did you go?"

"No. I was very happy to stay in Ireland, far away from all that pomp and celebration."

"Do you think she'll be a good Queen?"

"Difficult to tell at this point. Much will depend on if she marries, and who she marries if she does."

"I've read several stories in the papers that have suggested she might marry Price Albert."

"It's possible. Time will tell."

"Changing the subject: do you have a lot of friends in London?"

"Many years ago we did, when Elizabeth was alive. But after her death, I withdrew into my own world, and gradually lost touch with most of them; and for the past few years most of my time has been spent at Arden. I tell you this so that you don't expect too much. I'm not even certain as to how we'll be received; it will take some time to get back into the social circle and we don't have much time. I'm hoping that the party for Lawrence will be the perfect opportunity."

The weather was exceptionally sunny and warm, and the trip went without a mishap. They stayed overnight at a small Inn in separate rooms and arrived at his home the next afternoon. All the servants were waiting on the front steps to greet them, and he proudly introduced Cassie to them. After they went inside, the men commented that she was certainly a very attractive young woman, "young enough to be his daughter," one said; and the women were all a-twitter about what the future might hold. All they had been told by Albert, was that a woman was coming to arrange a Welcome Home Party for Lawrence. The talk in the kitchen was non-stop. "I'll wager ye that she's here for more than just plannin a party," the cook remarked waving a ladle in the air and twirling around. "Aye indeed," came a chorus of laughter. They all agreed that they had never seen the Master so happy since Elizabeth, and Lawrence left for the service. It had been many, many years since the house had been filled with joy and laughter.

The manor was a large three story stone building with forty rooms situated on two hundred acres. There were stables for the horses; a carriage house; barns; and other out buildings. Fortunately, for the past several years, even though he had been mostly absent, he had maintained a full staff of servants. As he and Cassie toured and inspected the home and grounds, it was evident they had kept the home and grounds in perfect condition.

Walking back toward the manor, John switched the conversation to the party. "I'll give you a list of the people I know here, and a list of Lawrence's friends. Since we don't know how many will come, it's important to get the invitations out as quickly as possible. I'll stop by my club and talk to as many of the men I can find. Even if only half of the people we invite come, we will still have over a hundred."

"What about the food?"

"Make up your list and give it to the cook, Martha, she's very good. Unfortunately, Martha told me that the pastry cook left three weeks ago," he paused for a moment. "Maybe the simplest idea would be to ask Martha for the name of the best bakery, and have them prepare whatever you want." He stopped and turned toward her, "Cassie, I'm putting it all in your very capable hands. You make whatever decisions you feel are necessary. I've already told the staff that you have full authority." He took hold of her hand and smiled, "I can't begin to tell you how very happy I am that you're here."

"I hope that I can live up to your expectations of me," she replied.

"Oh I have all the ...."

"Stop," she placed her fingers against his lips, "I'm sure that I can take care of all the preparations for the party; that's not what concerns me."

"What then?"

"It's meeting your friends. My husband and I were not really part of the social scene. When he came home from his voyages, he just wanted to relax, for us to spend time together. Oh, sometimes we'd go to a party, but we never really fit in."

"I don't care about....."

"Please let me finish, this is important to me." She held his hand tightly. "Before my late husband and I met, I was a typical socialite, and made all the annual events. But after we were married, that changed, he was gone for months at a time. At first, I attended the parties by myself, but I soon found out that some of the men were continually trying to ...." she paused.

"Seduce you," he finished the sentence.

"It was terrible. I finally stopped going. I haven't been to a party like this in several years, and I'm afraid that I'll do or say something that might embarrass you."

He squeezed her hand. "Don't worry. I haven't seen most of these people in years, some of them since Elizabeth was alive. I can't imagine anything you could say or do that could embarrass me." He looked her straight in the eyes, and with a very sober look said "tell me, you don't get drunk and dance on tables do you?" He burst out laughing.

"Well," she winked at him, "I was married to a sailor you know. Maybe I'd better just leave the champagne alone and drink the punch."

"I guess I'll just have to keep a close eye on you," he said as he pulled her close to him and put his arms around her. "This is going to be a wonderful party. Not just because Lawrence is coming home for a while, but because I want everyone to meet you. Before I met you I was a busy man; content perhaps, but not really happy. You've changed all that. I love you."

"Are the tables strong enough to dance on?" she asked as she twirled on the pathway.

"Why you little Vixen," he reached out to grab her hand, but she darted ahead with him chasing close behind. Just as she rounded the corner of the hedge, she ran headlong into Albert, followed by John who ran into them both.

Albert, taken completely by surprise by the collision, stood there speechless as they both began to laugh. A smile crept across his face, "It's good to see you happy again M'Lord; and you too M'Lady."

For the first time in more years than he could remember, no, since Elizabeth had given the money to the women in the street, Lord Bligh blushed.

Several days passed, very busy days, and then the replies to the invitations began coming in. Whatever doubts Lord Bligh might have had regarding who would come were quickly dispelled: everyone was coming. There were John's acquaintances who were interested in talking to Lawrence about the situation in India, the real situation. Several of them had been to India years ago, and the daily reports in the newspapers were so often conflicting it was difficult to know what was really happening there. Secondly, they were curious to meet this new woman in John's life.

Secondly, there were many of Lawrence's friends who had not seen or heard from him in years. It would be nice to see him again and renew old friendships. Most of the women his age had married, but there were still a doleful few who considered their invitation to his party a heaven sent chance. Eligible bachelors of his age; financial status, and social standing were exceedingly rare. Nothing less than death, or the second return of Jesus, would keep them from this party.

Last, but certainly not least by any means were the older women. Some were happily married and were simply accompanying their husbands in anticipation of an enjoyable social evening. Others, those who were not enjoying connubial bliss, or were widows; came for the adventure of the hunt. But regardless of their status, they were all simply mad to meet this new young woman John had brought all the way from Bristol, "just to arrange a party for Lawrence," they said with a sly smile.

The voyage from India had gone remarkably smoothly, no storms, and fair winds. Three days ago; they passed the Channel Islands and entered the English Channel, and now they were heading north-by-northeast in the Straight of Dover. Standing on the quarter deck, to his left he could see the white chalk cliffs of Dover; and beyond them the lighthouse at Margate. Just ahead lay the last few miles of a long journey.

"Helmsman, set your course to 300 degrees," the First Mate called out. "Aye, Aye," came the reply. He could feel the ship turning under him and heel slightly to starboard as the wind shifted in the sails. Within seconds, the crew was scrambling over the deck pulling on the sheets, trimming the sails for the new course. As the ship swung around and entered the bay, he could see the church steeples in Southend-On-The Sea; and beyond that the mouth of the Thames River over the port bow. Within three hours they would be tying up at the dock and he would be home for the first time in over nine years. Over the past four months, he had gone over what he might expect at home many times. But the sight of the Thames brought a quickened pulse he had not expected.

In all, he had spent almost ten years in India and he knew that it had changed him. He knew India, but how much did he really know of England? Whatever he might have known when he left would not be the same, because both he and England had changed. He had waved goodbye to his father as a naive young man in uniform, shouting the usual Hip, Hip, Hurrahs. He was returning as a veteran of many campaigns: a man who no longer had any illusions as to the glory of the British Empire. He had seen too many friends die, or get crippled for life. He was on his horse alongside and talking to Major Wilkin when a cannon ball ripped the Major's leg off. And when they carried his friend, the young Scottish Corporal into the hospital tent, he had literally grabbed the surgeons arm and stopped him from amputating his arm. "Damn it man, he's going to need that arm to fish for salmon when he gets home."

He had seen too much, the Union Jack was now soaked with the blood of too many innocent people. Now whenever he heard "God Save the Queen," he whispered to himself, "let God save her, I'm not gong to do it anymore." As for India, he thought of that young Indian officer who had died at his feet so many years ago. He knew that someday they would gain their freedom; perhaps not in his lifetime, but someday she would break free of British rule just as the American Colonies had.

With thoughts and ideas such as these running through his mind, he wondered how he would he be received by his father, his father's friends, and his own. It was possible he would be an outcast among his own Countrymen. And what of the English women; were they still the same pasty-white, foolish, ignorant of the real world girls he had known before. Pretty perhaps; and adept at all the social graces and bearing children; but totally inept at carrying on an intelligent conversation of anything beyond the latest fashions.

He felt a slight shiver run down his spine, as he thought of spending afternoons at lawn parties, and listing to meaningless twaddle about what was happening at Court and the theater. Although he considered himself to be reasonably good looking, he knew that regardless of his looks, he was a commodity that would be relentlessly pursued. He would be like one of those Scottish salmon that everyone was trying to catch. That thought alone caused more anxiety than facing a thousand charging fanatics. One could kill the fanatics, he thought to himself, but you cannot kill silly women, however much you might wish to. And lastly, he wondered when he should tell his father that he wasn't just coming home on leave; that he had resigned his commission and was home to stay.

John Bligh had arrived at the dock early, and watched as the ship bringing his son home began furling its sails. It was marvelous to watch as the Captain gracefully maneuvered his ship up the river with just the headsails; and how the small tug boat eased her along side the dock. Monkey's heads went flying over the gunwales down to the waiting dockhands, followed by the heavy mooring lines. Within minutes, the last of the sails were furled and the spring lines were doubled up. The boatswain's pipe sounded, and the gangplank was swung over the side and lowered into place. "All ashore, that's going ashore," echoed over the dock, and a single line of passengers began disembarking.

They caught each others eye at about the same time, John carefully watching the passengers coming down the gangplank, and Lawrence scanning the crowd for a familiar face. They waved at each other and a few moments later, to the great surprise of Lawrence, his father threw his arms around him softly repeating, "Lawrence, Lawrence, you've come back. Welcome home Son." He grabbed his son's duffle bag, "Let me carry this." He looked back to the carriage and called to Grove, "see to the rest of his luggage, we'll be in the pub across the street." With that, he took his son's arm and almost pulled him across the dock.

Lawrence, still in a state of complete surprise, followed his father across the street into the pub. No sooner had they stepped inside when John called out, "a round for everyone on me, my son is home." Lawrence looked at his father closely and saw the happiness in his eyes; it was very apparent that his father had also changed.

The carriage ride home dispelled any anxieties Lawrence had about how his father would receive him. They talked about India, London, politics, and Ireland. At last as they were approaching the manor, Lord Bligh said, "there is one other thing I must tell you, her name is Cassie and...."

Lawrence burst out laughing, cutting him off. "So that's it; another woman." He reached over and lightly punched his father on the shoulder, "and all this time I thought you were just happy to see me."

"Well certainly. I'm thrilled to have you home; but yes, it's true, I'm also in love, and anxious for you to meet her. She's planned your entire party, and is very nervous."

Lawrence looked out the window and seen the manor coming into view as they turned into the drive. On the steps he could see the familiar faces of the servants, and then he noticed a lovely woman standing next to Albert.

"Is that Cassie?" he asked pointing. "Well I'll be," he paused. "So how old is she?" he teased.

"Old enough to be your ....," he stopped and laughed. "Well let's just say she's old enough. Now mind your manners." The carriage came to a stop, and before Grove could climb down from his seat, John opened the door and they got out. Lawrence waved and called hello to all the servants, who sensing the moment, set custom aside and waved and called back, "welcome home Sir."

John motioned to his son to follow him as he walked up the steps toward Cassie, "Cassie, let me introduce my son Lawrence; Lawrence, meet Cassie."

Lawrence took hold of her hand. "When I left for India many years ago, my father was perhaps the most unhappy man in London, maybe in all of England. Upon coming home, I can see that you have made him the happiest man in the world. Cassie, it's truly a pleasure to meet you."

Leaning forward he whispered, "said he loves you. Has he asked you to marry him yet? We need to talk."

In that instant, Cassie who had been apprehensive about meeting John's son, knew that she liked Lawrence, and that this was going to be a wonderful, wonderful, party.

Chapter 14

Many years before, when John Bligh and his wife Elizabeth learned that she was pregnant; they were one of the happiest couples in London. He of course was hoping for a son to carry on the family name. She would have been happy with either a son or daughter, but prayed for a son for her husband's sake. But as they were to soon discover, not all children are a blessing.

From the time he was a very small child, Robert had been rebellious. Born into a family of privilege; having parents, especially a mother who cherished him; and surrounded by every toy a child could want; he constantly flew into tantrums. Believing that perhaps his behavior was caused by some unknown malady, they had him examined by the best specialists in England. Their conclusion: there was nothing medically wrong with their son; he was simply a willfully destructive child. Their suggestion: place him in an institution.

Elizabeth however, refused to give up. She spent countless hours with him, trying to teach him to play like other children. Breakable toys were replaced with solid wooden ones; windows were protected by wire mesh on the inside; and servants who had previously been kicked, bitten, or hit by a flying toy, looked very carefully before entering the play room. Because of his tendency to hit anyone, including his mother, John ordered Elizabeth to stay away from the playroom during the last four months of her next pregnancy. Their great hope was that when the next baby was born, it would have a mellowing effect on

Robert. But after Lawrence was born, it quickly became evident it only made him more selfish and unruly.

Privately, the servants whispered to each other, "Bad seed; that one will come ta no good end."

When he reached school age, one school after the other refused to have him. Left with no other options, his parents hired private tutors, only to have them quit within a few weeks. Eventually they found a very talented woman; a German teacher who also happened to be physically large and strong: a tutor who brooked no nonsense. If he threw something, she made him go and pick it up; if he ripped up his papers, she forced him to do them over again; if he struck her –which he did at first- he quickly learned that she would hit him back. It was a brutal contest of wills, but he did learn.

At the age of twelve, his father wanted to enroll Robert into a military school where rigid discipline might straighten him out. Elizabeth begged him not to, continuing to cling to the hope and belief that her love, and being at home with his parents, would somehow transform him. Out of his love for Elizabeth, he relented and Robert continued to live at home, much to the dismay of the servants.

When Elizabeth died, he rewarded her ceaseless love and devotion by refusing to go to the funeral. "So she's dead" he said without a trace of emotion, "everybody dies sometime." His father in turn, rewarded his son's callous indifference by placing him in a military school the following week. He continued to stay at the academy until he was eighteen, not because he showed any signs of changing, but because Lord Bligh made a very substantial donation to the academy to build a new athletic field with one key provision: they kept him there until he was eighteen. The day of his birthday he came into his inheritance; a Trust established by his mother, and left the academy for London.

For the first couple of years he spent most of his time in gentleman clubs, drinking and gambling with other men members of the same upper social strata. Because of his prominent family name and wealth, he was invited to society balls and parties where he met a number of young women. They were attracted to him by his crude manners and shocking language; he to their innocence. Convinced that if they submitted to his ardent kisses and fondling they could get him to marry and settle down; they soon discovered that foolish liberties quickly led to the loss of their virginity. It wasn't long before first one young woman, and then another, and another, found themselves pregnant.

One young woman's father, upon learning Robert had impregnated his daughter, was about to challenge him to a duel for his daughter's honor, when he was told Robert had spent over three years in a military academy and was a crack pistol shot. He settled for having his solicitor sue for several thousand pounds; and sent his daughter to France for the summer to have an abortion and be rid of a bastard child. Robert's continued outrageous behavior and refusal to conform to any rules of decent conduct, resulted in being barred from one club after another. Shortly thereafter, invitations to parties quickly dried up. He was now an outcast, banished from gentile society.

With a substantial source of income from his Trust, he rented a large house and soon found a group of friends more to his liking; together they continuing a life of drinking, gambling, and debauchery. His house became a haven for gambling and drug addicts, and women of the street who freely shared their bodies for a warm house, plenty of food, drugs, and drink. The rules of the house were very simple, get caught by the police for stealing and you were banished: period. Secondly, he had the right to bed any woman that stayed in the house, even if she was another man's wife or girl friend. Given the morals of those who came there, the second rule posed no problem. Realizing that the income from the Trust would not be sufficient to sustain his life style indefinitely; he determined that he needed to make some investments in the hopes of increasing his limited wealth. After considering the potential returns of several business opportunities, he decided that the slave trade offered the greatest potential quick return.

Trading in slaves had become a high risk venture: first because of the inherent danger in transporting the slaves; and secondly, because now there was a very strong anti-slavery movement in England. The general opinion of the Parliament was that if legislation banning slavery was not passed this year, it would be in the near future. Since the directors his Trust would never sanction such a risky venture, he carefully concealed the true nature of his investment by establishing an Import/ Export business allegedly dealing in African hardwoods. Had the venture succeeded, he would have easily doubled his money. Unfortunately for Robert, the slave ship floundered on one of the many treacherous reefs in the Caribbean. All on board, together with a large part of his Trust went to the bottom.

Having disappeared from the social clubs, and no longer having any contact with family friends and acquaintances; his Father knew very little about his present life except for the occasional letters addressed to him from solicitors demanding money and damages for one offence or another. For Robert's part, he cared nothing about either his Father, or his brother Lawrence, whom he had not heard from in many years, and assumed was still in India.

The family estate however, was something else. Under the English Laws of inheritance, in the event of his father's death, as the eldest son the estate would come to him. For that reason alone, he quietly continued to keep informed about his father's business dealings and his health. As for Lawrence, his younger brother had no right of inheritance; besides that, he was far away in India with a good chance of getting killed. Comforted by these dark thoughts, he continued his life of wantonness, satisfied that in time it would all work out to his advantage.

Then one day, his Bank mailed him a notice requesting that he come to the bank to discuss an important matter; it was tossed on a desk piled with other unopened mail. A week later, a second letter came marked urgent; again it remained unopened. Two days later, an officer from the bank personally came to the house and informed him that the balance in his Trust account was getting very low. Believing that there had been some mistake, he went to the bank and was shocked to discover that all the monies his father had paid to solicitors, tradesmen, and others for his misdeeds, had recently been deducted from his Trust Fund.

"No, no," he yelled. "He cannot do that."

"I'm afraid that he can Sir." The bank Manager said in hushed tones. "We sent you two notices attempting to alert you that we had received a Demand against your Trust Account from your father's solicitor. You never responded to our letters. In respect for your late mother, Lady Elizabeth, we sent Mr. Williams to see you. In the meanwhile of course, we had our legal department carefully review the Demand; it's all quite legal. It turns out that there is a clause in the Trust, permitting reimbursement in certain instances such as those costs your father had previously paid. We had no choice Sir, but to deduct the funds from your account." In one fell swoop, thousands of pounds were deducted from his Trust.

Returning home and looking through other mail he had ignored, he found a letter dated over a month ago from a detective he had hired to keep watch on his father. The letter informed him that his father had been spending a considerable amount of time at a place called the Captain's

Inn in Bristol with a young woman, a widow named Mrs. Smyth. The detective wanted to know if he should investigate Mrs. Smyth. That news brought him up sharp. Whoever she was, she could become a very serious problem because if his father remarried, it was possible he could lose his inheritance. He immediately sent a letter to the detective; investigate the woman at once.

The next evening he was in a tavern drinking a couple of his friends, trying to determine the best course of action to thwart this new threat, when yet another blow fell. He chanced to bump into an old acquaintance from his earlier days at one of the gentleman's clubs, who told him that his brother Lawrence had returned home.

With his money running out at an alarming rate, he calculated that would be broke in less than a year. As for any chance of loans backed by a very large future inheritance, he knew that no lender would consider such a loan if they discovered there was a possibility his father might remarry. Add to that the news that his brother was coming home, and he quickly realized that he was in a financial situation which was becoming more desperate by the day.

He was trying to come up with a good reason, any reason, to visit home, when his former friend informed him about the forthcoming 'Welcome Home Party' for Lawrence. That was the answer he had been looking for. Regardless of past problems, even his father would not object to him welcoming his brother home. That would also be the perfect opportunity to determine how serious his father's intentions were toward this woman from Bristol. With that happy thought, he ordered more whiskey.

One of Robert's basic problems was that he always had to do things his way. His friends, who were generally in a mental twilight from drugs and alcohol, did have occasional sober rational moments. During one such brief period, they told him to stay off the booze for a while and clear his head. The Home-Coming Party and meeting with his father and brother would be very important, and he needed to be as polite and conciliatory as possible. That would not be the time to say or do anything to further antagonize them.

"Who in hell asked you for advice," he responded, "and when was the last time you paid for anything? Now shut-up; I know how to handle this." He poured himself another whiskey. "What I've got to do," he said taking another swallow, "is find a way to bust up this new romance, to send this Smyth bitch packing. Bobby," he called to a man at the bar, "I need somebody to take a message to that detective - whatever his name is - and tell him to get over here. I need to know what he's found out about that whore."

A big smile crossed his face. "Maybe I'll go to Bristol and bed the bitch myself, wouldn't that be a joke. Then when I go to the party I could say, "Father dear, small world, we're both screwing the same whore." He let out a laugh, belched, emptied his glass and poured another. "Now that's a good idea," he said to himself, "I'll leave for Bristol tomorrow. If the bitch is willing we'll have some fun; if not, I'll still have fun." She wouldn't be the first he'd forced himself upon. Either way, telling his father he'd had her would do the trick.

No longer able to afford a private chaise, the following day he took a public coach to Bristol arriving two days later. Dressed in a neat dark brown coat, white hat, corduroy breeches, well polished boots, cloth leggings, buckskin gloves, and feeling very smug; he had a local cab take him to the Captain's Inn. The mental pictures of conquest he had conjured up were quickly dashed by a small note on the door that read: Closed.

"Damn it," he swore pounding on the door. A few moments later, a servant opened the door and informed him that the Inn would be closed indefinitely. Mrs. Smyth, the owner had gone to London, and they didn't know when she would return. The door closed and he walked back into the street. "Damn it! damn it! damn it!" he yelled, loud enough for passersby to hear. "I just wasted two days and money I can't afford to spend." As they looked at him, he pointed his walking stick at them and shouted, "so what the hell are you looking at?" The people scurried away fearful of what else he might do.

He turned around and looked out over the harbor. The sun was slowly drifting down toward the distant sea, igniting the clouds in a blaze of fire. The tall ships in the harbor turned to black silhouettes floating on a crimson sea, backlit by the changing light. He thought for a moment of how his father and this woman had looked out over this scene many times. A caring person would have felt a tinge of happiness for them. But Robert had never in his life felt, or cared, for anyone but himself.

He looked down the street, hailed a cab and told the driver to take him down by the docks. "Take me to an Inn that's cheap.....and where I won't get mugged during the night." Tomorrow he would head back home. He checked the money in his purse; not enough money left to hire a prostitute, but if he was lucky he might find a little tart and get her drunk enough to spend the night with him. His lusty thoughts were suddenly interrupted by a terrible thought. While he was here looking for a place to stay for the night, that bitch was in London with his father. "Shit," he said to himself.

The trip back to London did not go well. It had rained all night and twenty miles from Bristol, the coach broke an axel requiring the passengers to stay an additional night at a roadside Inn until it could be repaired. The next morning he awoke to the drumming sound of rain on the roof; more trouble. When the weather was dry, most passengers preferred to ride on top of the coach where they could watch the scenery and enjoy the fresh air. When it rained there were two choices, stay on top with an umbrella and hope to stay reasonably dry; or ride inside the coach where it was close, dark, and stuffy. He chose the inside and sat next to a huge fellow who, judging from the very strong odor, had not bathed in many months, if ever. Adding to his misery, the man kept dozing off, his massive bulk falling sideways squeezing him against the window that leaked. Robert would jab his elbow into the man to wake him up, but within a few minutes the scene – comical to everyone else in the coach - would repeat it self over and over again.

The going was slow on the muddy road, and desperation began taking hold of him. Considering the travel fares both ways, five nights of lodging, meals, whisky, and the wasted drinks on an over weight, middle aged woman who fell asleep as soon as she climbed in bed; this had been a very costly and fruitless trip. His financial affairs, his whole way of life was like a ship that had hit a reef and was beginning to go down fast, like his ill fated slave ship venture.

Years before, he had destroyed any possible chance of a good friendship with anyone from the society he had been born into; now he had no one with financial means to turn to for help. He also knew that once the Trust money was gone, his so called friends would leave him faster than the proverbial rats left a sinking ship. That also included the prostitutes and other loose women that shared his bed; for them it was strictly pay to play. If necessary, he could stop buying the whisky for his friends and cut down on the food, but he could not give up the women. Not because he was sexually driven, most of that was for show; in fact there were many nights he never even touched the woman lying next to him. He needed the women because he had a carefully hidden secret; he had always been deathly afraid to be alone in the dark.

Given the bleak prospects for his financial future, the most immediate problem was to find a way to destroy the relationship between his Father and that Smyth woman. As the carriage slowly lurched along the muddy road towards London; the seed of a plan began to take root. A very dangerous plan to be sure; but these were desperate times, and desperate times require desperate measures.

Robert arrived back in London tired, wet, and angry. The trip to Bristol had been a total waste of time and money, money he could not afford to spend. When the cab pulled up at his house, the detective just happened to arrive at the same time. "What bad news could he have for me now," he thought.

"Good afternoon Mr. Bligh, I hope your trip was profitable," he said in a mood far too cheery to suit Robert.

"It was a terrible trip," he snapped. "What are you here for?"

Sensing that this was not a good time to ask for his long overdue payment, he decided to postpone that until tomorrow in the hope that it would be a better time. "I just happened to be in the area and when I saw you arrive, I thought I'd stop and ask how the trip went."

"As I said, it was terrible, nothing went right. Now if you'll excuse me I need to change into some dry clothes." He grabbed his traveling bag and went into the house, where he was greeted by the sight of a couple having sex on the divan in the parlor. "What the hells wrong with you," he yelled, "don't we have enough bedrooms upstairs?"

"Who's that?" the woman asked sitting up.

"He's the bloke that owns the place," the man said pushing her back down. "Com'on now, let's get on with it."

Had he been in a better mood, he would have stayed and watched the couple, another perversion he enjoyed. But even that thought failed to brighten his dark frame of mind. He went upstairs to his bedroom to change into some dry clothes. The room was a mess; empty glasses and bottles on the dresser and floor, and plates with old dried food stuck to them. He looked at the bed, little doubt that the woman he had last slept with here, had been very busy entertaining in his bed while he was away. It was also evident from the smell that the bed linens had not been changed since he left. "Filthy drunks and whores, all of them. Why do I live like this?" he said angrily throwing the bed linens on the floor.

Leaving the bedroom, he went back downstairs to his office. A pile of mail was carefully stacked on his desk. He turned and walked to the kitchen, "I need a drink before I start sorting through that," he mumbled to himself.

Opening the cupboard where the whisky was kept, he found it empty. His angry screams could be heard halfway down the block.

"What was that god-awful yell?" the woman on the couch asked, getting up on one elbow and looking around.

"That's his highness, he's jes discovered there's no more booze."

Chapter 15

If Cassie had been overly concerned about the Party, she needn't have worried. The day dawned bright and sunny, and since it had not rained for several days, the beautiful grounds and gardens were dry and open for everyone to enjoy. Cassie made one final tour around the manor to insure that everything was in place, and had a last minute meeting with the Albert and the cook. Satisfied that all was in order, she went to her room to get dressed.

Although she realized that this was an important occasion, and that all of John's friends would be watching her very closely, she was remarkably at ease. Certainly she wished to make a good first impression, but knowing that John loved her, and that Lawrence had welcomed her with open arms had calmed her earlier fears. Now, having been living at the manor and dealing with the servants for close to a month, she could clearly see that John was his own man and very sure of himself. In his opinion, true friends were friends regardless of circumstance; and he was not one to make false apologies, or play political games to gain anyone's favor. If they liked and welcomed Cassie, fine; if they didn't, it made little difference to him. In that respect, he was much like her late husband who was fond of saying, "I am what I am," and she loved him for it.

Beginning in the late afternoon the invited guest began arriving, many ahead of the scheduled time in the hope of meeting and talking to John or Cassie before the actual party began. Some of the men were anxious to talk to John about what his future business plans were: did he intend to return to London and stay; and how was the situation at his estate in Ireland? Particularly, why did he spend so much of his time there? something they couldn't fully understand. And lastly, although few would have admitted to it, they were more than curious to meet this new young woman he had brought from Bristol.

The women of course were focused on one thing, or more precisely one person, Cassie. Who was she? From the day she arrived in London, the gossip began. In less than a forte night, numerous rumors had circulated throughout the social circles: He had met her in a dockside Pub in Bristol; she was just a close friend helping him plan the party; she was his mistress; that he had already asked her to marry him; she was already pregnant; ....

One particularly wild rumor had it that he had met her twelve years before when he and Elizabeth had visited Bristol on their way to Ireland; and that she had been his secret mistress ever since. Now of course none of the women placed much stock in any of these rumors, but gossip was such fun and it brightened - for a while anyway - their otherwise boring routine life. Truth be known, there were several women in the group, who given the chance, would have been very willing to be John's mistress.

As for Lawrence's friends, several of his former classmates from school had also joined the service. It would be very interesting to talk to them about their military experiences, and how they now felt about "the Empire." Others had become involved in politics, the only other vocation acceptable in aristocratic society. If one had money, it was not publicly talked about. Most of the young women he had known before he left had long since married and now had small children. He learned from a friend that one woman in particular, Sally Fairfield, had become very active in the fight against slavery, and had never married.

He tried to recall those early memories; if his recollection was correct, she was a tall slender, dark haired girl who had been very opinionated; and when it came to arguments, gave the boys measure-for-measure. Her R.S.V.P. had not been returned, but occasionally a guest would arrive, Invitation in hand explaining that they had been away from home and apologized for not having had time to return it. "Sally Fairfield," he thought to himself, "now she could prove to be interesting. It would be nice to see her again."

Dinner was served at Eight followed by dancing in the ballroom. Everyone was having a joyous time, and John, Cassie, and Lawrence were having a difficult time being pulled this way and that by all the friends wanting to talk to them. Cassie made it a special point to personally speak to as many of the women as possible, and tell them how she met John. When she told them that she owned and operated an Inn, a number of them audibly gasped. She also noticed that a couple of the younger women began whispering among themselves, "she owns and runs an Inn, how exciting!" When she approached them, they said would like to talk to her privately when she had more time.

It was about 9:30 PM; John had just walked across the dance floor to speak to someone, and Cassie was standing by herself watching the dancers and thinking about how well everything had worked out; it had truly been a wonderful party. She had met dozens of John's and Lawrence's friends, and sincerely felt that they had accepted her. As she stood alone sipping a glass of champagne; Robert, whom she had never met and who obviously had far too much to drink, walked up to her.

Stepping right up to her face he said, "So you're the little bitch that's been screwing my father to get his money."

Most women would have been shocked into silence, a few might have fainted. Cassie hesitated for a second then slapped him so hard across his face the blow could be heard around the ballroom; sending the young man back on his heels in surprise. Before he could recover his balance, she quickly stepped forward to his left, simultaneously gripping him around the neck just behind his left ear with her right hand, driving her thumb deeply into his neck. As he sank to his knees from the pain, the lower edge of her flattened left hand slashed downward smashing the bridge of his nose. The musicians stopped playing; the dancing stopped; and the guests turned and watched in astonishment as blood started gushing from Robert's nostrils, down the front of his clothing and unto the floor. It had all happened in less than five seconds.

As John came running toward her, he quickly glanced at Cassie and asked if she was alright; she nodded yes and released her grip on the young man who was desperately trying to stem the flow of blood.

"Whoever you are," she seethed, "get out of this house you're not welcome here."

A second later Lawrence appeared and he and John grabbed him by his collar and dragged him across the dance floor toward the door. Albert ran ahead and opened the door and stood back as John and Lawrence pushed him outside and threw him down the stairs where some of Robert's friends were waiting.

Returning inside, Lawrence glanced at Cassie and turned to his father, "now she is some woman!"

His father smiled, "she certainly is."

"My friends," John began holding his hand in the air, "let me apologize for what just happened. That young man is my other son Robert whom some of you know. He was obviously very drunk, and is not welcome in this house. Again, please accept my apology and continue to enjoy the evening." He motioned for the musicians to begin playing.

The evening; which had started to settle down to quiet conversation, instantly took on new life. No sooner had the music started than the hushed whispers and conversations began around the room.

"Did you see that?" one woman inquired.

"No, I was facing the other way, what happened?"

"Well," another woman answered, "it looked to me like John's son tried to hit Cassie."

"No," said another. "He said something to her – it must have been terrible- and she slapped him."

"More than slapped him I'd say. In seconds he was down on his knees bleeding all over himself? I think she broke his nose."

"I don't know what she did, but I'd sure like to learn that trick," a young woman replied.

John and Lawrence came back and began talking to Cassie, "What happened?" John asked. "Did he say something to you?"

"It's really not important John. Let's just forget that it happened."

"No, I can't do that. He said something that hurt you and I need to know what it was, please."

She whispered in his ear.

"Oh my God Cassie. I'm sorry that he said that to you, and the fact he was drunk does not excuse his behavior. Elizabeth and I did everything we could for him, but …."

She put her fingers to his lips, "I understand John. Sometimes a person is born and no one can understand where they came from. They're like someone from another family."

John turned to Lawrence, "tomorrow, there's some very important business we must take care of. I've put it off far too long." Looking at Cassie, "Cassie," he said smiling and taking her hand, "how about a dance? No, not just this dance," he added, "how about all the dances for the rest of our lives. Cassie; will you marry me?"

"I was beginning to think you'd never ask her," Lawrence quipped, and walked away.

"Of course I'll marry you," she answered. "Now let's start dancing."

As they waltzed around the floor, Lawrence walked to the front of the manor and looked out the window. He could see some of his brother's friends helping him into a carriage as Robert held a bloody cloth to his face. It had been his hope that while he was in India, that his brother had changed; and that they could really become close like he had been with the Corporal from Scotland. Judging from what he had just witnessed, it was apparent his brother had grown even worse. He shook his head, "Looks like I left one war, and came home to another." Had he over heard what his brother was saying to his friends, he would have realized how true that was.

Lawrence turned away from the window and walked around the house again, hoping that he would find Sally. Why? He didn't really know why. He just wanted to see her again, and see what she looked like now. But she wasn't there.

Late the next morning, Robert awoke with a terrible headache, and a swollen throbbing nose. Not only had his plan to embarrass Cassie and drive a wedge between her and his Father failed, but she had utterly humiliated him in front of everyone present. That was disgraceful enough; but the broken nose, and then being thrown bodily down the stairs in front of his friends was the last straw. Real anger was beginning to take hold of him now.

This was going to be more difficult than he had imagined; something more drastic had to be done, but what? He looked at the older woman in bed next to him, she looked familiar, but he couldn't remember if anything had happened last night. "Doesn't matter," he mumbled to himself gently touching his badly swollen nose and face. He climbed out of bed and half stumbled down the hall, calling to his friends sleeping in the other rooms. "We need to talk," he yelled in a nasal voice, "Get your lazy worthless asses out of bed."

From several rooms, a motley assortment of men and women appeared in the doorways, most of them half naked and still dazed from the drinking and drugs of the night before. Just in front of him was a totally naked slender pretty girl with short dark brown hair who appeared to be about twelve or thirteen. He reached out with his left hand, placed it around her neck and pulled her close to him.

"I haven't seen you here before, did you have a good time last night?" he said reaching down and fondling her tiny breasts.

She looked frightened and remained silent.

He bent over and started to kiss her, but pulled back in pain as his nose touched her. "I'll be better by tonight; think you can you give me a good time?" Looking at the woman standing behind her he said, "how's about the two of you with me tonight? that'll be a kick."

The young girl turned to the man she had been with the night before, "should I go with him?" she asked.

"Hell yes if that's what he wants. He owns this place."

"Where'd she come from?" Robert asked.

"Her mother sold her ta me last night. She was drunk and needed money for drugs, so I bought her fer a week."

"A week huh. Was she a virgin?

"Nah, her mums sold her lots a times before."

Robert looked at her young hard body as he pushed his finger in her navel, and then slowly ran them up her stomach to her breast and pinched her nipples; he really liked the young ones. "We're all gonna have some fun tonight," he laughed. "But right now I need to get something to eat; then you've gotta help me try and figure out what to do about my Father and that bitch he's with."

"Yea," someone called out. "Let's get something ta eat and help 'em figure out what ta do about his old man."

"Why don't we just kill the bastard so that Robert can inherit the money."

"I like that idea," one of the women said. "Just thinking of living in that big house makes me want to kill him myself."

"Com'on," Robert said. "We're not going to kill anybody. I need some serious thinking here, not that kind of bullshit."

After breakfast, the discussion of what to do began in earnest. For over an hour they drank and debated the possible options. Unfortunately, most of Robert's friends had never finished grade school. Whatever imagination they might have once possessed; had long ago been dulled by drugs and drowned in alcohol. Their solutions ranged from plain stupid, to super stupid, such as: "why not have yer own party and invite them ta come here?" Sometimes, even he grew weary of these idiots.

Later that day, the detective that he had hired stopped by. So far as he had been able to determine, his father had not changed his Will. The question was how long would it be before he did? Robert knew that whatever he was going to do, had to be done soon. After considering his limited options; murder began looking better by the hour. The next question was; if murder was the answer, who could he get to do it; and how much would it cost?

John Bligh did not like alcohol, and never drank more than a half glass of champagne, and that only in toasting at a dinner party. Consequently, the morning after the party he woke up early mentally alert and pulled open the drapes on another beautiful day. "Today's the day," he said to himself. "Today I'm going to draw up a new Will." He pulled on the cord by his bedside, when the servant knocked and opened the door he asked that his barber be sent up.

Down the hall, Cassie was already up and dressed. Running the Inn had conditioned her to rise early to check on the guests and her staff. She was already dressed and on her way down the stairs when she saw the barber walking toward John's room. "Please tell Lord Bligh I'll wait for him in the breakfast room," she said. When she walked in, Lawrence was already on his second helping.

"I was famished," he apologized, "and I didn't know when you and my father would be down. With all of the goings-on last night, I really didn't eat very much. Are you hungry?"

"Famished is the word my late husband, the Captain, often used. And if you had watched him eat, you knew he was telling the truth. Your father's so trim and athletic, the Captain was anything but. That's the difference between him riding and walking all over Arden; and the Captain walking the deck of his ship. Eventually that's what killed him; over weight; a sudden heart attack.

"I'm sorry. My father told me that you had loved him very much."

"It's true. And he loved me." She sat down at the table. "But that was years ago. Now, as you can plainly see, I'm in love with your father. Last night he asked me to marry him and I said yes. Why am I telling you this, you were there."

"Cassie I think it's wonderful, for both of you. For so many years he was depressed. Arden helped pull him out of some of that, but you're the one that's brought him real happiness." He took a sip of coffee, "there's something I have to ask you - I hope you don't mind. What exactly did you do to Robert last night?"

"Oh that," she laughed. "Many years ago, my husband Matthew returned from a voyage and brought an old shipmate with him that he hadn't seen for about fifteen years. After dinner, the three of us were sitting in the parlor talking. His friend had had a little too much to drink, and started becoming vulgar. Matthew got up and suggested it was time for him to go, and at that point he made an obscene remark toward me. Matthew walked over to him and gripping him by the neck, took him to the door and pushed him out into the street."

"After that unpleasant incident, he became concerned for my safety when he was away, so he taught me a few self defense tricks; like the one I used on Robert last night. Want me to show you how?"

At that moment John walked in the breakfast room.

"You're just in time for the demonstration," she said. "I'm going to show Lawrence what I did to Robert." With that, she walked over to him and placed her hand around the back of his neck and pressed her thumb gently just below his ear. "There's a nerve there; press hard and down they go regardless of how big they are. Then you bring your left hand down like this across the bridge of their nose. Hit it there and it breaks very easily."

"That's amazing," Lawrence said. "If I ever get married, I'll be certain to teach that to my wife. But not before I'm married," he laughed. "I'll also remember to be very careful not to antagonize you."

"Well you better not," John replied. She's going to be your step mother very soon."

Lawrence stood up and raised his coffee cup, "A toast. Here's to the most deserving couple I know. Cassie, let me welcome you into our family with a heart full of love for both of you. I can't think of a more wonderful home coming gift than the two of you getting married."

John walked over and put his arms around his son. "I'm so pleased that you were here for this. You don't know how much it means to have you here with us; even if it's only for a few weeks."

"Father, Cassie, I have a confession to make, and now is as good a time as any." They stopped and looked at him.

"I'm not home on leave. I resigned my commission. You're going to be stuck with me for a while. At least until I can figure out what I'm going to do."

John and Cassie glanced at each other and then ran over and threw their arms around him. When the servant walked in to see if they needed anything, he found the three of them arm in arm, dancing around the room.

When the servant walked back into the kitchen, he said, "I don't know what's going on in there, but they're sure happy."

John and Cassie; having decided that one big party was enough for a while, were married one week later in a quiet ceremony at home. Since neither of them had really been in London for quite some time, they spent the next three weeks investigating everything. They went to see the famous Shakespearian actor Macready play King Lear at the Globe Theater; spent two days at the new Polytechic Exhibit Hall which featured all the latest advancements in science and technology. They held their noses and gasped for air as they experienced the repulsive smells of chemicals in the Great Hall; and saw the newly developed Diving Bell for underwater exploration.

They were among the first to hear Charles Dickens recite his newly published book, "The Adventures of Oliver Twist." John bought Cassie an autographed copy of Elizabeth Barrett Browning's latest book of poetry, "The Seraphim and Other Poems."

London was alive with exciting events, plays, concerts, new restaurants, and of course shopping. Cassie had never had so many new dresses, shoes, and hats in her life. Every night they would come home exhausted; but the next day they would go out again. At the end of the third week,

Cassie told John, "That's it. I cannot go to one more play, or concert, or shop, or restaurant. You'll have to leave me and marry someone else, or go alone."

"You don't know how happy I am to hear you say that," he replied. "It's been wonderful, but I was beginning to think you were trying to do the old man in." He looked at her and smiled, "that's the price for marrying such a young and beautiful woman."

"Well I've been thinking," she said coming over and sitting on his lap. "These have been very busy weeks. Maybe something a bit more quiet is in order. What would you say to the idea of going to Arden? I'm sure there are a lot of things you need to check out there; and on the way we could check on the Inn."

"You're an absolute darling; it's a wonderful idea. Would you mind if Lawrence came along?"

"I want him to come with us. He's been looking around for weeks now for something to do; to get involved in. Maybe Arden is it. He's never been there has he?"

"No. I wanted him to go with me once, but that was when he decided to join the service."

"What's Ireland like? I've never been there either."

"It's a wonderful place, filled with wonderful people when you get to know them. I have a feeling that you'll learn to love Ireland as I do. But it's much different than England; the land; the people; their customs. It's hard to imagine...." he stopped. "Well I don't want to say too much, I want you to see and judge it for yourself. When shall we leave?"

"Let's tell Lawrence this afternoon, and see how he feels about going. I can be ready to leave in a couple of days." She looked at him. "Now tell me seriously, what do I need to pack, and for how long?"

"Riding and hiking clothes, lots of sweaters, and good boots; comfortable country clothing. There's little need of ball gowns there."

"What? No Ball gowns?   So this talk of us dancing forever was only a ruse to get me to marry you."

"It worked," he said with a big smile.

Chapter 16

Except for short trips down the River Thames aboard her former husband's ship, Cassie had never been on an actual voyage before; so she was both excited about the trip from Bristol to Kilrush, and apprehensive. She had heard some terrible stories about sea sickness, and did not relish the idea of leaning over the rail vomiting for two days. Besides, as the new wife of Lord Bligh, she believed she had a certain obligation to be at her best at his side. After arriving in Bristol and checking on the Inn, she went to the local apothecary shop to see if they had anything to prevent sea sickness: they did not. However, a young seaman who happened to be in the shop over heard her conversation with the druggist.

"Beggin yer pardon M'Lady, but I over heerd ye askin aboot sea sickness. My advice is ta keep yerself away from the smell of coffee and bacon; and if it's a follwin sea, keep as close ta the bow of the ship as ye can. Aye, it's the yaw that'll get land-lubbers every time."

"A follwin sea? the yaw? What are those?"

"A follwin sea is when waves come at the ship from the stern – behind ye. When that happens, the back of the ship lifts up on a wave and swings ta one side; then as the wave goes under the ship, the it drops down and swings ta the other side," He demonstrated with his arms and hands. "Up and over, down and back. Up and over, down and back."

"Oh, a following sea," she said, almost becoming queasy from watching him. "Well thank you very much for the advice. I'll try and remember that."

"Yer very welcome M'Lady. Where's ye shipping off ta?"

"To Kilrush, in Ireland."

"Well I'll be horn swaggled," he exclaimed. "You'll be traveling on my ship, the Mary Jane. You'll have some good company. I bin told that Lord Bligh and his son that jes returned from India will be on board. I also heerd Lord Bligh's got his self a new young bride. A fine fellow Lord Bligh is, 'ard to believe he's English. Oh, begging your pardon," he quickly added noting that she was English

"So you know Lord Bligh?" she asked, very interested in what he had to say.

"Aye, that I do," he replied with a smile. "I've 'ad the pleasure ta talk to him many times on the trips back and forth. He's nothin like those other hoity-toity English gentlemen," he said with contempt. "Just a real nice bloke who'll shoot the blarney with anyone; doesn't care if they're rich or poor as a church mouse. Not only that, but my cousin works on his estate in Kilrush, she tells me that everybody up in those parts loves him." The sailor paid for his package, and turned to leave, "T'was a pleasure meetin ye M'Lady. If ye need anythin while yer on board, just ask for Billy," he tipped his hat and walked out the door.

After he left, the druggist said, "Lady Bligh, why didn't you tell him who you were?"

"Oh heavens no," she laughed, "I want to see the look on his face when we meet again.... on board."

Cassie walked out the door feeling warm and wonderful inside. She had just talked to a total stranger who did not know who she was, and had no reason to lie. He had just confirmed her belief that she had married a remarkable man. And what the young seaman said was true; John was not Hoity-Toity like those other Englishman. She could hardly wait to get to Kilrush and Arden. She glanced in a shop window and saw her reflection, "You're a lucky woman Mrs. Bligh she said to herself. She continued walking back to the Inn feeling more alive and excited than she had in many years. It's going to be a wonderful trip. Just remember to watch out for the smell of the coffee, bacon.... and the yaw.

Except for the surprised look of embarrassment on Billy's face when he discovered who the lady in the store was, the trip was smooth and uneventful. The winds were fair as they left the dock in Bristol and headed south west and then west. The Mary Jane cut through the seas raising a lacy white wake that rippled along her sides. Half a dozen gulls would soar above the masts with wings outstretched; and would then would pull in their wings dip, and glide astern ever watchful for whatever scraps of food might be tossed overboard.

For the first couple of hours as they sailed out of Bristol Harbor, the rolling deck was a challenge and she stayed close to the base of the main mast; but after leaving the lighthouse at Barry astern, the Captain altered course to West by North West. The sails caught the powerful winds sweeping across the open sea, and the Mary Jane settled down with a slight list to starboard.

Cassie had never felt the steady wind of the open sea, heard the flutter and crack of the sails, or the sounds the wind made as it played through the sheets and shrouds. She walked over and leaned against the rail watching the waves, and noticed how they rolled under the surface in a steady line heading east; and felt the ship gently rise and fall as the wave slipped beneath the hull and continued on its journey.

All these new sensations filled her with deep emotions, and for the first time she truly understood why her first husband had so loved the sea. There was a captivating aspect to it that could never be fully conveyed to anyone who had not stood on a moving deck, or sensed the awesome power that held the ship in its grasp. Somewhere out there thousands of miles away beneath the rolling waves, Matthew had gone to his final resting place; and while she regretted she had not been there for his last moments, she was happy with the knowledge he had died doing what he loved. She blew a kiss out over the sea, "Goodbye Matthew," she called. As she turned around, she saw John and Lawrence walking toward her. A new life had begun.

Two days later, the Captain slid the Mary Jane gently up to the dock in Kilrush and made fast. The quiet routine of the open sea quickly gave way to the hustle and bustle of passengers disembarking; the shouts and occasional curses of the crew as cargo was being off loaded in huge nets that would rise from the hatches and be swung over to the waiting hands on the dock; while out going cargo was being readied to bring aboard.

She held John's arm as they walked down the gangplank. When her feet touched the land, she quickly gripped his hand tightly as an unexpected new sensation hit her; the land was not moving. For two days her sense of balance had been altered as her legs, body, and eyes had adjusted to the movement of the ship and the horizon. For a moment, her legs and eyes were confused by the unmoving land, and she felt as unsteady on the land, as she had at first been on the moving ship.

"It takes a few minutes to get re-adjusted to the land," John said, knowing exactly what she was feeling. "Just look over there at the Custom House for a moment," he pointed. "Your mind needs to adjust to a steady scene, instead of the moving horizon."

"That was a real surprise. Anything else I should know before I take another step?"

"Just that you had better keep a tight grip on my hand. Otherwise some of these handsome Irish rogues are very likely to think you're single and make a pass at you."

"They will, will they?" she said looking around. "You mean like that nice looking young man over there? Maybe I should have made the trip here long ago," she laughed squeezing his hand.

John pointed at Scattery Island in the distance. "Next week, after we get settled, I'll take you and Lawrence out there to see the ruins of the old monastery. All that's left is the old church called the Hill of the Angel, and the round tower. It was built by Saint Senan in the 6th century."

"According to the legend; an Angel placed Saint Senan on the hill as he fought and killed a horrible monster; so he built the church there. I personally think the reason he built the monastery out there was to get away from women; he hated them. The Vikings attacked and looted it in 816 and occupied it in the late 900's. The English destroyed it in the 15th century." They were still looking out at the Island when Lawrence walked up.

"The horses and carriage are being off loaded now. Grove will have everything ready in half and hour." He looked around at the buildings, shops, and in the distance Saint Patrick's. He also noticed some very pretty young women who were not at all like the pale-faced women he knew back in London. These had real color in their faces from being out in the sun; and flowing locks of black hair. "Say Father, when you wrote to me about Kilrush and Arden, why didn't you ever tell me about the attractive women here? I might have come home years ago."

"Well had the thought occurred to me; you can be sure I would have written you many, many letters about them. Keep in mind now, these are Catholic Irish Lasses, who are very suspect of young English gentlemen," he said as they walked across the street. "One other thing, unlike our demure English women - my Cassie excepted - they have been known to pack quite a punch."

Lawrence looked around again and smiled. He had a feeling he was going to like Ireland.

The trip going out to Arden was an unexpected experience for both Cassie and Lawrence. First they noticed the large number of people who walked along the road; adults and children. Even more surprising, was the considerable number who recognized Lord Bligh's carriage and called and waived hello as they passed. Three times, John stopped the carriage and got out to speak to someone. Each time he climbed back into the carriage, he told Cassie and Lawrence who the people were. He then suggested that they should have a party and invite the local folks. "Give everyone a chance to meet you and get acquainted."

Lawrence and Cassie looked at each other in surprise. These were common people, tenant farmers, laborers, and John was going to have a party and invite them all? That would have been unthinkable in England. Somewhere, back out there in the ocean, they had crossed an invisible line that John had crossed long ago. As Billy had told her in the Apothecary shop, John wasn't like the other Englishmen, everybody here loved him.

It was already becoming apparent that Ireland was much different than what they had known in England. And as for John, among his friends back in London he was quiet and reserved; but since arriving here they marveled at how alive he had become among these people.

The next time Grove stopped the carriage for John to get out and talk to a family, Cassie turned to Lawrence, "this is your Father's home, Ireland; and these are his people, his real friends."

The following two days were a whirlwind of activity. Shortly after they arrived at Arden, a wagon carrying their luggage arrived. As Cassie unpacked, she was so thankful for what John had told her to pack. She looked out the window and saw Lawrence walking across a field talking to one of the workers. She hurried putting the rest of her clothing away. "Time to get out there," she said to herself.

Next, accompanied by Neil, the three of them rode and walked all over the estate, meeting literally dozens of people. John walked more than he rode, and it seemed that he knew everyone he met by name. He would introduce Cassie and Lawrence, and then ask about their wife or husband, and how were their children.

"Lawrence," Cassie asked, "how many people does he know by their first name? there must be hundreds." And always it was the same, walk up and shake their hand, pat them on the back, talk and laugh. With every passing day, she loved him more and thanked God for the day he stopped at the Inn.

As for Lawrence, he was getting to know things about his father he had never suspected. When he had left for India, his father had been a very rigid, no nonsense businessman. A man who had little time for the pleasantries of life, and certainly no time for anyone that could not further his ambitions. The man he was observing now had obviously undergone a total change of character; and like Cassie, he thought it was wonderful. She had been right with her opinion about his father; this was his real home, and these were his people, his friends.

On Saturday afternoon, five days after they arrived they had their big party. Everyone had been invited including folks from Kilrush and Holy Jim's Canyon. Since there were not enough tables to hold all the food, planks laid across saw horses were set up on the lawn. John provided the food including dozens of chickens, lamb, and pigs for roasting, and their cook supervised the tenant farmers wives preparing everything picnic style. A large area of the lawn was roped off for a dance floor, and some of the local men provided the music. It was a gala event, and they later estimated that over three hundred people had attended.

Cassie and Lawrence had never met so many new people at one time: Catholic Priests, the Methodist Minister, local businessmen, tradesmen, blacksmiths, shopkeepers, millers, farmers with their wives and children, not only from Arden, but from miles around. Unlike the staid and proper dancing at the party in London, this was a foot stomping, hand clapping, swing your partner style of dancing that was all new to them. As for formal introductions, there were none. When the fiddles started it was grab the closest person, say hello, and away you went. Watching Cassie and Lawrence trying to learn to dance the Irish Jig brought howls of good natured laughing from everyone present

After the first few dances, Lawrence saw a lovely Lass across the way and asked her to dance. It was like a match tossed in dry hay. Before the evening ended, he had danced with close to two dozen women, young and old. Some who danced just for the joy of dancing; and a few younger women who began to think far beyond the party and dancing.

"Well Cassie," Father Grant said as he approached her, "it looks to me like you made a marvelous impression here today. I over heard a couple of conversations that questioned as to whether you were really English – incidentally that's good here. I must confess, when I first heard that John had remarried, and was bringing his new bride here, I had apprehensions. Praise be to Mary they were completely unfounded. John certainly found a priceless treasure when he met and married you." He then lit his pipe and added, "but as for you Cassie; I'm not sure you got as good a deal," he laughed.

"I can see Father,' John said walking up and hearing Grant's last remark, "that I may have to reconsider my support for Saint Patrick's, I understand that Reverend Swagart's church could use more financial help."

"Did you hear that Cassie? Your new husband is threatening to cut off his support for good old Saint Pat's."

He took a puff on his pipe, "Now if he was a Catholic, I'd order him to come to confession, and have him say a hundred Hail Mary's."

As the good natured banter between John and Grant continued, Cassie asked, "Now if I leave the two of you, it won't be drawn swords at dawn will it?"

"Pistols," John quickly answered. "Grant spent many, many years in the army. I wouldn't have a chance with a sword." Looking at Grant he asked, "you're not good with pistols too?"

"Very."

"Ah Cassie me darlin," John replied in his best Irish brogue, "ye may be a widda before our first anniversary."

She looked fondly at the two of them; shook her head and excused herself; walking over to Kathleen who was speaking to a woman she had not met. Cassie had met Kathleen in town one afternoon, but had never seen the other woman before. "Kathleen," she called as she walked up to them, "am I interrupting anything?"

"No," she replied looking at Bridgit, "we were jes discussin somethin that can wait fer another time. Have ye met Bridgit? Let me do the introductions." Thus began a friendship between the three of them that was destined to have long and lasting effects in and around Kilrush.

As the evening wore on, Fathers Carmichael and Grant, together with Reverend Swagart from the Methodist Church kidded with John that if only half their congregations showed up for services the next morning, he would have to make up for the short collections. John laughed and said he would be happy to, provided they stayed to clean up the huge mess after the party. They declined, deciding to take their chances on the collections. Finally, with everyone either too full, or too tired to dance or even talk, the party ended about midnight.

Chapter 17

Father Timothy wanted to go to the Arden Lawn Party, but deliberately stayed back at the church. His anxiety about Bridgit, which had been growing steadily since he heard that she had not attended Mass or confession for a couple of weeks; was somewhat lessened when he learned that she had been there talking with Kathleen. They had not spoken to each other since the 'incident' at her cottage, the term he used in his own mind; still being unable to emotionally cope with the fact that he had raped her.

It was evident that she had not spoken to anyone about what had happened, or word would certainly have reached the street by now. If she had spoken to Father Carmichael, he would have been called into the study. What he found most frustrating, was the fact that he did not know how she was. He doubted that she was pregnant, believing that she would have asked to see him. His deepest hope was that she was simply feeling humiliated and embarrassed, and that in time would resume her daily life. Life would go on, and in time the 'incident' would be forgotten. His greatest fear was that he would be exposed, expelled from the priesthood, and could possibly even be sent to prison.

Father Carmichael had suspected that something was wrong when he had visited Bridgit, and had hoped that she would have sought his help. Now he was chiding himself because he had not followed up on his initial instinct. The fact that something was not right was clearly evident from the fact that she had missed Mass and confession several times, something he could not ever recall her doing, even when she had been very ill. He was therefore relieved to see her at the party, but when she didn't danced- not even once - he knew that something was seriously amiss. The question was; what was wrong? and why had she not spoken to him about it.

Up to this point, he had not linked Timothy's sudden trip out of town with Bridgit's sudden withdrawal from society. The simple truth was that Carmichael had never been strongly motivated by sexual feelings and desires. Like the Apostle Paul, he was totally committed to his mission in life. Consequently, the second part of Paul's admonition, "that those who couldn't contain themselves should marry and not burn," had failed to register in his consciousness.

At the same time Carmichael was having second thoughts; Kathleen became aware that Bridgit was behaving strangely. She too noticed that Bridgit had not danced; clearly she was not herself. She chided herself; how could she have been so unaware of her best friend's sudden change. Later that evening after speaking to Father Carmichael and Grant at the party, she determined that tomorrow she was going to Bridgit's home find out what was going on.

It was a convergence of forces. Timothy, no longer able to emotionally deal with the unknown, decided to go and talk to Bridgit. The next morning, he left Saint Patrick's heading down the street toward her house. He had gone about half way, when he noticed Father Carmichael about two blocks ahead of him, heading in the same direction. It was possible that Carmichael just happened to be going in the same direction, but not to her home. A few blocks later however, he was certain Bridgit's was the destination. He decided to slow his pace, the last thing he needed was for Carmichael to turn around and see him. He stepped into the hardware store, walked around for a moment, and stepped back into the street just in time to see Kathleen meet-up with Carmichael. They spoke for a brief minute and together they headed toward Bridgit's. He could feel his heart beating faster, the heat beginning to rise in his face, and he began perspiring. What did they know? Why were they both going to see her at the same time? He felt a growing pit in his stomach, turned around and started walking back to Saint Patrick's. Perhaps later he would try again.

When Bridgit answered the knock on the door, she was surprised to see both Father Carmichael and Kathleen.

"We missed you yesterday at the party," Kathleen said stepping into the house, not waiting to be invited in. Father Carmichael followed closely behind her.

"I was at the party," Bridgit replied. "I talked ta ye, don't ye remember?"

"Yer body was there, but the Bridgit I know wasn't," Kathleen answered.

"That's right," Carmichael added, "and we don't see you around the church everyday like we used to." He took hold of Bridgit's hand, "I've known you all your life, you're almost like a daughter to me. Kathleen and I want to know what's wrong. Whatever it is, we love you and want to help. What's troubling you?"

Bridgit closed the door and sank into a chair. For several moments, she remained silent going over in her own mind what to say. Kathleen walked over and knelt down alongside the chair, taking Bridgit's hands into her own. "Yer the best friend I have. Everywhere I go, the folks are askin 'bout ye. Most everybody in these parts love ye, and…."

Before she could finish speaking, Bridgit began crying, softly at first, and then sobbing, the tears running down her face and splashing on Kathleen's hands. She leaned forward and whispered in Kathleen's ear, "I'm pregnant."

The words stunned her. She had considered any number of things that might be troubling Bridgit; a serious illness; financial problems; the recent loss of a trusted friend; but never in her wildest thoughts had she considered pregnancy. Even now it was unthinkable. She collected her thoughts and turned to Carmichael, "I hope ye understand Father, but Bridgit and I need ta talk alone for a wee bit."

Carmichael had watched this brief exchange and quickly understood that the problem, whatever it was, was a major one. "Certainly," he answered. "Whenever you need me, I'll be at the church. Don't get up, I'll let myself out." He excused himself and left.

During the next half hour, Kathleen learned about the terrible and traumatic events of five weeks ago, as well as what had happened in the days since.

"At first, I hoped and prayed ta the Blessed Mary that nothin would come of it. But a few days later, I missed my time of the month." Her sobs began to become less frequently and less intense. "I still hoped and prayed that maybe I missed the first one because I was so upset, but a few days ago, I missed the second." She looked up at Kathleen. "I'm pregnant, and I need ta know what ta do. That's why I've been stayin home, tryin ta figure it out." She wiped the ears from her eyes, "I didn't know where else ta turn, and I couldn't tell ye at the party; so I was gonna ta go ta yer house this afternoon."

"I'm sorry that ye didn't come and git me sooner, but here we are."

Bridgit got up and went into the kitchen. "I'll put on some tea, let's talk out here."

Like Carmichael, Kathleen had known her all of her life, and had attended Tom's funeral, the young man killed by the bull who she had been in love with many years before. Over the years they had become the best of friends and often worked together helping other people. She simply couldn't imagine Bridgit having an affair and pretending to having been raped, it simply wasn't in her nature. No, she was certain Bridgit had told her the truth; but who would rape her?

As if anticipating the question, Bridgit said, "Please do na ask me who did it. It's nobody's business but mine."

"But it is. He may rape another woman or girl."

"No. I know that will not happen."

"Ok, sayin yer right; but that still leaves folks wondering who he is. Now I don't have a doubt about yer chastity, or what ye told me. But truth be told Bridgit, there'll be a few men, and some wives, who may begin ta doubt yer story. Everyone 'round here knows that ye flirt and dance with some of the men, even married ones. Up ta now, all of the wives have trusted ye. With this happenin, some of 'em may start thinkin maybe it was their husband. No good man needs ta face a suspicious wife."

"It weren't any of the men I flirt and dance with, and ye kin tell all their wives I said so. But I still canna tell ye who he was."

"I canna understand why ye want ta protect an evil man, but ye must have a good reason. Now think of this," she said wrapping her fingers around her cup of tea, "Sean was at the party yesterday, and it seemed ta everyone there that he has really changed. If this had happened even six months ago, he would have been the first one accused. There are some who will still point their finger at him. Ye needs ta say somethin to put peoples mind at ease, and to protect thems that did na do it.

"No, it wasn't Sean. I haven't talked ta him, but I've heard he's really changed."

"That bein so, why don't we jes say that the man isn't from here, can ye say that?"

Bridgit thought about that for a second. Although she had determined that she would not reveal the man's identity, she thought Kathleen's suggestion to eliminate possible suspects was a good idea. While Father Timothy was here presently, technically he wasn't from around Kilrush, so that wouldn't be a lie. "No, he's not from here," she said, hoping that the Blessed Mother would forgive her for a little white lie.

"Good, that will help put a lot of minds ta rest. But understand, once this news gets out, the constable will be here ta question ye. This'll not be goin away." Kathleen knew that Bridgit was as devout a Catholic as Father Carmichael, so an abortion was out of the question. "Unless ye have a miscarriage, this baby is goin ta start showing in about three months. We need ta decide how ta handle this once word gets out."

"I've been thinkin on that. I'm gonna have the baby and raise it myself. I'll not turn it over ta the church."

Judging from the strength in her voice, Kathleen knew that she was as determined in this matter, as she had been about staying a spinster. "I'll support ye in every way I can," she said. "It won't be easy. There'll be gossip, hurtful and....."

They were interrupted by a knock on the door.

"I'll get it," Kathleen said, "stay here."

When she opened the door it was John Bligh.

"Well Kathleen, looks like you beat me here," he said. "Is Bridgit well?"

"She'll be fine John, but she doesn't want ta see anyone jes yet."

"Good to hear that she's feeling well. If there's anything that Cassie or I can do to help, don't hesitate to let us know." He reached into his coat pocket, "The other reason I stopped by, was because Cassie has some work for her. She made up a list of new linens, curtains, and some other things she would like to have made. Will she be able to handle that?"

"I'm sure she will."

"Good. Then I'll just leave the list with you to give to Bridgit," he said as he handed her the list. "Please be sure to tell her I missed dancing with her at the party; and we're looking forward to seeing her soon."

Returning to the kitchen, she handed the list to Bridgit. "Looks to me like ye have enough work there for at least a month."

"Seems like Cassie is really nice," she said glancing down the list.

"She's a good match fer John. In some ways she reminds me of Lady Elizabeth, very out-going, talks ta everyone. I think ye'll also like John's son Lawrence, when ye meet him. He's jes come back from India. I talked with him fer a spell; said he doesn't know what he's gonna do yet."

"I seen him there, but I really didn't want ta talk ta him. I was afeared that….."

"Afraid of what?" Kathleen asked. "Do ye think the man who raped ye was there?"

"No, I'm sure he's gone by now. I was afeared that one of the Lads would jes pull me out ta the floor ta dance. I did na want ta dance; I 'jes needed ta get out of the house and come ta the party, hear some music an folks talking and laughin agin."

Kathleen thought about what Bridgit had just said, not certain that it was the truth. She had understood Bridgit to say the man wasn't from Kilrush, so who might have been at the party that fit that description. She didn't have time to figure that out now, but she would give that a lot of thought when she had a chance.

"Well Bridgit, I think the shock part is over and yer on the mend. Now ye need ta start getting out more and seein folks; let 'em know yer alright." She wrapped her arms around Bridgit, "I love ye like a daughter I do." She let go and wiped the tears from her eyes. "Would ye mind if I told Father Carmichael about our talk today, he needs ta know what's happened ta ye."

"I'd like that. Tell him I'll be at church tomarra mornin"
She walked Kathleen to the door and said goodbye. It
had been a good morning, and she was beginning to feel
like her old self again. She walked out to the kitchen and
picked up the list on the table. After looking at it carefully,
there were several questions about the curtains. It was time
to go to Arden, see some of her friends again....and meet
Lawrence.

After seeing Father Carmichael heading towards Bridgit's
cottage, Father Timothy had returned to Saint Patrick's.
Half an hour later when he saw Father Carmichael walking
up the steps, he slipped out the back door and headed
toward Bridgit's house again. He was trying to get up
enough nerve to walk the last block when he saw Lord
Bligh go up the steps, knock on Bridgit's door, and then
saw Kathleen open it. Moments later he watched John
hand Kathleen some papers, and then leave. His mind
started racing. Why was everyone going to Bridgit's today'
had she said something? Had he been identified? What
was in those papers? A few hours ago, he had begun to feel
more relaxed. Weeks had gone by, nothing had happened,
and it seemed the crisis was past. Now he could feel the
anxiety returning with a vengeance.

He turned and started walking towards the hills outside of
town. He needed time to think and pray. At that moment
the noon-day bells of Saint Patrick's began to ring. He
recalled how inviting they had sounded the first time he had
heard them, believing that he would spend many happy
years at Saint Patrick's. Today they sounded more like a
death toll than a welcome to prayer. A new sense of
foreboding swept over him. He was now convinced that it
was just a matter of time until he was found out.

The following morning, Father Carmichael had two surprises shortly after breakfast. The first was Father Timothy, who asked if he could meet him privately in his study. Expecting to be asked for another short leave to visit his uncle again, he was completely caught off-guard when Timothy requested he be transferred to another Parish, preferably one in England as soon as possible.

"I've tried to fit in and make friends here in Kilrush," he began, "but have only become more frustrated. The Irish are very sociable, out-going. I was raised to be very reserved, and during the years in the seminary I wasn't able to change that. I believe that a place of service among my own kind of people in England would be better for the church and myself. I'd feel more at home there."

Carmichael listened and watched him closely. Part of what he was saying was true, but there was something more that wasn't being said. "My son, I'm very sorry to hear this; I must confess that I was not aware of these feelings. How long have you felt this way?" He did not wait for an answer but continued, "In fact, Father Grant told me that you had been making good progress in meeting the local people and participating in some local events. You were at Lord and Lady Bligh's party yesterday were you not?

"No, I stayed here at the church. I felt that I'd be uncomfortable there, especially with all the .... revelry."

"Revelry?" Carmichael exclaimed raising his voice. "Do you mean watching these folks enjoying themselves, and making the best they can out of a very hard life? Ireland's a heaven and hell rolled into one. It is a beautiful land filled with promise; but these people have been robbed of it, and forced into becoming serfs in their own Country; you can see that. These people deserve all the happiness and joy – 'revelry you call it' - they can get. Everyday I pray God's blessings on Lord Bligh for all he has done here, including yesterdays party." Almost out of breath, he stopped and sat down, surprised at how passionate he had become.

"I'm sorry, I didn't mean to imply anything sinful," he said realizing that revelry had been a bad choice of words. "Maybe I still have too much of the staid English in me. For that reason, I think England would be a place for me to become more useful to the Church. Would you write to the Bishop and request a transfer for me?"

Once again he found himself lying. Truth be told, he found the Irish people's ability to find joy in the midst of hardship an amazing quality. But lying; as he was quickly discovering, was a hard taskmaster, a growing monster. Unlike truth that could stand alone; a lie depended on other lies to support it; soon it became a fragile house of cards. Until six weeks ago, he couldn't remember ever really lying about anything; now his life consisted of piling lie upon lie.

There are those who would describe what happened next as coincidence, some would claim fate; others would say karma; still others the Hand of God. Call it what you will, it happened.

Carmichael got up, walked over to his desk and picked up an envelope. Turning to Timothy he said, "this is a letter from the Bishop requesting that I send one of our young priests to a Parish in the south of London."

"That's wonderful, an answer to my prayer," Timothy began, amazed at this unexpected stroke of good fortune. This would mean that he would not have to wait for weeks for letters to go back and forth, and even then possibly have his request turned down. If Carmichael was agreeable, he could leave right away. He watched as Carmichael slowly folded the letter, his fate hanging on how he would decide.

"I'm against it," he began, the words striking like a knife into Timothy's heart. "I do not feel that you have finished your training here, that there is still much you could learn. However, the Bishop has asked me to send someone and you are more prepared than the other Lads. I'll notify the Bishop that I have someone to send right away."

In less than a minute, he had gone from utter despair to hope. "Thank you Father Carmichael. Did the Bishop say when they would like someone?"

"Yes, his letter requested sending someone as soon as possible. I see no reason that you couldn't leave today or tomorrow if you like. Of course when you leave Kilrush will depend on when you can get a ship to Bristol. "

Trying very hard to control his excitement and the tone of his voice, Timothy carefully said, "well, since the Bishop has asked for someone as soon as possible, I could be ready to leave today, right after lunch."

Once again Carmichael listened and watched Timothy carefully. He was more certain than ever that there was a hidden agenda; what, he did not know. Of one thing he was certain, time reveals all things. "I'll be sorry to see you leave us, and I'm certain I can speak for Father Grant and the sister's as well. From the day you came, we felt that you would add to our mission here, and in time take a more senior position at Saint Patrick's. Father Grant will be especially disappointed. You know, he had great plans and placed a lot of faith in you."

The words cut like a surgeon's scalpel. He had destroyed not only Bridgit but himself. He looked down at the floor unable to speak, struggling to hold back the tears. Mustering every ounce of control that remained he looked up and in a stilted voice said, "it's with regret that I leave Saint Patrick's; a part of me will always remain here." His voice relaxed a bit and he continued, "you and everyone else here have been so wonderful to me, I could never hope to repay the debt I owe to all of you. But, I must leave. If I can be excused, I would like to go and say goodbye to everyone, and get my things together."

"You're excused. Unfortunately, Father Grant's away for the day. He'll be very sorry to have missed your departure."

He shook Carmichael's hand, greatly relieved at not having to face Father Grant. "I'm sorry I won't be able to say goodbye to him personally," another small lie he thought to himself, when will it end? Unlike Carmichael, Grant would have asked some very probing questions he did not want to answer.

Having packed his personal belongings and hastily saying goodbye to all, he headed toward the docks. Nearing the river, he made a short detour so that he could see Bridgit's cottage for one last time. The flowers in her garden were all in bloom, and as he watched, she came out the front door and began picking a small bouquet. "How very beautiful she is," he whispered to himself. Without thinking, he started to raise his arm and wave, and then caught himself, letting his arm sink slowly to his side. Bridgit looked at the flowers she had gathered and satisfied, went back into the house. She was gone.

He turned away, and as a dead man walked to the docks and a ship that would forever take him away from all he loved.

Chapter 18

Sean Egan had never been so happy. Since he had been converted, his life had taken a steady upward trend, and he had become a familiar and welcome sight around town. One of the reasons for this change on the part of the town's people, is that he had joined a small group from the Methodist Church that went about the community helping those in need. Recalling full well his former reputation, on his first few visits he went with one or two others in the group. As time went on, word spread that there was nothing to fear from having Sean come to your home and help. Even those who had previously suffered at his hands in one way, or another; gradually came to accept the fact he had truly changed and was no longer dangerous.

In the weeks and months that followed, another remarkable transformation began to take place. Miraculously, as he helped others and told them about his conversion, his jaw gradually moved back into alignment. And his arm, which had been partially locked into place because the bones had fused improperly, straightened out restoring full use. Sean had been transformed from the town drunk and bully, into the town's most active greeter who could be seen everyday walking down the street waving and calling, "hello; good morning; how are you today?" to all who passed by. He had also become the best friend of every stray dog and cat in town.

Prior to his conversion, he had worked at the local stable cleaning out the stalls when he was sober. Upon seeing how Sean had changed, the Owner began giving him other duties, and more responsibility. Within six months, the Owner's confidence grew to the point he would leave for hours at a time, placing Sean in complete charge. I addition, he told Sean he could use one of the horses whenever he needed one. Without a doubt however, the change that brought Sean the most joy, was that his mother had asked him to move back home.

These remarkable events and his physical recovery did not go unnoticed, especially among those who suffered from other physical aliments and deformities. The Pastor of the Methodist Church, Reverend Swagart, began having an increasing number of people from the town stopping by the church, asking him about Sean's healing. Soon, there were numerous requests for what they called, "healing prayers," either for themselves, or for another family members and friends.

Because the faith healing aspect of the scriptures had never been the focus of his ministry, Swagart began searching through his bible for every reference he could find regarding healing. Armed with new scriptural insight, his prayers began taking on a new authority as he would lay his hands upon the person, anoint them with a drop of oil on their forehead, and quote specific verses in his prayers.

Upon being ministered to in this fashion, and hearing scriptures quoted they had never heard before; those who came for healing prayers gained new confidence and their faith increased. As their faith increased, so did the number of healings. The Methodist Church which had struggled for so many years with only a handful of members, now grew every week. Within eight months, the numbers increased to the point that the church lacked enough pews to seat everyone; and Reverend Swagart was required to hold a second service on Sunday morning.

In the meanwhile, as Sean had been praying for new ways to be of service, it occurred to him one morning that he should go to Colin and ask his forgiveness. After lunch, he went to the Blacksmith shop and met Colin who was startled to see him. First by Sean's coming to ask for forgiveness; and secondly, how his body had been restored. Never one to hold a grudge, Colin forgave him, shook his hand, and introduced him to his wife Mary who had also just walked into the shop.

"We been hearing good things about ye, and how ye like to help people," Mary said. "Have ye talked ta Kathleen or Bridgit? They're always helping folks; maybe they could use yer help."

Sean wondered how he could have overlooked the obvious; especially since it had been Kathleen and Bridgit who had saved his arm, and probably his life. "No, but I thank ye fer remindin me, I'll go tamorra. Colin, anything I can do for ye?"

"Not unless ye happen to be going out to Arden. I got some drawings for John and Neil ta check over, and I'm bogged down here today."

"I'll take 'em this afternoon," he answered, grateful to be able to do something so soon.

"Thanks Sean, that'll be a real help," he reached into his pocket for some money.

"No money, please. Ye may not understand what I'm gonna say, but it was yer punch that saved me. That punch busted me up so bad, it stopped me from hurtin more people and ruinin my life. Because of that, I found Jesus, and he made a new man of me. So ye see, I owe ye my life."

Colin scratched his head. "Well... Can't say I ever thought of it that way. Fact is, I always felt real bad, ye getting hurt like that." He put his huge arm around Sean's shoulders, his hand completely enveloping Sean's upper arm, "Let's be friends?"

For a split second, Sean thought of how easily those arms and hands could crush him. A wonderful smile crossed his face. "Friends," he answered, realizing once again how Jesus had transformed his life, and now another former enemy had become a friend. "If ye got those papers, I'll take 'em to Arden."

Colin gave him the drawings and watched him walk back down the street toward the stable. "Life sure can be full of surprises," he said turning to Mary. "What did ye want ta see me about?" He picked up his hammer and tongs.

"Another surprise; a happy surprise," she said snuggling up tight against his chest, "we're going ta have a baby,"

Colin dropped the hammer and tongs, and swept her off her feet holding her in the air like she was a little girl. "A baby!" he shouted, "oh Mary," he whispered softly. "Now that's what I'd call a wonderful surprise, a super surprise."

"Hey Dad," he called to Ryan who was working out behind the shop. "Yer gonna be a grandpa."

When Timothy arrived at the dock, he learned that the only ship that was planning on leaving that afternoon, was a small fishing sloop. Walking down the dock toward the boat, he called to the Captain standing by the rail, "are you going to Bristol?"

"Aye, that we are, but it'll be 'bout two weeks before we get there. If ye can wait a couple of days, the Mary Jane will be here. She sails direct, and will get ye there in about five days."

"I'm in no hurry to get there, but I really need to leave today. Will you take a passenger?"

"That we will," he called back. "The mate will show ye where ta store yer gear. We're shoven-off in half an hour, don't be late."

Timothy took his bag and stepped aboard. Not wishing to be seen by anyone from the town, he went down to the galley and sat down. The cook brought him a cup of coffee, looked at his priests clothing and asked, "yer name's not Peter is it?"

Timothy looked at him puzzled, "No my name is Father ....," then he began laughing, "No, and it's not James, or John either; it's Timothy, and forget the Father part. How's the fishing?"

"Fishins been fair. So where ye headin, if ye don't mind me askin?"

"London, but I don't need to be there for three weeks."

"I've been ta London twice, last time 'bout four year ago. Hope ta never see it agin."

"What's wrong with London?"

"Big, dirty, smelly... too many people." The cook continued to talk as he checked his stores, "Ye kin keep yer big cities, I'll stick with the open sea and fresh salt air."

Timothy thought about what the cook had just said about London; big, dirty, smelly, and the Parish he was to report to was in south London, a bad section. Fortunately, he didn't have to get there right away. It would be good to have a couple of weeks away from everything and everyone. A chance to clear his head, and not be worried that today, or tomorrow, or the next day, someone would come looking for him about Bridgit.

"So why did you become a fisherman?" he asked the cook.

"My father, his father, his father....we've always been fisherman. 'Tis a good job, some years better'n others. When the weather's fair, and the fishins good, tis the best job in the world." He looked at Timothy, "so how'd ye get into that garb?"

Before he could answer, the Captain called for all hands on deck. It was time to cast off.

Still concerned about being seen by anyone he knew, he stayed below. He could hear the mate calling to the hands to cast-off the mooring lines, and set the jib; he could feel the ship beginning to move, and back out into the river. As the ship entered the strong river current, it rocked gently and he heard the mate give the command to hoist the mains'l. There was the sound of lines being pulled through sheaves, and the deep crackle of canvas being pulled up to the spar. He felt the deck under him dip to port as the sail caught the wind. He waited for about fifteen minutes and went up on deck. He walked to the stern and looked back at Kilrush growing smaller, and smaller, in the distance. Soon, it would be out of sight. If only it would fade from his memory.

The sea air was wonderful, and for the first time in days he began to relax. The Captain told him the ship was going to make a brief stop at Loop Head, and then sail south to Blasket Sound and across Dingle Bay on the way to Glenbeigh. Along the way, they would stop and fish in different spots the Captain had known from his youth, special places his father had shown him.

After picking up another crew member at Loop Head, the ship headed south and Timothy watched the men sit around on deck preparing the fishing lines and cutting bait.

"What are you fishing for?" he asked

"Atlantic Salmon. This time of year they start gatherin in the bays, and in a couple of weeks they'll start running up the rivers ta spawn."

"I had it for dinner once," he replied. "My parents took me to a fancy restaurant in London before I entered the Seminary."

"It's the king of fish, if ye ask me," the First Mate replied. "If we gets lucky on this trip, we may catch a few and sell 'em when we get ta Bristol. They'll pay a good price fer 'em there."

"What do you mean, get lucky?"

"'Tis a bit early for 'em ta come in this far. Still, 'tis worth a try."

While they were talking, Timothy noticed the Captain was taking bearings from the shore and checking is chart.

Looking up, he tapped the chart with his pencil, "Ok, Lads," he called, reduce sail and start feedin out yer lines."

Timothy had never seen anything like this before, and was both fascinated and excited watching these men work. For two hours, the ship barely moved along under shortened sail, rising and falling gently on the swells as the men held the lines, waiting for a fish to strike.

"Do na think they're here Captain," one of the men said.

"Aye. Well we canna stay here an wait fer 'em, the Captain replied. "We'll give it fifteen minutes more, then start pullin in yer lines."

That was the beginning of an unbelievable run of bad luck. Day after day, location after location, and not a sign of fish. The Captain fished over almost every spot he had marked on his charts; tried every trick he knew, and still no fish. On the sixth day one of the men said what several had been thinking, "there's a curse on us, that's what I think."

"I'm your Jonah," Timothy said.

"Who's Jonah?" someone asked.

"Another crew member called out, "he was a man who did na do what God told 'em ta do; and then sailed on a ship trying to get away from God. A real bad storm came on 'em, and the crew threw 'em over-board," another answered.

"Old superstition," the mate answered. "We do na believe in curses on this boat, 'tis jes bad luck, and we've all had it before."

"Aye, that we have," said the Captain laughing, "and Father, don't ye be worrying we're gonna throw ye overboard. Besides Lads, the story 'tis not about Jonah; or the great fish; it's about God's grace."

The Captain's knowledge of the scripture surprised Timothy, however he still wasn't so sure that he wasn't the source of their bad luck. Like Jonah, he was certainly trying to avoid God.

The next morning, when they arrived at the last location on the chart before heading into Dingle for supplies, there were three other fishing boats ahead of them. Sailing within hailing distance of one of the boats, the Captain called out asking how they we're doing.

"Nothin," came the reply. "Been here two days, an not a nibble; same with the other boats. We're heading back up north, to the grounds off Galway Bay."

The Captain thought for a moment about going with them, but since he needed to put into Dingle, decided against it. "Good luck," he shouted," as he waved. "Ok Lad's we're here, lets give it a try."

"What do you catch here," Timothy asked.

"Bottom fish mostly. If luck is with us, we may get a few good flounder."

"No Salmon," Timothy asked.

"Not here," the mate answered.

Once again, the men put their lines over the side, the Captain hoping that they might catch enough fish to pay for needed supplies.

"I'm thinking that we should have Father Timothy say a prayer," the Captain asked, "how 'bout it Lads? Sure's heavens above, he's read where Jesus helped his disciples when they needed help."

Caught unawares by the Captain's request, Timothy looked out to see every eye focused on him. "Now wait a....," he started to protest, but caught himself. Given the sinner he was, he didn't believe God would even hear the prayer; but then these men would not hold him accountable if the prayer didn't work.

"Our heavenly Father," he began, "just as you honored the hard work of Jesus' Disciples long ago and brought the fish to their boat, I ask that you do the same for these good men here today. Amen." That was it. He finished the prayer before some of the men had even closed their eyes.

It was not ten seconds later, that one of the men yelled, "fish on!" Then another, and another. As the first fish broke water, someone yelled, "salmon!"

"No one's ever caught salmon here before," someone yelled back.

"Well they have now," the man said heaving the fish aboard.

Within minutes, every man was yelling as they hauled in their lines and salmon bright as a new silver coins began coming over the rail and on to the deck. It was pandemonium as the men unhooked the fish, baited, and threw their line back in the water. Live salmon were flopping all over the deck, as no one took the time to throw the fish in the hold.

"Father Timothy, give us a hand," the mate yelled. "Toss the fish down the hatch."

Timothy looked at dozens, maybe a hundred or more, bright shiny silver fish larger than any fish he had ever seen, and still more coming over the rail. He reached out to pick one up, but it just slipped out of his hand.

"Ye gotta grab 'em under the gills like this," the mate shouted, "or around the tail."

Timothy reached down slid his fingers under the gills, lifted the heavy fish and dragged it to the open hatchway. "One down, a hundred to go," he yelled.

The intense fishing lasted for almost an hour, during which they boated almost three hundred Salmon. Then it ended as fast as it started.

Timothy, his arms aching from using muscles that had not been used like that in many years, pushed the last fish down the hatch with his foot. The deck was slippery with blood and slime, and as he turned around, he fell, sliding halfway across the deck before one of the men put his foot out and stopped him.

"Three cheers for Father Timothy," the Captain called out. "Hip, hip, hooray. Hip, hip, hooray. Hip, hip, hooray," the men yelled, raising their arms in a salute. "A man that can pray like that, we should make him part of our crew," one of the men said.

Timothy sat up hands braced against the deck, his priestly garb covered with blood and slime, and reeking of fish. He had never felt so good in his life. Here he was, a sinner trying to escape, and still the Grace of God had not departed.

Because the Captain wanted to off-load the fresh fish as soon as possible, he immediately set sail for Dingle. The price wasn't as good as he could have received in Bristol, but he considered it fair, and it saved valuable time. They picked up the needed supplies and in less than twelve hours, set out for the fishing grounds farther south.

For the next two weeks, Timothy began to enjoy life. He borrowed some clothing from one of the crew; packed his priests robes; and finally convinced the crew to call him Tim. He began learning how to fish; trim sail; handle the lines; read a compass and a chart. He took his turn at watch, and the wheel, and was starting to learn how to read the sky for signs of weather. They shared their stories, some true, some less true; they sang songs and sea chanteys, the words of some which burned his ears. Gradually, he noticed something else had happened to him, his shyness and clumsiness began to disappear.

One night, as they sat on deck, he related how and why he had become a priest. His mother, after loosing four children, two in childbirth, and two others to childhood diseases; promised God that if her next child was a boy and lived, he would become a priest: I was that son. My father died the year I entered the seminary, my mother two years later. But she died happy knowing that she had kept her promise to God.

"So ye have no kin?

"No, I had a younger sister, but she also died. All of my family is dead."

"No sweetheart?" a man asked. Suddenly realizing what he had just said he apologized, "beggen yer pardon Father."

"That's alright, it was a natural question. And remember, my name is Tim." He fell silent for a moment thinking about Bridgit; and wondering how these men would treat him if they knew the truth about him.

During those two weeks, the Captain and members of the crew became his friends, and it was a sad day for him when they slipped up to the dock in Bristol. After off-loading their catch, the Captain paid the men their share, including Tim.

"So now yer off to the Parish in London," the Captain said. "Well Tim, it was a pleasure ta have had ye on board. I'm a Quaker myself, as are many of the Lads. Yer the first Catholic most of us got ta know. It's possible some of ye Papist's might make it ta heaven after all - not the Pope of course -" he laughed.

"I was thinking the same about you Protestants," Timothy replied, joining in the laughter.

They said their farewells, and not telling anyone that he had changed his plans he started walking down the street. That comment one of the men had jokingly made about keeping him on as part of the crew had stuck in his mind. Now it had taken root.

Chapter 19

After leaving the dock in Bristol, Tim used some of the money from his share of the catch to buy some street clothes: new pants; a shirt; sweater; coat; shoes; and a cap. Dressed in his new attire, he took a coach to London. Two days later, he hired a cab to take him to the Parish Church where he was to report for service. Still dressed in street clothes, he looked at the church; and decided to first checkout the neighborhood streets. Once a neighborhood of lovely old homes, and small parks; it had become a seedy area of low income workers; people on the dole; drunks; secondhand stores; pubs; and brothels. Having recently left Kilrush, and spending three enjoyable weeks on a fishing boat, he shook his head whispering to himself, "I'm not ready for this." He turned around, hailed a cab and headed for the docks along the Thames River.

With his recent fishing experience, he knew what kind of clothing and miscellaneous gear he needed, and a local pawn shop was able to provide him with everything at minimal cost. An added benefit was that it was used, so that he did not look like a total novice. Sea bag slung over his shoulder, he toured the docks checking the fishing boats to see who was hiring. It wasn't long before he signed-on, the boat leaving in two days.

Since he expected to be at sea most of the time, he rented a small room in a nearby boarding house under the name Peter Wilson, his given name. Uncertain as to his longtime future, he hid his priest's robes, rosaries, crucifix, and other religious articles in a bag under his bed. He looked at himself in the mirror and adjusted his sweater; as of today he would be a fisherman.

Two days later, the Captain told the crew that he had bad news, the new spar would not be ready for another three days. With extra days to fill, Peter decided to use the time to talk to local fisherman, pick up a few tips, and explore the area. That night he was having supper in a pub when he overheard the name Lord Bligh in a conversation from the adjoining table. He casually glanced over and saw two men; one neatly dressed, the other with tussled red curly hair looked more like a street ruffian. Although they talked in hushed tones, from what he could make out, it sounded like the well dressed man was discussing hiring the other to murder Lord Bligh and his wife. At length the two men concluded their agreement and walked out. After they left, Peter walked up to the bar and asked the bar tender if he knew who the men were.

"Don't know who the well dressed bloke is, but I see him here now and then. He was a big spender until recently. Understand he's got a big house down the street. Rumor has it the place is filled with drunks and whores. I think the other chap's name is O'Toole. Don't know his first name, not from around here. Do you know them?"

"No," he replied. "I thought they looked like someone I knew."

Finishing his dinner, he went back to his room and considered what he had just heard. The series of recent events were difficult to attribute to mere coincidence. He just happened to arrive in this part of London this week; the fishing boat, which was scheduled to leave this morning, was delayed; out of dozens of Pubs, he had supper in the same one that a stranger used to meet a possible assassin; of all the tables in the pub, he sat at the adjoining table. He recalled a story the Captain had told him after the "Jonah" incident. "When God strikes his harpoon in ye, ye can run all ye want. But when he's ready, he'll pull ye back in.

But ye must understand the difference; the Whaler wants ta kill, God wants ta save." Peter felt his back muscles twitch; the harpoon no doubt.

That night he wrote a letter to Father Grant about the plot kill Lord Bligh and his wife, that he had chanced to overhear. Unfortunately, he did not have any details except that he believed the assassin's name was O'Toole. He went on to describe O'Toole as best he could remember, especially the tussled red curly hair. He made no mention of what he was doing and signed it, your friend, Father Timothy.

Unable to go to the local Police Station for fear of revealing who he was, he wrote a second letter stating the same facts, and mailed it to Scotland Yard. In two days he would be gone, and without a signature or return address, they would have no way of finding him. Hopefully, they would contact the police in Kilrush and alert them in time to prevent the murderous plot, if that's what it was. The next morning he took the letters to the post office and paid for the fastest mail service.

With nothing else to do, he went to the dock and went aboard the fishing boat. Two other crew members were there, and they spent the day getting acquainted. Peter was fascinated listening to them tell stories of other fishing trips, being caught in terrible storms, broken masts, taking on water, and of the friends they had lost at sea. Although he was very new to all of this, he could sense the deeply felt comradeship fishermen had for each other. Regardless of where they came from, or on what other boats they had crewed, in their own way they were brothers. Although he had never thought of it before, he began to realize that it was not by mere chance that Jesus chose most of his disciples from men who were fisherman.

Eight days later, two letters arrived at Saint Patrick's. The first was a letter addressed to Father Carmichael from the Bishop in London, notifying him that Father Timothy had not reported in; did he have any information regarding his whereabouts? The second was Timothy's letter to Father Grant. After discussing the letters with each other, a decision was made that Carmichael would write to the Bishop, stating that they had received a brief letter from Timothy mailed from London two weeks go, but no forwarding address was given. The second and most critical matter was the alleged death plot against Lord and Lady Bligh. They both agreed that Grant should leave immediately for Arden.

Lawrence was just going through the gate on his way to town when Grant came galloping up the road like the devil was behind him. Reining his horse to a stop next to Lawrence, he asked where his father and Cassie were.

"Out in the stable, why?" he asked.

"Follow me," Grant said spurring his horse up the lane, "I need to speak to them immediately, and you need to hear this."

Lawrence, bewildered at what could be so important, kicked his horse and followed Grant like it was a cavalry charge.

John and Cassie heard the horses coming and stepped out of the stable to see what the commotion was all about. Grant pulled his horse to a stop, almost leapt out of the saddle, and quickly hurried John and Cassie back into the stable, with Lawrence right behind them.

"There's a plot to kill you both," he exclaimed. "We just received a letter this morning from Father Timothy in London. He stated that he was in a Pub having supper, when he overheard two men discussing a plot to have you assassinated."

"But why," Cassie asked. "Who would want us murdered?"

Grant looked at the ground for a second, and then directly at John. "We don't know. Timothy said the one man was well dressed, but he never heard his name mentioned. After the men left, he asked the bartender who told him the man was a regular in the Pub, but he didn't know who he was."

"Oh John," Cassie said putting her arms around him. "It must be some kind of mistake, who would want us murdered?"

"It's possible it's a mistake, but we cannot assume that."

"Did Father Timothy say who the second man was?" Lawrence asked.

"He said the man's name was O'Toole, no first name, and the bartender claimed he wasn't from around there. Timothy also gave us a partial description and said he had tussled red curly hair."

"You said the letter came this morning," John asked.

"Yes, the post mark was eight days ago."

"Eight days. That means that it's possible this O'Toole could already be here in Ireland," Lawrence said.

"Which is why I road up here like a bat out of hell; begging your pardon M'Lady," he said looking at Cassie. "My old army ways are not completely gone yet."

"Unfortunately," John said, "other than an alleged plot, and someone named O'Toole, we know nothing. We don't even know if this O'Toole was coming here, or waiting for us to return to London."

"True," Grant replied. "But Timothy got the impression from the men's conversation that it was to be very soon."

"Has the Constable in Kilrush been told of this?"

"I'll tell them as soon as I get back to town. I wanted to warn you first."

"I think we need to spread the word in town to be on the lookout for a man with tussled curly red hair," Lawrence said. "It's reasonable to assume that if he comes here, he will arrive by boat at Kilrush."

"Assuming that's true," John said, "you cannot arrest a man simply because he fits the description. We'll need more than that. I suggest that if he is spotted, we keep tabs on him, but not tip our hand."

"Good idea. In the meanwhile," Grant added, "I would suggest that you and Cassie stay here in Arden, and not go roaming about the fields like you usually do."

"I'll see that they stay close to home," Lawrence said. "Something else just occurred to me. If the plan is to kill them both, then it's logical the attempt would be while they are together."

"But why?" Cassie asked again.

"The estate," John answered. "I think the stranger's my son Robert. He's my eldest son, for him to inherit the estate, both of us would have to be dead."

"But he wouldn't resort to murder."

"After what you did to him at the party Cassie, I wouldn't put anything past him."

"I've seen men murdered for their boots M'Lady," Grant replied. "Well, I've got to get back to town. I'll alert the Constable, and tell a few people around town to keep their eyes peeled for O'Toole." He stated walking out of the stable to his horse, "Lawrence, can I talk with you for a minute?"

Once they were out of earshot from John and Cassie, Grant began. "I didn't want to say anything in front of Cassie, but I believe that the plan is to kill them here in Ireland. First, if it is your brother he won't want to be connected to this; so the farther away he is; the better. Secondly, he chose an Irishman, someone who will blend in with the locals. Put the word out to your workers and tenants to report any strange men they see around Arden to you immediately."

"I'm beginning to feel like I'm back in the Army," Lawrence quipped.

"Well be thankful for the training, it may come in handy."

"For Queen and Country," Lawrence said saluting.

Mounting his horse, Grant leaned over and whispered, "I'd go easy on 'for Queen and Country' in these parts; unless you want to get yourself killed too."

Lawrence laughed, "thanks for the tip, I'll try to remember that."

Grant left, and Lawrence went to look for Neil. It was time to organize some surveillance.

A week passed without anything happening, and John was beginning to get restless. "I can't stay here in Arden cooped up like a chicken," he said to Neil and Lawrence. "there's important business to attend to in town. For one thing, Colin has been making new parts for the Mill, I need to see him. Besides, if as you suspect the plan is to kill us at the same time, I should be reasonably safe if I'm by myself. Cassie will of course stay here close to the house."

"Maybe you're right," Lawrence replied, "to be on the safe side, I'll go to town with you." They headed toward the stable.

"Good, I'd like to have you along," John said beginning to feel like he was regaining control. "While we're in town, let's check with the Constable and see if he has learned anything more about this O'Toole. And Neil, forget the fields for today. I'd like you to stay as close to Cassie as possible."

"Yes Sir," he answered smiling, "I'll do my best". Like John, Cassie was anxious to get this over with, and get on with all the things that needed to be done."

The trip to town yielded nothing definite; no one had reported seeing anyone matching O'Toole's description. However, the Constable said they had received an urgent dispatch from Scotland Yard, claiming they had received a letter about the plot from someone named Tim, no last name given. Scotland Yard said that O'Toole's first name was Brian, and that he had killed another man two years ago, but they were not able to get enough evidence to convict him. Consider him to be very dangerous.

"Well it's not much, but it's something," John said.

They were walking out of the Constable's office when Sean came running across the street toward them. "He's here, O'Toole's here in town. I jes seen 'em goin in the Pub."

"Good work Sean. Looks like we might have something at last," Lawrence said patting him on the back. "Father, I suggest that Sean go back to the Pub and see if he can learn anything more."

"Excellent idea," John replied. "Wait a minute, Sean, do you still drink?"

"Not anymore," he said with a big smile, "but I'll have the bartender, Sam, fix me up with something that looks like a drink."

"Good. Find out everything you can; buy him drinks; get him drunk." John reached into his pocket and handed Sean a wad of money. "Whatever you find out, come to Arden and let us know as soon as you can."

Sean left them heading back to the Pub, John and Lawrence informed the Constable about what had just happened and left for Arden. This was the break they had been hoping for, now if only Sean could get some good solid information.

It was just after daybreak the following morning when Sean came riding out to Arden with news of the plan. Sean told them he pretended to be someone that the Bligh's had wronged, and he was looking for revenge. "Do ye suppose God will forgive me the lie? It was fer a good reason."

"I've no doubt he will," John said. "So what did you learn?"

For the next half hour, Sean told them that he had bought O'Toole a lot of drinks, and that O'Toole wanted to know if there were any Englishmen in town; said he hated the English.

"Did he ask anything specific," Lawrence asked.

"What's that mean, spe….?"

"Specific means something special to what you're talking about. For example, did he ever mention the name Bligh?"

"No."

"Did he say why he came to Kilrush?"

"Said he was jes passin through, lookin fer a farm ta buy."

"How long is he planning on being here?"

"Did na say. But tamorra, he said he wants ta rent a horse and go ridin ta look a farm ta buy. Should I rent him a horse?"

"Yes, and don't say or do anything to arouse his suspicions," John said. "I'll have some of our tenants stationed all along the road, pretending to be working in the fields to see where he goes. When are you going to meet with him again?"

"Tamorra night in the Pub."

"We'll just have to wait and see. When you get back to town, tell the Constable what you just told us. Tell him that I request that he not follow O'Toole, or let on in any way that we're on to him. Same thing with the Lads in the Pub, tell them to keep quiet. When this is over I'll give them a party they'll never forget."

Brian O'Toole had not gotten this far in life by being stupid. When he was eleven years old he had been arrested for being a pick-pocket. For that offence, he spent three years in prison where he was beaten and raped by older boys and men. He vowed to himself, he would never get caught again.

Having a quick mind, he learned a great deal about the criminal world while he was in prison: the most important lessons being, what not to do. By the time he was released he had made several important decisions: small petty crimes carried too much risk of getting caught. Always work alone; partners just increase your chance of going back to prison. Never break into the homes of the rich to steal jewelry. First, there are too many servants around that might see you; secondly you had to sell the jewels to a Fence with the result being less profit, and someone else that could later identify you.

The result of his prison education was that he only robbed rich men when they were alone, generally when they were leaving a brothel. He only kept cash, jewelry which could later be identified was thrown in the river. Since the men he robbed could easily afford whatever he took, and did not want to report to the police they were robbed coming out of a brothel, the crimes were seldom reported. For over ten years he plied his profession very carefully; and never committed a robbery in any area of London more than once in a six month period. The result was that while the police suspected him, they never had any substantial evidence that could be used to arrest him.

His simple robbery system changed when a wealthy man he was robbing asked him if he wanted to make some real money, big money. He said he was interested, and the man asked if he was willing to kill his business partner. Having no moral scruples about murder, he accepted the job and made more money in one night than he had the entire previous year.

Several months later, he was offered another contract killing job; this time by a man who wanted the husband of a woman he loved murdered. During the next five years, he killed nine men. Each killing was carefully made to look like a robbery gone bad. Scotland Yard and the police became very suspicious because of the similarity among five of the killings; but again, there was no evidence to tie him to the crime. While he was paid well for each of the murders, he was waiting for a big score; a job that would pay him enough to leave England, go to America and buy a pub. He realized that while he had been very careful, there was always the element of chance. Thus far, luck had been with him, but nothing lasts forever, especially good luck. He knew that time was running against him. Then he met Robert Bligh.

The first time they met, they were both extremely careful about what they said. Neither being certain they could trust the other. Robert checked again with the person who gave him O'Toole's name; and O'Toole checked to find out more about Robert. One week later they met again, and briefly discussed the generalities. Robert said he wanted a man and his wife killed, and asked about the price.

When O'Toole first heard that he was to kill a man and his wife, he said no, and got up from the table to leave. Robert caught hold of his coat sleeve and whispered, £25,000. O'Toole sat back down, but demanded £40,000, claiming that killing men was one thing but he had never killed a woman. When he learned that the couple was Lord and Lady Bligh, the price jumped to £100,000 pounds. Further, he demanded £5,000 in advance, and non-refundable if Robert changed his mind. Robert balked at the sum, but since he needed someone now, and also because he would inherit an estate worth tens of millions of pounds he agreed. Their third meeting was the one in which they discussed the details; that was the meeting Timothy chanced to overhear.

When O'Toole arrived in Kilrush, his plan was to simply spend a couple of days looking around the area and checking out the local law enforcement. If anyone asked him why he was in town, he would say that he was just a businessman passing through, possibly looking to buy a small farm. Consequently, when on his first day in town a total stranger came up to him in the Pub and started buying him drinks, his guard went up and he started to become suspicious. When he noticed that the bartender was pouring Sean's drinks from under the counter, he became very cautious; falsely assuming that Sean and the bartender were planning on getting him drunk and later robbing him.

The second thing that initially caused him some anxiety, was when Sean mentioned the Bligh's by name, and said that they had wronged him and he would like to get even. However, the more he thought about it, the more he felt he was over reacting. After all, he had asked about Englishmen in the area, and said that he hated them. In the end, he concluded that Sean had just responded to his own questions and statements. Tonight he would guard against any potential robbery attempt, and get a good night's sleep. Tomorrow he would begin to find out the habits and routines of the Bligh's.

Chapter 20

O'Toole was surprised to find Sean working at the stable the following morning. Sean acted very casual, and said he had enjoyed meeting him yesterday. O'Toole replied that he always enjoyed a morning ride and just wanted to look around the countryside. When Sean asked when he would return, he answered by lunch-time.

At this point in time, O'Toole only knew what Robert had told him about his father's estate in Ireland, which was very little. He said that his father owned a large estate called Arden somewhere near Kilrush: where exactly he did not know since he had never been there. Robert told him that his father spent most of his time at the estate, so he was certain that some of the locals must know him, and could certainly tell him where Arden was. Since he had not really spent any time, or communicated with his father for many years, Robert had no way of knowing about the profound social transformation in John's life, and described him as heartless and arrogant.

He described Cassie as an attractive woman in her mid-forties, with short curly red hair. O'Toole was completely unaware of the fact that Lawrence, Robert's brother was in Ireland, because when he and Robert made their contract for murder, Robert did not know that Lawrence had gone to Arden with John and Cassie. With this scant knowledge, O'Toole mounted his horse and set off down the road in hopes of getting some solid information.

The easiest way to have gotten information he wanted, was to simply ask. But not wishing to draw any attention to himself, he needed a less direct approach. As he passed Saint Patrick's church, he saw a priest working out front.

"Excuse me Father, I'm looking for property in this area, and was told that there was an estate near Kilrush for sale. Would you know anything about that?"

The young priest, new to Kilrush, said there were several estates in the area but didn't know if any of them were for sale.

"I see. What's out this road?" he asked pointing.

"Mostly little farms. But if you go out ten miles, there's a very large estate called Arden."

"How big?'

"I'm not sure, but it's thousands of acres. I've only been there once."

"Too big for me," he laughed. "Well, I'll just keep looking. Thank you for the information." He jerked the reins and started on down the road in the direction of Arden.

The young priest waited until he was a block away and ran into the church looking for Grant, "he just came by. Said he was looking for property to buy. He's headed out toward Arden now. Do you want me to follow him, or do anything else?"

"No. Not for now. But when you see him come back into town, let me know."

In London, three hundred and eighty miles away as the crow flies, the detective Robert had hired, hailed a cab and set out for Robert's house. He had two objectives: first to get the long past due money owed to him; and secondly, to give Robert a bit of very important news. Arriving at the house, he knocked at the door. It was only after loudly knocking the fourth time that Robert, still dressed in his robe answered the door.

"What are you doing here this early in the morning?" he snapped stifling a yawn.

"It's after ten o'clock, and I didn't want to miss you. I have some very important news."

"So what is it?"

"Not until I get my money first."

"You'll get paid, now what's the news?"

"Its critical news, but you'll not get a word of it 'til I get paid."

Robert reached out to grab him, but he ducked to one side. "Either pay me, or I'll sue. And if I sue, you'll not get the information."

Having just paid O'Toole £5,000, Robert was getting desperately low on money. But if the detective had important news, 'critical' was the term he used, he had no choice. "Com'on in," he said. "How much do I owe you?"

"Eighty two pounds," he said following him into his office.

That was more than Robert expected, but then he had not been keeping track of his bills. He pulled a locked metal box out of a desk drawer, and counted out the money. "Here's your damn money, now what's the critical news?"

The detective counted the money, put it in his pocket and said, "Your father changed his Will. He disinherited you, cut you off without a shilling."

The news hit Robert like a blow to the stomach. For a few seconds he sat there at his deck holding the cash box without saying a word. Placing the box back in the drawer, he asked, "Are you certain?"

"Positive. Got the news directly from a clerk who works for your father's solicitor. He told me that originally, your father was going to leave you £10,000, but after what you did at the party, he told his solicitor to disinherit you. Said he saw the Will himself, cut you off without a shilling he did. Everything goes to his wife and your brother.

Robert sat silently in his chair staring out the window for a moment; then he got up and showed the detective to the front door, "thank you for the information," he said in a trance-like voice.

"Is there anything else you want me to work on?" the detective asked as he walked down the steps.

"No, no. Nothing I can think of right now."

He closed the door and slowly walked back to his office. "What to do now," he mumbled to himself running his fingers through his hair. He was certain that by now, O'Toole was in Ireland, planning for the assassination. If he was successful, O'Toole would come back and want the rest of his money, which he would not have. O'Toole wasn't someone you wanted to cross, and would most likely kill him. In any event the £5,000 was gone, no point in fretting about that. What he needed to do now was to stop O'Toole. What had been a desperate financial problem, had now become a very volatile dangerous situation. Until today, money had been the problem, now his life was at stake.

On his way back upstairs to his bedroom to get dressed, a half naked woman passed him on the stairs. Under ordinary circumstances, he would have stopped and talked to her, made some crude vulgar remarks, and most likely reached out and groped her; today he didn't even notice her. He pushed the bedroom door open and turned on the gas lights. The young girl in bed partially sat up and looked to see what was going on, and then lay back down pulling the blanket over her head.

He glanced in the mirror as he put on a shirt and decided to get a shave at the local barbershop. A plan was beginning to form in his mind as pulled on his pants and rushed back down the stairs. Going back into his office he pulled out the cash box. "Damn it," he yelled," looking at the little amount of cash left. He hadn't planned on paying the detective this morning, and realized that now he would have to go and get more money out of his Trust, which would entail another argument with the Bank Trustee.

Only two weeks before, the bank had reluctantly given him the £5,000, allegedly for the purchase of property in Ireland. Oh well, couldn't be helped. "Damn it!" he yelled, "when will this ever end?" and headed towards the barber shop.

Sitting down in the barber chair, he told the barber that he wasn't interested in any of the usual conversation this morning. With the hot towel wrapped around his face, it gave him time to think and he began to formulate a plan of action. First, he had to get to Ireland as fast as he could and tell O'Toole that the assassination plan was off. If he was lucky, he could do that without his father ever knowing he had been there.

Grant was leaving the church on his way to see Sean, when he ran into Bridgit, wearing a pretty new dress.

"You look especially nice this morning," he said. It certainly is wonderful to see you out and about town again."

"Well I feel wonderful," a big smile crossing her face. "I'm on my way ta Arden, Lady Bligh wants me ta sew up some new curtains fer her."

"Will you do me a favor," Grant asked. "I have a message for Lord Bligh, would you deliver it for me?"

"Be happy ta, what is it?"

"Come in here for a moment," he said walking into the hardware store. "I'll write it down for you."   He quickly wrote a note telling John that O'Toole was seen heading out toward Arden, no doubt a reconnaissance mission of sorts. Very doubtful he would make any hostile action yet. I'll keep in touch. Grant.

Bridgit took the note, "I'll see that Lord Bligh gets it right away."

"Thanks Bridgit. Will we see you at church tomorrow?"

"I'll be there."

Grant continued on down the street, first stopping by the Constable's office to keep them informed as to what was happening, and then on to the stable to see Sean. He had been giving some thought as to how Sean had handled the situation in the Pub, and felt it had been too obvious. He suggested that tonight, Sean should just stop by the Pub, meet with O'Toole and say he was busy and couldn't stay. It was very important that O'Toole not have any idea he was being watched. "Don't say anything about the Bligh's, don't even mention their name. If he should ask you why you are angry with them, just say it was because they sold you a bad horse. Leave as quickly as you can."

Sean agreed, but was disappointed. He had lain awake half the night thinking of clever questions to ask O'Toole.

O'Toole was leisurely riding along, carefully observing everything along the road: the grade, ditches, culverts, the wooded lots adjacent to the road, the bridges, other roads that connected; the distance between farm houses and cottages, everything he would need to devise a plan. In his mind he was beginning to imagine how the attack would be carried out; his escape route; and most importantly, how to create the appearance of an apparent highway robbery that had turned bad.

Of course he still needed to know when the Bligh's came to town together, but first he needed to pick the right place for the ambush. He had just stopped and dismounted next to a creek to let his horse drink, when a coach with Bridgit went by. There was just an instant when their eyes met, but it was enough for her to identify him to the Bligh's when she arrived at Arden. O'Toole swung back into the saddle wondering who that attractive woman was, and continued down the road. He was so intent on his search that he never noticed there were dozens of pairs of eyes watching him from the fields.

Back in London, Robert had never moved so quickly in his life, but then his life had never depended on moving fast. Immediately after getting shaved, he was at the bank requesting fifty pounds; allegedly to go to Ireland and check out the property he was buying. Because they had previously given him money for the purchase; fifty pounds more seemed reasonable, and they quickly they gave him the money. Leaving the bank, he returned home and quickly packed his bags.

"I'll be gone for a couple of weeks, you're all on your own," he said to a couple in the parlor on his way out the door. He caught a cab and went to the coach station where he bought a ticket to Bristol. If all went well, he could be in Kilrush within five days, a week at the latest, and hopefully find O'Toole in time to stop the plan.

He was lucky. No sooner had he arrived in Bristol than he was able to book passage on a ship leaving for Kilrush that same afternoon. He was starting to feel a bit better when the ship left the dock and headed out into the channel. From now on, it depended on the weather, and again luck was with him. Clear skies, and moderate winds drove the ship on its northwesterly course.

He leaned on the rail staring at the horizon. While he knew they were making very good time, he still realized that every hour counted. He was still thinking that he needed to get there in time to stop O'Toole, when the idea hit him. "Of course," he said to himself loud enough for the elderly man standing next to him at the rail overhear.

"Excuse me, did you say something?" the man asked.

Robert looked over, "sorry, just thinking aloud."

He turned and walked toward the stern, "I don't want to talk to O'Toole; I need to kill him before he kills my father. I'll tell the authorities that I learned of the assassination plot and raced up here, hoping to be in time to save him."

It was a wonderful idea. First, he wouldn't have to be worried about O'Toole demanding more money; secondly, it could even ingratiate him to his father. After saving his life, perhaps his father might even reconsider the Will, or at least offer him some money. With these happy thoughts in mind, he went below to his cabin to clean and reload his pistol.

O'Toole returned from his excursion having learned a few important facts about the country side, but was not satisfied as to where to carry out the act. There were two basic problems: the first and most critical, was how to escape. Most of the road to Arden was across open land, and the few wooded areas were far too small to hide in for any length of time. The second problem was the assassination itself. Killing the Bligh's was one thing; but if he carried it out on the road, there would also be a coachman and possibly a footman or two. He had no intention of getting involved in a gun fight or creating a bloodbath. He needed time to consider alternative plans.

That evening, O'Toole was looking forward to meeting with Sean again over supper. He had certainly seemed to be very talkative the night before; hopefully he would provide more information tonight. That hope was crushed when Sean came in and apologized, saying that he had other business and could not stay.

"How about supper tomorrow night?" O'Toole asked.

Sean thought about that for a moment and agreed; that would give him time to meet with Father Grant and decide what he should say… or not say.

"See you tomorrow night then Sean."

After telling the waiter what he wanted for supper, he asked, "so what do people do in this town for excitement."

"Not much. Have a few pints at the pub; some folks play cards. The dance on Friday night is the biggest event around here."

Friday night he thought, that's two days away. "Where's the dance held?"

"Saint Patrick's, down the street."

"So it's a big thing here, lots of people come?"

"Maybe couple hundred, if it's a nice night."

"Mostly members of Saint Patrick's, right?" He knew the Bligh's were not Catholics so that wouldn't be of any help.

"No. Lots of folks from around here go. Those that live outside town ride in on wagons that picks 'em up. Some come in from Arden, and if Lord and Lady Bligh are home, they usually come."

"Who did you say usually came?" he asked pretending he hadn't heard.

"Lord and Lady Bligh. They own Arden, a big estate 'bout ten miles from here. No better folks anywhere, they do lots of things ta help the town. Most everybody 'round here loves 'em."

The waiter's description of Lord Bligh as being easy going and friendly certainly didn't square with the cold, stiff, arrogant father Robert had described. But no matter, he was hired to kill Bligh whatever he was. "And you say they come into town for a dance at the Catholic Church? Isn't it kind of strange that rich people would do something like that?"

"Fer other rich people, but they're not like that. They come and kick up their heels and dance with everybody. Ya shudda seen Lady Bligh tryin to learn the Irish jig. We was all laughin so hard, our sides hurt."

At that point the bartender called to the waiter, and told him other customers were waiting for service.

"Sorry, gotta go."

"Thanks for the information," O'Toole called as he walked away.

That was the best news he had received since he got here. Finishing his supper, he paid his bill and stepped outside. It was a warm summer evening, and what would be more natural than sightseeing, so he began walking in the direction of the church. The street was lined with stores; shops; and numerous other buildings and alleys to duck into. And with the big dance there would be hundreds of people; loud music, talking and dancing …. this could be the perfect setup.

For the next hour, he casually strolled around the church; checked out the dance area; walked down side streets and alleys; carefully familiarizing himself with places to hide if the need arose. Satisfied that his plan was good, he headed back to the Pub. Earlier, he had noticed a couple of attractive women near the Pub, and now with a couple of days to kill, he might get lucky.

After he finished his supper and left, the bartender questioned the waiter about what he and O'Toole had talked about. The bartender quickly passed the information on to Sean; who passed it on to Father Grant; who rode out to Arden and talked to John and Lawrence.

Nor had O'Toole's stroll around the church gone unnoticed, at least a dozen individuals had watched his every move since arriving in town. The local Constable knew more about O'Toole movements than he did about his deputy's.

"Judging from the way O'Toole looked over the church and surrounding streets," Grant said, "he may be planning his move during the dance; with all the activity it would be an ideal opportunity for him."

Lawrence agreed, "perfect place for an ambush. It would be fairly easy to shoot someone from a dark doorway, and in the following confusion simply blend into the crowd. We need a street map of the area."

"I'm one step ahead of you," Grant answered, pulling one from his robe. He laid it on a table and John, Lawrence and Grant huddled over it marking the key points that needed to be guarded. "I'll talk to the Constable when I get back to town. He only has two men available, but if you can provide six other men, he said he'll deputize them. With the eight men, we can cover these potential escape routes. What do you think?"

"Looks good to me," John answered, "what about you Lawrence?"

"Very good. My main concern is you and Cassie being out in the open and exposed."

"I think I can help with that problem too," Grant said. "First, I believe they should both come. We need to be able to draw O'Toole out. If he learns they're not there, it's doubtful he'll show up. But there needs to be very strict rules: First, they never get within fifty feet of each other; secondly, they keep moving, even when they are talking with someone. He'll be looking for a chance to get them close together. We cannot give him any opportunity to get off a single shot, let alone two.

John listened and watched the two men discuss strategies. He felt especially proud of his son who had proven himself over the years. Now that his and Cassie's lives were in danger, he could not think of any men better trained and experienced to protect them.

"I also have another little surprise for our friend. I started asking around for look-a-likes for Lady Bligh, and three women from the area with fairly similar characteristics – age, size, and hair color - have agreed to come to the dance. We also have a nun at the church, Sister Lillian, who is about the same size as your wife, and has short curly red hair, although she's not nearly as attractive. I think we can safely assume that O'Toole has never actually seen Cassie, so seeing several women with similar appearance will really confuse him."

"Do you really think that's safe Grant, asking these women to become potential targets?" John asked.

"I do. It's very doubtful he would shoot at anyone unless he was certain it was the right person. And since we know he was hired to kill both of you, he would not risk shooting at just one of you and give himself away. He must be able to quickly identify and target both of you.

As for you John," Grant laughed, "Reverend Swagart has offered to loan you one of his collars for the evening. I'd let you have one of mine, but they'd be much too big."

"So if I understand your scheme correctly, a Sister will be dancing while pretending to be Cassie; and I'll be disguised as a minister," John said. "I almost feel sorry for O'Toole."

"That's what you get when a military man becomes a priest. A very devious combination."

"If this wasn't so serious, it would be a lot of fun," Lawrence laughed, "but I agree with Grant, keep him confused. There is always the outside chance that O'Toole might do something really stupid, but from what we know he's a very careful man; the odds are against it. My feeling is he would wait for a better opportunity."

"Obviously, my greatest concern is for Cassie's safety," John replied. "If there is any real chance of her getting hurt or killed, we will stay home."

"The problem with that John, is that we need to catch this man as soon as possible. We need to draw him out, and catch him with a gun on his person. Good people do not come to dances with a loaded gun hidden in their coat."

"He's right father. If we miss this chance, O'Toole will try something else; like an ambush along the road, where we won't have any control. Unless Grant and I are wrong, the dance gives him what he thinks will be the perfect chance. What he doesn't know, is that we know who he is, and that we're ready for him."

"Are we agreed then on the plan?" Grant asked.

"Let's do it," John replied. "Cassie and I will be there."

"Good. Now let's start getting everything in place," Lawrence answered.

"There are only two more things to cover," Grant said. "John, will Cassie lend Sister Lillian a dress for the dance? She told me she hasn't worn one in many years."

"I'll have her get one for you before you leave. You know," he said with a chuckle, "it will be quite amusing to see the look on some of the folk's faces when they see Sister Lillian dressed up like that."

Grant laughed, "It will certainly raise a few eyebrows. It's doubtful she would even have considered it, except it's for a very worthy cause."

"What's the second thing?" Lawrence asked looking at Grant.

"We all pray for a lovely summer evening. We don't want rain to mess up this chance."

"Well Grant," John chuckled, "since you have a direct line to heaven, I see no reason for Lawrence or myself to worry about that; right son?"

"Absolutely. Isn't that why they pay priests such big salaries?"

"Well if that's true, I can assure you that Saint Patrick's never got the word. Now if you'll get that dress for me, I'll get back to town."

"I'll pick out six good men and send them into town Friday afternoon to be deputized," Lawrence added.

With the plan set in motion, they shook hands and parted.

It was now just a matter of time, and waiting.

Chapter 21

A stranger walking down Francis Street, the main street of Kilrush Friday afternoon, would never have guessed at the level of tension in the air. The six men from Arden had arrived in town; and after the Constable had deputized them, he took them out one at a time to where they were to be posted and keep watch, but not before the dance started.

At Arden, it was decided that John would ride into town with Neil a half hour before the dance, and Lawrence and Cassie would come together in the carriage twenty minutes later. In the Nun's quarters at Saint Patrick's, Sister Lillian tried the red dress on four times, and stood before a mirror smiling - just to make sure it fit properly- she told the other sisters.

The Constable and his two deputies were in the police station re-checking the street map, when a man entered and introduced himself as a detective from Scotland Yard. He had just arrived in Kilrush, and explained that the Yard had received a letter about an assassination plot. Since London was anxious to both prevent another murder, and hopefully arrest O'Toole, they had sent him to see what he could do.

The Constable quickly filled him in on the dance that night, and details of the plan that had been worked out and set in motion.

"That's quite a plan," the detective exclaimed, "who worked it out?"

"Father Grant and Lord Bligh's son, Lawrence."

"A priest and the man's son!"

"Aye, but not your typical priest, or son," the constable answered. "Father Grant spent over twelve years as an

Officer in the Army before becoming a priest; and Lawrence, Lord Bligh's son recently returned from India, he was a Major. I think both men are very responsible and know what they are doing; but you need to talk to them yourself. First, you might want to go to Saint Patrick's and meet Father Grant. Lawrence Bligh's at Arden, the Bligh's Estate, but he'll be here in town later today."

The detective thanked the Constable and left, heading straight for the church. He could hardly believe this stroke of good luck. When he had left London, there really wasn't any solid information to go on, let alone a plan. He had come here hoping for some help from the local police, and a slight chance to apprehend O'Toole before he killed anyone. As for stepping into a carefully laid out plan, such a thought never crossed his mind; nor did he imagine the level of experienced help he was about to get. Up until an hour ago, he had viewed this trip largely as a waste of time; a long shot. Now as he walked up the church steps, he was already beginning to anticipate a promotion.

"I'm looking for Father Grant," he said to a Sister sweeping the entrance.

"This way Sir."

The detective followed her and was looking at the beautiful stained glass windows, when a voice interrupted his thoughts.

"I'm Father Grant, how can I help you?"

They had been talking for about ten minutes when Lawrence walked in, having decided to come in early in the event of any last minute changes. Grant and Lawrence were delighted that Scotland Yard had sent someone. The detective told them that they had tried to arrest O'Toole once before on the charge of murder for hire; but when they went to his house, he was gone. That was a about two years ago.

"We suspected he went to France," the detective said, "so everyone at the Yard was surprised when we learned of this new plot."

For the next hour, the three of them went over every detail as they pointed out to the detective where the dance would be held, the streets and alleys, and potential escape routes, and where the deputies would be posted. The detective shook their hands and thanked them again, and again. He was now so certain of arresting O'Toole and a good promotion; he mentally began spending his raise.

At three o'clock another ship docked at Kilrush, and for the first time Robert set foot on Irish soil. During the last two days with plenty of time to think, he had changed his plan again. Originally, he was just going to go to the hotel where O'Toole was staying and shoot him. He would then explain to the local police that he had heard about the plot to kill his father, caught the first ship to Kilrush, and had shot the assassin before he could act. Second thoughts however, had convinced him that might not work. It would only be his word against that of a dead man.

The new plan was that he first locate the hotel where O'Toole was staying; tell him he came to help, and find out when and where O'Toole planned to carry out the killing. His pitch to O'Toole would be that two of them working together had a much better chance of success. He would have an accomplice, and still get all of his money. In truth however, Robert planned on shooting O'Toole just before he had the chance to kill his father and Cassie. By killing him in the act he reasoned, the police would have no questions regarding the shooting.

It didn't take long to find the hotel where O'Toole was staying. Unfortunately, O'Toole wasn't there, and the desk clerk had no idea when he would return. Uncertain as to what to do next, he went to the Pub for something to eat. While he was sitting at the bar, he overheard the waiter talking to another patron about the dance that night.

"Gonna be a big one tonight, and I heerd that Lord and Lady Bligh will be here agin. Did ye see her last time? Sure is a pretty woman."

"I not only see'd her, I danced with her," the man laughed. "Maybe ifin I'm lucky, I'll get ta dance with her agin ta night."

Robert couldn't imagine his father or Cassie attending a street dance; and as for dancing with common people, there had to be a mistake. He called the waiter over, and asked about where the dance was held and when it started. Like O'Toole, he was very surprised to learn of his father's and Cassie's Irish life style. Finishing his sandwich and beer, he stepped outside and walked down the street to check out the church. He was halfway down the street when O'Toole walked into the Pub, unaware that Robert was in town and looking for him.

At seven o'clock, people began drifting into the church yard; by seven-thirty a couple of hundred were milling about waiting for the dance to start. Father Carmichael, who had started the Friday night dance over twenty years ago, stood up an asked everyone to bow their heads in prayer. As the last words left his lips, the fiddles struck a chord, and seconds later the ground was covered with dancers swinging their partners; while those on the sidelines began hooting, hollering, slapping their legs and clapping their hands.

Spaced around the periphery of the dance area, the deputies clapped their hands to the music while they kept a careful watch on the streets and alleys. John, with his cleric's collar, Grant and Neil casually walked around; while Lawrence and a local girl danced. Cassie sat talking to Kathleen and Bridgit. She had sent Sister Lillian two dresses to choose from: one black the other a bright red.

Sister Lillian, reasoning would never get a chance like this again, decided to go in grand style and chose the red one. She was a bit nervous at first, but after the second man asked her to dance, she accepted and went whirling across the floor. "God's grace is sufficient," she kept whispering to herself. Upon seeing her, John, Neil, and Grant, started laughing.

"What did Sister Lillian do before she became a Nun?" John asked.

"I'm not certain, but it's evident she learned how to dance," Grant answered.

On the other side of the floor, Carmichael caught sight of her and turned to Agnes, "looks like she's having a wonderful time; may I have this dance?"

Stunned by the request; she watched as Sister Lillian swished by, and replied, "if she can do it, so can we." With that, arm-in-arm, they stepped into the whirling crowd.

"On seeing Carmichael and Agnes dancing, Grant exclaimed, "the confessional's going to be a very busy place tomorrow."

"Sister Agnes, still in shock at what she was doing, asked Carmichael, "is what we're doing right?"

"David danced before the Lord," Carmichael replied. "Isn't that what we're doing?"

Agnes thought about that, not certain it was the same thing, but she was having to much fun to stop and debate theology at this point.

Later, when Grant and John stopped by and congratulated Carmichael on his dancing, he reminded them, "don't forget that Monday we're having a meeting of the emergency committee. I received word yesterday that there was a small crop failure near Enna. I didn't mention it before because I know you have to focus on the immediate problem."

"I received that news too," John said. "But I've been so caught up with this O'Toole thing, I put it out of my mind."

"We'll have plenty of time for that later," Grant replied, wondering to himself about how much time they might really have if the crop failures started spreading.

Because it was still light outside, O'Toole stayed in the Pub, carefully and slowly sipping a drink. He was waiting for it to get darker, and he intended to be stone sober for this nights work. Two blocks away, Robert sat in his hotel room rechecking his guns, knowing full well that against O'Toole he wouldn't get a second chance. Sighting down the barrel of his pistol, for the first time he was grateful for all that military schooling his father had forced on him.

An hour later, dusk was falling and O'Toole walked out of the Pub. Not wishing to be seen, he took the back streets to get to the church, and took up a position in a dark doorway in an alley facing the dance area. From here he could watch for the Bligh's. Then, when the right opportunity presented itself, dart out, shoot them, and dash back into the darkness.

It was after he had been watching the dancers for a few minutes that he seen the woman with the short curly red hair. "There she is," he mumbled to himself; "now where's her husband?" He was still scanning the dancers trying to pick him out when, a few moments later he noticed another woman with short curly red hair; then a third, and a fourth. Several women with similar features, was something he had not anticipated; he had no idea which of the women was Lady Bligh.

Across the dance floor, the detective from Scotland Yard thought he saw some movement in the alley, and told John and Grant he was going to investigate. When Lawrence came dancing by a moment later, John informed him, and told him to keep very close to Cassie, who was now dancing with Neil. Having also been alerted by the detective, the Constable, who came dressed in plain clothes, walked around the area alerting the other deputies.

Meanwhile, a couple of hundred dancers having no idea of the intense drama that was taking place, were having a wonderful time swinging their partner, who more often than not, was not their husband or wife.

At seven-thirty, Robert left the hotel and he too, took the side streets and alleys to get to the church. His focus was not on the dance floor, but on the dark areas surrounding it. If O'Toole was there, that's where he would be hiding. When he got to within a block of the church, he cocked the pistol and kept it in his hand hidden just under his open coat. Simultaneously, the detective walked slowly around the end of the dance area while keeping his eye focused on the spot where he thought he had seen something; he too, took out his gun and held it in his coat pocket. He was half a block from where he seen the movement; when O'Toole, realizing that he could not identify Lady Bligh, decided it was a hopeless situation, and decided to join the party and have a good time.

Just as he stepped out of the darkened doorway and into the light, Robert came around the corner, saw him and fired at almost point blank range. O'Toole stumbled backward and fell to the ground. The detective, not being able to clearly see either man, assumed that O'Toole had fired the shot and had just killed someone else. He drew his pistol and yelled, "police, drop your weapon."

Robert was so intent on watching to see if O'Toole moved, he never heard the detective's warning. Then out of the corner of his eye he caught sight of the man coming toward him, he instinctively turned toward him with the gun still in his hand. The detective seeing the gun now pointing at him, immediately fired at the man who he believed to be O'Toole. Robert was hit in the chest and spun around by the shot, completely bewildered. The gun fell from his hand as he sank to his knees, blood pouring through his fingers as he clutched at his chest.

Because of the loud music, dancing, talking, and other noise; very few of the people at the party heard the gun fire. John, Grant, and the deputies having been alerted, were already on their way to the scene when they heard the shots. The detective, his pistol at the ready ran over to

Robert who was trying to lift his head, and motioning for him to come closer. Seeing that the man was fatally wounded and wanted to tell him something, he stooped down to listen. In a low voice, Robert told him who he was, and said that he had come to try and save his father, Lord Bligh, from an assassin. As he finished speaking his head fell back to the cobblestone walk. He was dead.

The detective quickly stood up and walked over to O'Toole, who knowing that he was dying, coughed through the blood in his throat and pointed at Robert lying a few feet from him, "he hired me to kill his father and his wife." There was a slight gurgle in his throat, and he slowly exhaled in a long sigh. The detective felt a sudden cold chill in the air that raised the hair on the back of his neck; but he did not see the Angel of Death dressed in black, who had come to collect the souls of Robert and O'Toole.

Having first taken Cassie to safety, Lawrence ran to catch up with his father and Grant. Together and out of breath, they ran up to the detective expecting to see O'Toole lying in the street. They were completely taken by surprise when they saw two dead men.

"They're both dead M'Lord," the detective said pointing to Robert and then to O'Toole's body a few feet away. "This man said he was your son Robert, the other man over there was O'Toole." He then explained the rapid series of events, in which Robert had shot O'Toole and when Robert ignored his warning, he had shot Robert.

John knelt down and looked into Robert's face, "he was my son. He hired O'Toole to kill me and my wife." He looked up at the detective, "but why is he here, and why did he kill O'Toole?"

"He told me he came here to stop O'Toole, before he could kill you."

"I would rest easier if that was true," John replied. "The thought that he had at last ...." he paused, not certain of how to finish.

"I don't believe he changed father," Lawrence said. "I think that somehow he found out that you had changed your Will."

"That would explain it," Grant added. "Killing you would not gain him anything, but O'Toole would still demand his money, or kill him."

"I suspect you're right," John replied, "but we'll never know for sure." He turned to Lawrence, "Son, will you take Cassie home. Grant and I will stay here and help the detective complete his report, then I'll ride back home with Neil."

John knelt down again and placed his hand on son's shoulder. Despite all the terrible things he had done, even the plan to kill him, he still felt a sense of remorse, of loss. "Elizabeth," he whispered, "I'm so glad that you were not here to see this day."

Robert's body was shipped back to London for burial. Because of Lord Bligh's social prominence, Scotland Yard agreed to release a brief statement saying that Robert Bligh, eldest son of Lord Bligh, had been accidentally killed while visiting Ireland; which, if one stretched the truth a bit was technically true. There was a private family funeral service, and he was laid to rest in the family plot next to his mother who had so loved him.

Silently standing over them both, was the beautiful marble angel with out-stretched wings.

It was over.

Chapter 22

Following Robert's funeral, John and Cassie decided to stay in London for two more weeks. This would give John a chance to meet with some of his other business partners, and discuss some problems which had been neglected because they were difficult to handle by mail. This also permitted Cassie to spend some time with Albert and the cook, regarding preparations for their plan to return in late Fall, and spend the winter in London. On their way back to Arden, they would stay at the Captain's Inn, which was still closed to the public, and make a decision regarding finding a Manager to operate the Inn, or sell it.

Lawrence, having no business interests in London; decided to spend a few days trying to find an old friend; Sally Fairfield.   Unfortunately, conversations with a number of his friends and acquaintances provided no clues as to her present whereabouts. Recalling that she had once been active in the fight to abolish slavery, he was able to find the address of their meeting hall, and went there in the hope that someone might be able to help him locate her. When he rang the bell, a short stocky woman in her early fifties opened the door.

"Good morning madam. My name is Lawrence Bligh, and I'm searching for Miss Sally Fairfield. I know that several years ago...," he was cut short by the woman's response.

"Sally Fairfield!" she exclaimed, "why sure, I know her well; but don't stand out there, come in, come in."

"So you know Sally?" she said leading him into a small library stacked floor to ceiling with bundles of papers, pamphlets, and posters.

"We were friends many years ago, before I joined the army and went to India."

"You don't say. Are you still in the army?"

"No, I saw enough in twelve years. I resigned my commission last year."

"Saw enough of what?" She picked up a stack of papers and held them in her hand looking at him.

"I couldn't tolerate the way our government treated the Indian people; and even many of our own enlisted men. I felt it was unjust."

"Well….you don't have to go to India to see that. There's plenty of injustice right here in England. If you really…," she stopped. "Forgive me, I started to get on my soapbox again, a habit that's difficult to break." She placed the papers on an empty chair. "You were asking about Sally. She lives in a boarding house about three blocks from here. She never married – what man would put up with her independence - to say nothing about her schedule. She almost killed herself with exhaustion working on the slavery campaign. When we got word that Parliament passed the legislation ending it, she collapsed; was in bed for almost six weeks recovering."

"I well recall her independent spirit," he said with a big smile. "Is she alright now?"

"Oh she's fine; a tough trooper that one. We're trying to get her to help us again; women's suffrage. We're tired of men taking forever trying to decide something, and then usually getting it wrong."

Not wishing to fall into that baited trap, he asked, "Do you think she'd mind if I called on her?"

"I think that's a wonderful idea. She needs to get out and see something of life before it passes her by." She took a scrap of paper and wrote down the address. "Now when you see her, tell her Mildred - that's me - said to take the day off, go out and have a jolly bit of fun. I can get along without her today."

Lawrence thanked her and decided to walk the few blocks to the address Mildred had given him; wondering why she was living in a boarding house. She came from a wealthy family, had something happened?

The house was a very large white four story home with Greek style pillars across the front porch. The Landlady asked him to wait in the Parlor while she went upstairs to let Miss Fairfield know that she had a visitor. A few moments later Sally came bounding down the stairs, two at a time. He looked at her as she walked toward him. She had visibly grown older; was as slender as he recalled; and now had a few strands of gray mixed in with her long black hair: the result of a lot of stress he thought to himself. If anything, she had become lovelier with maturity.

"Larry," she called out, I thought you were still in India, when did you get back?"

"About four months ago. Didn't you get the invitation to my home coming party?"

"Why no, I didn't. Really too bad, because I would have enjoyed coming. Who else was there?"

"Most everyone we knew. Billy and Reggie couldn't make it, Billy's still in India, and Reggie's in China. Poor Charles was killed in South America."

"I heard about that. Terrible blow to Clair, she was left with their two children you know."

"Yes. Alice told me at the party. I'm afraid I completely lost touch with all of you while I was gone. She said that everyone's married and have children now." He laughed, "Looks like we're the only holdouts."

"But you were in India fighting for the glory of the Empire," she said, a slight tone of sarcasm in her voice.

"Yes indeed. While you were here fighting to free the slaves, I was busy fighting in India trying to make more.

Not actually, but figuratively speaking." He looked down and shook is head, "I'd rather not go into all that just now if you don't mind."

They talked for a few more minutes in the parlor, and then he asked her if she would like to go for a walk, and have lunch.

"Now before you say no, Mildred gave me strict instructions to tell you to take the day off, and have fun."

"So you met Mildred, the Iron Lady," she gave a sly smile. "Did she try and bait you with her "men make all the wrong decisions" speech?"

"Yes, and luckily I avoided the trap. Otherwise I suspect I'd still be there."

"Very true. Well, since she said I should go out and have fun, I guess I don't have a choice; let's go." And with that, she called to the landlady, and said she would probably be out for the rest of the day.

For the next three days they walked in the park; went to the Zoo; toured the Pavilion; and got to know each other again. Over lunch one afternoon, he asked her why she was living in a boarding house.

"Several reasons. About a year after you left, my father lost much of his fortune...bad investments. When he died three years ago, the estate went to my brother James. We never got along; and whatever the subject was, we were almost invariably on opposite sides. He's adamantly opposed to women having anything to do with politics; and virtually disowned me because of my involvement in the slavery issue. It became impossible to stay home. Since I had been left a modest Trust fund, I decided to go out on my own. With my busy – no, frantic schedule – a boarding house seemed to be the perfect solution."

"Has it worked out?"

"Some good, some bad; I do miss being around family." She paused for a moment, "Speaking of family; how's your father and brother Robert?"

"My Father's fine; Robert's dead. We buried him last week."

"I'm so very sorry," she said reaching out and touching his hand. "What happened?"

"One day, I'll tell you the whole tragic story; but not today. This is to be a day of fun."

Later that afternoon, when she mentioned that she was undecided about getting involved in another major campaign, and thought perhaps she might take a little vacation and get away from London, he seized the moment.

"Have you ever been to Ireland?"

"Ireland. Now there's a place I want to visit some day. Their poetry; their music; the tragedy of the place, and the people…. In some strange way, even though I've never been there, even the name Ireland, brings out the melancholy in my soul."

"Sally," he took her hand, "come to Ireland with me. My father has an estate near Kilrush, I've spent the past two months there; you'll love it.

"I don't think so Larry. I've heard about the rich English Lords and how they exploit the Irish. And as I recall, your father is quite ruthless. I can only imagine what he has done up there."

"You would not recognize my father. He is no more the man you knew back then, than…" he was at a loss for words.

"Than I'm the sweet shy, naïve, wallflower you knew a dozen years ago, right?"

"Exactly," he laughed. "Believe me, you will absolutely love my father, Cassie his new wife, and Arden."

"Cassie, a new wife? And who's Arden?"

"Arden's the name of their estate."

"Arden? as in the Forests of Arden in Shakespeare's play? Somehow I have trouble equating romance with your father. Are we still talking about John Bligh?"

"One and the same. As I told you, he's a transformed man."

"And he remarried?"

"Yes, her name's Cassie. He met her in Bristol when he stayed at a small Inn she owns."

"Your father, Lord Bligh, one of the richest men in England married a woman that owns a small Inn? If anyone else had told me that, I'd have thought they'd had too much to drink." She watched him for a minute just to make certain he wasn't playing a joke on her. Satisfied that he wasn't, she agreed.

"Larry, I'll come with you. First, because it will give me a chance to see Ireland and be with someone I know. Secondly," she made a deep curtsy, "to see for myself just how much His Excellency, Lord John Bligh has really changed, or this is some Irish blarney."

"Wonderful," he laughed. "How soon can you be ready to leave?"

She thought for a moment. "Actually, I've nothing to keep me here now. I can be ready to leave tomorrow."

"Then tomorrow it is. When you pack, there's no need for fancy dresses, or ball gowns there. Practical outdoor clothes; sweaters; riding boots; that sort of thing."

"Country clothes; I'm beginning to like the idea even more; never really been the ball room type you know. I go to a party now and then, but only to keep in touch with old friends. I haven't danced in years."

"We're going to change that."

"But you just told me not to bring any fancy dresses or gowns."

"I'm talking about Irish dancing. You'll have the time of your life. Now let's get back to your place so you can start packing. I'll pick you up in the morning at eight o'clock sharp. Dress comfortably. Remember, it's a two day coach ride to Bristol, where we'll get a ship to Kilrush; a small town on the Shannon River. Arden's just a few miles from there. You're going to love it."

As he left her standing on the porch, it was hard to say who was more excited. One thing they both knew for certain; a new chapter was opening in both of their lives.

Chapter 23

After all the excitement surrounding the assassination attempt on the Bligh's died down, life in Kilrush returned to normal. Sean met with Kathleen and Bridgit, and they began working together more often. The women enjoyed having Sean to handle the wagon when it was needed, and other more physical tasks. Sean welcomed the chance to repay them for helping to save his life.

Bridgit's daily life had returned to normal, with the exception that because she was pregnant, she became very conscious of physical activity and took care to not over-do it. Although almost everyone knew what had happened to her, it was seldom discussed publicly. Privately, speculation continued to circulate as to who the man was that had raped her. Supposedly, he was no longer in the area; but still, many women wondered if that was really true and paid particular attention to strangers in town.

The daily routine at Saint Patrick's resumed. Fathers Carmichael and Grant took a trip up north to view the crop failure near Ennis first hand; and returned home more determined than ever to get the emergency plan fully operational. For the next two weeks, Grant traveled to all of the local farms, encouraging the owners and tenants to come to the meetings. Time after time, in meeting after meeting, he would tell his audience how critical this emergency planning would be if there was a local crop failure. His reception was almost always the same indifference, with typical statements from the listeners such as: "It's different here; they didn't know what they were doing; they planted bad seed potatoes." There were a number of folks however, who began taking the possibility of a disaster seriously, and promised to attend the meetings at Saint Patrick's. In this regard, he found the situation very much like army life: everything became far more complicated than was originally believed; and took far longer to accomplish.

Neil made plans for the harvest at Arden, and while waiting for the Bligh's to return, reviewed the contracts they had for the sale and shipment of grain, potatoes, and dairy products to England. Their business enterprises were flourishing; and he was encouraged by the feeling that Lawrence was beginning to share in his father's and his own vision for a major agricultural industry centered in Arden. Having heard through Father Grant that two small farms were going to be sold in the area, Neil made a detailed inspection of both farms so that when John and Lawrence returned, they could discuss a possible purchase.

Two weeks later, the staff at Arden had a surprise when Lawrence and Sally arrived unannounced. Even more surprised, was Sally's reaction upon hearing from the house staff and tenants that, Lord Bligh, Mr. Bligh, or John, depending upon who was speaking, was a kind, marvelous, and generous man.

"Aye Lassie, never was there a man more kind, or giving than his self. You'll see it fer yer self when he gets back."

During the next two days, Lawrence took Sally to Kilrush where he introduced her to Fathers Carmichael and Grant; Agnes, and several of the Sisters. As they walked down Francis Street, a number of people came up to Lawrence welcoming him back and asking when his father and Cassie were going to return. They warmly welcomed Sally, and told her how fortunate she was to be a friend of the Bligh's.

"Now mind ye, I canna say many good things about the Lad here," one elderly man said poking Lawrence in the ribs, "but his father is one of the finest that ever set foot on our fair Irish soil. Course, he can never become a saint ye understand, 'em not bein Irish; but he's getting close."

Having met and spoken to perhaps three dozen or so Irish people, Sally was struck by their wonderful sense of humor; especially considering the hard life they had and the persecution they had endured generation after generation. There were a very few people she met, who had allowed their hatred of the English to color every aspect of their lives; and would have blamed bad weather on them if they could have figured out a way to do it. For individuals such as these, life was a miserable existence, and continual thoughts of vengeance consumed them. Overall, despite their unending daily hardships, she became convinced that the Irish were a happier people than the English.

A week later, John and Cassie returned. Their departure from Kilrush with the body of Robert had been on a dark note; and it was wonderful to come home to such a very warm welcome; with the added surprise of seeing Sally there.

"Lawrence, why didn't you tell us Sally was coming?" his father asked as he put his arm around her and gave her a hug, something her own father had never done. "Please forgive my son," he said to her with a smile, "We raised him well, but he must have forgotten his manners in India."

"It's a pleasure to meet you Sally," Cassie said giving her another hug. "The night of the Party, Lawrence kept wandering around the house looking for you. He was very disappointed when you didn't come."

"Disappointed!" John added, winking at Sally, "the next day, he moped around the house like a lost puppy."

"Don't believe a word of it," Lawrence replied, somewhat embarrassed as he saw Sally watching him with an amused look.

John and Cassie took her by the arms and led her out towards the stable, Lawrence following. "So tell us all about yourself, we want to know all the details," Cassie asked. "Lawrence said that you had been involved in the fight to end slavery. What a wonderful thing to do."

Sally was overwhelmed by their greeting. She couldn't recall the last time she had been hugged and fawned over since she was a little girl. For the next hour, they asked her questions; answered her questions; told stories, and joked. She carefully watched John and Cassie, and it quickly became apparent they loved each other, and made a wonderful team. When Neil joined them, she noted how he was treated, not simply as their farm manager or a hired employee; but as one of the family, almost like another son.

She had only been there a week, and already she was beginning to feel closer to the Bligh's than to her own family. As they headed back toward the house, she walked along side Lawrence a few steps behind John and Cassie. Looking around at the buildings; the rolling hills; the fields of growing crops; cattle and sheep; scattered patches of woodland; and workers talking and laughing, she realized that she was more at peace with herself that she had been in many, many years.

Later, back in the house, she watched John go to the kitchen and give the cook a package; some special spices he brought back from London, plus a box of real chocolates.

"Chocolates!" she exclaimed loudly motioning for the other women to come over. "And will ye jes see what this sweet man brung us." She took a piece and bit into it, "tis right from heaven it is. Who da ever thought I'd live ta be so blessed." She passed the box around, "take a piece, and tell me ifin it isn't made by the angels themselves?"

Then there was the wagon load of gifts for the staff Cassie had purchased. Toys for the small children; crates of books; some new tools; and bolts and bolts of cloth for the tenant's wives. It was very obvious that what Lawrence had said about his father was true. He was not the man she had known before. Whatever had happened in his past, had truly transformed him. He in turn, transformed those around him. She was beginning to understand why these people loved him so much. In many ways, he had become like a loving and benevolent father to all those at Arden.

One week became two, then three. She met more and more people including Kathleen, Bridgit, Sean, Colin, and Mary, his very happy pregnant wife. She went to the dances, learned the Irish Jig and other dances; danced with more men in a few weeks than she had in the previous dozen years. She was having the best time of her life; and day-by-day, she was falling in love with Ireland and its people.

Summer ended, the crops were harvested; it had been a good year. A couple of temporary storage buildings had been constructed to hold some of the grain until the silos could be built. Finally, the plans for the new silos arrived at Arden, and John, Lawrence, and Neil began talking to some local contractors, requesting construction bids. Their goal was to have them up before the cold winter rains began.

In the meanwhile, Cassie and Sally began spending more time together. Cassie began telling her of various needs in the community; and explaining to her how Kathleen, Bridgit, and Sean; working with the Methodist Church, had developed a Helping Hand program. With a little more organization and money, Cassie believed they could do much more.

"Sally, there's so much more that could be done here. From what Lawrence has told us, we know that you're good at organizing projects. So we have a proposition for you: if you'll work on getting everything organized, John and I will supply the money."

Sally thought back to how hard and long they had struggled to get people involved and raise money for the anti-slavery campaign. Here, if she was willing to help, she was being offered whatever she needed.

"I'd love to help in whatever way I can. But understand; I just came up here for a short time as Lawrence's guest, and yours of course. I never intended to stay."

"Neither did John when he came here years ago, nor did I when I first came here with John on what I thought would be a kind of short holiday while he showed me around Arden. Now strange as it may seem to you, we're more at home here than in London. Oh we have friends back there; but here, our friends are like our family. Since living here, I've discovered that Ireland is a kind of magical place. It opens your eyes and quickens your spirit in a way I never experienced in England."

"I must admit that in the short time I've been here; I've begun to feel 'the magic,' as you call it."

"Sally, I lived in Bristol for many years; yet, with the exception of an Easter or Christmas service now and then, I never attended church. But here, John and I are very involved at both Saint Patrick's, and The Methodist Church; which is strange considering we're not either Catholic or Methodist. And look at the friends we have here: Catholic Priests; Sisters; Protestant ministers; farmers; blacksmiths - the proverbial butcher, baker, and candle-stick maker - not even counting the scores and scores of our tenants and workers here at Arden.

"John has told me that for all the years he had business partners in London, he never knew the names of their wives, or children – he never cared. But here in Arden, he knows the name of every tenant farmer, the farmer's wife, their children's names and ages. There's something here - a spiritual force perhaps - which draws you closer to the land and the people around you."

- "Sally," Cassie said taking hold of her hand, "John and I have already talked about this. We want you to stay for as long as you wish; and I know that Lawrence wants that too.

John and I will be returning to London sometime in late October; Lawrence said he plans on spending the winter here. If there's nothing back in London for you, why not stay here for the winter?"

It was all coming so fast. A few weeks ago, she was living alone in a boarding house, wondering what she should do next. With the exception of the few women she worked with on various campaigns, she really had no friends. In fact, even they were more like acquaintances than friends. Before Lawrence showed up that morning; she had no social life, and had not been out with a man in four years. She was well aware of the fact that the life she had been living was an empty life.

"Thank you for the kind offer Cassie, but I really need some time to think about it. If I do decide to stay, what about my place in London? I'll have to do something about that." She paused for a moment, "do you really think Larry wants me to stay? He seems to be happy when I'm around, but he never really….." her voice trailed off.

"He's just like his father, the slow but sure type. John would come to Bristol, stay at the Inn; we'd go to dinner; the theater; take long walks; he'd hold my hand, this went on for a couple of years. I was beginning to think I'd die of old age before he made up his mind; finally he did. Give Lawrence some time," she smiled. "Now I know what John's going to do before he does. Lawrence is just like him….well, maybe he's a little faster," she laughed.

"You're sure?"

"Very sure. When he came back home, one of the things he talked to us about was how different the women in England were from those in India. In India, the ones he went out with were strong, independent, knew what they wanted, and were willing to stand up and fight against a culture that suppressed women. He considered the English women as being silly; preoccupied with fashion; gossip; and the next party. He wants a woman who will stand up and fight for what she believes; and could care less about the latest fashions, or being in the society column."

"I never read the society pages."

"My point exactly. As for staying here for the winter, and what to do about your place in London; what life has taught me is that if you make the important decision first, the others seem to come easy. '

'Now, changing the subject; Father Grant asked about you yesterday while we were in town. He wanted to know if you said anything to us about helping with the Emergency Plan. I told him you hadn't said anything to us."

"That's something else I've been thinking about. When he found out about my work in England, he asked me to consider helping with the organization and speaking to the women. I told him I'd let him know."

"Well between the Helping Hand project and the Emergency Plan, looks like you'll have a very busy schedule here if you decide to stay." She turned to leave, "John and I are going riding; he wants to check out the area up by Holy Jim's Canyon."

"Holy Jim's Canyon? I haven't heard of that before. Is it a religious shrine?"

Cassie started laughing, "I'm not going to tell you. Have Lawrence take you there some day." She walked out of the room still laughing.

Despite the general happy mood of the people; the good harvest; the fact that there had not been any local crop failures; and no out-breaks of contagious sickness; Father Carmichael could not rid himself of the dark cloud over his head. There was something ominous in the air, unseen as yet, but it was there. For a couple of weeks, the urgency of the Bligh situation had over shadowed this feeling; but now it was back and stronger than ever. Day and night he prayed that God would reveal the nature of the danger, but no revelation came.

Sister Agnes, never known for being tactful, told him not to worry, it was just old age creeping up on him, "I'd be concerned too if I was that close to Saint Peters Door."

He smiled and thanked her for her compassionate concern. They had been together for over twenty years, and had long ago decided to be outspoken and frank with each other. "The simple fact is we need each other," he had told her years ago. In some ways, they were like an old married couple; sometimes tender; grouchy at other times; maybe a bit harsh on each other; but beyond all that; they both knew that life would lose some of its joy, and be more difficult without each other.

"As for getting closer to the next life," Agnes, "that brings me joy, not sorrow. No, that's not the source of my uneasiness. I just need to keep praying until God decides to reveal the nature of this dark cloud hanging over me."

Father Grant, while not having the same strong feelings Carmichael possessed; had listened to stories Sister Agnes related about previous times Carmichael had sensed something long before it happened. Consequently, he put great stock in Carmichael's spiritual gut feelings as he called them. For that reason, even though they didn't know what the future had in store, they did everything they could think of to prepare for it, whatever it might be.

Accordingly, they held the emergency planning meetings every month; put up posters around town; and continued to invite everyone to attend. It was slow going at first, but gradually the attendance increased. Grant continued to promote the idea of changing a large portion of the land from raising potatoes to grain. His efforts were greatly helped by John and Neil who pointed to what they were doing at Arden. To further their goal, John had purchased the mill in town, and had it rebuilt increasing the capacity.

At every meeting, Grant would repeat again and again, "think about it folks, you can store grain and it will keep, potatoes will not. If there are no potatoes, what are you going to feed your family and animals with?"

There were some stubborn farmers who insisted there would always be potatoes. "Maybe not as many taters in a bad year, but I reckon there'll always be 'nough ta survive. And ifin there's not 'nough ta feed the pigs, we'll jes have ta kill 'em. Besides, why should I hafta learn how ta grow grain?"

The breakthrough came when Sally become involved in the Emergency Plan. Her previous organizational and speaking skills were just what Father Grant had been praying for, and he quickly made her a crucial part of the leadership. Unlike Father Grant, who gifted as he was, she was able to talk to the women in a way that convinced them of the urgency to be prepared.

"But that's exactly what I told them," he would say to Sally after a meeting. "Why do they listen to you, but not me?"

"Because I'm a woman and you're not - in case you didn't notice," she would tell him with a big grin. "If it wasn't for the women, slavery would still exist. It's even possible you men would still be living in caves wearing animal skins," she laughed. "And unless I'm mistaken, Jesus mother was a woman; where would your church be without her?" she asked picking up some papers. "You know," she said looking straight at him, "I'm beginning to think God might be a woman."

Grant picked up a piece of paper, crumpled it into a ball and threw it at her. "Yer goin too fer now Lassie," he said in his best Irish accent while reaching for another piece of paper.

She ducked his throw, and threw another back at him. "With throws like that, it's a good thing you're no longer in the army, they'd never win a war."

"That so," he countered as he fired three paper balls in rapid succession, hitting her twice.

She was raising her hands in surrender when Father Carmichael walked into the room, saw her raised hands, and noticed paper balls all over the floor. "I'm happy to see that the meetings are going so well." He reached down and picked up a ball, trying to decide which one to throw it at. He turned suddenly and threw it at Grant, just missing him. A paper ball firefight ensued, until all three collapsed into chairs laughing.

"Sally," Carmichael said between breaths, "you're one of the best things that has happened to Kilrush since John Bligh came to us. Please, don't ever leave us."

"Now wait a minute, she's a member of the Anglican Church," Grant said.

"Nobodies perfect," Carmichael said smiling at Sally. "Now that I think of it," he added as he fired another ball at Grant, "I seem to recall you once belonged to that church."

"That seems so long ago, it was in a different lifetime," he replied picking up the paper ball, "even a different world."

"Interesting that you should say that," Sally said. "Ever since I came to Ireland, I've felt that I was in a different world; a place not so much of things, but of people."

"Aye, and that's the difference Sally. Things have a way of creeping into a person's life and taking over, even when they don't mean it to be so. In a strange kind of way, the poverty of Ireland has been a blessing to its people. Saint Francis of Assisi discovered that truth over four hundred years ago, and gave away everything he owned. Now mind you, I'm not saying what he did is for everyone, it's not. God has place for everyone in his Kingdom, the rich and the poor."

"And the greatest secret in life," Grant said, "is finding your place in his Kingdom. I found mine here at Saint Patrick's."

In his voice, Sally heard the calmness and assuredness she had been seeking for. Since coming here to Ireland, Kilrush, and Arden, she had begun to find a new joy in life. Perhaps in time, she thought, she too would have the same inner peace.

Chapter 24

The following week, Lawrence took Sally on a ride out to Holy Jim's Canyon where she recognized several people from the dances and waved hello; then they rode to the far end of the lake where Jim lived.

She looked at the small cabin, "Ok, so this is where Jim lives; but you still haven't told me who Jim is?"

"I'm Jim," he called out coming around the corner of the cabin, "and this is my wee little castle." "Lawrence, who's this pretty Lass ye brought along?"

"Jim, this is Sally Fairfield, a good friend of mine from London. She's staying with us for a while at Arden."

He looked at her with a peculiar gaze and smile as if he recognized her from the past. "'Tis welcome ye are."

After the introductions were completed, she told him about her comment to Cassie about the Canyon being a religious shrine, he laughed.

"Can't say I ever heard it called that before, but why not." He motioned for them to come inside his cottage and sit down. "When ye really think about it, since the Earth is the Lord's, I guess ye could say it's all a religious shrine; or should be."

"I think I'll try to remember that," Sally replied. Like those before her who had been invited inside, she was surprised to see the walls lined with books, very good books.

"I do a bit of readin now and then," he remarked, "ta try and keep up with what some of the better minds in the world are thinking."

She walked around the room, here and there pulling down a book, noting that almost every book had little slips of paper protruding, marking particular pages. "Read all of these?" she asked.

"Some several times: what about yer self; do ye read much?"

"I did until about six years ago, and then I became so busy I didn't have time."

"Unfortunate, but ye are ta be forgiven."

"Forgiven? why is that?"

"Because ye was investing yer life ta end a great evil," he stood up and bowed. "When Lawrence mentioned yer name I recognized it right off. I followed the progress of yer committee in the papers, and count it a privilege ta have ye in my humble cottage. So tell me about yer work; what ever led a Lass like yer self ta join the struggle against slavery?"

"The great injustice of it; because it was driven by greed; because it was inhumane..." She looked at him intently, "but then you know something about that here."

"Aye, we Irish have faced our own form of slavery by some of the same greedy men. Not with shackles and chains mind ye, but more insidious forms of bondage; being impoverished; denied education; hunger."

Lawrence listened to them, quickly noting that a bond was forming between them. Given time, he was convinced they could become very close friends.

"Well, t'was a grand and noble thing ye did Lassie; though I'm sure there was a lot of people would rather have seen ye tucked in a casket."

They talked for over an hour, and Sally quickly came to realize that Jim was not what he appeared to be a first glance. Beneath that rough exterior was a very widely read intelligent man with deep convictions. It was obvious that he could have made something of himself. Why she wondered, had he decided to come up here and almost live as a hermit?

After they left and were heading back to Arden, she spoke up, "I just can't understand why a man with his intelligence hasn't made something of his life. What's wrong with some men?"

Lawrence reigned in his horse, and told her to stop and turn around.

"See all that?" he said sweeping his arms across the horizon, "it all belongs to Jim. Over a thousand acres; the cattle; sheep; the cottages along the creek… everything. He's a very wealthy man, and his name is not really Jim, its Percy Kilpatrick. But I must caution you; everything I just told you is a secret; and you must never, never, tell this to anyone else. Father Grant; Carmichael; John; Cassie; Neil; and myself; plus a couple of others, and now you, are the only ones around here that know the truth about him. I don't know why he's chosen to live this way. I just know that he's an eccentric; a remarkable man who helps many, many, people around here; and he prefers to do it anonymously."

"But why is this called Holy Jim's Canyon?" she asked.

He laughed as he told her about Jim's interesting way of keeping unwanted people away from his place. "The only reason your ears didn't get singed, was because you were with me. Believe me, he spares neither man, woman, or beast with his sharp foul language."

"Why that old rascal. As for getting my ears singed, I don't think he could have used any foul language that hasn't been personally directed at me before. You may not know it, but the woman you're looking at has been called an ugly bitch; nigger lover; and a whore more times than some of the women working the streets. It really hurt when I first started working on the campaign, but after a while it rolled like water off the ducks back. Sticks and stones, as the old saying goes."

As she glanced back at the land and the cottages, she thought of all the priests and ministers in their churches; and wondered how many people like Jim did God have tucked away here and there, quietly doing good works.

"I owe you an apology," she said as they started back down the road.

"What for?"

"My earlier comment about what's wrong with some men."

"Oh that. I thought you were talking about me again," he laughed. "Come-on, I'll race you to the bridge." He snapped the reigns and headed down the road at a gallop, Sally in fast pursuit.

The days and nights began turning cold. One morning everyone awoke to see frost covering the land and trees like millions, and millions, of tiny diamonds.

"Gonna be a cold winter," Neil said to Sally as he saddled his horse.

"What makes you think that?"

"Caterpillars had heavy coats this Fall; sure sign. So, are you staying here for the winter? You know we all want you to. Very pretty around here with the snow, though we don't get much here. But when we get one of those blizzards, we hitch up the horses and the big wagon. You know the wagon we used for the hayrides? John had Colin make some iron runners for it so we can use it as a sleigh. We throw on a bunch of blankets and everyone has a grand time. If there's enough snow, sometimes we go tobogganing." He tossed a bridle over the horses head. "The farming's over, it's our time to relax."

"What's a toboggan?"

"A long narrow, flat wooden sled with a curl at the front end. Several people sit one behind the other and when everybody's ready, the man at the back gives a shove to get her moving, jumps on, and down the snow covered hill you go like the wind."

"Sure sounds much nicer than walking the dirty streets of London in winter."

"Never been to London, but from what I've heard, I'd never want to live there; maybe a visit sometime." He swung up into the saddle, "Going to town to see Colin. If it makes a difference Sally, my wife also wants you to stay."

She watched him ride down the lane toward the gate, and then headed back toward the house. "Why am I taking so long to make this decision?" she asked to herself. "No one's waiting for me in London." At that moment she made her decision: she was going to spend the winter and Christmas at Arden.

As Neil rode into Kilrush, Father Grant happened to be standing in front of the church,

"Neil," he called, motioning for him to come over. "I need to talk to you."

Neil steered his horse toward the church, leaned forward in the saddle, "Morning Grant."

"If you have a minute come inside: it's important."

As they entered the study, Carmichael was sitting in his chair, a letter in his hand. "You know that ominous feeling I've had for months? Looks like this might be a reason for it," he waved the letter in the air. "This is from the Bishop in Galway. Several of the English Landlords there have started evicting their tenants."

"Why?" Neil asked.

"To free up more land for planting grain, and raising cattle."

"What about the families? Where are they going?

"They're being driven off the land by the sheriff, and their cottages are being torn down so they cannot return. Some of them are lucky and have a family they can move in with; a very few others are migrating; I expect some will come here. The less fortunate, elderly, and sick, are living in the ditches along the road."

"Can the Landlords do that, legally I mean?"

"With their money, the Landlords buy whatever justice they want." Carmichael got up from his chair and walked towards his desk. "Neil, I jotted down a few thoughts for John. Thank the Blessed Mother he's is nothing like many of the other English landholders, but he's still part of their society. I've written to him in the hope that he may be able to help. Would you please take this to him when you return to Arden?"

"Of course. I need to see Colin for a few minutes, and take care of a couple of other things here in town; then I'm heading right back."

As they left the study and walked back outside, Neil put his hand on Grant's shoulder. "You know that I managed Arden for several years before John bought the Estate. Before that, I worked for several other English land owners. With a couple of exceptions, my experience was that they detested the Irish, and were completely indifferent to the needs of the tenant farmers: some were arrogant beyond belief. Once I learned what they were really like, I couldn't work for them anymore and left. To be honest, I don't think they'll listen to John, but I could be wrong."

"Thanks Neil. Unfortunately, being Catholic works against our getting deeply involved. It's hard to say who they hate more, the Irish or the Catholics; but let us know if there is anything else we can do."

When John read Carmichael's letter, Neil saw a side of John he had not seen before, a very angry man. John crumpled the letter in his hand, "Bastards." He paced around the room considering his options. "We should just go up there and kill the bloody bastards."

Lawrence, who had just walked into the room asked, "What's going on?" He hadn't seen his father like this since before his mother died.

John handed him the crumpled letter, "Seems like some of our peers have decided to eliminate the tenant farmers from their estates; throwing them out like so much garbage. There are times Neil, that I feel ashamed to be English."

"The English don't have a monopoly on cruelty, we've had our share of Irish bigots right here," Neil replied.

"I saw plenty of that in India," Lawrence remarked. "The question is what can we do about it? It's their land, how could we stop it?"

"Legally, we can't," John replied. "What I'm afraid of, is that if this starts spreading it could trigger another revolt, a backlash by the Irish. People killed; livestock slaughtered; trees cut; estates burned down."

"As certain as I'm standing here," Neil added, "I've no doubt that terrorist groups are already forming to take revenge. It's been very quiet around here, but not so in some of the other counties."

"What do you mean?" Lawrence asked.

"Look, the Irish talk among themselves; stories; rumors… things the men talk about at the Pub; but things you'll never hear because you're English. Doesn't make any difference how good you are; fact is you're still English. Folks around here know you and trust you, but in most other places they'll look at you as just another greedy, crooked, Englishman."

"Still, we need to do something," John said. "Maybe if we invited a number of them to come here to Arden, and see what we've accomplished here, it might change their thinking and some of the evictions."

"It'd be great if that happened," Neil replied, "but you're up against several hundred years of distrust and hatred on both sides."

"Lawrence, what do you think?"

"I think we should give it a try," Lawrence answered. "Let's send out some invitations. It's possible that if they see first hand how Arden works to everyone s benefit, some of them might reconsider what they're doing."

"I'm still doubtful; but it can't hurt to try," Neil added.

"Good, that settles it. Neil, I'll prepare an invitation and send it out tomorrow. I want you to notify everyone here about what we are doing. We don't want our people becoming alarmed when they start seeing carriages with footman, and regally garbed English lords arriving and walking all over Arden."

"That will be quite a sight for certain. I doubt that many folks here have ever seen anything like that. I was always amused watching them when I worked on their estates. Carefully walking around like they were afraid they might get a spot of dirt on their clothes." Neil did a mock imitation of their walk, nose in the air. "John, I'll tell you something I never told you before; it's what I - what we all - expected when the news came that an Englishman was going to buy Arden. You have no idea of how relieved we all were when you and Lady Elizabeth arrived, and we got to know you."

"For your information Neil, it wasn't long before you met me that I was just like that. My nose was in the clouds. But gradually, Lady Elizabeth brought me back to earth; taught me how to become a human being; to realize that but for God's grace and blessing, I might have been a common beggar on the street. She was a saint, and I'm happy that you got to meet and know her. Much of what Arden has become, were her ideas."

"True it is she was a saint. Lawrence, you should have seen the folks here when she came to visit; they all loved her like she was one of them, and that's how she always acted. No that's not right, she didn't act, she was one of them - of us. And the sorrow and grief we all felt when she died....it was like our own mother, or sister had died."

Lawrence was overcome by this expression of affection for his mother. Although several individuals had expressed to him how much they had cared for his mother, this was the first time he had heard Neil say it so clearly. It was also the first time he heard his father give the credit to her for beginning his transformation; and that she had been so instrumental in developing Arden. He wondered what she would say if she could see Arden now.

It was silent for a moment, then John spoke up. "Let's try and get everyone here in a fortnight. I'll have Cassie talk to the cook and prepare something that should suit their fancy. Lawrence, we don't have enough accommodations here. Go to town and reserve some of the rooms in the hotel for our guests. They'll think they're roughing it, but it's the best we can do. Neil, talk to the staff and the tenants and explain what we're doing. We want Arden to sparkle like a diamond; that includes the tenant's cottages."

"Lawrence, I think you and I should go to town and talk to Carmichael and Grant. They need to know what we are doing, and also let some of the towns folk know. Having several English Lords coming into this area at the same time, and unannounced, could cause a potential problem."

The special meeting plan was set in motion and the days went by quickly. Soon letters began arriving at Arden: seven accepted the invitation, three declined claiming they had other commitments. Fortunately, the day they began arriving turned out to be beautiful and sunny. One of the guests arrived on horseback with a single servant riding along side. The others came in their carriages drawn by impeccably groomed teams; coachmen, and footmen in livery. One Lord even had several uniformed armed body guards riding along side his coach.

John looked at Lawrence and Neil, "I think they're going to be in for a surprise about how we do things here."

"I think shock is a better word," Neil responded.

The first thing that shocked the visitors, was the simple farm house instead of a grand manor. The second surprise was that instead of servants, John and Lawrence personally greeted them wearing common ordinary country clothing; while Neil had arranged for several of the tenant farmers to help handle the horses and take them to the stable. It was all intended to be very informal.

By noon, everyone had arrived and lunch was served. Afterward, riding horses were provided and the guests were taken on an extensive tour of Arden. John, Lawrence, and Neil answered dozens of questions about the operation. It became clear that four of the guests were very interested in how Arden had been developed, and observed the remarkable friendly relationship between the Bligh's and the Irish staff and tenants.

"This all looks very nice, but how do you handle the problem of stealing?" one asked.

"We very rarely have that problem," Neil replied. "We're like a family, why would we steal from each other?"

"Come now," an obviously hostile Lord exclaimed looking at Neil, "you're Irish, of course you'll cover up for your friends. I dare say, John, you don't know how much is being stolen from you."

"On the contrary, Neil and I work side-by-side everyday. There isn't anything that goes on here that I'm not aware of."

"You work side-by-side!" another asked, "Do you mean that you're actually involved in the daily operations. Isn't that what your manager is hired to do?"

"Neil does that, and superbly I might add. But we discovered that by working together, we get much more accomplished. And there's an added benefit; when the staff and tenants see us working together it creates a wonderful atmosphere. And now that my son Lawrence is here, it's even better."

Several of the guests started talking among themselves, some obviously intrigued by this novel idea, others saying that Bligh was kidding himself.

"Let me ask you a question," John said. "How many of you know the names of your tenant's?" he paused; "their wives? their children?"

"Whatever for?" two or three men asked simultaneously.

"Several reasons. First, because they live on your property, and should be given simple dignity. They address you by name, right? Then why not have the courtesy to do the same. Secondly, never forget that it's their labor that adds to your wealth. The better you treat them, the better their work. This also relates to the problem some of you have with theft. The scripture says, 'whatsoever a man sows, that shall he also reap.' When you treat them badly; cheat them of their just due; they will treat you the same."

"Are you accusing us of stealing from our tenants?"

"Certainly not. I'm not accusing anyone here of anything. I'm merely pointing out that common courtesy is one of the factors that has made Arden so successful."

John headed toward the dairy barn, and motioned for them to follow. "One of the reasons I invited you here, was for you to see for yourself what we've accomplished here; and secondly, to see how we've done it."

"It's true," Neil spoke up, "as simple as it may seem, the fact that John knows the name of everyone here - including all their children's names - increases production; eliminates theft, and if you don't mind my saying so, makes Arden a happy place to live."

"John?" one asked, "you let your manager call you by your first name?"

"Yes, I suggested that many years ago, but it took him a while to get used to the idea. Seemed rather silly for us to spend all day working together, and require him to call me M'lord. Besides, what's a title? Everyone here including myself, inherited their title; we never did anything to earn it. Had circumstances been different, Neil might have been born Lord McLeod, and I plain John Bligh."

Looking around and seeing the expressions on their faces, it was obvious he had stepped on some toes with that last remark about inherited titles.

By six o'clock the tour was finished, and the guests were invited into the house. Wine was served in the parlor, and the questions continued until dinner was served at eight. After dinner, John carefully brought up the subject of evicting tenants from the land.

"Now that you have had the chance to see how we operate Arden, you can see that the real key to our success is how we treat our people, the workers, and our tenants. Now we could gain another hundred-fifty acres or so by eliminating the tenants. I had my Son and Neil calculate the potential profit from another hundred-fifty acres of grain, or using it as pasture for cattle. The figures they came up with, shows that we would actually lose money."

"Lose money, why is that?" one asked.

"I'd like to answer that," Lawrence replied.

"We'd lose for a couple of reasons. First, most of the tenants live on small plots that are not well suited to grain crops, and are marginal for cattle. More importantly, by providing them with their own cottage and a good safe place to raise their families; they work harder and increase the yield on the land we do farm. If we moved them off the land, several things would happen. Our production per acre would go down off-setting any gain from the additional acreage. Secondly, we would open ourselves up to hostility – like the stealing you mentioned earlier. Not only from the tenants we evicted, but also by all of their relatives and friends that live in the immediate area."

"It's guaranteed trouble," John added. "I don't have to tell you that we English landlords, are generally not liked, even hated here. Why would we want to deliberately increase the hostility, when the potential gain is slight, if at all, and the potential loss very great."

He looked at Lord Stuart, "William, I noticed that you came here with an armed escort. Why was that?"

"Because you never know when one of these dirty Irish thieves is going to try and ambush you along the road."

"Interesting. Lady Bligh, Lawrence, and I, ride our horses and walk all over this area for miles around by ourselves, and never give a thought to being ambushed. Why do you suppose that is?"

"Because you've become one of them," he said standing up and throwing his napkin on the table. "You work side-by-side with your Irish manager," he sneered with contempt; "he calls you by your first name; you don't demand the proper respect; and you treat these people as your equals." He was becoming angrier by the second.

"Look at you; you've become a disgrace to your Class, and the English race. If it was within my power, I'd strip you of your title."

"Lord Stuart's right," Lord Clark said. "This is our land, and we will do whatever we bloody well choose to do with it. I don't care if I lose money by throwing the Papist trash off my estate. I'd rather see it become a useless bog than to have them living on it."

"I agree," Stuart added, "and I'll tell you this, we'll never be able to fully develop Ireland until we get rid of every last one of them. If your idea of having us come here was to try and convince us to stop evicting tenants; let alone treating the Irish as equals," he looked at Neil, "you wasted your time and ours."

"I'll not spend another minute here listening to this rubbish," Clark said getting up from the table so quickly that he knocked over this wine glass. "If you want to become like the Irish, do so; but don't ever attempt to speak about it to me again. And as for you gentlemen," he said looking at the other guests, "If you value your social standing, I suggest you think twice before joining this Irish loving traitor."

The room fell silent as Stuart and Clark stalked out, talking to each other. At last, one of the others spoke up.

"I don't quite know what to say. I inherited my estate from my father. As far as I know, he never came to Ireland to see it; always had an English manager. It lost money year after year; so when he died, I decided to come up here and see it for myself. I quickly discovered that the manager hated the Irish, and they hated him. If the estate made any money, the manager pocketed it and blamed the loss on the tenants."

Another spoke up, "My situation is similar; bad manager; unhappy tenants robbing me blind. What I have seen here today, gives me hope that it can be turned around."

"But where can we find good managers like Neil?"

"I suggest that you ask him," John replied, "perhaps he knows someone in your area. But remember, you've got to become personally involved. The manager's important, but it's when the tenants see you in the field; when you talk to them; ask about their families; see if you can help them in any way, that's when the trust begins."

The meeting continued. More questions, and more discussions. Two of the landowners expressed concern about the trouble Stuart and Clark could make for them. While they liked some of the ideas they were hearing, their fear of possibly losing their social standing tipped the scales to continuing managing their estates as before.

"Please understand," Lord Harrison said, "I do not hate the Irish, but I must leave the decisions to my manager who does. He's the one who lives here; I do not, nor do I wish to. If he believes evicting some tenants will benefit the estate, I will not interfere with that decision."

"He's right," the other man said to John. "With your wealth and power, you can afford to stand against Stuart and Clark, I cannot. They could crush my family."

"I'm sorry that you feel that way," John answered. "As for Stuart and Clark, you greatly over-estimate their power and influence. A few years ago, they did everything they could to defeat the anti-slavery advocates; who were mostly ordinary citizens without titles or political power; but in the end they lost. England's changing, the Queen herself has less power, and as you well know the members of the House of Lords are now elected. I think you'll find that while Stuart and Clark have some influence, it's far less than they imagine it to be."

"I believe that," Harrison said, "but my wife is very involved in the social circles. She would be beside herself if we were to be shunned. I can't make a decision like this without talking to her first. To be honest, I don't think she would risk it."

"Of course you must discuss this with her first; unless you want to live on your roof," John replied.

"Live on my roof? I don't understand"

"There's a passage of scripture in the Old Testament that reads, '...better to dwell on a housetop, than in a house with a contentious wife."

"I can certainly agree with that," Harrison chuckled. "Perhaps I'm wrong and she will agree, at least to some of the changes. I'm going to do my best, simply because it's obvious they would solve so many problems."

"I've been listening carefully to everything that's been said here tonight," Lord Baltimore said, "add that to what we saw on the tour of Arden we had earlier; and I'm convinced this is the way to go. When I get home, I'm going to have a very serious talk with my manager. I have a feeling that he'll be willing to make some changes."

"I can't say the same about my manager," Lord Blakely replied. "My feeling is that he will not want to change so I might have to consider replacing him. As for Stuart and Clark making trouble, let them try. Our family has been around as long as theirs."

"Longer," Baltimore chuckled.

When it became apparent that Baltimore and Blakely were seriously considering beginning to make changes in the way their estates were being run, Lawrence spoke up.

"If you're willing too give this plan an honest try, Neil and I will personally come to your estates to help you get started. No point in your trying to reinvent the wheel. We've made the mistakes here, and are willing to share our knowledge of what works."

"Look at what you have now," John added, "and what you could have. When you carefully consider all the factors involved, it's really quite simple.

At that moment, Cassie and Sally entered the room, "Gentlemen, it's after ten o'clock; if you intend on continuing the meeting, we'll make some coffee for you."

"Thank you Cassie," John said, "I didn't realize it was that late. Gentlemen, I suggest we call it a day. Tomorrow after everyone gets a good nights rest, and for those who are interested, we can continue this discussion in the morning after breakfast."

Four of the guests said they wished to meet again in the morning; the fifth said he would like to, but unfortunately had a crisis he had to get back and attend to. Could he please come back another time?

"Certainly, you're welcome anytime. Would you mind telling us what the problem is? Perhaps we could offer some advice."

"One of the tenants stole a lamb and killed it to feed his family. The manager plans to have him publicly whipped tomorrow afternoon, and then turned over to the local Constable for prosecution."

"And if he's convicted - as surely he will be - then what happens?" John did not wait for an answer. "He'll be sent to prison and his wife and children will be left without support. Am I correct?"

"Yes."

"What happens to his family?"

"The manager will evict them."

"I'd like to make a suggestion if I may," John replied.

"Please. I'm very interested in hearing how you would handle the problem."

"When you get back," John began, "tell your manager to have all of the tenants - men, women, children, and other workers if you have any - assemble on the lawn. After they are gathered together, have the man who stole the lamb brought to the front - don't have him bound, that's very important - and make certain that his family is standing next to him. Tell everyone present what he did; and even though they know that stealing is against the law, remind them again."

"Now here is where you depart from the past; look directly at him and his family, and let everyone know that you are not going to either whip, or prosecute him; but that he will have to repay you for the value of the lamb - you can work up some kind of arrangement. This will be the result. He and his family will be very grateful; you keep a tenant who will now work extra hard, his wife will see to that. But in addition, you will begin to win the honest respect of your other tenants and workers. Remember, it's not fear, but respect that you're after. Never forget that fear only works to a certain point, and will eventually result in violence. Respect however, very seldom fails."

"The second part is, ask if anyone else is having a problem feeding their family. I suspect you will have several raise their hands. Meet with them personally, and find a way to help them. It will cost you very little, and you'll be amazed at the results."

"My manager won't like that. He says we've got to set an example."

"But you are setting an example; applying God's grace instead of the law. I can assure you from our experience here at Arden, that it works wonders. There may be a rare occasion when the offence demands that you must resort to the law; but I do not believe that sending a man to Prison and evicting his family from their home over the loss of a lamb, is one of them."

"I'm going to do it. The manager has punished people in the past, and it never really changed anything. I can see how your approach can bring a fundamental change, a change for the good. Thank you."

The other guests had listened intently to John, and it was evident from the look on their faces, and the glances they gave to each other, that something was beginning to work in their minds.

"Grace instead of the law, a very interesting approach," Baltimore said.

"Oh I didn't come up with the idea," John answered, "Jesus did."

After they had said goodbye to their guests, John, Lawrence, and Neil looked at each other.

"I think that perhaps we began making a difference today. We can't expect to win everyone over, but two out of seven is a start. Possibly, even one or two more. What do you think?"

"Far better than I expected John," Neil said. "I thought they'd all react like Stuart and Clark."

"Lord Stuart and Lord Clark to you, you un-respectful Irish Papist," Lawrence said as he poked Neil in the ribs.

"I'm sorry, there's just something in my blood -Irish blood - that begins to boil with arrogant people like that. Why are they like that?"

"Poor up-bringing. They've already forgotten that same arrogant attitude cost them thirteen colonies," Lawrence said laughing. "Seriously, it's little wonder that they fear for their lives. If I had their attitude, I'd never leave England."

"The sad part of it all," Neil said, "is that they just might get murdered, and then the English authorities will come down on us again."

"Which is why we must work that much harder to begin to change their attitude," John added. "Well, I'm going to call it a day; see you all in the morning."

That night, as these very different men climbed into their beds, there were those who could not imagine how anyone could be so blind to the obvious fact that they were of noble linage; and that God had bestowed upon them their wealth and position at birth for the purpose of taking dominion over the earth and everything on it, including the Irish. At the same time, others were beginning to seriously question those long held beliefs, which had been instilled in them from childhood; while the last group had already come to the realization that for whatever purpose he had in mind, God had blessed them; and now they had the responsibility to pass the blessing on to others.

Winter came; and one morning Sally awoke and when she looked out her bedroom window, Arden had been transformed into a misty white world. During the night, a heavy fog had rolled in off the ocean, crept silently up the river and reached its fingers out across the hills and valleys. The temperature dropped and the fog turned to frost, coating the grass; shrubbery; trees; the wire fences; encasing everything with billions upon billions of tiny diamonds.

Dressing quickly, afraid that the enchanting vision would vanish, she ran down the stairs and out the door. Neil and Lawrence were standing there on the porch talking.

"I've never seen anything like this before," she said excitedly, "how long will it last?"

"Pretty heavy," Neil replied. "I think it might last till early afternoon when the sun breaks through; but I can recall times when it lasted for several days."

"Larry, I'm so happy you asked me to come to Ireland, and stay through the winter."

"I'm even happier that you decided to stay. Neil and I were just talking about getting the toboggan ready. There's a chance that if it stays cold, we might get a little snow in the next couple of days."

She looked at Larry, Neil, and the glistening landscape around her. Her decision to stay had been the right one. Now she had more decisions to make; what to get everyone for Christmas.

Chapter 25

Kilrush 1841. It had rained most of the night, a cold March rain that sent the chill deep into one's bones. Inside Bridgit's cottage, Sean placed another block of peat in the fireplace to keep a cheery fire going, while Kathleen and Sally kept vigil by Bridgit's bedside. About three in the morning, her labor pains began. While Kathleen had been mid-wife at dozens of births, as had Bridgit; for Sally, this was an exciting new experience. Doctor Cain, a very close friend of both Kathleen and Bridgit, had offered to personally handle the birth; but since there were no apparent complications, they thanked him for his offer and suggested he get a good nights sleep and stop by in the morning. Accustomed to long hours and sleepless nights, he readily accepted their offer.

The excitement of witnessing and helping deliver a baby put Sally in a state of high anxiety, and she paced the floor like an expectant father; while Kathleen dozed off in a rocking chair, a quilt wrapped around her legs.

"When the pains start comin faster, put some pots of water on the stove ta heat, and wake me," Kathleen had told her.

Throughout the night, Sally and Sean talked about his life before he was converted, and she about her family in London and her political work. About five-thirty, Bridgit's pains intensified and began coming much faster. Sally woke up Kathleen, and Sean stoked the fire in the stove and put on the pots of water. Although she never said anything to either Bridgit or Sally, Kathleen did have a concern she had discussed with Doctor Cain; Bridgit was thirty-six, and the fact she had never had children before. His opinion was that because Bridgit was in excellent health, he saw no need to worry. "However," he said as he left, "if you start to have any problems at all, send Sean to get me.

At six-thirty in the morning the baby's head crowned, and Sally watched in wonder as a new life entered the world. "It's a girl," she yelled, "it's a girl."

Bridgit looked at Sally and smiled. "I asked the Blessed Mother for a girl," she whispered.

Sean was in the kitchen praying and thanking God for his many mercies, and asking his blessing on this new life.

Having done this so many times before, Kathleen let Sally cut the cord and told her she could wash and clean up the little darling. Although Sally had held her nieces and nephews many times when they were babies; she discovered that there was something transforming in witnessing the birth, and carefully washing the tiny little pink fingers and toes all so perfectly formed.

"Grace." Bridgit said in a low voice as she held Kathleen's hand. "I want her name ta be Grace."

"Why Grace? I do na recall anyone in yer family named Grace," Kathleen said as she placed the baby next to Bridgit.

"It's God's Grace, that I'm thinking of. When I vowed that I'd never marry, t'was knowin I'd never be blessed with children." She cuddled the baby in her arms, "Now here I am with a beautiful little girl."

Sally watched her cradle the baby next to her, and listened intently to what she was saying. She had been raped, and yet from that terrible event she was able to find a blessing. It reminded her of something Sean had said earlier when he was telling her about his own transformation.

"In everythin, every disaster, there's a seed of greater benefit. Out of the fight with Colin came my salvation. The secret is ta look beyond the grief ta find it. I coulda remained bitter and let it turn ta hatred for Colin. It woulda destroyed my life. Instead, I found Jesus, a new life, and now Colin is my friend. From Bridgit's tragedy came a beautiful little girl."

"So you think that bad things, disasters, come from God?"

"No, no, that's not what I'm sayin. Bad things kin happen ta anyone; but God can take it and bring a blessin out of it, ifin ye let him. Think about this; when ye sailed up here from Bristol the winds came from the west. When ye go back ta Bristol, the winds will be from the west, jes like before. Tis not the wind that determines the ships course or destination, but the Captain."

Sally thought about the winds in her own life, was she now letting the wind control her destiny, or was she in control? As she started walking into the kitchen, there was a knock at the door. When she opened it, she saw Doctor Cain, Lawrence, John, and Cassie.

"Looks like we all decided to come at the same time," John said smiling. "How's Bridgit doing?"

Kathleen walked out of the bedroom, "she's doin fine, t'was an easy birthin."

"You mean the baby's already been born?" Cassie asked.

"Darlin little girl," Sally answered with excitement. "Kathleen, is it alright if they go to see them."

"Bridgit would never speak ta me agin, ifin I didn't let ye."

The women all rushed towards the bedroom, leaving the men standing there by themselves.

"Looked to me like Sally is pretty excited about this," John said grinning at Lawrence. "What do you think Doc?"

"My experience has been," Doctor Cain said lighting his pipe, "is that whenever a baby is born women's maternal instincts start kicking in. At such a time, men - single men in particular - should be on their guard."

"Against what; whom?" Lawrence asked.

"Why single women of course," he laughed. "Like Sally there," he pointed his pipe toward the bedroom.

The men gave the women a few minutes by themselves to fuss over mother and child and then they went in to offer their congratulations. Doctor Cain took a couple of minutes to examine the baby and told Bridgit she had a very healthy little girl, who he did not doubt would grow up to be as lovely as her mother.

They had been visiting for half an hour when there was a knock on the door; it was Fathers Carmichael and Grant, followed by Agnes and two other sisters. Minutes later, several of the neighbor women stopped by to see the new baby. The little cottage was becoming packed, so Kathleen started shooing some of the visitors out. The parade of friends and neighbors continued well into the afternoon; by which time Bridgit, Kathleen, Sally, and Sean were very tired. Kathleen said she would stay and help Bridgit for the next two days, Sally eagerly agreed for the next two, while Sean said goodbye and headed home.

After everyone had left and quiet returned to her cottage; Bridgit nestled Grace, who was fast asleep, against her. She looked out the window and saw a little yellow finch perched on the tree. Her mind went back to another day nine months ago, and she thought about Father Timothy. Grant had told her he never reported to the church in London, and she wondered where he was. Did he even know that she had become pregnant?

The following afternoon, a fishing boat pulled into Kilrush for repairs and supplies. A heavily bearded, deeply tanned man stepped ashore. He wore a thick Irish sweater; had a knit woolen cap a-top his head; a pipe tucked into the corner of his mouth; and a small seaman's bag slung over his shoulder. Because this was a fishing port, and dozens of men with similar descriptions filled these docks everyday, he went completely unnoticed.

After securing a room at one of the small Inns near the waterfront, he stepped out into the street and started walking toward the center of town. Occasionally, some passerby would bid him good afternoon, but for the most part he was ignored, just another person on the street. After walking for several blocks with out being recognized, Peter was satisfied that his appearance safely protected his identity.

Although he was unaware of it, he had little to fear. It had been nine months since he had 'disappeared,' the term the Bishop of London used in the letter he sent to Father Carmichael. The last time anyone at Saint Patrick's had seen him, was the morning he ate breakfast before leaving for London to report to his new Parish. An inquiry at the dock in Kilrush disclosed that a Priest, identity unknown, had been seen boarding a fishing boat bound for Bristol. Several weeks later upon being located and questioned, the Captain of the fishing boat said that Father Timothy had indeed left the boat in Bristol, supposedly heading for London. According to the police, no one had seen him since that day.

During that time, he had continued leading his new life as a fisherman. Four months ago, while he was ashore in Bristol, he chanced to over hear another fisherman mention the name Kilrush. Curious, he approached the man and mentioned that he had a friend there that he had not heard from: what was the news from Kilrush? The man told him that the town was pretty much the same; but that there had been an assassination attempt on an English couple several months before. Peter's ears perked up at this news.

"Do you know what the couples name was?"

"Bligh. The only reason I remember it was because of old Captain Bligh. No relation I was told."

"What happened?"

"Seems as though the authorities had been tipped off and were waiting for the man. Nothing happened to the Bligh's; but what was strange was that there were actually two men killed. One killed the other, and a detective from Scotland Yard shot and killed him. Turned out one of the men was Bligh's son. After the family estate was what I heard."

Two months before, Peter had heard that the Bligh's were unharmed, but this was the first time he had heard the details of what had happened. "Must have been quite a bit of excitement."

"That it was, talk of the town for days," he paused. Can't think of any other special news," he paused again, "wait a minute, a woman was raped in her own cottage, but that was months ago. Folks said that she was very well known and active in the community. Shocked everyone."

"Did they catch the man?" Peter asked.

"He disappeared, and the woman would not say who he was. Sad part is the bastard got her pregnant. Gonna be tough on her."

This was bad news, really bad news that Peter had not expected. His hope and prayers that the entire incident would be forgotten, or at least relegated to the past, were shattered. "Terrible thing," he remarked. "Well, thanks for the news. One of these days I'll take a trip up there and see how my friend is doing." They shook hands, wished each other good fishing, and walked off in different directions. He mentally calculated the time, if the pregnancy was normal she would be due in March. What ever fishing boats he went out on now, he had to make certain he could get back to Kilrush in March.

The months went by, and despite talking to a number of
people who had been to Kilrush he could never get any
new information.   It was frustrating not knowing about
Bridgit's condition, whether she was doing well, or ill. It
was possible that she had even had a miscarriage; it was the
not knowing that drove him crazy. Now here he was in
Kilrush just blocks from her cottage. Somehow, he had to
find out how she was, without revealing himself.

After careful consideration, he felt the hardware store
would be his best bet. He had seldom gone there when he
was a resident at Saint Patrick's, and local gossip was a
stock in trade in such places. The barbershop would have
been better, but he did not want anyone getting that close to
his face. He casually walked down the street and entered
the hardware store. When asked if he could be helped, he
replied he was thinking of buying a new knife.

For fifteen minutes he looked at the knives and then
meandered around the store. No one else entered the store,
and becoming concerned about lingering too long, he left.
Next, he tried the Pub, choosing a stool at the far end of the
bar. The bartender engaged him in typical small talk and
asked him if he was a stranger in town. He answered that
he was, just here for a couple of days while some repairs
were being made to the ship.

"So what's your town like?" Peter asked.

"Nice town, nice people fer the most part," he answered
washing a glass.

"So what do you do for excitement?"

"The bartender looked up, "if I get yer meanin, I know a
couple of gals here that…."

Peter waved his hand, "no, I wasn't thinking of that. I
meant are there theaters; dances – what goes on here?"

"Oh, sorry about misunderstandin ye.   Saint Patrick's
down the street has dances on Friday nights, and there is a
small playhouse two blocks from here. Local group, I think

they're doin some play from Shakespeare; not anything I'm interested in myself."

Peter realized that this line of talk would take forever to get what he was after, so he decided to get to the point. "I'm thinking of movin up this way, that's why I'm asking about your town. This isn't a roudy place is it; barfights, killings, that sort of thing? That's why I want to leave where I'm at now."

"No, no, really a quiet place. Though there's an occasional incident." The bartender walked away to serve another customer. When he returned he continued, "the biggest thing was when two men tried ta kill Lord and Lady Bligh, but that t'was months ago. The police got the men, shot and killed 'em both. Lucky for 'em being killed like that. The Bligh's are very special folks 'round here. I think the crowd would've torn them apart limb from limb ifin they'd gotten hold of 'em."

He left to take care of another customer. He returned, "biggest news now is that Bridgit had her baby, little girl."

"What's so special about having a baby?"

"Ye really have ta know the story. Bridgit is loved like a saint round these parts, helps everyone. She was raped by some low life - never would say who did it - we all figure he left town. Anyway, Sean – chap that lives here in town - popped his head in the door yesterday morning and said the baby was born 'bout seven o'clock. Said Bridgit named her Grace."

"Tragic, but bad things can happen in any town. How's her husband taking this?"

"Oh, Bridgit's not married which makes it even worse, her being unmarried and alone. Father Carmichael told her ta give the girl ta the church ta raise. She wouldna have any of it, gonna raise the girl herself." He left to check on another man who had just walked into the Pub and sat down at the bar.

Peter finished his drink, left his money on the bar and walked out. He headed up the hill where nine months ago he had spent the afternoon in bitter remorse over what he had done. Now he was looking down toward her cottage where a new life was just beginning. More than anything, he wanted to see her and his baby girl, but he knew that was not possible, not yet anyway. For close to an hour he sat on a large rock, watching the cottage in the hope that she might walk out the door. He watched as Kathleen came out into the yard for a moment and then went back inside, but that was the only activity. He noticed a young couple, hand in hand, coming up the hill and decided he had better leave and head back toward his ship.

Returning to the dock, he learned that the repairs to the boat could not be made for a couple of weeks. Since they were not critical, the Captain had decided to depart on the morning tide. With no other business in town, he went back to his room and spent the night alone, thinking of all the things that might have been. In the morning, sea bag over his shoulder, he boarded the boat and said farewell to Kilrush again.

Three weeks later, a package addressed to Bridgit arrived at Saint Patrick's. Because Father Carmichael was not feeling well, Father Grant took the package to her cottage. By now, Bridgit was beginning to return to her former self, and when the knock came at the door, she welcomed Grant with a warm smile and cheery good morning.

"Got a package for you," he said. "Came to the church this morning."

"That's strange, I didna order anything."

"Got your name on it, but no return address," Grant said. "Open it up, see what's inside."

Bridgit opened the box and found it was packed with clothing; a beautiful dress and robe for herself; some baby clothing; and a silver baby's cup engraved with the name Grace. In the bottom of the box was an envelope with money, close to twenty pounds, enough money to take care of her and Grace for many months. She sat down holding the money in her hand.

Father Grant, puzzled by this surprise package, asked if she knew who it was from.

"I'm not sure; but it might be from an aunt I haven't seen in many years," she answered, silently asking Mother Mary to forgive her a small lie.

Father Grant looked at her knowing that was not true, Carmichael had told him that her only living relative was a cousin living in Canada. "Well it certainly is a wonderful surprise, whoever sent it. A real blessing I'd say. Actually, another blessing considering little Grace."

"True it is," she answered. God's grace 'tis wonderful is it not." She looked around the room filled with gifts from dozens of friends she had helped over the years. In the corner was a beautiful carved cradle the Bligh's had shipped over from London. And now, there was this unexpected package. There was no name enclosed, but she knew instinctively that it was from Father Timothy. Like everyone else in town, she had heard that he had disappeared on his way to the church in London; no one knew whether he was alive or dead. Now she knew he was alive, but said nothing to Grant. She had no idea of how he had learned of the birth, and that it was a little girl named Grace, but somehow he had. He was alive and well, and for that she was thankful.

Grant congratulated her again and left. Back at the church he told Carmichael about all the gifts, including the silver cup with Grace's name on it; and Bridgit's story about them being from her aunt. Carmichael shook his head, "We both know for a fact that's not true. I doubt her cousin even knows anything about Bridgit, being she left so long ago."

"So you think it's from Father Timothy?" Grant said.

"I'd almost bet my soul on it. I've gone over the incident a hundred times in my head. If it had been any other woman, she would have named the man who attacked her. But for reasons we may never know, Bridgit has vowed never to say who it was, and if we know anything about Bridgit, it's that she keeps her vows."

"Personally, I see no reason to notify the Bishop in London. What do you think?"

"I believe that would serve no purpose," Carmichael answered. "Father Timothy has determined to leave the priesthood, at least for now. The matter is now between him and God," he paused, "and perhaps Bridgit. One other thing, this is just a secret between us. Don't even let anyone else, not even Bridgit know that we know."

"I totally agree with that. You know, we're beginning to have a lot of secrets around here; Jim; Bridget; Father Timothy; Lawrence asking Sally to marry him."

"What's that about Lawrence and Sally?" Carmichael asked, a note of excitement in his voice.

"Sorry. Lawrence just told me last night he was going to propose, didn't get a chance to tell you before."

"What a wonderful day it is," Carmichael exclaimed rubbing his hands together. "Showers of blessings all around us." He grabbed Grant's arm and did a little dance. "Now tell me if this doesn't beat army life?"

Chapter 26

Lawrence and Sally were married in London one month after Grace was born; creating one of the largest social events of the season. Remembering the social concerns of some of the English Lord's who had attended the meetings at Arden, John had Carrie and Sally make a special point of inviting them and their wives; who upon receiving an engraved invitation from Lord and Lady Bligh, were delirious with excitement. It had been rumored that Queen Victoria might be there; and possibly Prince Albert, whom the court gossips were claiming she would marry. All of this high society falderal wearied Sally, who given the choice would have preferred to elope; or have a quiet wedding at Arden. But as she was learning, the high social status of the Bligh's carried a price tag, 'no-blesse o-blige'. After their honeymoon, they returned to Arden and had a huge party for everyone in the area, which they both enjoyed more than the party in London.

Five years had passed, and Arden continued to grow larger. Two adjoining farms had been purchased, and the business enterprises now employed over two hundred people. The efforts of John, Lawrence, and Neil had been successful in encouraging a number of other English Landlords to cease the practice of evicting tenants, and adopt some of the business models developed at Arden. Unfortunately, due to their dislike or even outright hatred of the Irish, other land owners rejected their appeal; and appeared to be waiting for a good excuse to evict every tenant on their property.

Lawrence and Sally now had three year old son, Nathan John; and a baby girl, Elizabeth Cathrine. John and Cassie, while still active at Arden, had turned most of the operations over to Lawrence and Neil; and were now content to divide there time between London, Arden, and traveling, and do whatever they could to spoil their grandchildren. Cassie decided not to sell the Captain's Inn, but hired a full time manager. Whenever she and John, traveled through Bristol, they would stay at the Inn and visit the restaurants and shops they had enjoyed before they were married.

Neil, his wife Sarah, and their three children had, for all intents and purposes, become part of the Bligh family. John and Cassie treated Neil like another son and his wife Sarah like a daughter. Their children were in turn, three more grandchildren for them to dote upon. Now that Lawrence and Sally were married with their own children, the two families spent much of their time together.

Over the years, the free 'Honeymoon at the Inn' idea John had suggested, had become so well known, that it generated marvelous word of mouth advertising, bringing in more business and profit than the cost of the program. This success prompted them to purchase an old Inn in Kilrush under a fictitious name. After completely refurbishing it, they hired a manager to operate it in the same manner as the Captain's Inn, including the free Honeymoon at the Inn. Within a year, business had almost doubled.

Father Carmichael, now eighty-one, was noticeably slowing down. His mind was as sharp as ever and his spirit unflagging, but the years had taken their toll on his body. He simply no longer had the energy and stamina to keep up with a growing Parish, and the escalating number of events which demanded increasing amounts of attention. On awaking every morning, his first praise was thanking God for being able to wake up; the second for Father Grant who now handled almost all of the day-to-day activities of the church. "God's eternal circle continues," he would say to himself, "Grant is now to me, what I had been to Father O'Conner, and he to the Priest before him."

There was one question that continued to trouble him; why had he felt this strong urging from God to start the Emergency Plan? Almost six years had gone by, and except for an isolated emergency here and there, there appeared to be little reason for its existence. Father Grant however, reminded him of Pharaoh's dream of the fat and lean cattle, which foretold a disaster that was many years in the future. God gave you this warning; be prepared. Our task is to be ready, whenever it may come.

Within four months of Sally joining Fathers Carmichael and Grant, the Emergency Plan they had started, had grown and flourished under her leadership. The Emergency Council, now comprised of twenty representatives from Kilrush and several surrounding towns, met once a month; and because of the growing crowds, the meetings had been moved into the main sanctuary. A comprehensive plan had been prepared and instituted for the development of several storehouses around Kilrush to be filled with non-perishable food stocks; medical supplies; and tools.

In addition, each year a small percentage of perishable food stocks, such as potatoes, fruits, and vegetables were to be stored in cold cellars, and then distributed in early summer before the next harvest came in. This proved to be a very popular idea, because the months of May and June had historically been a period of shortage, and occasionally near famine.

Pleased and grateful beyond words for how his idea had blossomed, Father Carmichael still attended every meeting regardless of how tired he was, and in a faltering voice gave the benediction.

The Bligh's had totally rebuilt the old Grist Mill in town, and combined with their grain silos at Arden, they provided an ever increasing supply of available grain and flour year round. In keeping with John's increasing philanthropy, they set aside fifty acres in Arden on which to raise potatoes which went directly to help feed the poor; and the surplus into the various storehouses.

What was particularly satisfying to the Planning Council's Leadership, was that the local town's people and area tenants who had originally scoffed at the Emergency Plan idea, were now offering suggestions. At one of the meetings, a tenant suggested that when anyone purchased a new tool, the old tool should be donated to the Emergency tool supply. Colin then offered to fix any tools that needed repairs without charge. Within three years the storerooms were filled; and as additional supplies came in, storerooms in areas outside of Kilrush, such as Holy Jim's Canyon, were added.

At Saint Patrick's, Sister Agnes, who had taken a very bad fall and broken her hip two years before, had reluctantly turned many of the kitchen responsibilities over to Sister Lorraine, and was doing her best to teach her how to make a good Mulligan Stew, but with little success. Whenever it was served, Carmichael would later call Agnes aside, "no need to worry, it's you they'll be asking for at the Great Feast in Heaven."

Sean, under the teaching of and leadership of Reverend Swagart had become something of a traveling evangelist. The amazing testimony of his conversion had even been printed up in a small tract that was handed out wherever he traveled. The sub-title on the cover read, "Even the Town Dogs Knew He Was Saved." In all the towns around Kilrush, whenever he spoke he always drew a big crowd because many of the residents could recall first hand what his former life had been like; and the now famous fight with Colin.

Occasionally, even though they were members of Saint Patrick's, Colin and Mary would attend a service, and Sean would invite them to come up to the platform as he spoke.

Standing between them, his arms around their shoulders, he would introduce them as being included among his best friends. In one service, a man in the back of the church jumped up and asked him how stupid could you be, picking a fight with someone as huge as Colin. It was the perfect opportunity, and without missing a beat; Sean launched into a long list of all the stupid things alcohol made a person do, and how it had almost destroyed him.

One of the results of his ministry almost led to a personal disaster. Two very zealous Catholic members of Saint Patrick's made a plan to ambush and beat him up. Fortunately, Father Grant got wind of their plan, and called the men into the church study.

Grant asked the men what on earth were they were thinking about with such a terrible idea; assaulting a fellow believer.

"He's taking people away from our church," one said.

"He's teaching heresy," the other added.

"Heresy you say? So you're both theologians now?" Grant asked in a sarcastic tone.

"No, but tis plain as the nose on yer face that he's teachin people whats wrong."

"What exactly is he saying?" Grant asked.

"Well fer one thing, he never mentions the Blessed Mother, or the Saints; and another thing is they let everyone take communion themselves without a priest."

"And they even drink the wine!" the other man exclaimed.

Carmichael and Grant tried very hard to keep from showing their amusement.

"Does he teach his listeners about Jesus, that Jesus died for our sins?" Grant asked.

"Oh sure, he does that."

"Have you ever heard him tell people that they should leave the Catholic Church?" Carmichael asked.

The two men looked at each other, "I never heard 'em say that," one answered and the other agreed he hadn't either.

"Let me tell you a story from the bible," Grant said. "One day, the disciples came to Jesus because they wanted stop other men from preaching, just like you're doing. Do you know what Jesus told them?" He didn't wait for their answer, "Jesus said if they're not against us, they're for us, forbid them not. What you should remember, is that Sean is leading people to God, the same thing we are trying to do here at Saint Patrick's. Now here's the important part, because of Sean's unique story of his conversion, he's able to reach some people who would never listen to us."

Having previously assumed that Father's Carmichael and Grant would have supported their plan, they now scratched their heads. "But I thought the Catholic Church was the only true church," one said.

"Well it's true some Priests teach that," Carmichael replied. "But here at Saint Patrick's we believe that any church that brings people closer to God is a good church. Certainly, we like to have as many people come here as possible. But the fact is that there are some folks that would never become a member here. Would you agree with that?"

"Sure," they answered together.

"Good. Now you both know Lord and Lady Bligh, and Lawrence and Sally Bligh. Wonderful people, right?" Grant asked.

"Some of the best."

"But they're not Catholics and never will be. Should we deny them the chance to worship God, just because they want to attend a different church?"

"No, I guess not. Never thought of it that way," one of the men answered.

"What you should be thankful for is that God saved Sean, and both of you know very well what he was like before. Now he's preaching and bringing others into the Kingdom of Heaven. I suggest that you start praying for him."

The two men thanked Carmichael and Grant, and walked out of the church talking to each other about what they had just learned.

"I always thought that ifin somebody weren't fer ye, they were agin ye. What Father Grant said Jesus taught is jes the opposite."

"Maybe we should get one of those bibles we can read for ourselves, the ones printed in English," the other answered. "They sell 'em at the Methodist church."

"If some of our friends see us comin out of that church with a bible, we may be the ones getting a shellacking."

"Yer right. Let's talk ta Sean and have him get us one."

Two more years passed, and life for Bridgit and Grace would have been very hard had it not been for her exceptional reputation before the rape. The fact that she had lived an exemplary life, and had spent much of her time helping others, acted as bread upon the waters. Now, it was returning as blessings. Rather than whispering in corners, and treating her with disdain, the town's people treated both she and her daughter with respect and love.

At age seven, Grace had grown into a slender pretty girl with long dark pigtails, freckles, and dimples. Unlike her mother when she was a young girl, Grace was a tomboy. While other girls her age were playing with dolls, Grace was climbing trees with the boys. While the other girls were carefully brushing their hair, she would tie hers in pigtails as fast as possible to get it out of the way. While the other girls were beginning to learn how to sew and cook, she was at the stable learning how to care for a horse;

watching Colin repair a wheel; or at the hardware learning about how different tools worked. One day while Bridgit was talking to Kathleen, she said, "when I named her Grace, how little did I realize how much of it I'd need ta raise her."

"Do na fret, she's a special child she is," a neighbor told her. "When I was her age, t'was the things the boys were doing that always interested me; never cared a jot about dolls, cookin, and such. She'll come 'round."

"Blessed Mother Mary let it be so," Bridgit whispered looking heavenward.

Because it was just the two of them, Bridgit was able to spend a great deal of time with Grace, and taught her to read at an early age. In addition, she began teaching her the history of Ireland and England using books the Bligh's had loaned to her. One evening, after they had finished a lesson, Bridgit sensed the presence of her grandmother in the room. She and her grandmother had been very close, and she began to recall all the wonderful stories her grandmother had told her about the Little People. When she passed away shortly after Tom died, the loss was beyond losing her grandmother; her link to the past, and other worlds, magical worlds, was suddenly gone.

"Grace," she said as she was picking up the papers from their lesson, "have ye heard of the Little People?"

"One of the girls at school said she saw a Leprechaun once, but the teacher said there was no such thing; and that the stories about the Little People were just myths."

"Would ye like me ta tell ye some of the stories my grandmother told me about the little people when I was yer age?"

"Really?" Grace ran across the room to her and gave her a big hug. "Are they true? About the Little People I mean?"

"No, I do not think so, but there are a lot of things we canna see but still believe. We canna see Jesus; or Mary; or the Saints; but we still believe in them."

That night, Bridgit began telling her about her Grandmother; and about the Fairies, the tiny supernatural spirits which possessed special beauty, grace, and a magical glow about them, and that they had wings and could fly. "Some people say that they can create illusions; sometimes they become frightening; and at other times alluring. My grandmother said that the King of the Fairies is called Oberon, and his wife's name is Titania. Some people believe that they live underground in special cities. My grandmother told me that once when she was out walking, she saw them in a forest, dancing around a ring of mushrooms under an ancient tree."

"What did they look like? Did they see yer Grandmother?" Grace asked in excitement.

"She said they were very tiny, about the size of a finger, and had human like bodies with wings like glass ye could see through. She said they danced and flew 'around and 'round and the air sparkled. When one of them flew close to her and seen her, they all vanished - poof! - in the blink of an eye."

"Wouldn't it be wonderful ta see 'em?" Grace asked as she spread her arms and pretended to fly around the room.

"Yer great grandmother seen lots of things, most other people never see;" she said in a soft voice remembering how much she missed her grandmother.

She started to tell her that her grandmother had been born with a veil over her face, a sign that she would be able to see spirits, and the future, but changed her mind. Her grandmother had been ostracized and suffered because of being able to see and know things others did not. A century before she might have been branded as a witch and burned at the stake; and even today such things still frightened some people. People were uncomfortable being around someone who might know something about them they did not know themselves. She decided that Grace did not need to hear that about her grandmother, maybe when she was older she would tell her.

"Another time, my grandmother said she was walking near the old stone bridge, the one by O'Flynn creek, and she heard this very faint tapping sound." Bridgit tapped with a pencil on the arm of her rocking chair, tap, tap, tap.

"She stopped and listened carefully; the sound was coming from under the bridge. She quietly climbed down the bank and there under the bridge, was a Leprechaun making a shoe."

"A shoe?" Grace exclaimed.

"Yes, Leprechauns are cobblers, and most often when ye sees 'em, they're workin on a shoe. She told me that this one was about this high," she indicated with her hand, "and he was wearing a red square cut coat laced with gold a waistcoat; buckled shoes; and had a cocked hat on his head. He looked up and saw Grandmother and they stared at each other for along time. She wanted to be able to follow him when he left and find the pot of gold he had buried – Leprechauns are very rich ye know."

By this time, Grace was sitting at her feet enthralled at these stories she had never heard before, and about her great grandmother. "Did she find the pot of gold?"

"No, because the Leprechaun tricked her. As long as ye watch them, they canna escape. So they try an trick ye inta lookin somewhere else. She said that as she was watchin 'em, a trout jumped in the creek, and when she looked ta see it, the Leprechaun vanished. The Leprechaun made the trout jump ta trick her, they're very clever and cunning."

"If I ever see one, he will na trick me," Grace exclaimed. "I'll get the pot of gold for ye mother."

In the weeks and months that followed; Bridgit continued to tell Grace many more stories of Fairies; Trolls; Sprites, and the Fairy Rings of mushrooms. She also told her the stories of the Tuatha De' Danann, the peoples of the goddess Danu. The tales of the ancient ones who inhabited

Ireland centuries before the Irish people came. She told her of the great battle of Magh Tuiredh, when King Nuada, who lost one of his arms in the battle, defeated the Fir Bolg; and how in the second battle, King Nuada was killed by the poisonous eye of Balor, King of Fomorian."

"So then Balor became the King?" Grace asked, mesmerized by these tales and stories she never heard in school.

"Only for a little while, and then Lug killed Balor with a spear."

"Did she tell ye other stories about things she seen?" Grace asked.

"She seen lots of things, but I'll tell you about them some other time."

One afternoon several weeks later, Grace came running home from school and up to Bridgit who was working in the yard. "Mommy, I saw somethin strange on my way home today."

"What was that Sweetheart?" Bridgit asked.

"It was a figure like a man dressed in black in a potato field."

Bridgit stopped hoeing, disturbed by what she had just heard. "It was probably jes a priest walkin across the field, or maybe farmer."

"No, it weren't a man. It floated above the ground, and was going back and forth across the field. My friend Jenny was with me, but she didna see it. What was it, Mommy?"

"Oh, I'm sure it was nothin, maybe a bunch of small birds, ye know how they fly in bunches sometimes." She tried to dismiss it, but she felt a sudden chill and pulled her shawl up around her shoulders. "Honey, will ye stay here and peal some taters fer supper. I need ta go and see Aunt Kathleen fer a spell."

Kathleen was standing in the front yard when she saw Bridgit walking down the road toward her, and raised her arm and waved. "What brings ye here/" she called as she got closer.

"Need ta talk ta ye about Grace; she seen somethin."

She looked at Bridgit and smiled. "I knew ye would be comin some day, let's walk a spell." They headed out across a field.

"Sometimes when we would be talking," Bridgit began, "ye would tell me that Grace was 'a special child,' what did ye mean by that?"

Kathleen knew how sensitive Bridgit had been about her grandmother's 'gift,' as they called it. Because of that she had purposely said nothing to her about Grace's birth. Now it was time to tell her. "Grace was born with a veil."

Bridgit stopped dead in her tracks and looked at her. "But ye never said nothin ta me, and Sally never said nothin."

"Sally didn't know. When Grace was born, I immediately pulled it away. I don't think Sally seen it, an ifin she did, she had never seen a birthin before, so she wouldn't know what is was. When did ye suspect something?"

"Today, when Grace came home from school. I knew that's she's got the gift."

"You said she saw somethin?"

"Aye, a black spirit floatin over the potato fields."

"Mary Mother of God preserve us!" Kathleen cried out. "What did ye tell her?"

"I told her she was jes imagin, that it was a flock of birds."

"Did she believe ye?"

"I'm not sure, she didna say anythin more."

"It's started then. Soon she will start seein other things. What are ye gonna do?"

"Tell her the truth. I've already told her about my grandmother seein things, but never about the gift."

"She needs ta know." They looked at each other, and started walking back toward the house. "Seein the black spirit over the fields; tis a bad sign it is. We need ta tell Father Carmichael and Grant. Carmichael will understand, do ye think Grant will?"

"I do na know, him bein English an all. Will ye come with me tomarra afternoon ta the church?" Bridgit asked. "I'll bring Grace with me."

"I'll come with ye." They walked in silence for a few moments and then Kathleen asked, "How long do ye think we have? – about the black spirit I mean - they've already had some crop failures up north."

"Not too long I'm fearin. Tonight, I'm gonna ask Grace if she's seen anythin else."

"Ye have ta tell her 'bout the gift, she needs ta know."

"Aye, that she does, but I'm gonna tell her not ta say anythin ta anyone else." She looked at Kathleen, "we need ta keep this a secret as long as we can."

The next afternoon, after telling Carmichael and Grant about Grace's gift, Carmichael walked to the window and clasp his hands. "It's the thing I feared most," he said, "there's going to be a crop failure here."

"Do you really believe that?" Grant asked. "Grace imagines seeing a black figure floating over a field, and somehow that portends disaster. I cannot believe it."

"Father Grant, you're in Ireland, a land steeped in superstition; but there's a good side to it. The people here are more likely to believe in the strange and unusual. I met Bridgit's grandmother over fifty years ago. In fact when I heard about her gift and what she was telling people, I called her in to see me and told her to stop. I said that what she was doing was not from God, and I doubted she could really see the future. After all, I was a Priest, I had studied for years at the Seminary; why would God choose her, someone without any religious education, and give her such a gift."

"She smiled at me, and I'll never forget what she said. She told me the scriptures tell us that sometimes God uses the nobodies ta confound the wise? God once used a Prophet's mule ta tell 'em he was wrong? Why did God pick John the Baptist - a nobody - to deliver his message, when the Temple was full of Priests? And why would he pick Rahab, a harlot to help the spies in Jerico? Then she took hold of my hand, 'Father Carmichael, she said, yer a good man, but do na box God in. He will choose whoever he pleases, whenever he pleases.'

"I didn't want to admit it but she was right; and at that moment I began to gain a better understanding of God. We often say, 'God works in mysterious ways,' but do we really believe it?"

"Alright, that much I will agree with," Grant said. "But as to predicting the future, or knowing things about people, how can you believe that?"

Carmichael picked up a bible and handed it to Grant. "Open it up to any of the Prophets, go ahead. Now read a passage."

Grant opened the book of Isaiah and read a prophesy of the future, then he turned to another, and another. "Again I must agree, but these men were true prophets."

"Did the people they talked to and prophesied to believe them?" he didn't wait for an answer, "no they did not, in fact many times they killed the prophets." He walked toward the window and looked at the cemetery.

Finally he turned toward Bridgit, "There's more to this story. Your grandmother then began telling me personal things about my own life that no one knew, some of my innermost thoughts: for example, why I never accepted the position of a Bishop. Only Rome knew what I had written in my letter to the Pope."

"It was then I knew that your grandmother had the gift, or whatever you want to call it. God gave it to her so that she could help others." He walked over to Bridgit and took hold of her hand, "I never told you this before, but your grandmother and I spent many afternoons together, and she would tell me things, things that later came to pass." He paused, his mind going back to a different time. "One day following Mass, she told me I should go and see Carl Cunningham, that his soul was not right with God, and he would not be with us much longer."

"I remember Carl," Kathleen said. "He was killed working on his farm."

"Yes," Carmichael sighed. "Carl was a healthy young man, plenty of time I thought. I was busy, and so I put-off going to visit him. A week later he was killed when a large bolder rolled over on him. I've never forgiven myself for that."

Bridgit and Kathleen listened to all this in amazement. The fact that Father Carmichael and her grandmother had been close friends and that he listened to her, was a total surprise.

"Bridgit, there is one other thing I must tell you. The day you were baptized, your grandmother told me that you would have a daughter who would help save her people. I naturally assumed that one day you would marry and have this daughter. When Tom was killed and you vowed never to marry, I thought that in time you would change your mind; but the years passed and you never did. Eventually, I began to believe that her prophesy would never come to pass; and then Grace was born."

"His prophecies are true and just," Grant added.

"But she was born…" Kathleen's voice trailed off.

Carmichael finished the sentence, "Out of wedlock?... Yes, but so was Solomon, and God chose him to become King of Israel." He paused to let that sink in. "Now to the matter at hand: Grace has seen something supernatural, perhaps a warning for us. The question is; are we willing to believe what she saw, and what do we do about it?"

Grant, ever the practical man, suggested that they should wait for a second sign. Besides he pointed out, the potato crops were ready for harvesting. Therefore, if what Grace saw was a warning, it must be for a future time: but when?

They all agreed that what he said was true, and decided to wait until something else happened to confirm the warning, if that is what it was. In the meanwhile, they also agreed that Grace should not be told about her gift just yet; but encouraged to tell her mother whenever she sees something unusual, or strange. "However, they added, "be careful not to say anything that might alarm her; or cause her to feel that she is different from the other girls her age. We don't want to do something that might cause her to withdraw from her friends." There was one point on which they were all very emphatic; under no circumstances should anyone else be told about Grace's gift.

After Bridgit and Kathleen left the study, Grant looked at Carmichael and smiled; "another secret."

Thirty miles off Loop Head, the fishing schooner Gideon, her hold filled with herring, set her course due East for Kilrush. It was the beginning of July when the Irish people, who lived on potatoes most of the year; happily celebrated their harvest of new potatoes with fresh herring.

At the ship's wheel was Peter, now a Second Mate. After several years of crewing and learning his new profession on boats out of London, he signed on with the Gideon which put into Kilrush several times a year. This gave him the opportunity to quietly, and without anyone's knowledge, periodically check on Bridgit and Grace and make certain they had everything they needed. Twice a year, a package would arrive at Saint Patrick's addressed to Bridgit, and

Father Grant would deliver it to her cottage. Each time, she would pretend it came from her Aunt, and Father Grant would go along with the pretence. While Bridgit had her suspicions when the first package arrived many years before, after the second package came six months later, she was certain it was from Father Timothy. Thus their little game continued; Carmichael and Grant strongly suspected that it was from Timothy but said nothing to Bridgit. She was certain it was from Timothy, but said nothing to them.

What none of them knew, was that he had changed his name to Peter and became a fisherman. His appearance had changed dramatically. His hair was now long, pulled back and tied behind his head in a pony tail. A thin scar crossed his right cheek; evidence of when he was working forward and a sudden gust of wind brought the jib sweeping sharply across the deck and the clew struck him in the face. His face and hands, were now weathered from constant exposure to the sun, wind, salt water, and the sea air. For the past four years, he had become a regular although infrequent visitor to Kilrush and freely walked about the town, passing people on the street he had known years before without being recognized.

When he was in port and the weather was nice, he would sit on a large rock on a hill near Bridgit's cottage, and watch them working in the yard, or Grace playing with her friends. At other times he would sit on a bench in front of the hardware store, and watch them as they went shopping, or walking on their way to church. Once, when he was sitting on the bench in front of the dry-goods store, Bridgit and Grace came walking out of the store. Grace, not watching where she was going ran right into him, tripped, and fell. He reached down took her hand and helped her to her feet. Both she and her mother apologized, and he mumbled not to mind, it was an accident. For a split second, his eyes and Bridgit's met, and then he turned his head away.

As they left and walked down the street, Grace said, "That man smelled really fishy."

"That's because he's a fisherman, he works on one of the fishing boats we see down at the dock sometimes."

"Do all fishermen smell like that?"

"I suppose so," she answered absent mindedly as she felt a strange stirring in her memory. It was his eyes; she whispered to herself, there was something familiar about his eyes. She turned around to look again, but Peter was walking across the street in the opposite direction. What if it was Father Timothy? He had done a terrible thing to her, and yet without that incident, she would be alone and not have her wonderful daughter Grace. That he truly cared, was evident from all the packages and money he had sent to them over the years. Believing that she would never see him again; she had never really thought about how she would feel and react if they ever met again, or what she would say to Grace. Perhaps it was time that she did.

For Peter, it had been a totally unexpected and wonderful experience. For a few brief seconds he had actually held his daughter's hand; and heard both her and Bridgit's voices as they spoke to him. He determined that somehow he must meet them and reveal his new identity. What he needed was the right opportunity; and a reason, or excuse. He glanced back just in time to see them turn a corner and disappear. He shook his head as he talked to himself; he needed more than just a good reason; he needed courage.

The years had passed rather quietly in Holy Jim's Canyon. After the very real scare of the dam failing several years before, the local residents had made a determined effort to maintain the dam and the land around it. Stone walls had been constructed to keep livestock away, and a regular watch had been set up to check the dam at least once a week, and daily during heavy rains. Several new cottages had been built by an anonymous benefactor for families which had been evicted from various estates; and had moved to the Canyon to be closer to their relatives. A special pride for their little community developed among the residents, and it was evident in the number of flower gardens that were appearing around the cottages.

Miraculously, the identity of Jim continued to remain a secret, due in large part to his Manager who went to remarkable lengths to avoid accidentally disclosing his real name. Over the years, Jim, Lawrence, and Sally had become very close friends. To avoid undue suspicion, they decided that it would not be a good idea for Lawrence and Sally to regularly visit Jim at his cabin. Instead, Jim would occasionally meet them in town where he was not well known. Because he was very much involved in the Emergency Plan, but anonymously, he would go to Arden for secret meetings with the Bligh's, Carmichael, and Grant. He was a bona fide eccentric who preferred that the general public and his neighbors view him as a poor, semi-recluse, with a penchant for foul language. In reality, he delighted in secretly giving things to people in need, and had personally funded the storeroom that had been setup at the Canyon, as well as building the cottages, making certain however, that none of the residents knew he did it.

To everyone's great relief, the rest of the year passed without major incident or further supernatural signs. When Christmas came, the weather was mild; the churches had their pageants; gifts were exchanged; and most everyone agreed that despite a few minor problems, it had been a good year in Kilrush.

Chapter 27

Irish hopes ran high in the spring of 1845, and it was generally believed that there would be a bountiful potato crop that year. In London however, Parliament was not so sure about the future of potato crops in Ireland or England. Accordingly, it was their plan to begin replacing the historic dependence on potatoes, by introducing Indian corn from America which, up to that time, was generally unknown as a food in Britain. As a first step, they planned legislation to repeal the Corn Laws which had restricted the importation of foreign grown corn. The major difficulty in effecting their plan however, was that unlike English laborers, workers in Ireland were seldom paid cash wages. Consequently even if the Irish wished to buy the new corn, they had no money to purchase it. In an effort to redress this unique problem in Ireland; the British government began a system of public works in Ireland, primarily road building projects, to provide the workers with cash money.

Government work programs such as roads and bridges; took lengthy periods of time to develop and implement, and time was not on their side. In addition, there were major difficulties in deciding where to build public roads in Ireland. Most of the existing roads were old farm lanes crossing private property. Consequently, the government saw little advantage in spending taxpayer dollars to improve private land holdings.

The potential Irish labor force proved to be an even greater difficulty. Men, who for generations had worked on farms, or their own land, were reluctant to leave them and work on road projects, especially if they were not close to their homes and family. Furthermore, having always raised their own food and being independent, the concept of receiving wages and buying food was foreign to them; and to some extent they believed it would make them dependent upon the hated English. Given the two choices, most opted to stay on their small patch of land and grow potatoes, and a few turnips.

That spring the planting went well, and soon the fields were green with the promise of a good year. Throughout May and June the plants flourished, and the first new potatoes were harvested in time for the early July herring festivities. A week later however, during a routine morning field inspection Neil noticed a brown spot on the leaves of some of the potato plants along the edge of the field. He quickly dismounted and began carefully going through the rows of plants. Within minutes, he knew from experience that they were in trouble; the Blight had struck.

He raced back to the house and alerted the Bligh's, and then began sending the tenant farmers into the infected fields to harvest as much as they could. By tomorrow, he knew that the leaves of the plants would be almost covered with spots, turn black, and would wilt, leaving just a green stalk. The following day the stalk would break off. Within 24 to 48 hours there would be nothing left to salvage. The potatoes would have shriveled to the size of a nut and be just as hard.

For the rest of the day, Neil, Lawrence, and John checked every field in Arden. Late that afternoon, they met and assessed the damage: approximately fifty percent of the fields had been infected by the blight. For reasons beyond their, or anyone's comprehension; one field would be infected while the adjoining field might remain untouched.

"Neil," Lawrence asked, "do you think other parts of the County have a similar pattern of infection?"

"Hard to say. No one knows what causes it, why it hits one field and not the next, or why we can go for years without the blight, and then suddenly it appears."

While Lawrence had read and heard about the Blight for years, this was his first actual in the field experience, "and there's never any warning signs?"

"None. You'd expect to be able to see something in advance, but you don't. One day everything is fine, and the next a field totally infected; total destruction almost overnight. I read a report a while back that said there was a new Blight that came from America, but I don't know if it's true. Anyway, we've had this problem for a couple of hundred years, and no one's figured out a way to predict it or prevent it."

"Well, what we need now is to find out how widespread this is," John said. "Lawrence, first thing in the morning, ride into town and see what you can find out there. Neil, go and check with some of our neighbors. I'll go up and see Jim; find out how the Canyon area is. We can all meet back here tomorrow evening. We need to know what were up against. Neil, do you think it will spread to the other fields?"

"It's anybody's guess. The next week or two will tell us."

In the next few days as the reports came in from outlying areas, it was apparent that this was a very widespread crop failure, effecting about half the summer crop. Unknown to the residents around Kilrush, the blight had spread throughout much of Ireland, and parts of England. Further away, France, Belgium, Holland, and even Italy also had major potato crop failures. Consequently, potatoes quickly became scarce driving up prices and shipping costs. To exacerbate the food shortage problem, crops which might otherwise have been sent to Ireland, were shipped to the Continent where they commanded better prices. As the news of the extent of disaster spread like a wildfire; there was a grave and growing concern with the realization that not only families; but entire communities, and even counties might be facing a potential famine. Unfortunately, the full extent of the potential disaster would not be known until the late harvest in August. If that crop also failed, it would be a major crisis.

In Kilrush, a meeting of the Emergency Planning Group was hastily convened at Saint Patrick's. While their planning and storerooms could help in the short run - until the late harvest in August came in - the loss of that crop would empty the storehouses within a few weeks unless drastic measures were quickly instituted. The primary goal now was to supplement the loss of half the summer crop. Accordingly a strict rationing system was put in place. Whereas the typical adult ate six to nine pounds of potatoes per day, the ration was limited to four pounds for each adult; and three pounds for children under the age of twelve. In addition to the potatoes, a measure of ground grain was distributed for each person together with instruction on how to prepare it.

In this regard, Kilrush was better prepared to deal with the crisis because the Bligh's stored a major portion of their grain at Arden, and had their own mill in town. Other towns and counties faired less well because the English landowners shipped their grain to England. Despite this advantage, the Emergency Planning Group calculated that in the event the August crop failed, their supplies would help prevent full fledged starvation, but there would still be prolonged hunger. Without Carmichael's spiritual warning however, the Emergency Plan would not have been created, and serious widespread starvation and possibly death would have been upon them within four to five months.

To further bolster the Plan, it was decided to take an inventory of all the local livestock, and try to determine how the food supply could be augmented with meat. It was pointed out that this idea carried its own risks, because the great majority of the people were not accustomed to regularly eating meat. Furthermore, with no means of refrigeration it would be impossible to keep the meat for more than two or three days. The people in town could pick it up on a daily basis, but for those in the outlying areas it would spoil before they could get it back to their homes. Salting and pickling was a possibility, but they lacked an adequate supply of salt, and barrels in which to store the meat.

One of the farmers pointed out that many, if not most, of the tenants kept a few pigs and a cow on their property, which were fed with cast-off inferior potatoes. With the crop gone, it was only a matter of time before the pigs and cattle would have to be slaughtered, or else they would die of starvation. Again, the lack of refrigeration became the curse.

"Why don't we build a large smokehouse in town and make it available to anyone that wants to use it. The smoked meat will keep for months."

Someone else then suggested that they could also smoke fish.

By the end of the meeting there had been several good ideas which could immediately be acted upon, and the general mood was optimistic, but guarded. As of today, it appeared from the reports that roughly half the potato crop was lost. If the losses increased....well, no one wanted to think about that now. The two major jobs now were to get the word out to everyone regarding the rationing plan; and start work on the other ideas that had been adopted. Lawrence agreed to meet with several of the local businessmen and contractors and begin building the smokehouse. A fishmonger said he would get word to the local owners of fishing boats about bringing their catch to Kilrush for smoking. It was past nine o'clock in the evening when the last few people left the church and headed home. Tomorrow morning, all the many years and months of planning would be set in motion.   Father Carmichael waved them all goodbye, content in the knowledge that many lives would be saved.

"Thank you Father," he said as he looked up into a sky filled with stars, "thank you for the warning, and now we pray that thy provisions will be sufficient."

A week later, thirty miles off Loop Head, the fishing schooner Gideon was hailed by another fishing boat just out of Kilrush. "Ahoy", the call came across the water, "we need ta come along side."

The Gideon headed into the wind and slowed until she just had steerage way as the other boat came within about thirty feet.   The Gideon's Owner's given name was Captain, a name given him by his father against his mother's objections. As he grew older, he shortened it to Cap to avoid confusion at sea. As the other boat edged closer, he went to the starboard rail and called over, "Do ye need help?"

"Nay Cap, we jes come out from Kilrush. Have ye heard about the crop failure?"

As his words 'crop failure' came across the waves, every man within earshot went to the rail. "We've been on the banks for over a week, and know nothing about it," Cap called back. "How bad is it?"

"Very bad, very bad.   When we left early this morning, they figured they'd lost about half the crop. We jes came out here searchin for other boats ta pass the word.   The town's building a smoke house and want us ta bring in whatever we catch." He waved farewell, turned his boat and fell off into the wind.

"We've about half a load," Cap said turning to Peter. "I'm thinking maybe we should make a run to Kilrush and find out what the situation is first hand." Turning to the helmsman he called out, "fall-off ta Starboard and set a course for Kilrush."

"Aye, aye," came the reply. The ship which had been barely moving and gently riding the swells, swung to starboard and quickly heeled as the sails filled with wind. Peter's legs and body automatically reacted to the sloping deck as he watched the crew trim the sails.

"I've got a cousin that lives near Kilrush," one of the men said to Peter, "he has a wife and six kids."

"Does he farm his own land?" Peter asked.

"No. He rents a small patch, maybe an acre. If the blight hit 'em, they'll have nothing; no food, or money for rent. It's why I left farmin years ago; not knowin from one year ta the next what's gonna happen. I miss my wife and family, but I've always been able ta make enough money ta feed 'em and pay the rent by fishin."

They both looked east toward the empty horizon. At the speed they were making, they would begin to see the land in a little over an hour. First, they would see just a very thin dark strip on the horizon that would appear as the ship rose on a swell, and then disappear as it slipped into the trough. Mile by mile the dark strip would grow larger, and larger. In time, they would be able to make out distinct features such as the lighthouse at Loop Head, which marked the north shore of the mouth of the Shannon River. If the wind held, they should be docking in about six hours.

Two hours later, they could see the sails of other fishing boats, two of which were heading for the river, evidence that news of the disaster had spread quickly among the boats. Many of the men on the other boats lived in and around the Kilrush area, what were they thinking about? How would this news affect the boat crews? For some of the men, just being away from their families for weeks at a time was difficult enough. It would become intolerable being at sea for weeks at a time, knowing your family might be without food and struggling to survive.

Peter leaned against the rail and began thinking of how this terrible news would change everyone and everything in Kilrush. Although he had heard fragments of talk about an Emergency Plan, it had been started after he had left Kilrush, so he did not know either the scope of the Plan, or even if it was intended to deal with a crop failure. He was certain that Fathers Carmichael and Grant would be working feverishly to helping whatever way they could. Had he made a mistake in walking away from the Priesthood?

His thoughts were interrupted by a voice at his side. "Thinking of Bridgit and Grace?" Cap asked.

He was stunned by the question. How did Cap know about them? Who else knew and how much did they know?

"Ah Peter; did you think we didn't know what you were doing when we pulled into Kilrush? Mike was the first one to see you climb the hill and watch the little cottage; that was two years ago. After that, we all kind of watched you and wondered. Another time, one of the other lads saw you dropping off a package." Cap put some tobacco in his pipe and lit it, drew on it a couple of times and continued. "None of our business mind you; just curiosity I guess you'd call it. So who is she?"

"The woman I love and wanted to marry, but she would not have me."

"And the girl?"

Peter looked down at the frothy tops of the waves slipping along side the hull; bringing him ever closer to Kilrush and whatever fate held in store for him. "My daughter," he said without looking up.

Cap put his hand on Peter's shoulder, "Pretty girl; does she know?"

"I'm not sure, but I don't think so." Turning to face Cap, he felt a sudden rush of relief, of freedom to talk about what had been pent-up in his heart and soul for so many years. "I don't look like I did seven years ago; even Bridgit wouldn't recognize me now. Over the years, I've tried to keep watch over them and help them, secretly of course. That's why I send a package every six months or so; to make sure they have money and some other things to make life more enjoyable."

"Does she, Bridgit that is, know it's from you?"

"No, I never put my name on it, or include anything that would identify me."

"Rather strange I think, doing something like that. I've a feeling there's a lot more to this story than you're telling me; but that's ok, I'm sure you've got your reasons." He puffed on his pipe, and then pointed the stem at the tiny white point on shore, "there's the light house, bring her a couple of points south. And Peter, they'll never be a better time than now to go to them. For all you know, Bridgit has known all along who her mysterious benefactor is." He started to walk away and turned to look back, "one last thing, you're a good man Peter, or whatever your real name is; if you ever need my help, just ask."

Cap and every man in the crew liked Peter, but they all knew that he had something else in his background; something that had nothing to do with boats, the sea, or fishing.

While he had worked very hard at becoming a skilled seaman and fisherman over the past seven years, most of the men around him had been fishing since they were boys of ten or twelve. Several of the men, including Cap, had followed their fathers, who had followed their fathers, to the sea. Thus while he was good at what he did, every now and then a situation would arise that only long experience knew how to handle. He would have liked to stay by the rail and spent his time thinking about how he would approach Bridgit, but now there were too many things to do, especially with other boats heading for Kilrush. Fortunately, they had been one of the first boats to get the news, and the Gideon was a fast boat. With good sailing and a bit of luck, they would be able to tie up to the dock and unload, and not have to anchor in the river and wait their turn.

"Mike," he called pointing to the boat off their starboard side, "tighten the down-haul and the jib sheets, we don't want the Galilee beating us to the dock, do we?"

"No Sir," he called back, a big smile on his face.

"Ok boys," Peter called, "we've got bad news waiting for us, so let's show the Galilee our stern and have some fun now."

The Captain of the Galilee seeing the Gideon preparing to race, called to his crew, "beat 'em ta the dock and I'll buy ye a couple of pints; look lively now!" Looking across the waves, he waved at the Gideon: the race was on.

For the most part, fishing was a solitary profession. Days and weeks, spent working the banks alone with only your crew members to talk to. Occasionally, if the fishing was exceptional, several boats might be fishing within a quarter of a mile of each other, but even then it was almost impossible to converse with the other boat. One of the few times they could forget the fishing, was a day like today when they had a chance to race another boat to port. When that happened, every man stopped whatever he was doing and within moments, ordinary fisherman transformed themselves into a racing crew.

"Looks to me Peter," Cap said, "she's riding high; must be carrying a light load."

"Aye, that may be; but we're the better boat," Peter said smiling.

Turning to the helmsman Cap told him to come five degrees to starboard. "I want to get closer to him. We're up-wind and have the steady wind, if we can disturb the air before it reaches them, I'll give us an advantage."

Peter laughed, "I read about that in one of your books on seamanship."

"So you've been reading them?"

"Yes Sir. I figured sooner or later, I might get a chance to use some of what I've learned."

The Captain of the Galilee watched as the Gideon slightly altered course and began moving closer to them attempting to cut off their wind. To prevent that, he could fall off slightly to starboard, but he knew the Gideon would continue to press him; eventually it would put him too close to the south shore of the rivers entrance. His other options were to fall astern of the Gideon then cut to the north and get upwind of her; or crowd on more canvas and try and pull ahead of the Gideon; both choices carried risks. If he chose the latter, there was less than a fifty-fifty chance he could get ahead of the Gideon before he ran into the shallow water of south shore. If he chose to drop behind and swing around her, would he be able to make up the lost distance?

"Ease the sheets Lads," he called out. This would spill the wind from the sails slowing the boat. As the Galilee started to drop back, he ordered the helmsman to get ready to bring her to port on his command; at the same time he told the crew to get ready to haul in the sheets as soon as they could clear the stern of the Gideon. The crew watched with anticipation as their rival pulled ahead. "Another minute....wait....wait," the Captain called as he watched the distance open. "Now!" he yelled, and the crew hauled in on the sheets bringing the sails amid ships. Immediately, the ship responded and heeled to starboard as her sails filled with wind; at that instant the Captain signaled the helmsman who spun the wheel, swinging the ship to port.

On the Gideon, Cap, Peter and the crew watched as the Galilee first slowed and fell behind, then cut across their stern. Cap chuckled, "Jimmy's no fool," he said referring to the Galilee's Captain. "He knew he would run out of sea room when we got to the entrance. He's gonna try and do to us what I tried to do to him, get upwind. I've raced Jimmy many times, sometimes he's won, other times I have. This time I'm gonna stand back and watch the fun," he drew a puff on his pipe, "it's your show Peter."

Peter looked at Cap and smiled, "Thank you Sir," he said surprised and pleased that he was given command for the race. This was going to be a real test of his ability, and he had no intension of losing. His mind raced quickly as he considered what to do next. Walking back and standing next to the man at the wheel. "Bring her to port, and then parallel her heading," he said pointing at the Galilee. "We don't want to let her get a chance to up-wind us."

At this point, they were approximately six miles off the entrance to the river which is about eight miles wide. The Captain of the Galilee, who had intended to cut around the stern of the Gideon and then turn to starboard and make a run past her on the windward side, was now blocked by Peter's move. He knew that as they entered the river, two things would happen: first they would run into the heavy swells as the out going tide met the easterly moving ocean swells. Secondly, they would be sailing into the wind which was now coming down the river.

Ordinarily, ships entered the river on the incoming tide which avoided the heavy swells, and also gave them the advantage of sailing with the current; but this was not an ordinary day. Entering against the tide and wind would require that the ships would have to alter course [tack] at least twice. His hope was that by timing his course changes correctly, he could out-maneuver and slip past the Gideon. For the moment he was content to let the Gideon stay ahead off his starboard bow. He smiled to himself, knowing that he had an ace up his sleeve.

Peter looked back and waved to Jimmy who waved back. His timing had been perfect and Cap patted his shoulder, "good move, I don't think Jimmy suspected that; but you've not won yet."

Both ships were now on a north by east heading which would bring them through the river's mouth and moving closer to the north shore of the river. The steady north-easterly wind coming off the open sea would soon be blocked by the land, and they would be buffeted by the wind coming down the river. Close to shore, they could encounter 'cat's paws', strong gusts of wind that dropped off the hills to the river without warning and swirled around causing havoc with sailing vessels. Peter's challenge, was to sail just close enough to the north shore to avoid potential cat's paws before changing to a south by east course, but still continue to block the Galilee.

About three miles ahead, he noticed that there was a large flotilla of fishing boats, scattered across the middle of the river. These were the small boats of local fisherman of varying size, with one to three men and women using hand lines to catch whatever they could. If he changed course now, he could safely pass them on the west, forcing the Galilee to follow him. "Come to starboard," he called to the helmsman. "Keep as close as you can to the small boats, we don't want to leave room for the Galilee to slip between us and them."

His plan would have worked, but for the unexpected. When he looked back, he could see that the Galilee did not change course and follow him. Jimmy, the Captain of the Galilee was going to try and make a run between the north shore and the fishing boats. In addition, Peter could see that he was hoisting gaff topsails, hoping to catch the wind coming over the hills. If he succeeded, his daring move would place him far ahead of the Gideon. Peter looked up at the bare spars of the Gideon in the false hope of seeing what he knew was not there, their gaff topsails. Having earlier decided that this short fishing trip to the local fishing grounds would be a good chance to mend them, they had left them with the sail maker in town. Peter looked over at Cap.

"Jimmy's a fine seaman," Cap said. "He's taking a gamble that he can get past the small boats before he has to change course. If he makes it, he'll win."

Peter watched the sails of the Galilee fill as she worked her way upriver between the shore and the small boats. For the moment, Jimmy's plan was working; but Peter knew that before long, the Galilee would be heading directly into the wind. At that point, Jimmy would be forced to turn south and head right into the cluster of boats. Peter was not the only one watching the Galilee, there were a hundred pairs of eyes on the small boats watching the Galilee sail this narrow channel between them and the shore, and wondering if she was suddenly going to turn into them. If she did, any small boat in her way would be swamped, or possibly cut in pieces.

Jimmy looked ahead, about a half mile more and he would be clear of the last of the small boats, not any to soon as he was losing the wind and the Galilee was quickly losing speed. All he needed was another five minutes, minutes which seemed to drag on-and-on. He looked up as the sails began to luff. The crew was working feverously, alternately forcing the main boom from port to starboard and then back again, hoping to catch every bit of wind they could and keep the ship moving. Suddenly without any warning, there was a tremendous cracking sound as a cat's paw caught the main gaff topsail, shattering the main mast just above the gaff.

In an instant, the men directly below were running for their lives as hundreds of pounds of heavy timber, blocks, shackles, tackle, and rope came hurtling down toward the deck. The small boats closest to the Galilee instinctively knew what would happen next; and began frantically hoisting their little sails, and pulling hard on their oars to get out of her way as she slowing swung south toward them. As her bow came around, the sails which had been slack, caught the steady wind coming down river and quickly filled, driving the Galilee into the cluster of boats. On board the Galilee, the crew didn't need any orders as to what to do next, and immediately released the sheets letting the wind spill from the sails. With the top section of the main mast gone, part of the support for the forward mast was lost. This was no longer a race, it was making every effort to avoid losing the forward mast; crushing or swamping the small boats; and drowning the people in them.

On board the Gideon, Peter, Cap, and the crew watched as the Galilee very slowly made her way through the small boats, which were scattering to make room for her. Peter, having already passed to the south of boats, gave the command to bring the Gideon to port and set a course to the east in order to meet the Galilee. Fifteen minutes later as they pulled up along side, they saw that the crew aboard the Galilee was still busy cutting away the tangle of lines, blocks, and the broken mast.

"What can we do to help?" Cap called to his friend Jimmy.

"We're ok, nobody hurt, jes my pride," he called back. "Lost a bit of tackle," he said looking up. "For a minute or two, I thought we might lose the forward mast, so far so good," he said knocking his fist on the rail, "but we'll have ta be careful taking her in.

"Thought you were going to make it," Peter said. "It was a bold move, but the luck wasn't with you today."

"No it weren't," Jimmy said. "Still, it was a lot of fun while it lasted, aye?"

"Sure was, we'll have to do it again," Peter called. "We'll follow you in. When we get to Kilrush, suggest you go head and pull into the dock for repairs. We'll anchor out."

"I've another idea," Jimmy called back. Looks like you've got a good load of fish, we don't have many.

Besides, we've got ta go slowly. You scoot on ahead. We'll anchor until you off-load, and then switch."

"It's a deal. If you don't need our help now, we'll run in ahead of you."

"Be off with ye then, we've handled far worse than this," Jimmy replied.

"Indeed he has," Cap told Peter. "He was dismasted once off Loop Head in a terrible storm. While the crew was working to cut away the rigging, a couple of the sheets ran under the boat and fouled the rudder and they lost control. Jimmy took a knife and swam under to free it, but while he was doing that, the boat broached. A couple of huge waves washed over the boat, and took two members of the crew with them. You know Sean don't you? His father was one of them. For a while it looked like the boat would go down, but Jimmy's a real fighter. He later said he had worked too long and too hard for his boat, and Davie Jones wasn't gonna take it from him." He re-lit his pipe and puffed on it a couple of times. "He'll be fine."

As the Gideon pulled away, Peter looked back and waved. These were good, fine, hardworking men, and he was very proud to be one of them. These past years had brought a new appreciation and understanding as to why Jesus had chosen so many fishermen to be his disciples; and why he spent time in their boats fishing with them.

"When I get to heaven," he whispered to himself, "it's going to be so much more fun talking to Peter, James, John, and the others: we now have a lot in common."

"Did you say something?" Cap asked.

"Talking to myself," he answered, "doing a lot of that these days."

"Seems to me you've got a lot to talk to yourself about. While on the subject, have you decided on how to meet with Bridgit and her daughter?"

"Aye, straight on. Walk up, knock on the door, and see where it goes from there."

"Good idea. The simplest plan is usually the best; less chance of getting tangled up in unnecessary complications. My prayers are with you."

"Thanks, they mean a lot to me. Now let's get to Kilrush and see how bad the situation is there."

For the last few miles, with the exception of occasional orders regarding changing course or trimming sails, the crew remained silent, caught up in their own thoughts as to what awaited them. Whatever the situation, it would be easier on the single men. For the married men, they would be torn between returning to the sea; or staying ashore trying to care for their families: a terrible catch 22.

Back in Kilrush, Bridgit and Grace had just left a meeting at Saint Patrick's. Father Carmichael and Grant had very discreetly questioned Grace to find out whether or not she had seen or dreamt of anything unusual lately. Grace came away from the meeting very puzzled, asking her mother why the Priests would be interested in her dreams.

"Oh I'm sure it's jes because they like ye and want to know how yer doin.... if anythins bother'n ye."

"Well nothin is," Grace replied, not fully comprehending the magnitude of the impending calamity that was beginning to happen all around her. "I'll race ye ta the top of the hill," she said as she began to run ahead of Bridgit.

Bridgit, so very happy and proud of her, watched her dart ahead. As she began running to catch up, she realized that soon, very soon, she would have to tell Grace about "the gift." When she did, she knew that it would begin to change her; and part of her youth and innocence would be lost forever. Ever since the meeting with Fathers

Carmichael, Grant, and Kathleen; she understood that it was only a matter of time before she had to tell her.

At first, she told herself she would tell her sometime within the next couple of months. Then as Grace began having more dreams, it was next week, or the next. Finally, Grace's increasing questions made her realize that now was the time. Tomorrow, she kept telling herself, I'll tell her tomorrow. But as the days turned into weeks, that tomorrow had never come. She looked up the hill at Grace and stopped for a moment, then started walking; all the while watching Grace still running as free as the wind. Now, the crop failure changed everything and brought tomorrow with it: it was waiting for them at the top of the hill.

"Look Mommy," Grace called, "there's our house; it's so pretty with the flowers around it." Turning around she pointed to the river; "some fishing boats are comin in. Let's go down ta the dock and see what they caught."

Bridgit marveled at the wonderment in a child. She and Grace had been to the top of this hill dozens of times, perhaps a hundred; and yet each time Grace reacted like she was seeing everything for the first time. Reaching the top, she stood behind her and wrapped her arms around her looking out over the river. "'Tis beautiful ta be sure. Look at how the wind fills the sails of the boats."

"Have ye ever been on a big boat like that?" Grace asked.

"No. Once when I was about yer age, my father took me fishing in a small boat like those down there," she said pointing to a boat with two men in it.

"What did ye catch?"

"Jes a few small trout; but they was good eatin."

"Can we go fishin some day? I'd like ta catch a fish. Did my father like ta fish?"

The last question was like a small dagger. For the first few years, Grace had not asked any questions about her father, but during the past two years the questions became much more frequent. "I suppose that he did, most men like ta fish," she answered. "Oh, look there!" she said pointing to the Galilee and hoping to change the subject, "part of the mast is gone. They musta had an accident."

"Can we go down ta the dock and see it when it comes in?" Grace asked excitedly. "I like ta see the fish they catch. Once, one of the fisherman let me hold one, it was slippery and I couldn't hold it. It was smelly, like that man I bumped into." She started walking down the hill.

As Bridgit walked along side her Grace turned to her and said, "Mother, I forgot ta tell ye I had a dream about that man, the one I bumped into at the store. I dreamed he came ta our house."

Bridgit wanted to stop, but didn't want Grace to think there was anything special about the dream. "When was that Sweetheart?"

"A few days ago. I'm sorry I forgot ta tell ye. He was very nice and said he remembered me from the store."

"Did he say why he came to our house?"

"He said he wanted ta talk to ye, and see if we we're ok, and did we need anything?"

"I told him ye were workin in the garden behind the house. He said he would go back ta talk ta ye. Then I woke up."

Grace started skipping down the hill, and Bridgit's heart began beating much faster. She had long suspected that this day might come; now the question was, what would she do when it did. Grace's dream, coupled with the crop failure, now convinced her that day was very soon. Her hunch had been right about the familiar look in the fisherman's eyes; she was almost certain that it was Father Timothy. He had become a fisherman.

"Being forewarned is being forearmed," she said to herself. Now it was time to seriously think about what to say to Father Timothy when he showed up; and even more important, what to tell Grace? As for telling her about 'the gift;' she would tell her tomorrow.

Chapter 28

As the Gideon gently slid into the last open berth along the dock; Peter jumped down to the dock before the mooring lines were secured, and quickly headed toward the Dock Managers Office. Sticking his head inside, he told them that they needed to off-load their catch as soon as possible; the Galilee was damaged and on her way in. There was a shuffling of chairs as two men got up and went outside, yelling at some dock hands to look lively.

Aboard the Gideon, a hoist had already been rigged on a boom and the crew was lowering nets into the hold. Within fifteen minutes, net loads of fish were being swung over the side into wagons where they were being salted down. In slightly more than an hour, the Gideon had unloaded their catch and was slipping away from the dock, making room for the Galilee which was about a mile away; slowly making its way up the river under shortened sail.

Peter had originally planned on staying ashore, but that was before the accident on the Galilee. Now, considering all the attention the damaged boat would draw, he decided it would be better to stay on board until later that afternoon. At this point, he didn't want to risk any chance of being recognized, however remote the chance might be.

Meanwhile, as Bridgit and Grace walked down the hill, she told Grace that rather than going directly to the dock, she had to stop by Saint Patrick's first. "I need ta talk ta Father Grant for a minute Sweetheart; then we'll go down ta see the boats unload."

"Can I go watch the boats while ye talk to Father Grant?"

Although she had no idea of what boat Father Timothy worked on; she was not willing to risk the chance of Grace running into him by herself; she said no, this time she wanted to be with her. Grace thought that was kind of strange, because she had been to the docks by herself several times. Almost everyone knew Bridgit and Grace, and she was as safe there as she was at home. Bridgit could see that she was disappointed, but assured her that talking to Father Grant would only take a few minutes. As they approached the church, Grace saw one of her friends and Bridgit told her to run along and play. Actually, she was happy this happened as she preferred to see Father Grant alone. Grant, who was just walking out the side door as they approached, saw them and waved hello.

"Father Grant," she called, "I need ta talk ta ye for a minute."

"I was just on my way to check the storeroom, so far it looks like we're going to be ok," Grant replied. "What can I do for you?"

"Important news I have for ye," she said, and proceeded to tell him about Grace's dream.

Grant looked at her rubbing his hand along his chin, "Assuming the dream is true, we don't know when that might happen. It could be today, tomorrow, or months from now."

"I jes got a feelin it's gonna be soon, and I need ta be ready. What am I gonna say ta him? What'll I tell Grace?"

"How you feel about him is the key to the situation," Grant replied. "It's been evident for many years now that he cares very much about you and Grace. I believe he's still in love with you. What if he tells you he's sorry for what he did, but that he loves you and still wants to marry you. What'll you say to him?"

"That's why I wanted ta talk ta ye first. I'm not sayin 'tis true, but jes supposing mind ye, that I've grown ta love him because I've seen how much he cares for us. I know

now that he never meant ta hurt me. 'Twas a terrible mistake he made. But he was a priest; what will the church do ta him, or the Constable?"

Grant thought for a moment, "nothing," he answered. "Father Timothy is free to renounce his vows to the church, just as other priests have. In fact, Martin Luther left the church and married a nun. As to the law, you never revealed the name of the man who attacked you; no charges were ever filed, so I doubt anything could be done. And if you never say anything when he returns….," he paused for a few seconds, "no, the law wouldn't do anything. As for Father Carmichael and I, what happened back then would forever remain a secret."

"Thank ye Father. Understand, I'm not sayin I love him, but I need ta know where we would stand."

"What about Grace?" Grant asked.

"I'm not sure, but I think she senses something because of the man in her dream. With the gift an all, she's not like the other girls her age. She seems ta understand things in a way different from us."

"How well I know that," he laughed. "For what it's worth, I'm certain that Grace will have no problem accepting "Father Timothy - or whatever name he goes by now - as her father. Like you, she has also seen his kindness over the years. When he comes, she will welcome him as the mysterious person who sent presents to you both. And as for being her father, what child doesn't want a father?"

Bridgit stood there silently thinking about everything that had happened during all these many years. "Thank ye, and I believe yer right about Grace," she replied turning to leave. "Say hello ta Father Carmichael for me. We're goin ta the dock and watch 'em unload the fish."

"Say a prayer for him Bridgit. He caught a cold yesterday and hasn't been doing well. He needs to stay in bed and rest, but you know how he is. Incidentally, your garden's still ok isn't it?"

"Aye it is, but Alice's patch down the street is gone, blight took it all. I told her ta help herself ta our garden. Be sure ta tell Father Carmichael that Grace and I will be prayin fer him ta be sure. Grace!" she called loudly, "let's go see the boats."

They were halfway to the dock when Bridgit heard someone call her name. Looking across the street she saw Lawrence and Sally walking toward them.

"We haven't seen you for a while," Sally called walking toward them. "Grace, you sure are getting to be a pretty girl; did your mom fix your braids?"

"Yes Mrs. Bligh," she said proudly turning around.

"Well we'd like to invite you both to come out to Arden again. You know Grace, I think there's a nice pony out there that misses you."

"That's right," Lawrence added. "This morning when I gave him some oats, he asked me when you were coming back to play."

"Really? Can we go ta Arden Mommy?"

Before Bridgit could answer, Sally said, "I've got another sewing project for you. So while Grace is riding the pony, we can talk about it. Where're you headed now?"

"Ta the dock and see the boats unload the fish," Grace said excitedly. "Do ye want ta come with us?"

"That's a great idea," Lawrence answered. "I've got to meet Father Grant in an hour to go over the plans for the smoke house. But", he said turning to Grace, "that leaves lots of time for us to go see the smelly fish," he pinched his nose with his fingers. "I noticed that one of the boats coming in looked like it had been damaged." Taking her hand he said, "young lady, I think you and I need to go check that out. Do you like to race? I'll bet I can beat you to the dock."

"No ye can't," Grace said pulling her hand away and starting to run.

"Go ahead," Sally said laughing, "it'll give us a chance to talk."

As Lawrence started running down the street trying to catch Grace, Bridgit took hold of Sally's arm, "I need ta tell ye something." Sally listened in amazement as Bridgit told her the entire story, including Grace's dream. "I'm telling ye this in confidence because yer one of my best friends. I don't know when he might come, he might even be on one of the boats at the dock now. Course he won't look the same like he did before. The day we seen 'em, he was hardy lookin with his beard and long hair pulled back; an being out ta sea all the time his skin was kinda brown. It was only when I looked inta his eyes that I thought I recognized him."

"Looked into his eyes? When was that?"

"A few months ago, when Grace ran outta the store an right inta him sittin on the bench."

"Did you talk to him?"

"No, we jes apologized. But when he looked at me, I seen somethin in his eyes that looked familiar. It was after we got home that I remembered seeing his eyes before."

"So you haven't seen him since then?"

"No."

"Well, Larry and I won't say anything to anyone. Who else knows?"

"Fathers Carmichael and Grant, and Kathleen are the only ones that know. Oh ye can tell John and Cassie, they've been wonderful ta Grace and me, and I'll tell Sean, because he's been a good friend, but nobody else. So ye can see, there's not many that knows."

"What do Father Carmichael and Grant think?"

"They suspected it was Father Timothy after the first package came. Course ye know he never showed up at the church in London seven years ago; and nobody knew where he was. An ta think he's been coming and goin, and watchin me an Grace right here in Kilrush all these years; and sendin us the packages....," her voice trailed off.

The warm smile that brightened her face as she said this, told Sally all she needed to know about how Bridgit really felt, but she didn't want to push her. "Well Bridgit, we want you to know that we'll support whatever decision you make. What's Father Timothy's name now?"

"I don't know, but its fer sure he don't go by Father Timothy anymore," she laughed.

"Well whatever he calls himself; he's proven himself to be very concerned about you and Grace, and did what he could to provide for you."

They were now approaching the dock and could see Lawrence and Grace looking at the damage on the Galilee. "Did ye see the fish?" Bridgit call to Grace who was sitting on his shoulders.

"No, we was too late. They said the Gideon caught some, but she went back out there," she said pointing, "so that this boat could tie up at the dock."

"I'm sorry ye were too late, t'was my fault."

"That's ok Mommy, Mr. Bligh has been telling me about what happened ta the boat, look at the broken mast and all that rope. He put me up on his shoulders so that I could see better. It's better than seein the fish."

"She's a wonderful girl, Bridgit," Lawrence said. "If you ever decide to get rid of her," he kidded, "we'd like to adopt her."

"Well the next time she burns the taters, I might jes do that. What do ye think Grace? They've got a pony."

"Oh Mommy, ye wouldn't really give me away would ye?" she answered with a very serious tone in her voice. "I wouldna trade ye for a hundred ponies."

"We was jes foolin Sweetheart, I'd not give ye up in a million years" she went up and took hold of her hand. "I'd die without ye fer sure."

While Bridgit, Grace, and Lawrence were busy talking and having fun, Sally was carefully observing the men on the Galilee; and not seeing anyone that matched the description Bridgit had given, turned and looked toward the Gideon, anchored about a hundred yards away.

On the Gideon, Peter, who had been standing by the rail watching the Galilee, suddenly noticed Bridgit and Grace, and the couple they were with. Whoever they were, it was evident that with Grace sitting on the man's shoulders, they were close friends. Then a thought occurred to him; what if that man and Bridgit were going together, and the other woman was a friend? The possibility of another man hadn't occurred to him before, but he had been gone for seven years, a long time; that could have changed everything. He needed to find out before he went to see Bridgit. Many of the previous anxieties, which he had finally put to rest; rose again in his mind like tormenting specters. "No," he said to himself, "I'll not be putting this off any longer."

At that moment, his eyes and Sally's met, and he watched her turn and pull on Bridgit's sleeve. She turned around and looked in the direction Sally was pointing. For a split second Bridgit looked directly at Peter, and then started talking to Sally. A few seconds later, Lawrence and Grace turned around.   Grace immediately recognized Peter, "there's that man Mommy," she said and started waving.

Peter, seeing Grace wave, waved back not certain what it all meant. Why would she be waving at him? Could she have remembered him from that brief moment in town? Much more likely, she was mistaking him for someone else, but who?

Lawrence, noticing all this waving back and forth, asked what was going on; and who was the man on the boat?

Before Bridgit or Grace could answer, Sally said, "I'll tell you all about it later." As they left the dock, Bridgit turned and looked back; Peter was still standing by the rail watching them. Sally took her arm, "come to Arden day-after-tomorrow," she whispered, "we need to talk some more."

Late that afternoon after the crowds had left the dock; Peter came ashore in the long boat and had supper at the Pub, where he learned that the couple he had seen on the dock was Lawrence and Sally Bligh, John Bligh's son and his wife. He also heard once again the story of how John's oldest son Robert had hired a man to kill John and his wife Cassie, and the entire story of what had happened. "Seems somebody in London heard about the plot and tipped off Scotland Yard," the waiter said. "Sure was a lot of excitement around here for a while." It was evident that this story would be told, and retold, for many years.

Peter thanked the waiter and let out a silent sigh of relief; the man was not a rival suitor and he could proceed with his plan. Tomorrow afternoon he would go to see them, and by tomorrow night he should know one-way or the other, where he stood. As he stepped out into the street, it suddenly occurred to him that he hadn't heard anything about the crop failure, and concluded it wasn't as bad as they had thought. If this was true, that was the second piece of good news today. He crossed his fingers, "now Lord, let me get the best news of all tomorrow."

Having decided that he wanted to get a good-nights sleep in a real bed, and a warm bath and shave in the morning, he checked into the hotel. He got two of his wishes, the warm bath and shave. As for the good nights sleep, a terrible dream about the day he raped Bridgit made him sit bolt upright in the bed. During the first couple of years after the incident, it had been a reoccurring nightmare, but then it stopped. Now he was wide awake, and thoughts of Bridgit, Grace, and what tomorrow held in store would not stop long enough for him to fall asleep. It was a long, long, restless night.

The morning dawned bright and clear, a good sign. During breakfast, the conversation at the adjacent tables was about how well the emergency plan had worked; starting construction on the smokehouse; and the hope and prayer that the August crop would escape the blight; all good news so far. As he went to pay his bill, the cashier was talking to a man he thought he recognized, but couldn't be quite certain. The man was telling the cashier that Father Carmichael had come down with pneumonia and was seriously ill. After he left, Peter asked the cashier who the man was, and was shocked to hear that it was Sean Egan.

"Sean Egan?" Peter asked. "I seem to recall that he was a drunk and badly crippled from a fight several years ago."

"Aye, that he was. A devil if ever there was one."

"What happened to him?"

It was a golden opportunity for the cashier, who had actually witnessed the fight between Sean and Colin, to re-tell the wondrous story of the fight with Colin: the terrible beating Sean had suffered; and his subsequent conversion at a revival meeting."

Peter had known about the fight, but not about Sean's conversion. "And that's the same man?"

"Indeed. He's now one of the finest men you'll ever meet. Always working to help others; even the men and women he hurt before are now his friends." The cashier handed Peter his change, "Never really had much use for religion myself, but after seeing what happened to him, it turned me into a believer."

"Amazing story of God's grace," Peter replied.

"Aye, that it is. If it worked for Sean, there's hope for anyone. Well, top-o-the morning to you."

Peter walked out of the hotel restaurant feeling good, very good. So far there had been two good signs: a nice warm sunny day, and now by coincidence - if you believed things happened by chance - a story of God's ability to save anyone. "So even the women he had hurt, were now his friends," he said to himself. "Well God, my prayer is that Bridgit, who I hurt very badly, will love me." He started walking back to the dock and stopped in his tracks as he was struck by an unimaginable idea. Turning around, he headed toward Saint Patrick's.

As he approached the church, a Sister came out the front door and began sweeping off the steps. "Excuse me, Sister, if Father Grant's here, would you tell him and old friend is here to see him."

"And your name Sir?"

"Peter," he answered, "No wait; tell him Timothy."

The sister disappeared into the church, and Peter waited on the steps, his breakfast churning in his stomach. It was not a long wait.

Suddenly, Father Grant came running out the door, and down the steps. "Timothy, or is it Peter now?" he exclaimed throwing his arms around him. "We've been expecting you. Father Carmichael would be here, but he's ill. I sent the Sister to tell him you're here."

Peter was speechless. Before he could even say a word, Grant was going back up the steps two at a time, and motioning for him to follow. "Com'on, he'll be waiting to see you. We've got a lot to talk about."

Peter followed Grant down the hall past the study where he had last spoken to Father Carmichael, and up a flight of stairs to a small room in the back. The door was open, and Grant tapped lightly to announce their presence, and stepped inside. Peter looked at Carmichael who was in bed in a sitting position propped-up by several pillows. It was evident that his body had failed during the years he was away; but he quickly learned that his mind and wit was as sharp as ever.

"So Timothy our prodigal son has returned," Carmichael whispered.

"And he's changed his name, its Peter now," Grant said.

"A wonderful name. I think there was someone in our church history a long time ago with that name, remarkable coincidence," he tried to laugh, but it started him coughing.

"It's wonderful to see you both again," Peter said taking Carmichaels hand and glancing at Grant. "I must confess that it's been a long time since I spent time in the company of priests."

"No, that's not true Peter. Perhaps not in the presence of Roman Catholic priests, but God's priests are everywhere. I see them every time I walk down the street; waiting on you in the restaurant; the hardware store; the woman selling flowers on the corner; why Peter, you yourself are a priest. As Saint Paul wrote, we are all kings and priests."

"I broke my vows when I walked away from the church seven years ago."

"To the Catholic church perhaps, but not to God," Grant replied. "Father Carmichael and I have had many discussions about you. It's our opinion that God never intended for you to be an ordained priest. That was something that your parents, especially your mother, instilled in you. Isn't that true?"

"From the time I was a small boy. There was never any thought about my being anything else but a priest."

"You're not alone Peter. There are hundreds of priests and protestant ministers who are in the wrong profession, for many different reasons," Carmichael said. "But tell us, when you left here and went to London, why didn't you report to the church there?"

"Well, it was rather strange. On the way to London I spent two weeks on a fishing boat. At first, I wore my robes, and then a few days later I started helping the crew when I could. Knowing that I was a priest, one of the men would bring his English bible on deck, and they started asking a lot of questions, some of them really hard to answer. The Captain was a Quaker, most of the others were also Protestants; I was the only Catholic. It was a wonderful feeling, talking to them. Sometimes we would get in arguments, but they accepted me and I began to feel at home with them."

"In a way you never felt that you fit in here, right?" Grant asked.

"Yes. Out there on the boat, it was easy to share my faith as we worked together. Here, I always felt that I was separated from the people, even though I didn't want to be. So when I got to London I packed away my robes; changed my name; bought some clothes for fishing, and signed on with another boat."

"Doing what it appears God wanted you to be doing I'd say," Carmichael added.

"God's always way, way ahead of us, but he's also very patient. When the time is right, he finds ways to move us to where he wants us to be. For example, isn't it remarkable that you just happened to be in the right London Pub dressed in your street clothes, in time to over hear the plot to assassinate the Bligh's; and send those anonymous warning letters to Scotland Yard and to us. You saved their lives Peter."

"You knew that was me?"

"Just like we've known from the beginning that you were sending the packages to Bridgit and Grace."

"That too! Does she know?"

"Oh, for the first couple of years she tried to convince Father Carmichael and me that they came from an aunt up north. But she knew…. we all knew the truth."

The room was silent for a few moments. Peter got up from his chair at went to the window. "I'm going to see her today." He turned around to face Carmichael and Grant, "I've never stopped loving her….and now there's Grace." He paused for a moment and then in a much stronger tone of voice continued. "Something very strange happened yesterday. We anchored out so that the Galilee could tie up at the dock - she lost part of her mast. Anyway, Bridgit, Grace, and John Bligh's son and his wife came down to the dock; looks like they're close friends."

"Yes they are, and Bridgit and Grace often go to watch the boats unload the fish," Grant said. "She enjoys watching the boats."

"Well, while I was watching them, Grace waved to me; I thought she had mistaken me for someone else. Several months ago I was sitting on a bench down the street, and she ran into me as she came out of a store; she and Bridgit were embarrassed and apologized. I can't imagine that she would have remembered me."

"Good memory for faces, I guess," Grant said with a sly glance toward Carmichael. "So you're planning on going to see them today?"

"I've got to. I need to know if she will forgive me for what I did to her."

"That's all?" Grant asked.

"No. The truth is that I would love to marry her, take care of her and Grace. But...." He hesitated, "but after what I did...."

"That was a long time ago," Carmichael said. "Bridgit's a remarkable woman. What you did was horrible – and mind you, I'm not excusing what you did, especially since you were a priest. But out of that tragedy Grace was born; a wonderful daughter she would otherwise never have had."

"I've asked God a thousand times to forgive me for that."

"If your first prayer was truly sincere, God forgave you; and the other nine hundred and ninety-nine were wasted. But God's forgiveness does not wipe away all the consequences; those we continue to live with," Grant replied.

"So you think that I should go to her? That's what I want to do."

"Absolutely," Carmichael said, "and I think...," he started coughing and placed a cloth over his mouth.

"We believe," Grant continued, "that you need to talk to her. We don't know what she'll say to you, keep in mind, it's not just her now, but Grace as well. Still, the matter needs to be resolved, for everyone's sake."

They were interrupted by a light knock on the door. Grant opened it and a Sister told him that a man was down stairs waiting to see him.

Turning to Peter he reached out his hand and took hold of Peter's hand, "I have to leave, and I think Father Carmichael needs to rest; it's been good seeing you again. Go see Bridgit, then please come back to see us again."

Carmichael took the cloth away from his mouth, "you're always welcome here....and loved," he said struggling to hold back another coughing spell.

Peter reached out and placed his hand on Carmichael's shoulder, "Thank you. Thank you both."

Grant and Peter left the room and started down the hall, "one quick question," Peter asked; "when you met me on the steps out front, you said you had been expecting me. What did you mean by that?"

Grant glanced at him and smiled, "I'll tell you about that next time we meet."

Chapter 29

Bridgit's cottage was a little over five blocks from Saint Patrick's, but it took Peter almost two hours to cover the distance. Several times he walked to within sight of the cottage, slowed his gate, lost his nerve and turned back. This time he determined there would be no turning back. Setting a brisk pace, he strode the last block, walked up to the door and knocked. Having rehearsed many times what he would say when Bridgit opened the door, he was surprised when Grace opened it.

"Good morning," she said. "I recognize ye, yer the man from the fishing boat, we've been expecting ye."

Caught completely unawares by Grace and what she said, he stood there speechless for a few seconds, and then came to his senses. "So you're the pretty girl that waved at me from the dock"

"Aye, I recognized ye from the day I ran into ye at the store."

"I remember that day," he said with a smile. "I think I had my legs and feet striking out too far from the bench."

"No Sir, t'wasn't yer fault. I weren't lookin where I was goin. If ye want ta see my Mother, she's out back workin in the garden." Before he could answer she said, "follow me," stepped past him and started running around the side of the cottage calling, "Mommy, he's here."

He was completely bewildered by this unexpected turn of events. In his mind, he had imagined he would knock at the door, Bridgit would answer, hopefully invite him in and they would quietly talk inside her cottage. Somehow, he had totally forgotten that Grace would be there. Now he was following her to the garden, and totally mystified by hearing Grace calling to her mother, "he's here," as if they were expecting him. Then it occurred to him that while he was walking around getting up the courage to come to her cottage, Father Grant stopped by and said he would be coming: that would explain it.

Hearing Grace calling, Bridgit stopped raking, turned around to see her, and saw Peter twenty feet behind. Even though she knew that this moment had been coming, her heart began pounding and she was happy to have the rake for support. Grace, totally unaware of the history involved, was all smiles as she ran up to her mother and turned around to face Peter.

"Mother, he want's ta talk ta ye, the man from the boat," she said happily. "It's jes like in my dream."

"Aye, that it is Sweetheart. Why don't ye go and play with yer friends fer a while, so's we can talk private."

"Ok, I'll go ta Mary's. Nice ta see ye again," she said to Peter, and then took off running across the yard.

"Good morning Bridgit," Peter said slowly walking toward her. "I guess that Father Grant came by and let you know I was coming."

"No. I haven't seen him since yesterday, but we knew ye was comin."

Once again, Peter was confused. Everything in his carefully laid out plan had been turned upside down; and what was the reference Grace had made about a dream? But all that could wait, he was here at last.

"It's wonderful to see you again Bridgit," he began. "As you can see, I'm not a priest anymore, and I changed my name to Peter.

"Peter," she said pronouncing his name quietly, "'tis a nice name. And ye became a fisherman."

"Aye, that I did. Over seven years ago, when I left here. It was by accident. I got on a fishing boat so I could get away from here as fast as I could. After I spent two weeks with the crew, I knew that's what I should be doing."

"Maybe it wasn't an accident that ye got on that boat," Bridgit answered.

"No," he said with a slight smile, "judging from everything I've learned in the past seven years, it seems many of the things we think are accidents, or coincidences, have been planned by God."

"Would ye include Grace?" she asked, again taking him by complete surprise.

He looked at her trying to decide how to answer her question. Was it a statement he should agree with? Did she think God had planned the entire incident, and they were merely pawns in His grand scheme of things; or was this a trick to see if he would blame God for what he had done. He had to be very careful here; better to ask another question. "I'm not sure what you meant by that?"

"Do ye think that maybe God wanted ye to rape me, so's I could have Grace?"

"Heaven's no!" he exclaimed. "God would never do such a thing. What I did was because of what I wanted; I loved you and thought you loved me. Before we say anything else, I want, I need to beg your forgiveness. It has haunted me all these years."

"Is that why ye sent the packages ta Grace and me, ta ease yer conscience?"

"Yes…. I mean no. I sent them because I never stopped loving you, and wanted to do everything I could to help you….and Grace of course."

She had waited too long to miss the chance for a least a little revenge. "So yer sayin yer conscience didn't bother ye?"

His mind was getting more confused. He could recall listening to the men on the ship telling stories of how women would take a man's statement and twist it around. If ye say it black, they'll claim ye said it was white; and if ye tries ta correct 'em, they'll want ta know why yer changing yer story. One of the crewmen even suggested that it wasn't the serpent in the Garden of Eden that took advantage of Eve, but the other way around.

"I sent the gifts because I loved you, and yes it did help to ease my conscience. I was afraid to come, so I sent the gifts. What I want you to know is that I loved you then, and love you now….here today, this minute."

"So ye was afraid after what ye done," she said her voice rising. "Like a little boy that breaks a window and runs way; a coward."

He stood there stunned by the words and the sharp bitter edge in her voice. This was not what he had expected. Was this her rejection of him? He knew that was a real possibility, but not this. It was over. He had come to her cottage to find out once and for all, now he knew.

"Yes, I…."

"Stop! she yelled as she dropped the rake and ran towards him putting her fingers to his lips, "do na say anythin more. T'was a terrible thing I said ta ye, Mother Mary forgive me." She looked up at him, "I remember even as ye were doin that ta me, ye kept sayin that ye loved me, and I know it was true." She pressed up against him, putting her face against his chest. "I love ye too," she whispered.

In a split second, his heart and mind went from hopelessness to joy. He reached out and put his arms around her. "Then I'll ask you again what I asked you so many years ago, will you marry me?"

She kept her face buried in his sweater and softly said, "I want to, but I need ta talk ta Grace first. It's not just me now, she needs ta be told yer her father." She pulled away from him and looked up into his eyes, "come inta the house, there's some things ye need ta know about Grace."

"She's not sick, is she? Is there something wrong?" he said following her to the house.

"No, she's fine. But Grace's not an ordinary girl." They went into the parlor and sat down. "Do ye remember her sayin, he's the man in my dream?"

"Yes."

"Do ye know what it means ta be born with a veil?"

"No. What kind of veil?"

For the next hour, she explained everything to him: her grandmother; the prophesy about Grace; her birth; the Church: Fathers Carmichael and Grant; Grace's dream about the crop failure, and of course Peter returning to their cottage.

"So that's what Fathers Carmichael and Grant meant when they said they had been expecting me; and what Grace said when she answered the door."

"Aye. Ye must know that Grace doesn't understand all about 'the gift,' that's what we all call it. She's only seven years old, and if we told her everythin, it could steal her childhood from her, we do na want that. So I jes quietly ask her now and then if she's had any more strange dreams, and make nothing of it. Other times, she tells me on her own. Yer daughter's a very special girl."

That was the first time Bridgit had matter-of-factly acknowledged Grace as his daughter in a tender and loving way. "Our daughter," he replied, "and even if there was 'no gift' as you call it, she would still be very special."

At that moment, Grace came bursting through the door, breathless from running. "Mary had ta go ta town with her brother, so I came home; I'm hungry. Do ye want ta stay and eat with us?" she said turning to Peter."

"His name is Mr...."

"Williamson, Peter Williamson," he quickly added realizing that Bridgit had never known his given name. .

"I'm pleased ta meet ye Mr. Williamson," she said as she did a little courtesy.

"Likewise Grace," Peter replied and reached out and touched her hand.

At the touch of his hand, Grace stood upright and looked into his eyes. "Yer my father, aren't ye?"

"Grace!" Bridgit exclaimed, "why would ye say such a thing? Did someone say something to ye?"

"No one said anything ta me. When his hand touched mine, I knew he was my father."

"What do ye mean ye knew; how could ye know that?"

"I do na know mother. It jes came inta my head sudden like when he touched my hand. Ye are my father aren't ye?

Peter glanced at Bridgit, "yes I am Grace, and I'm very proud to be your father."

"Yer the man that has been sendin us the boxes with the clothes and toys, for which I thank ye. Have ye come ta be my real father and stay here with us?"

"Would you like that?" he asked startled by her directness.

"Morein anythin. If ye do, then I would have a father like my friends, and we could walk ta town and go ta church tagether. Will ye put me up on yer shoulders like Mr. Bligh? Would ye take me fishin?"

"Grace!" Bridgit said, "ye shouldna be asking questions like that."

"Its fine Bridgit, she can ask all the questions she wants." Turning back to Grace, "I'll carry you all over town on my shoulders if you want me to," Peter answered, "and you, your mother and I will go on picnics, and we'll go fishing."

What ever concerns and anxieties Peter and Bridgit may have had about Grace's reaction to the news that he was her father vanished in seconds.

Grace wrapped her arms around his waist and held him tightly for a few seconds then turned to her mother. "I've been prayin every night ta Mother Mary for a father, like my friends have, and she answered my prayers." She turned to go to the kitchen, "Father, are ye gonna stay and eat with us?"

Peter took Bridgit and held her in is arms. Never in his wildest dreams had he imagined how glorious this day would turn out to be. Not only had Bridgit agreed to marry him, but Grace was already calling him father. The next matter to be resolved was when and where they should get married. Bridgit was just about to whisper to him that a quiet ceremony here at her cottage would be fine, when Grace called from the kitchen.

"I forgot ta tell ye mother, I had another dream last night," she said as she ran back into the room. "I forgot about it till jes now."

A sudden chill came over Bridgit, and Peter could feel her body grow tense.

"What was it Sweetheart?" she asked fearful of another ominous sign of another crop failure.

"We was all at a big party at Arden. Fathers Carmichael and Grant was there, and you and father, and me, Aunt Kathleen, and Uncle Sean....lots and lots of people. You and father danced, and he danced with me standin on his toes. Can we eat now, I'm hungry."

Bridgit let out an audible sigh of relief; "Well with all yer, playin, dreamin, and talkin, I guess I'd better feed ye before ye starve ta death." She reached out and pulled Grace into her arms, "yer the most wonderful daughter any mother ever had."

"And the prettiest girl a father ever had," Peter added. "Say, I've got an idea, why don't we all go down to the hotel and have something to eat there."

"Really!" Grace exclaimed with excitement. "I've never had anythin ta eat in a hotel. What can ye eat there?"

"Oh lots and lots of things. They have a piece of paper called a menu that lists all the different kinds of food, and you tell the waiter what you want."

"And they cook it and bring it to ye?"

"Yes. And do you know what the best part is?"

"What?" she asked, her eyes bright with curiosity.

When you're finished eating, the waiter picks up all the dishes and takes them to the kitchen to be washed. You don't have to do anything."

"Mommy, can we go… please? Tomarra, I'll tell my friends I ate at the hotel."

"Well…. maybe this once. Since yer so hungry, it'll be nice ta let them do the cookin."

Perhaps somewhere in the long history of Kilrush, there had been a happier family that walked down the street on a warm sunny day; had lunch and chocolate cake for dessert at the hotel; but it's doubtful.

The next morning when Bridgit and Grace arrived at Arden, Sally told Grace to go down to the stable; her pony was waiting for her. "Larry and our children are there," she said to Bridgit, "they'll have a lot of fun. No sooner was Grace out of sight, than Bridgit's words started pouring out like water from a broken dam.

"Wait, wait, wait," Sally said holding her hands in the air, "let me go and get Cassie; she'll want to hear this too." A couple of minutes later Cassie came in from her flower garden and the three of them talked, laughed, and cried for over an hour.

"It's a miracle Bridgit, a real miracle," Cassie said. "Of course, you'll have the wedding here at Arden, I'm so excited, just wait till I tell John. You know he loves you like a daughter, and Grace is another grandchild. Bridgit, would you consider having John give you away? He's not your real father of course, but it would make him so proud."

"Well, we was thinking of jes a small weddin at home, Peter and I…," Sally cut her off.

"A small wedding! nonsense. Cassie and I will host one of the biggest and grandest wedding parties Kilrush has ever seen. We'll invite everybody; it will be wonderful, lots of food, music, and dancing. Bridgit, you should ask Fathers Carmichael and Grant to conduct the service, they will love to do it. Have you told Kathleen yet?"

At that instant, Bridgit remembered Grace's dream. "It will be jes like the party in Grace's dream, everybody will be here," she said quietly.

"What dream?" Cassie asked.

"The dream Grace had two nights ago about a big party at Arden. She said everybody was here, and I was dancing with Peter."

"Two days ago? Peter hadn't even come to your house yet."

Bridgit then told Sally and Cassie about when Peter touched Grace's hand, she knew he was her father. "'Tis the gift, it's growin stronger."

"We had heard about the dreams," Sally said. "Father Grant told us about Grace's dream, or whatever you want to call it, about the dark figure floating over the fields."

"And now you're saying that just by touching someone, she pick's up on things in their mind?" Cassie asked.

"I do na know how it works, or why it's only at certain times. My grandmother, bless her soul, could sometimes jes look at a person and know some secret in their life. She told me, it was always something that could help the person, not harm them."

"So now you think Grace has this....gift."

"Aye, but I do na want her ta become afraid of it; or the people around her ta become afraid of her."

"It's a two edged sword, is what it is," Cassie replied. "It can be a blessing if used wisely, but a curse if not."

"Aye, an my Grace is but a sweet young girl. That's why it scares me so."

"Well, enough about the gift, for now anyway," Sally said to change the subject. "We need to start working on the wedding plans. Now this is one idea....."

Two more hours went by and the table was littered with notes, schedules, and other details of what was going to be a major social event in Kilrush. Bridgit was frightened; over-whelmed; and overjoyed; all at the same time. As to what opinions Peter might have regarding the plans, Cassie and Sally reminded Bridgit that a wedding was a woman's thing; all Peter had to do was to be there on time.

To prevent Peter from becoming upset and possibly interfering; it was decided that Bridgit would not tell him about the big wedding plans; but simply ask him to accompany her to the church and meet with Fathers Carmichael and Grant. Prior to their meeting, Cassie and Sally would meet with the Fathers and lay out the entire plan; telling them that it would be a wonderful gift for Bridgit who had done so much for the community. Consequently, when Peter and Bridgit arrived at the church a couple of days later, Peter was quickly outmaneuvered, not by Bridgit who remained surprisingly quiet, but by Carmichael and Grant, who after listening to Cassie and Sally, had immediately become avid supporters.

"Peter, it's a marvelous gift they're giving to Bridgit," Carmichael said.

"And with you joining in," Grant added, "the community is much more likely to welcome you, and forget the past."

"It's plain to see I've been set-up by the women," Peter said laughing while pointing to Carmichael and Grant, "and their religious co-conspirators. Well, count me in. Bridgit and Grace deserve every possible happiness."

"It's settled then," Grant said. "Bridgit, let us know the date, and if you need anything from us. Father Carmichael and I have discussed the wedding itself, and are looking forward to a garden service. It will be beautiful this time of year. Peter, we are assigning you one small job, as a priest it shouldn't be too much trouble; you pray for a lovely day and no rain."

"A former priest," Peter exclaimed.

"There are no former priests in God's kingdom," Carmichael replied.   "You may be a fisherman by profession, but you'll always be a priest in God's sight."

Bridgit began to weep quietly, "I'm so happy," she said quietly. "Not jes fer me and Grace, but ta see how ye have welcomed Peter; the three of ye together again as friends," she started crying even harder."

"Women," Grant said, "they cry when their happy; upset; sad…. and there will be times Peter, when you won't know which is which."

"Before I entered the priesthood," Carmichael said, "my parents expected me to get married. My father told me the secret of a happy marriage: Son," he said, "a happy wife, is a happy life."

Chapter 30

When the news initially spread throughout Kilrush and the surrounding area that Bridgit was getting married; at first there was a shock of surprise; and when the individuals and groups learned that the man that she was marrying was Father Timothy, who now called himself Peter, there were gasps of amazement. All in all however, the consensus was that it was a miracle, a wonderful miracle. As for the revelation that Father Timothy was the mystery man who had raped her; when the full story was related of how he had done so out of misdirected love; had secretly provided for Bridgit and Grace throughout all of these years; and had now returned and again asked her to marry him; all but a few self righteous bitter souls nodded their heads in approval. Several of the men commented that not every man was cut out of the right cloth to be a priest, and most acknowledged they would not be able to do it. Father Timothy they said – or Peter, as he now called himself - had proven himself to be an honorable man. Life's too short: if Bridgit's willing to forgive him, let bygones be bygones.

There were also two or three of the local married women, who, after years of quietly suspecting their own husband might have been the un-named culprit, gave them a special hug and kiss that night. Upon receiving this totally unexpected warm expression of affection, the husbands asked what it was for; and were given the usual reply, "it's nothing, nothing at all dear." The poor men unable to sleep; lay awake that night searching their memory for something they might have done, and wondering exactly what 'nothing' meant.

The forth-coming wedding quickly became the most talked about social event of the year. Father Carmichael had almost fully recovered from his illness, and he and Father Grant worked out a special ceremony where they would share in officiating. Cassie and Sally kept the cooks busy for days preparing food; while John, Lawrence and Neil had several of their tenant farmers clearing brush and grooming the grounds to accommodate a large crowd of visitors. Ropes were placed around Cassie's flower garden, in the hope of keeping the energy driven children from trampling it to death. Several wagons at Arden were readied for service; and a number of the local shop keepers in Kilrush arranged for their carts and wagons to assist in transporting guests from town to Arden and back. Neil had some men build a dozen large serving tables from wooden horses and planks. With the very large number of guests expected, it was decided that eating would be picnic style, so word was spread for people to bring a cloth or blanket to place on the ground.

With unbounded joy, Bridgit worked on her wedding gown and a dress for Grace who was to be her flower girl. Peter, who had gone back to sea for two weeks, prayed ceaselessly for no rain. In fact, after the first two days out, the entire ships crew, Christian or not, prayed with him. The Archangel Michael personally took special note of the great number of prayers coming from the Gideon, and passed the request on to God.

Days passed, weeks passed, and the great day dawned at last. It turned out to be a beautiful warm sunny day, as grand as Ireland ever experienced. Wagon loads of men, women, and children descended upon Arden. Many of them were friends and acquaintances of the Bligh's or Bridgit; plus dozens of others who simply took advantage of the open 'everyone welcome' invitation. The women and older girls yearned for a chance to go and see a truly Grand Wedding Party; and the men their chance to look around Arden which had become quite famous; not to mention the unlimited free food and drink.

The wedding ceremony, one of the happiest ever performed by Fathers Carmichael and Grant, took place at one o'clock; followed by the reception which lasted until ten o'clock that evening. Huge amounts of food and drink were consumed, followed by dancing, and more food, and more dancing. For the women, Cassie had arranged for each to receive a small gift, a memento of the occasion. For the men who were interested, Neil set up a tour of the facilities at Arden. The children were treated to cart and pony rides.

Because many of the local people were quite poor, special instructions were broadcast around the area that no one was expected to bring a gift. The goal was to have as many people that wished to come, and enjoy the event without any obligation. Some of Bridgit's closest friends did bring gifts, which for the most part were things they had made themselves. The grandest gift was given by the Bligh's; a week honeymoon stay at the Captain's Inn in Bristol, together with all travel and expenses paid, plus money for shopping. Despite Bridgit's offer to have Grace come to Bristol with them; Grace decided that riding a pony everyday would be a lot more fun than shopping and walking around Bristol; so she eagerly accepted the chance to stay at Arden while they were gone.

Despite the early summer crop failure and crisis, the late summer and fall of 1847 had turned out to be good for most people. The greatly feared total crop failure had not happened, and that fact alone made it a good year in the eyes of most. Whatever else life might dish out - and disappointments were as common as shamrocks in Ireland - having enough food to eat and a roof over their heads was the greatest blessing. Anything beyond that was considered a serendipity, a special gift from the Blessed Mother herself.

Christmas came and Saint Patrick's sponsored a big production Christmas Pageant complete with the holy family: the wise men; shepherds; and even a couple of live sheep brought in by a local farmer. As the evening drew to a close, Father Carmichael looked out over congregation; the grand parents; parents; children; grandchildren; widows and widowers, the flock he had faithfully shepherded for so many years. He felt a hand rest on his shoulder.

"Psalms 100 verse 5," Grant said softly.

"For the Lord is good; his mercy is everlasting, and his truth endureth to all generations." Carmichael replied.

"Good. Just checking to see if you still remember," Grant chuckled.

"I was remembering something else; something that Bridgit's grandmother told me many years ago, that we are temple builders."

"Temple builders?"

"Yes. You recall that Jesus told his disciples that he would tear down the temple and rebuild it in three days - speaking not of Solomon's Temple - but of us, the believers. As we do God's Will, we too share in that spiritually building-up of those around us, helping to make them into a temple unto the Lord. It's a wonderful thought, you and I, the Sisters, Bridgit, Kathleen, Sally, John, Cassie, Sean....everyone who does anything for the kingdom of God, is a temple builder."

Carmichael reached out and grasped Grant's hand, "I want you to know that you are the man I prayed for years ago. A temple builder, a true man of God to take over this church and Parish when my time came. I never imagined that he would send a former military man; but then, God is full of miracles and surprises."

"Indeed he is. I have only to look in the mirror to see that. But as for taking over when you time comes, that's a long way off."

Carmichael squeezed Grant's hand, "You're not kidding me, and I hope not yourself," he looked directly at Grant. "I had a dream last night. An Angel in shimmering white robes came and took hold of my hand. I remember passing right through the wall of my room, and as we slowly rose into the sky, I looked down and could see Saint Patrick's, just as a bird would see it. Then as we went higher, I could see the town and the fields, the river and the sea, it was beautiful. I imagine that's how God must see us."

"A wonderful dream," Grant said.

"Aye, that is was, and more." Carmichael looked at Grant, "It was the same kind of dream that our little Grace has. I tell you this so that you can be prepared. My dearest friend, I will not be here for the spring planting."

Grant looked at Carmichael and wrapped his arms around him; "how will I ever be able to continue here without you."

"God will see to it that you are able. Ere the lamp goes out, he has another prepared."

"But mine is a feeble candle next to your bonfire."

"Don't be overly modest, remember that God chose you. Many times, I've thought about when you came here. Out of thousands of priests serving in the church, he by-passed them all and reached down and chose an ex-Army officer – not even a catholic - to come to Saint Patrick's. It reminded me of how he did the same thing in Jesus time and chose John the Baptist to spread his word. One of the greatest truths we can rely on; is that God doesn't make mistakes."

"It will never be the same without you."

"And it shouldn't be. I was here for my appointed time, just as you will be for yours. God is always moving forward. The day you stop moving with what the Spirit is doing, you'll be left behind, and the ministry of Saint Patrick's will begin to whither." He let go of Grant's hand, "now enough of that. I think they be waiting for us downstairs in the reception hall. I understand the Sisters have baked up a lot of cookies, and I intend to get my share."

Grant watched Carmichael head down the hall toward the stairs. There was no doubt that times were changing, and Saint Patrick's would change with them. But still, he would dearly miss this man who had helped change and enrich his life in so many ways.

Winter passed. It had been very mild, so mild that everyone was eager for Spring to arrive. The farmers walked their field everyday, trying to decide when to begin planting. A few young men, heedless of the advice of the older experienced farmers, began too soon and then watched in dismay as heavy late winter rains washed their seed away.

Father Grant was also watching, and waiting. One morning in early April, Sister Annabelle knocked on the study door and told him that Father Carmichael had not come down to breakfast, a meal he never missed. "Should I take a tray to his room?"

"No Sister Ann, that won't be necessary; I'll go up to see him. Thanks for letting me know." Before he even climbed the stairs, he knew his friend was gone. He had not seen the shimmering angel, but he had heard the rustlings of his wings.

Grant had seen many men die on the battle field; in hospitals; even some members of the church here in

Kilrush; but he had never known anyone as close to God as his friend.

When he entered Carmichael's room, he could see the old man lying peacefully in his bed. One look told him that he had taken hold of the Angel's hand. Unlike the typical pallor of death; his countenance was almost radiant, and a wondrous smile was fixed across his face. Grant sat down on the edge of the bed and placed his hand on Carmichael's head as if he was giving a blessing. "Farewell old friend, we shall meet again in a land even fairer than Ireland."

On the dresser, Grant found two sealed envelopes. One addressed to Sister Agnes, the other to himself. When he opened the latter he found a simple Last Will and Testament.

Dear Grant:

Would you please see that these final requests are carried out. I leave my rosary and crucifix to Sister Agnes. I request that the cup given to me by the Pope be used as the communion cup at every Mass. My old bible filled with a lifetime of scribbled notes, I leave to you. Since I have no living relatives, please distribute all of my other personal items as best you see fit.

Your eternal brother in Christ,

Samuel Carmichael.

The news of Father Carmichael's death traveled faster than the news of last year's crop failure. Within hours, dozens of members and local residents stopped by the church. Sean, upon hearing the news, said he would ride out to Arden and let them know; and then go on to Holy Jim's Canyon. Upon learning of Carmichael's death, Jim exclaimed with a catch in his voice, "I've lost a wonderful friend; this community has lost a saint."

After Grant told her of Carmichaels passing, Sister Agnes quietly went to her room clutching the rosary and crucifix he had left her. There, sitting on the edge of her bed she opened and read his letter.

My Darling Agnes, it began, and in the letter his love for her poured out like champagne from an uncorked bottle. All those things he could not tell her while he was alive because of his vows to the church. She read the letter over and over again until she knew the words by heart.

"Samuel, my Samuel," she cried, "you promised me that I would go first, that you wouldn't leave me alone. Why did you leave me" she sobbed, "why did you leave me alone?"

Sister Agnes had been in love with Carmichael for over fifty years, almost from the day they first met. He had arrived at Saint Patrick's two weeks after she had been transferred from a convent. She closely watched this young priest, now in his early thirties. Unlike other priests she had met, he was exceptionally intelligent; ambitious; and sure of himself. Where others viewed him as somewhat aloof, she recognized that as reserved strength. When the insurrection came in 1798, his steady leadership not only endeared him to the local people, but strengthened her growing love for him.

But while those around him noted that that he certainly had strong feelings for her; he was very careful to keep his distance, and never acted in any manner that would cast a shadow across her character or his. If there had ever been any outward show of personal affection between them, it was limited to the occasional incidents where he would take hold of her hand while they were discussing something; but then that was his custom with almost everyone. Even so, those who were close to both of them sensed that there was a much deeper bond between them: not outwardly evident, but surely it was there.

As for Agnes, the mere touch of his hand sent waves of ecstasy coursing through her body. She full well knew that their relationship would never go beyond what it was; but simply being near him was enough for her. Many years ago, the local County Bishop had given her orders to transfer to another Parish; she refused, flatly stating that if she was forced to go she would leave the Church. Since she was such a great asset to Saint Patrick's, the Bishop decided that it was better to leave her where she was. After her second refusal, he began to believe that he and the Holy Father in Rome had something in common, very stubborn but valuable subordinates.

When Carmichael died, her reason for living ceased to exist. Grant, who had long understood their special relationship; went to her room several times and talked with her, but to no avail. She sat on a chair, refusing to leave her room or eat. Two days later she suddenly stood up and looked toward heaven, "I'm coming Samuel, I'm coming my love," and with those words still on her lips she collapsed and died, his letter still clutched in her hand.

Because Sister Agnes had died so soon after Carmichael, they were buried on the same day in the cemetery next to the church. Hundreds attended the Mass, and the church grounds were filled with families; in some cases two, three, and in a few cases, four generations; plus hundreds of others, many of whom did not attend Saint Patrick's. In serving the people of Kilrush for over sixty years, Father Carmichael and Sister Agnes had moved far beyond being a Priest and a Sister; they were family.

As the afternoon of the funeral wore on, numerous individuals came up to Father Grant, took hold of his sleeve and told him they were sad for Father Carmichael's passing, but were so grateful that God had sent him to take his place. Several remarked, "Only a man such as yerself could ever fill his shoes." Of all the honors and medals he had received during his military career, none brought him more joy than hearing these folks, his flock now, saying they knew God had sent him.

As Bridgit, Peter, and Grace left the little church cemetery, Bridgit told him there was something she had to do. "After Tom was killed, for the first couple of years I would go ta his grave almost everyday. I'd just sit on the stone wall and talk ta him, tell him what was happenin. After a while, I couldn't remember what he looked like and I felt so ashamed I stopped goin. Would ye mind goin there with me?"

Breffa Cemetery is very old, and is laid out with individual square or rectangular family plots enclosed by a low stone wall, with a single headstone on which the names and dates are inscribed. A few of the more prominent families erected a monument of some type; generally a Celtic cross above the headstone.

As Bridgit walked among the family plots, she would point them out to Grace and Peter, and read the names, many of them distant relatives, or friends of her parents; among them some of her own friends who had died young. When they came to their family plot, Grace began reading the names of her mother's great grandparents; grandparents; her parents, and her brother and sister who died in early childhood.

"These are our family Grace; someday, a long time from now God willing, our names will be written there."

"No they won't," Grace said.

"Grace!" Bridgit exclaimed, "why would ye say such a thing. "Don't ye want to be laid ta rest with yer family when yer time comes?"

"Aye Mommy, but we will not be here then."

"And jes where do ye think we will be goin?"

"I do na know, but there's lots of mountains covered with trees, and deep valleys with villages. It's not like here."

A shiver went down Bridgit's spine as she wondered what Grace's statement meant. She had seen something, but what? Before she could ask another question, they came to Tom's grave. She ran her fingers over his name and the date he died, "so long, long ago," she whispered.

"Take your time Sweetheart," Peter said softly combing his fingers through her hair, "Grace and I will walk around a bit."

Bridgit nodded a thank you and sat down on the stone wall. "It's been a long time Tom," she began. For the next half hour, she related all the things that had happened over the years, the terrible loneliness she had felt at first. Her meeting and then working with Kathleen; and about Sean, the town drunk and bully who had become a preacher. She told him about John and Cassie, Lawrence and Sally – English people mind you - and Arden. She laughed when she told him about Jim who lived in Holy Jim's Canyon, of whom they had heard stories when they were young, but had never met. She began crying when she told him that Father Carmichael and Sister Agnes had been buried today. Lastly, she told him that she now had a wonderful daughter named Grace; and how she came to marry Peter. She sat there silently for a few moments longer; wiped the tears from her eyes and stood up.

"Goodbye Tom," she said softly touching the headstone again. But even after all of these years, she couldn't stop the tears.

Chapter 31

Despite evidence to the contrary, the people continued to cling to the old belief that if the potato blight destroyed a crop one year, the following year would yield a more bountiful crop. Since the previous year's early crop had failed, expectations ran high that this year would be a very good crop. As further encouragement, it appeared that heaven sent exceptionally nice spring weather, and the planting went quickly.

However, not everyone in Ireland believed in the old superstition, including Neil and Lawrence. Based upon what they had been hearing from government spokesmen and reading in various agriculture articles; many members of Parliament had serious doubts about successful future potato harvests. Accordingly, they were making a major effort to replace the Irish people's dependence on potatoes, with imported American corn.

American corn was a new crop; one that neither Lawrence, or Neil had any experience in growing. Their plan was to take several of the potato fields that had failed the previous year, and plant them in American corn; what they needed was someone with experience. In anticipation, three months earlier Lawrence had placed several Help Wanted advertisements in London and New York City newspapers. They received several replies, including one from an American farmer who was coming to Ireland to spend the summer visiting relatives nearby. Since his letter came just four days before he was scheduled to arrive in Kilrush, they had no choice but to wait and meet him at the dock.

Percy Shea was a first generation American, but as Irish as Irish could be. When he stepped off the Mary Jane, he could easily have passed for a local, right down to his Irish brogue. As he stepped off the gangplank, he was followed by his portly wife; two strapping teenage sons; and two pretty younger daughters. It was evident from the way they were dressed that life had been very good to them in America. Percy Shea had the appearance of a very successful farmer. It was a good sign.

Lawrence and Neil stepped forward and introduced themselves. Percy reached out with both hands, and with a grip like a vise, shook Lawrence's and Neil's hands.

"Pleased ta meet ye both. This here is Ruth, my sweet bride of twenty years; my sons Michael and Jerry; and my little angels Lorraine and Megan. So this is Kilrush," he said looking around. "My parents left here in 1798 right after the Rebellion, if the British had caught my father they woulda hung him... and maybe my mother too," he laughed. "Oh the stories they told us about this place; the wonderful people; the town; the rebellion; and of course old Saint Patrick's. They never stopped telling us about the church and a wonderful young Priest, Father Carmichael. In fact, he was the one that saved their lives, and several others. He hid them in the Church's wine cellar when the British were searching for them. He'd be in his eighty's by now. Is he still alive?"

"He went to be with the Lord a couple of weeks ago," Lawrence answered.

"I'm sorry to hear that - not that he went ta be with the Lord - but that we won't be able ta meet him. My father passed a year ago, Mother is still with us but failing. It would have been wonderful to talk ta Father Carmichael about them. Jes ta see if everything they told us was true," he laughed.

As they started walking down the dock toward the street he asked, "So where's this little farm you boys have? I'm plantin close to two hundred acres now. Ruthie and I have the biggest farm in Jefferson County, Ohio," he said with obvious pride.

Neil looked at Lawrence, "Well we're not thinking of planting all our land in corn, we just want to try it out in a few fields and see if it will grow here. We realize we're quite a bit farther north than you are."

"According to your advertisement in the paper," Ruth asked, "you call your farm Arden. Is that from the Arden in Shakespeare."

"Yes it is," Lawrence replied. "The name was given to it by the former owner, and when my parents purchased the estate they kept the name."

"How wonderful," she said with a smile. "I'm looking forward to seeing it, assuming of course we - that is you and my husband," she quickly added, "can reach an agreement."

It was evident from the tone of her voice, that while Percy may be an excellent farmer, Ruth was the business woman. Whatever deal was made, she would be the one making the decision, but carefully letting her husband believe it was his.

"Well we're looking forward to having you come out to Arden. We think you'll enjoy seeing how we do things here; and having Percy let us know what he thinks about our idea to grow corn. Today, you can get settled in and rest up. Tomorrow, we'll send a carriage for you about 10:00 tomorrow morning."

"All of us?" Ruth asked.

"Why certainly. You need to meet our wives and some of the people Percy would be working with…. if this idea works out."

Ruth was obviously surprised by this, and pleasantly so. One of her hopes for this trip was to meet people other than 'just Percy's relatives.' Ruth was a very big frog in the pond back home, and she had no idea of who the Bligh's were, or the other people they would meet at Arden tomorrow. All she knew at this point was that this was her chance to meet some local farmer's wives.

"Do you hear that children? We're going to see an Irish farm tomorrow, isn't it exciting?"

From the glum expressions on the children's faces, Lawrence and Neil could tell it sounded like just more of what they had at home, and there was no excitement in that.

"Well, we'll see if we can come-up with something fun for you kids to do while we're talking business. Boys, have you ever fished for trout?"

"No," one of the boys answered, "all we got is ponds with sunfish and bullheads."

"I saw a picture of a trout in a magazine once, sure was a pretty fish," the older boy exclaimed.

"Well," Neil said demonstrating hooking a fish, "when you hook them, they run back and forth very fast and jump clear out of the water trying to throw the hook."

"Are they good to eat," a very pragmatic Ruth asked.

"Delicious," Lawrence answered. "If you boys can catch them, we'll have the cook fry them up."

"Are they hard to catch?" the younger boy asked.

"Sometimes they can be very hard to catch, but we'll see how it goes tomorrow." He looked at the girls who didn't look interested in the least bit. "Do you girls like to ride Ponies?"

"We've never ridden a pony before," the oldest girl answered. "Sometimes Daddy lets us ride with him on a horse."

"Then I think you girls are going to have a lot of fun tomorrow," Neil answered.

"Will they be safe?" Ruth asked.

"They'll be fine. There will be some other children their age, and a couple of adults to supervise them," Lawrence replied. "Well, I think we have everything taken care of here; we'll see you in the morning at Arden."

As Lawrence and Neil walked away, Percy turned to Ruth, "they sure seem to be a couple of nice fellas."

"I thought their considering the children was very special," Ruth added. "Not what I expected from businessmen. I'm lookin forward to seeing their farm, what about you?"

"Very much, very much," Percy replied watching them walking down the street.

"I'm gonna catch more trout than you," the younger boy said to his brother.

"Go catch your smelly old fish; we're gonna ride a pony," the girls yelled in unison.

"Looks ta me like tomorrow's gonna be a big day for everyone," Percy said. "Now let's get checked into our hotel, and get something to eat. I'm starved."

The following morning when they arrived at Arden, they were at first impressed with the lovely tree lined drive to the house, the manicured lawns and flower gardens. It was quickly becoming evident that Arden was more than a typical farm. As the carriages pulled up to the porch, there was a small delegation waiting to greet them. Lawrence introduced them to everyone, and said they would start a tour of Arden as soon as they got the children taken care of.

About fifty feet from the front porch, was a wagon ready to take the boys to the lake behind the dam. The son of one of the tenant farmer's was about a year older than the boys, was very keen on trout fishing, and knew the lake well. When Neil asked him if he'd like to take the day off and take the boys fishing, he jumped at the chance.

"We've got a boat there," he said as the boys climbed on the wagon and they started down the road. "When we get there, I'll show you how to rig the poles and lines."

As they left, Megan, the youngest girl asked, "Where's the pony?"

"Megan," Ruth scolded; "mind your manners."

"She's fine," Sally answered taking Megan's hand. "Com'on girls, let's walk down to the stable and see if they're ready." She reached down and also took Lorraine's hand, "are you ready to go riding?"

They nodded their heads.

"Then let's not keep those ponies waiting." Turning to Percy and Ruth, "com'on down with us, the other children are already there."

"While we're in that area," Neil said, "we'll show you our dairy and cheese operation."

"You have a dairy and make cheese?" Ruth asked.

"We ship cheese to over twenty countries now, in fact, we just added the United States a few months ago."

Ruth glanced at Percy. Arden was very much more than a typical farm.

"So how many acres do you have," Percy asked?" Guessing perhaps five hundred or so.

"Last year we bought another small farm that adjoined us to the east, so that brought us up to about 7,200 acres," Lawrence answered. "Of course not all of that is farmable. There's the land the tenant farmer's homes and gardens are on, that's probably a couple of hundred acres; a few orchards; couple of peat bogs; some rocky out croppings and odd areas, that sort of thing; plus the five or so acres here around the house that we never plant. We probably farm about 6,000 acres, and run the cows on another 500."

Percy and Ruth both gulped at the same time. Whatever their original impression had been, Arden was far beyond that. Ruth was mentally trying to compare Arden with where they lived back home, and quickly determined that it was larger than most of the farms in Jefferson County combined.

As they approached the stables, John and Cassie came out to meet them; "Mr. and Mrs. Shea, let me introduce you to my father Lord Bligh, and my stepmother, Lady Bligh."

John and Cassie could see from the dumb-founded confused look on their faces, they had never been introduced to anyone with a title before now, and were at a total loss of what to say or do.

Sensing their bewilderment Cassie quickly stepped forward, "We're very pleased to meet you. I'm Cassie and this is my husband John, please forget the Lord and Lady; we save that for the Court in London."

Lord, Lady, Court in London.... Ruth, who was never known back home to be at a loss for words, found herself unable to speak. But her mind was already beginning to think of the grand and glorious stories she would tell her gossiping friends when they returned home.

Percy however, was his usual self. "Hi, I'm Percy and this is my wife Ruth," he said reaching out his hand. "We're pleased to meet you. This certainly is an impressive operation you have here," he said looking at the stable. When we decided to reply to your son's ad, we had no idea of how large Arden is."

"Well it was only 3,200 acres when my first wife and I bought it," John said, "but we've added a few acres since then. Neil was the estate manager when we bought it, and now he and Lawrence run everything. Cassie and I just have fun now. In fact, we're taking your daughters and the other kids for a nice ride, and a picnic if that's acceptable to you?"

Ruth, having finally found her voice answered; "that would be wonderful."

Besides their two daughters, there were six other children who were jumping up and down as three men brought out the ponies, one for each of them. "A couple of other adults are coming with us in case any of the children need assistance" Cassie said. "Plus we have a wagon loaded with hay; food; and toys. If any of the children get tired riding their pony, they can ride in the hay wagon."

"Looks like you've thought of everything," Ruth said, secretly wishing she could go along, but she knew she needed to stay with Percy. At that moment, a man came out of the stable leading two of the most magnificent horses Percy had ever seen.

Noting the look on his face, John walked the horses over to him. "They're Arabians. Cassie and I bought them last year while we were in Egypt; and had them shipped here. Fabulous horses." He whispered in the ear of one of the horses, which nodded. "Just telling him how proud we are of them," he said to Percy.

"You talk to them?" Ruth asked.

"All the time. Something Neil taught me many years ago."

"When are we goin?" one of the children asked.

"Right now," Cassie replied. "Tom, would you help Megan and Lorraine get on their ponies, this is new for them." Looking around at the other children, she saw that they were already mounted and anxious to get started.

Ruth watched as her girls were seated on the ponies, and then saw John and Cassie mount their horses and lead their little troupe off across the field. She hadn't been on a horse since she was a young girl, and never gave it a thought back home. But now she was beginning to sense new awakenings, feelings she had never had before. When they got back home; they were going to get some riding horses, ponies, and build a stable. Percy didn't know it yet, but things were going to change.... really change.

For the tour of the fields, Lawrence and Neil had a nice comfortable carriage waiting for Percy and Ruth; while they rode along side pointing out various features and the fields they wanted to plant in corn. Every now and then they would stop, and Percy would get out of the carriage to inspect the fields and offer his opinion as to would it be suitable for raising corn. Ruth stayed in the carriage, not really paying attention.

On their voyage to Ireland, she had laid out very specific terms she intended to demand before Percy accepted the position: she intended to drive a hard bargain. All of that changed as of this morning at the stable. Now she was continually scanning the fields and the horizon for signs of the children and the Bligh's. Her new goal was to become friends with Lord and Lady Bligh, Lawrence, Neil and their wives; and spend as much time as she could at Arden. In fact, she little cared if Percy got paid anything, well maybe that was going a bit too far. After the fourth stop, she leaned over to him and whispered, "it looks very good to me Sweetheart, I think you should take the job."

He looked at her. 'Sweetheart'? She hadn't called him that in years, and 'take the job' just like that? This, after all the little lectures he had heard on the ship about not rushing into anything? Then it dawned on him and he smiled, "If that's what you think dear," he replied chuckling to himself. She was going to be the new Duchess of Jefferson County when they returned home; and this trip was going to be far more expensive than he had planned. Still, they were going to have a grand time, a very grand time.

Lawrence and Neil had also been carefully watching. As they pulled their horses up to a stop a little ahead of the carriage, Neil leaned over to Lawrence, "Did you see Ruth's face down at the stable? It's amazing how some people are affected by a couple of Titles, even these Americans who claim they don't believe in them. I don't think Ruth is going to be nearly as hard to deal with as we first imagined."

"Maybe we could get them to pay us," Lawrence laughed.

"I was wondering if the boys caught anything?" Neil replied, "I think we just got ours."

Chapter 32

As had happened the year before, disaster came silently like a thief in the night. On July 12th, the potato fields were lush and green. On the 13th, they were black rotting masses. It also quickly became apparent that this year's crop failure was far beyond the previous year. Last year, there were scattered fields hit by the blight, this year it seemed that almost every potato field had been destroyed.

Neil was a very early riser, up before the roosters had cleared their throats; and generally began his day before breakfast by checking the fields adjacent to his home. As he stepped out on his back porch, an unmistakable stench reached him; rotting vegetation. He bolted down the stairs and ran to the barn. He didn't waste time saddling his horse, but rode him bareback out of the barn heading for the potato fiends. Even in the early morning light of daybreak he saw devastation all around him. Turning his horse, he headed for Lawrence and Sally's home. He was halfway there when he met Lawrence.

"Looks like we have trouble," Lawrence called out. "Couldn't sleep last night, so I was up before daybreak and went out on the porch, that's when the smell hit me."

"Same here... looks bad, very bad," Neil replied, "three fields near my house are completely gone."

"So are the ones in the south quarter," Lawrence answered pulling his horse up along side Neil and noting the missing saddle. "Kinda in a hurry this morning?" he laughed.

"Oh I jest wanted to remind myself of what it was like before I started living next to you rich people," he replied with a chuckle. "Seriously," he said patting the neck of his horse, "I wanted to talk to you as soon as I could. Lucky you didn't sleep last night."

"A blessing in disguise, my mother would have said," he paused for a couple of seconds remembering her then continued. "Neil, I don't think we'll be able to salvage much of anything. Looks like it's going to be worse than last year; seems more widespread."

"I agree," Neil said, "we should immediately begin harvesting the good fields before we lose them too. Small potatoes are better than none. "

"Good idea. Get everyone; men, women, and the children into the other fields as fast as you can; save whatever's possible. I'm going to town to see Father Grant and tell him to start getting ready for whatever lies ahead."

As he turned to ride away, he pulled up his horse and looked back, "Neil,' he called, "send out a couple of riders to check the other farms. You might also want to put a saddle on your horse," he added laughing, "we've got a long day ahead of us, and your ass isn't as tough as it was before us rich people came along."

When Lawrence reached Saint Patrick's, there was already a small crowd of townsfolk standing by the front steps listening to Father Grant telling them to remain calm. "We don't know how many of the fields have been effected; perhaps it's only the small fields here in town." He uttered the words with a silent prayer, hoping that it was true. But when he saw Lawrence riding into town at a gallop this early in the morning, he knew it was not.

Before Lawrence reached the church steps, he was surrounded by the crowd yelling and asking questions asking about what he knew about the blight. Holding up his hand, he asked the people to stand aside so that he could talk to them from the steps.

He dismounted and waved to the crowd, whispering to Grant that he needed to talk to him privately.

"Good morning," he called out. "I know you're worried, but right now we need to remain calm while we determine how widespread the blight is. Right now, Neil has riders out checking for miles around. By tonight, we should have a good idea of what we're up against. In the meanwhile, you should go home and carefully check your own plots, and those of elderly neighbors. Dig up everything that's not rotted. If you have a good field, dig that one too. Save everything you can."

"Please folks," Father Grant called out raising his arms, "go home and do what he told you. We'll meet here tonight at six o'clock."

They watched the crowd disperse and walked into the church.

"Very bad," Lawrence began. "Looks like most of our potato fields were wiped out. We have everyone that can walk in the fields harvesting everything not hit with the blight."

"Worse than last year?"

"I think so, so does Neil. What's the condition of the storehouse?"

"Actually, it's in pretty good shape considering last year; but if what you suspect is true, we both know we'll never be able to meet the needs of a major disaster. We'll need outside help."

"That's what I was thinking as I rode into town. After Neil gets the reports from the riders, we'll know more about how extensive the blight is. I've a gut feeling it's very widespread this time."

"If you're right - and I hope and pray you're not – we'll need help from London; and only God knows if that will ever come. I don't need to remind you that Ireland is not on their priority list."

"You'll get no argument from me on that score. We'll need every friend and acquaintance we know in London to help us."

"I'll send a letter to the Bishop there and ask him to start rallying support," Grant offered.

"Good. As soon as I get back home, I'll tell Sally about the situation. She'll fire-off letters to John and Cassie who left last week for Italy, and all the political leaders she personally knows. I'm sure she'll also ask for help from the women's groups she used to work with. Were lucky that she's knows a lot of good people there."

"She was a wonderful help last year. Considering her past political involvement and connections to Parliament, she may prove to be even more of a help this time. We're very fortunate now to have her here, and you're a lucky man to have her as your wife," Grant said patting Lawrence on the shoulder. "Well, there's lots to do; we'll see you later this afternoon.... right?"

"Yes. Neil and I will be here before the meeting so we can brief you on what we've learned about the area."

With that, they parted. Father Grant heading back to his study, and calling to a young priest to round up everyone for an emergency meeting in his study – now! Lawrence walked down the church steps, mounted his horse and headed for the Methodist church. Reverend Swigart had a number of English members in his church, and this blight was going to hit them as much as the Irish. There was also the possibility that those members might have connections in London who could help.

Reverend Swigart, who had been up very late the night before visiting a sick family; had slept in later than usual and met Lawrence at the door in his nightshirt.

"Lawrence," he exclaimed, "what brings you knocking at my door this early?"

Over the next few minutes Lawrence brought him up to date on the blight that had struck overnight; the meeting with Father Grant, and about the meeting scheduled for that evening at Saint Patrick's.

"In the twinkling of an eye," Reverend Swigart said looking at Lawrence. "One day, or one minute all appears well, and in the next everything has changed." He looked down and suddenly became aware that he was standing on his front porch in his nightshirt.

"Speaking of changing, I'd better get inside before any of my women parishioners see me. Now that would be some gossip we don't need."

"Oh, I don't know," Lawrence laughed. "I think that maybe we're going to need all the smiles and laughs we can find. Now speaking for myself, it would be different."

"And why is that?"

"I don't sleep in a nightshirt." He turned and rode away leaving Reverend Swigart laughing on the porch, and wondering what Mrs. Swigart might think of that idea.

———————————

Neil was standing on the porch when Lawrence returned. He told Neil about the meetings with Grant and Swigart, and the meeting scheduled for six that night.

At that moment, Percy Shea and his wife Ruth walked up on the porch.

"What is that terrible smell?" she asked. "We had our bedroom window open last night and it woke me up early this morning. Smells like something's rotting."

"The blight," Neil answered. "It hit last night, wiped out over half our fields.

"The potato blight!" Percy exclaimed. "We've heard and read about it, but thought the stories had to be exaggerated. We have corn blights from time to time, but nothing wipes out an entire crop overnight. If a blight hits us, it might destroy maybe twenty – thirty percent, but never the entire crop."

"Well the potato blight does," Lawrence answered. "Green healthy plants one day, black rotting stench the next. No one knows what causes it; and there's never any kind of warning; no sign of a problem."

"Good heavens," Ruth exclaimed. "From what we've seen since we've been here, everyone lives on potatoes and almost nothing else. If there are none, what are these poor people going to do for food?"

"Well now you know why we have been so anxious to grow corn," Neil answered. "We don't look at it as just another crop to market. Lawrence and I have been very concerned about the potential disaster a major blight would cause."

"That's why we invited you over here," Lawrence joined in. "We wanted to see if we could successfully grow corn; and how quickly we could develop corn as a secondary food supply."

"I'll be the first to tell you," Neil added, "that the Irish are a stubborn lot, and we don't take to change easily. They've grown and eaten potatoes for uncounted generations. So growing corn is one thing, getting them to eat it will be another. But if they're faced with starvation, eat it they will."

"You don't need to tell me how stubborn the Irish are," Ruth spoke up. "I married one. I've seen this man," she said pointing to he husband, "cut off his nose to spite his face more than once."

"Now Ruthie Dear," Percy said walking over and placing his arm around her shoulders, "Larry and Neil have a very serious problem to deal with; they don't need to hear about our little differences."

"Little differences!" Don't Ruthie Dear me," she fumed, "if it wasn't for me, we might not have a farm."

Seeing where this was headed, Lawrence jumped in before Ruth really got going. "You're right Percy, we have a very serious problem, and we're going to need all the help we can get. You've been here for almost three months now, and have met quite a few people in town that like and respect you."

At the mention of respect, Ruth straightened her shoulders and a slight smile crossed her lips.

The look did not escape Lawrence's gaze. "Ruth, there's going to be a meeting at Saint Patrick's at six tonight, and Neil and I would like you to come and start talking to the local women about corn; how to cook it, different ways to prepare it."

"The corn won't be ready to harvest for at least two – two and a half months," Neil added. "If we're lucky - and we won't know that 'till our Riders get back later today – we believe there'll be enough potatoes to last until late August. Of course everyone will have to cutback and eat less, but we think it will work."

Lawrence listened to Neil, knowing that neither of them really believed that; but at this point what was needed most was to instill confidence in the future. Percy, Ruth, and their family would be returning to America after the corn harvest. In that sense, the potential famine wasn't their problem. But in the meanwhile, using them and their personal experience with corn as a major food source in America, could help turn the local Irish folks total reliance on potatoes around.

"The problem here Ruth, is that these folks know nothing about corn. We need to begin teaching them now about how to prepare it. We can't wait until the potatoes run out and they begin starving."

"Do you really think it could come to that?" Percy asked.

"Yes, I've seen it many times in my life," Neil answered.

"Do you have any corn?" Ruth asked.

"We have some seed corn left, right Percy?"

"Maybe a hundred pounds."

"Well it's not the best for cooking, but I can use it to get started," Ruth answered. "I can teach them how to make a corn chowder; corn casserole; corn pudding; corn bread..." her mind was already moving into high gear. She was also beginning to think about how her heroic efforts to save the starving Irish would play out at home.

"Good, that's all we need at this point," Lawrence said. "I'll have one of our men take it to the mill and have it ground. Now if you'll excuse us, I think Neil and I would like to get some breakfast."

As they walked away, they could hear Ruth and Percy talking about the blight and potential famine. Not having enough to eat was almost beyond their comprehension; let alone nothing to eat, and people actually dying from starvation. This was something they had not expected on their trip to Ireland.

The Riders returned late in the afternoon exhausted, and with very bad news. They had visited almost every farm and estate within twenty miles of Arden. Again, it was the same mysterious pattern; one field would be totally destroyed, while the adjacent field remained untouched. The major difference this year was that far many more fields were gone. Based on what they had seen and learned, they estimated that approximately seventy percent of the fields had been destroyed.

Lawrence and Neil thanked the men and told them to go home and get some rest. Tomorrow, they wanted them to ride to the adjoining Counties and see what the situation was there. The situation was bad enough as it was, but if the other counties had suffered similar losses...they shuddered to think of the implications.

Upon learning of the extent of the crop losses, Sally began writing letters to everyone she knew in London that could possibly be of help. It had been several years since she had been actively involved in politics; but many of her former friends and associates were still active, and they in turn had contacts. By late afternoon, she had written over thirty letters; and on each one she included a postscript about the detailed report that her husband was preparing, to be sent later. She also wrote to John and Cassie, and included a request from Lawrence to immediately purchase and ship five hundred pounds of ground corn to Arden. Getting up from her desk, she said she would personally take the letters to the dock later today, and see that they were on the first ship heading for England.

As luck would have it, the Mary Jane was in port and leaving for Bristol the following morning. Assuming a good passage, the mail would reach London in less than a week; the sooner the better. As she handed the mail to the Captain, she looked and saw Bridgit and Grace standing at the end of the dock. She thanked the Captain, called to Bridgit and began waving her arms.

"It's so good to see you again," she called out. "Hello Grace, you sure look pretty today."

"We're waiting for my Daddy," Grace said spinning around to show off her dress.

"The Gideon's on her way in," Bridgit added. "Peter's been out for a week and we've missed him."

"It's wonderful knowing that you're all so happy." She paused briefly and then said, "I'm sure you heard about the crop failure. I came down to mail some letters to friends in London. We're going to need outside help this time."

"I know," Bridgit replied "It's gonna be very bad this time"

"Lawrence and Neil sent Riders out early this morning, they came back a couple of hours ago and said about seventy percent of the crops had been destroyed."

Bridgit glanced at Grace and then stepped close to Sally and spoke in a low voice. "Grace had another dream; a very bad dream. She saw a woman holding a rotten potato in one hand, an a dead child in her arms."

"My God!" Sally exclaimed, "did you tell anyone?"

"We went to see Father Grant two weeks ago. He thanked me and said all we could do was to pray that it wouldn't come true." She looked at Sally, "but I knew it would. Will ye and Lawrence be stayin here in Ireland? Bridgit asked.

"Oh yes, yes. There's going to be so much to do. Will you help us get ready?"

"Grace and I will do everything we can. Have ye talked to Sean?"

"No, I haven't seen him in a couple of months."

"He's been preaching in England; just got back two days ago. He's becoming quite famous ye know. Ye'll need ta talk with him."

At that moment, Grace began yelling, "I can see the sails. I can see the sails Mommy."

Sally looked down river, "I can see lot of boats and sails Grace. Are you sure it's your Father's boat?" Sally asked.

"Oh ye can be sure of it," Bridgit answered with a big smile. "Before ye can see the boat, she knows it by the sails. Never bin wrong yet,"

"I'd like to stay until he comes in and say hello, but I have to get to the church. Did you know there's a meeting tonight at six?" Sally asked.

"We'll be there," Bridgit answered.

"Well I have to leave. Say hello to Peter for me, and I hope we'll see you later. Bye Grace," she called. But Grace was far too intent on watching the Gideon grow larger and larger as it came up the river. She held her mother's hand and squeezed it. Very soon her Daddy would be home again.

The meeting at the church was not as successful as they hoped it would be. Despite Neil's account of the extensive crop losses; there were the usual unconcerned responses.

"We've had it worse than this before; the fall crop will be fine; we'll survive, we always do. Besides, we've got the storerooms now ta tide us over, so there's little to fret about." They drove Lawrence, Neil, Sally, and Father Grant crazy.

But while the local people were unfazed, Ruth was beside herself. Her carefully planned cooking demonstrations attracted only two women, Kathleen and Bridgit. All the rest of the women politely thanked her, but said they saw no need to learn how to cook corn. Come fall, there would be plenty of potatoes.

"My Lord," she later told the others back at Arden, "and I thought Percy was stubborn."

"We never said it would be easy," Lawrence laughed. "You just have to keep hitting the Irish on the head until you get their attention."

"And sometimes they die before that happens," Neil added, which brought a round of laughter from around the table.

It had been a very long trying day. It felt good to laugh.

The following morning, the ten men selected to ride to the adjoining counties stood by the porch as Lawrence and Neil gave them their instructions. This was not to be a haphazard inspection tour, but a detailed plan complete with written daily reports. All of the men selected could read and write, and were good communicators. They would be sent out in pairs, the belief being that four eyes and four ears were better than two. Because appearance would be important, each man was given two pairs of pants, two shirts, and a light top-coat. Each man carried a letter of introduction stating that he was a representative of the Arden Estate in Kilrush - which had become widely known over the years - that could be presented to local officials; owners of estates; and anyone else who might wish to question them. Each team was provided with sufficient money for food and lodging for twelve days, although the plan called for them to return in ten days. In addition, in the event of a real financial emergency, each team carried a letter of credit from the Bank of London.

Looking out at the men assembled on the lawn; for a fleeting moment Lawrence's mind went back to India and those times when he would address his troops before a battle. In a very real sense, their present situation was a battle; one in which survival itself could be at stake.

"Men," he began slowly, "we are in a battle. Not against an opposing enemy of men with weapons, but against something just as deadly; the possibility of wide spread famine. An enemy that you well know could not only kill you; but your wives and children; your parents....your friends."

He watched the changing expression on the men's faces, and could tell by how they shifted their weight and stood more erect that they were listening to what he was saying; that this was a critical moment in their lives, and that of their families.

"You're going out on a very important mission. Neil and I want you to carefully observe everything you see, and listen to what you hear. Jot down notes in the booklets we gave you: how many fields destroyed; how many acres; how many fields didn't get hit by the blight; the attitude of the local people; the estate owners; town officials. In regard to the English Land owners and local officials, don't be intimidated by them. You represent Arden and the Bligh family which, as most of you know, is one of the wealthiest and most powerful families in England." He let that sink in for a moment, and then to lighten the mood added, "besides, those stuffy English Lords put their pants on one leg at a time, just like you do." That brought a big laugh from the men and others gathered around.

Neil spoke up, "Remember, we don't want rumors, or gossip; there'll be plenty of that right here in Kilrush: we want facts. Facts so we can carefully plan our strategy to deal with this crisis."

The men stood silently listening to Lawrence and Neil, proud to have been picked for such an important mission. With only two exceptions, these men had been ordinary tenant farmers before they began working for the Bligh's at Arden. Only one had ever been more than fifteen miles from where he was born. Now they had been chosen to become the representatives of one of the most famous estates in south western Ireland, perhaps in all of Ireland. In fact, the produce from Arden was now sold in numerous countries throughout the world. Never in their lives had they ever imagined they would ever be given such an important task, and they could see the pride in the eyes of their wives, children, and friends.

"Neil, anything else you want to add?"

Neil shook his head, "I think that covers it."

"Ok then," Lawrence said as he and Neil stepped down off the porch, "time to get started."

There was a flurry of good-byes, and kisses from wives and children. Lawrence and Neil went to each man, shook their hand, and made a personal comment about how much they trusted their judgment and were counting on them. The men could not have been any more proud had they been appointed by the Pope himself.

"Mount up," Neil called.

"God speed," Lawrence called as he waived his hand.

The men, sitting tall in their saddles astride beautiful riding horses, rode slowly down the drive, listening to the cheers and good-byes from their families and friends.

Very soon, they would separate into four teams. Two teams heading to Galway and Tipperary, the Counties to the north and east; and the remaining two teams going to the dock in Kilrush, where they would take a boat to Limerick and Kerry Counties on the south shore of the Shannon River.

The next ten days were at one and the same time, frantic with activity, and agonizingly slow waiting for the men to return. Everyday was filled with making preparations for dealing with the extent of the crop failure as they knew it; while at the same time trying to anticipate what would be needed if the disaster deepened and became more widespread. Lawrence and Neil's belief that it was going to be more severe was supported by the fact that in the days immediately following the first failure on the 12th, additional fields were hit by the blight. Their decision to immediately harvest all their fields had been the right one.

Meanwhile, other farmers and individuals agonized over whether to gather-in an immature crop of young potatoes; or have faith that the blight had by-passed them. Most of those who left their crops in the field lost everything in the following days. But not every field was destroyed.

Everyday brought more rumors and gossip from travelers passing through town. "Total disaster, not a single potato left anywhere," one hysterical woman said as she boarded the boat to Bristol. "I'm not gonna stay here and starve ta death." Other more rational strangers passing through town still painted a picture of a major disaster, although they avoided being fatalistic.

Lawrence and Neil believed that if what they were hearing was even half true, the price of potatoes, which had already started to rise, would quickly skyrocket. Not wasting any time, Lawrence and Neil made an open offer to buy the crop from any field that had survived, at a price slightly above the prevailing price.   These crops were immediately harvested and turned over to the Emergency Planning Group.

In the meanwhile; counting the days until the Riders returned with their reports, Father Grant, Sally, and the others on the Planning Committee; laid out detailed instructions for the distribution of the potatoes and other food stocks which had been placed in storage.

It was a case of prepare for the worst, and pray, pray, pray, for the best.

Chapter 33

On the tenth day, two of the teams returned as planned. The two remaining teams, which had been delayed awaiting a boat to ferry them back across the river, returned late the following morning. Recognizing the critical importance of their mission, the teams had been on the road from before sunrise to well after dark every day trying to cover as much territory as possible. They returned with notebooks packed with data; and spoke for hours providing additional details not recorded in their books; personal stories of the people they met; their attitudes; hopes; and fears. Having spent twelve to fourteen hours a day, much of it on horseback, all of the men were bone tired.

Their reports were far more than Lawrence and Neil had hoped for. Despite their lack of much in the way of formal education; the reports they brought back were nearly as good as any Lawrence had received from his officers in India. The meeting went on past lunch as each man added what he could to the record. Finally, very late in the afternoon shortly before dinner time; Lawrence stood up and stretched.

"Men," he began, "I can't begin to tell you how very, very, proud I am of you, and what you've done. You don't know it, but these reports will help us save hundreds, maybe even thousands of lives. Not just here at Arden - we're fairly well off here - but in Kilrush, and other towns and Counties."

"What happens now Sir?" one of the men asked.

"Well, you men get a chance to rest for a couple of days; catch up on some sleep; maybe go fishing. I'm going to take your reports and condense them into a single report that I'll have printed. I'll then send copies to key political and social leaders here in Ireland, and in England. You men don't know it, but Governments are like the military; they never do anything unless there's a report. That way if something goes wrong, the leaders have someone else to blame it on."

"Kinda like my wife, they is," one man called out. "If anythin goes wrong, 'tis always because of somethin I did or said."

"Ye must be married ta my wife then," another man called out, causing a round of laughter.

"Lads, your families and friends here were very proud of you the day you left. Within a few more days, folks for miles around here; in London, and even in Parliament will know your names. I'll condense your individual reports, but your names will be listed big and bold as the men that gathered the information."

"But before you let your heads get to big for your caps," Neil spoke up, "there'll be some English Landlords that will hate you even more. Never forget, they'll not lift a finger to help the Irish, and they certainly don't want the government to help."

"True 'nough," a couple of the men answered.

"I heard a man in the Pub say that they want ta rid Ireland of the Irish. Kin ye imagine such a thing, Ireland without the Irish?"

"Well, that's not going to happen," Lawrence said. "There will always be an Ireland, and the Irish living here if we have anything to say about it…right?"

"Right ye are," they answered in a chorus.

"Ok now, skedaddle," Lawrence said with a wave of his hand. "Neil and I have a lot of work to do. Neil, are the packages ready?"

"Right here," he answered. As the men left the room each was handed a package containing a handsome bonus.

"Take your wives and children to town and have some fun while you can. The miseries will be on us soon enough."

After they had left, Lawrence looked at Neil. "I figure it will take me about two days to get the report written. With luck, the members of Parliament will have copies in their hands in a fortnight. Sally will also send copies to some of the people she contacted."

"While you're working on that; I'm going out with Percy to check the corn fields," Neil replied. "Later this afternoon, I'm going to town with Sally. She wants to meet with Father Grant and the Planning Committee and see how the plans for the store rooms are coming along." As he started to leave the room, he turned around and looked at Lawrence. "Did she tell you she saw Bridgit and Grace, and about Grace's dream?"

"She did. Terrible dream. Did Grace say she recognized the woman in her dream?"

"No," Neil answered. "But I know who she is. She's Ireland."

The next two weeks were a flurry of activity. The report had been mailed to dozens of political and social leaders in both Ireland and England. Responses were mixed. The Society of Friends (Quakers), immediately developed plans to setup soup kitchens in various cities and towns in Ireland, including Kilrush.

Sally, fully aware of the political implications in asking the British government for help - which was the central purpose behind the Report - left for London two days after they were mailed. She arrived in London just as they were being delivered to the recipients. Within days, she was involved in meetings from morning until late at night. Wherever she went, she carried extra copies of the Report; and was tenacious in getting the listeners to understand the potential magnitude of the crop failures. In meeting after meeting, the primary objection to offering any help; was the common knowledge that Ireland had suffered from numerous potato blights in the past, and had always managed to survive. Why should anyone believe this failure was any different from those in the past?

Furthermore, why should English taxpayers be expected to bail out the stupid; stubborn; Irish who continued to cling to raising a single crop that they knew was susceptible to repeated failures? A few of her closest friends pulled her aside and told her quietly that she had been in Ireland so long, she had forgotten the English hostility, not just to the Irish, but to Catholicism.

"They will not say this to your face Sally, but among themselves the talk is why should we help save the Papists?"

Upon reflection, she realized that her friends were right. She had been living at Arden and among the Irish Catholics for so many years, that the hostility to Rome had faded from her mind. Thus far she had been trying to swim upstream, trying to save a nation the English detested

Overnight, she changed her tactic from seeking help to save the masses of faceless Irish Catholics; to help save a starving family. She appealed to women's groups, "what if it was your children who were starving?" she asked.

Many of these women, who had themselves struggled to feed their own families from time to time; could readily identify with that cry for help. This new appeal spread quickly as these groups spread the word; and some political leaders began to accept the idea that something had to be done to help Ireland.

Sir Robert Peel, the Prime Minister of England, was sitting at his desk when Peters, his Secretary, entered the room and announced that a Mrs. Lawrence Bligh was waiting outside, and wished to see him.

"Mrs. Bligh?" he asked, "does she have an appointment?"

"No Sir Robert, she does not."

"Mrs. Lawrence Bligh," he mumbled to himself, "wait…I have it. Her husband, Captain Bligh sent that Report on the famine to me - and almost everyone else from what I have heard." He rummaged among the stacks of files on his desk, "ah, here it is. "When did we receive this?"

"Two days ago," Peters replied.

"I really need to read it before I talk to her," Peel whispered to himself as he flipped through the pages. "Looks very thorough. Says here he served in India, with Major Wilkins. Good man, Wilkins."

"Yes Sir Robert. What shall I tell her Ladyship?"

"Tell her I'm too busy now; perhaps tomorrow. And Peters, tell her I have her husbands Report. You understand it's not necessary to tell her I haven't read it as yet."

"Certainly Sir," Peters said smiling.

Moments later, Peters came back into the room. "Excuse me Sir Robert, it's about Mrs. Bligh. She still insists on seeing you today; and asked me to tell you that Sally's back. She said you would know what that meant."

"Sally?" he exclaimed getting up from his desk. "Good lord Peters, it's been so long that I forgot that she married Lawrence Bligh." He hurried out from behind his desk. "Well don't stand there Peters, show the Lady in."

As she entered the room, a hundred memories came flooding into his mind. "Lady Bligh," he said as he greeted her at the door. "I must apologize for not recognizing your married name, it's been so long. So tell me all about yourself and what you've been doing all these years. You realize of course that when you left London, things were never the same. No one else seemed to be able to," he carefully searched for the right words, "stir the pot quite as well as you did," he said with a chuckle as he took her hand.

"It's wonderful to see you again Sir Robert, and the name is Sally," she said as he lead her to a sofa and they both sat down. "So, I was a pot stirrer," she said with a laugh. "A good one I hope."

"The very best."

It was like old times for both of them. For over an hour, they reminisced about the political battles they had waged over ridding the Nation of Slavery. She told him how relieved she had been, when she learned that he had escaped the assassination attempt on his life a few years ago.

"It was tragic that Drummond, your Secretary, was killed. I always liked him, and he was always so kind to me," Sally added.

"It was a terrible time," he replied. "The assassin; Daniel M'Naghten, was criminally insane. Peters, came to work for me shortly after that. He's a good man, but Drummond had been with me for so many years he knew my idiosyncrasies and moods. I miss him."

"So now that you've moved into your new building; how do you like it? Must be a big change after all those years in old Westminster."

"It has been quite a change. The fire was back in 1834; so its taken almost thirteen years to rebuild. Did you know that it was Lord Melborne himself who had them bring the fire engines right into the Hall. His quick thinking saved the Chapel crypt, the Jewel Tower, and Westminster Hall."

"Well he did have some experience at putting out previous fires," she laughed.

He chuckled, "You're referring to his wife's affair with Lord Byron; and the attempt by Caroline Norton's husband to blackmail him. There wasn't any evidence, so of course the blackmail attempt failed. Nonetheless, both unfortunate for William. Still, we all had a great deal of respect for his integrity; and the Queen continued to write to him for years for advice –which she was not allowed to do - until she married Price Albert."

They turned to lighter subjects, and she laughed when he told her that a sigh of relief went up from several members of Parliament when they learned that she was getting married; and would not be joining in the campaign for women's suffrage.

"Is that right?," she smiled. "Maybe it's time for the 'Pot Stirrer' to return." She congratulated him on the recent passage of the Factory Act, restricting the number of hours that women and children could work in a factory. "Quite an achievement considering the fact that your father was one of England's leading Industrialists; not to mention the fact that so are many of your supporters."

"It had to be done," he replied. "It was not simply the long hours; but the hazardous conditions under which they worked. Hardly a week went by, but that some woman or child was getting maimed or killed operating a dangerous machine. The new safety regulations are modest; but they're a start, a move in the right direction."

The room was silent for a moment.

"Sir Robert, you know the reason for my visit. I know that if anyone can help with the growing crisis in Ireland it is you."

"Sally I...."

"Please let me finish. Have you read my husbands report?"

"No, not yet. I was planning on taking it home tonight."

"It's critical that you read it. This blight will not be like those of previous years."

"Come now Sally, how can you say that?"

Sally stood up and walked around the room, her fingers lightly touching some of the books on the shelves. "I'm going to tell you something," she said turning to face him.

Something that a few years ago I myself would not have believed; but I'm a believer now because I've witnessed it."

For the next twenty minutes she told him about Grace and the gift. Her dreams, and the fact they all had come to pass just as she dreamed them.

"I've heard about people that were said to have been born with a veil. But I've never met anyone who claimed to possess 'the gift' as you call it. And you say this girl's last dream was of a woman with a rotten potato in one hand and a dead child in the other?"

"Yes. A frightening, terrible, dream." She came over and sat down close to him. "I believe the woman is Ireland, and the child is the future. Unless something is done quickly...." her voice trailed off.

"Sally, I give you my solemn pledge that I'll study the Report tonight; and will do whatever I can to help." He paused, placing his fingers around his chin in thought. "One thing that could help is repealing the Corn Laws. That would free the government to buy large quantities of American corn and ship it to Ireland."

"That would be marvelous," she exclaimed standing up again. "Do you really think Parliament would do that?" I haven't been around here for several years, but unless something has changed, you'll be fighting against your own Party...again."

"No question about that. Our Party is still mostly the land owners, including your Father-In-law... and your own husband. They'll view a motion to repeal those laws as interfering with market prices."

"Don't worry about my husband Lawrence, or John Bligh. I spoke to John the day I arrived in London. They'll do everything they can to help and support you. The same goes for Cassie, John's wife. She said she'll talk to the wives of the land owners, and tell them that this is not about grain prices; the market; or money. It's about saving families; men, women, and their children."

At that moment Peters walked into the room. Twice before, he had entered the room to inform Sir Robert that he had another appointment waiting. Each time, he was told to tell the person that he was in an important conference, and would be with them shortly.

Before Peters could utter a word, Sir Robert waved his hand. "Yes, yes, Peters. Sally...," he quickly corrected himself, "Mrs. Bligh, and I are just finishing. Tell whoever it is that I'll see them in five minutes."

Peter gave a slight bow of acknowledgement; walked out, and closed the door.

"I'm truly sorry, but I really have to get on with business. It's been grand seeing and talking to you again." They got up from the sofa and walked toward the door. "Sally, I want you to know that there are some of us here that have missed you." He paused for a moment and took her hand, "you were ever the champion of the Angels of our better nature. Will I see you again before you return to Ireland?"

"John and Cassie have been traveling in Europe, and just returned home from Italy. They're having a small dinner party next week. Would you and Lady Peel join us?"

"We would be delighted," he replied walking her to the door. "My wife simply adores Cassie, says she sparkles with life," he said with a little chuckle. "If you don't mind my saying so, both John and Lawrence appear to have found themselves exceptional wives."

"Now you've confused me," she replied. "Am I an exceptional wife, or a pot stirrer?"

"I'd say you are an exceptional pot stirrer," he said with a warm smile. "When I see your husband, I'll ask him about the wife part."

"When I get back to Arden, I'll be sure to tell Lawrence he married an exceptional pot stirrer," she said laughing. "Now don't forget about coming to dinner, I'll have an invitation sent to you tomorrow."

Five days later, true to his word; Sir Robert Peel proposed a Bill to the Parliament for the repeal of the Corn Laws, touching off a fierce political battle. Repealing the Corn Laws, Peel argued, would permit the government to buy large quantities of corn from America, and ship it to areas in need of food in both England and Ireland. The opposition replied that it was not the responsibility, or the duty, of government to feed people; especially in Ireland. Everyone knows they have crop failures every few years. Start feeding them now, and it will never end. Those people need to take responsibility for their own fate.

Peel continued to argue against great opposition from his own Conservative Party; insisting that the government did have a responsibility to care for its citizens. "They desperately need food; and we have a means of getting it to them."

The English owners of large Irish estates, the backbone of his own Conservative Party; believed that Peel had betrayed them, and fought to block the repeal by publicly claiming that it would disrupt the free market. In reality however, they viewed the potential famine as a god given chance to legally evict the tenants from their property, and convert the land to raising cattle. After all, they pointed out; it was not them, but God who was responsible for the terrible Blight.

Still others, out of their deep hatred of the Irish - even though they had no financial interests in Ireland - used their wealth and political influence in an attempt to keep the British government from doing anything to alleviate the growing crisis in Ireland. Despite the opposition; public awareness of the crisis was growing, and attitudes were changing. Eventually Peel was successful, and the Corn Law was repealed; permitting a government subsidy for the purchase of food for Ireland.

In an age when the prevailing political attitude was that government should not interfere with commerce, his action was considered to be much too radical. The result was that his own Party turned against him; and he was forced to resign as Prime Minister.

"Sally, Sally "he whispered to himself, "there's a very dear price to pay for listening to the angel of one's better nature."

Chapter 34

John and Cassie, who had become increasingly disturbed by the daily reports in the London newspapers about the growing food problem in Ireland; decided to cut their holiday short and return to Arden with Sally. Although they were anxious to get to Arden; they waited a fortnight until Sally finished with her scheduled meetings, in order that they could travel together. They did this for two reasons: first to spend more time alone with Sally and get a real sense beforehand of what was happening in Arden and Kilrush. Secondly, because there were increasing reports in the papers of hungry, desperate, and occasionally violent Irish immigrants arriving in English sea ports. Under those circumstances, they did not want Sally traveling alone. The following week they all boarded the Mary Jane, bound for Kilrush.

John and Cassie, who had not been in Kilrush for almost two months, were shocked at the scenes that met their eyes as the Mary Jane tied up at the dock. Instead of the neat orderly dock; fishing boats off-loading their catch; and a few local residents just walking along the dock; there were dozens and dozens of hungry people milling about waiting for the next fishing boat to pull in, hoping to be able to snatch any stray fish that might slip through the cargo net during the off-loading. The fish were devoured raw on the spot; while distraught mothers franticly tried to keep their hungry children from getting trampled in the rush.

"These people aren't just hungry," Cassie remarked, "they're starving. My God John, what's happened here?"

In town, the streets and walks were crowded with hundreds of desperate people; young and old alike; and there were long lines in front of the newly opened soup kitchens.

"What's that," Cassie asked pointing. "I don't remember that being here before."

"A soup kitchen to feed the hungry; its run by the Quakers," Sally answered. "As soon as the news of the extent of the blight reached London, they began sending food and supplies. Wonderful people; I'll introduce you to some of them later."

"Look at the Workhouse!" John exclaimed pointing down the street.

Two blocks away the government workhouse, which had been opened years ago when the Poor Law was passed; had previously seldom held more than a score of people on relief. Now however, because English Landlords were evicting increasing numbers of families from their small plots of land for failure to pay rent' the workhouse was filled to capacity; and the Overseer had no idea of what to do with the scores of homeless, hungry, men, women, and children that came walking into Kilrush every day. Even had he wanted to help feed those in the streets, English law forbid helping anyone outside the Workhouse.

As they got closer to Saint Patrick's, here and there they recognized a familiar face; but for the most part, the hungry masses were strangers from outside Kilrush.

"I had no idea it was this bad," John said as they walked up the steps of Saint Patrick's. "We read articles in the papers almost everyday; but we assumed that the reports were highly exaggerated, written by reporters eager to make a name for themselves."

"It wasn't this bad when I left four weeks ago," Sally said carefully looking around, "but then most of the people still had something left to eat."

"What about Arden?" Cassie asked noting that the door to the church was closed and locked as they reached the top of the stairs.

"I'm sure Arden is ok," Sally answered just as Father Grant opened the door.

There was a flurry of greetings as Grant welcomed them all back; and told Sally how much everyone had missed her while she was away.

John and Cassie, who had largely turned the management of Arden over to Lawrence and Neil, had spent most of the past two years traveling the world; interspaced with short visits to London and Arden. Consequently, with the exception of a weekly letter from Sally, and the periodic financial reports sent by Lawrence, they had little direct contact with what was happening in Ireland.

Father Grant escorted everyone to his study where he quickly brought them up to date on the status of the church's store rooms and the Emergency Plan. "The simple fact is that the blight is far beyond anything anyone expected. If we had a hundred times – a thousand times – what we have, we could not meet the needs of our own members; let alone the hundreds that are coming into town."

As he collapsed into his chair, it was evident that Grant was nearing a state of exhaustion.

"Who else is here to help?" John asked.

"We have two young priests; Father Edward - you know him Sally -; and Father Phillip from France who just came three weeks ago. They're both over-whelmed at what's happening. We also have five sisters; but three of them are very young and have little experience. But then, no one has dealt with anything like this before."

"Besides the church staff," he continued, "Colin and Mary are here much of the time. His blacksmith business is virtually dead now; so they spend their time here doing what they can to help. Kathleen comes whenever she can;

but she's been so busy out in the country – she and Sean take a wagon out helping the elderly and children on the road. Bridgit and Grace are usually here everyday when Peter is out fishing; and then there are a few others who stop in and offer their help. Reverend Swagart's just as swamped as we are. "

"Have you heard anything about the conditions in Holy Jim's Canyon?" Sally asked.

"Nothing. I've wanted to get out there and see Jim, but haven't had the time. Come to think of it; I don't recall seeing anyone from the Canyon in town recently."

"Maybe Jim's been to Arden," Sally replied. "In any case, we'll send someone out there to check on them." She paused and continued, "Incidentally, we were surprised to find the church doors closed and locked. The doors were never locked before."

"It was a difficult decision," Grant answered; "but last week we finally had to close and bolt the doors. If we didn't, the church would be over-run, and there are those who would steal everything that wasn't nailed down to sell for food money. I don't think our members would ever do such a thing; but the town's filled with strangers, as I'm sure you noticed."

"What happened?" Sally asked. "It wasn't this bad when I left a month ago."

"Several things," Grand answered. "More and more fields were being hit by the blight everyday. The Emergency Plan guidelines we set before you left had to be changed. The mounting fear now is that the fall crop will also be lost; so the Planning Committee had no choice but to impose even stricter rationing; in reality, bare survival allocations. Had Lawrence and Neil not purchased the crops from the local farmers a few weeks ago and placed them into the store rooms; those fields would have rotted, or quickly have been stripped clean by neighbors and strangers desperate to feed their families."

"We've talked to hundreds of women and men," Grant continued. "Over and over they would relate stories of how their, and their neighbors, potato fields had been wiped out by the blight. Within a few weeks, they had picked and eaten whatever turnips or other crops they had. Once they were gone, the men, women, and children, were scouring every field searching for nettles and whatever edible weeds they could find. Those who had owned pigs; were soon forced to slaughter them because of a lack of anything to feed them. With no way to preserve the meat; a lot of folks then got sick from eating too much pork, or bad pork."

Sally told Grant about her meeting with Peel, and other members of Parliament, and the repeal of the Corn Laws.

"I read about that Sally," Grant answered, "and it's wonderful what you helped accomplish. But I'm convinced that the British government is not moving fast enough to deal with a rapidly escalating catastrophe."

As he started to get up from his chair, John noticed that he staggered slightly. "How long since you've had a full nights sleep?"

Grant offered a feeble smile, "It's been a while."

"Well we're going to take care of that; you're coming home with us. Sally, go get Father Edward and ask him to meet us here."

A few moments later, Father Edward returned with Sally. There was a brief meeting during which they discussed Father Grant's state of exhaustion, and the need for him to get some solid rest.

"We've been after him for weeks now to get away from here for a few days," Father Edward replied, glancing at Father Grant and the others. "Under the circumstances, there is just so much you can do. Father Phillip, the Sisters and I can handle the situation here for several days."

"But this is a battle," Grant replied, "and......"

"It's not all going to be fought today, or this week," John said cutting him off. "I'm ordering you to go to Arden for a few days. Even the best generals need their rest."

"Aye, aye, Sir," Grant replied saluting John, and sinking back into his chair.

"Good, that's settled. Now General Grant, go pack your night shirt. You're going with us to Arden."

Grant got up and placed his arm around John's shoulders as they walked toward the door. "You know John, I think you'd have made a hellava good military man; if you'll pardon some old army language," he chuckled. "I'll get my things and be back in a minute."

As Grant left the room, Edward spoke up. "I know I can speak for Father Phillip and the Sisters when I tell you how grateful we are to you for taking him away from here. We've been talking to him for weeks to slow down, but he wouldn't listen to us. At the rate he's been going, he'd kill himself."

"It can be a lesson for all of us," Cassie said. "There are terrible days ahead and we all need to use all the strength and wisdom we can find to get through them. You know, I think we should invite Fathers Edward, Phillip, and the Sisters to Arden as well. I'm certain they all need a rest."

"Wonderful idea," John said. "Father Edward, why don't you make up a schedule to have everyone including yourself, come out two at a time. You can start as soon as Father Grant returns."

"I'd like to expand on that," Sally said. "From what I've been hearing today, it would be a good idea to setup a meeting at Arden. We could invite all the key people from the area to re-assess the situation. That way we would all be working together on the same plan; and it would give everyone a chance to take a break from the daily stress."

"Great idea Sally," Cassie replied. "We need to use Arden as a place of rest and re-cooperation. Only God knows how long this nightmare may last."

"And only God knows if Parliament is going to do anything more to help," John added.

John was right. God knew that Parliament had little intention of offering more help; and there were members who were angry at what little had been done.

By early September, it was evident that the fall crop was a total loss, and the numbers of people applying for relief had increased dramatically. Thousands of homeless and hungry Irish men, women, and children were already pouring into English seaports. Unless they wanted an uncontrollable flood of starving refugees; like it or not, the British Parliament was being forced to take further relief action to save England, if not Ireland.

Sir Robert Peel, although no longer the Prime Minister; began working a comprehensive relief plan. Road construction was increased in Ireland to provide work for the men; and the Relief Commission laid out a plan on how to deal with the food and medical crisis. Unfortunately, the plan was based on previous partial crop failures, and stated that no relief was to be offered to those who suffered from 'ordinary distress.'

The order was absurd on its face, because the Poor Inquiry Commission had previously stated in its Report, that close to 2.5 million persons - almost one-third of the population of Ireland - were in a state of semi-starvation every year, regardless of whether or not the potato crop failed. In Ireland, 'Ordinary Distress' was the norm, not an exceptional condition.

The new plan called for Indian corn purchased from the United States; to be distributed to the starving multitudes now estimated at over a million, and growing by thousands every day. Once again the government's plan was ill conceived.

Commonly called flint corn because the kernels were so hard it could not be properly ground with stone mills; Indian corn required steel cutting blades, of which very few existed in England. The result was that the government had tons of corn arriving daily from the United States; but lacked the proper mills to grind the corn into digestible corn meal in sufficient quantities.

The third aspect of the plan was to provide medical help. It was well known from previous blights that typhoid fever; cholera; and dysentery, quickly followed hunger. Accordingly, instructions went out to every government Workhouse to build or rent a separate building to treat the ill. Because it was common for sickness to claim more lives than starvation itself; the Orders stated it was imperative that those who were sick be kept at a distance from the Workhouse itself, to avoid spreading disease and exacerbating an already grave situation.

In many areas, the governments actions had totally unintended results. Irish men, attracted by what they considered to be high wages; abandoned farming to work on the roads. To add to the growing labor problem; the great majority of these men had been farmers all their lives, and knew nothing about road construction. The end result was the government spent huge sums of money for roads that were so poorly built as to be almost useless; and at the unanticipated expense of losing experienced farmers.

On one point the members of Parliament agreed; central to the success of the governments plans, was the willing co-operation of the Irish landlords, which proved difficult for two reasons. First, many of the Irish landlords were nearing bankruptcy. As each new English landowner sought to surpass his fellow landowners; they built more grandiose mansions; larger stables; and added more servants; all of which required increasing sums of money. The cost of building and maintaining these huge estates placed the owners in a vicious financial cycle. They needed not only the profits from their crops, but the rents from their tenants to operate and survive. Thus when the crops failed, they lost income from both sources, which necessitated borrowing money. Given their continued and excessive borrowing; it was only a matter of time and the fickleness of nature that brought them to the brink of insolvency. All that was required to nudge them over the edge was a major crop failure. Even many of those who genuinely wanted to help their tenants, lacked the resources. Now the dance had ended, and the Piper had to be paid.

From the typical tenant farmer's perspective, however bad the situation had been before the blight, it grew much worse. In previous times, tenants had been given a lease for a period of years with the right to construct some type of housing for their family; an arrangement that offered the tenant a small degree of security. As the population grew, the demand for land dramatically escalated. Many Landlords, wishing to maximize their income and gain more control over the tenant farmers, no longer offered leases; and developed a system of subdividing the land into increasingly smaller plots of land. A ruthless land policy that became known as 'conacre.'

Under the terms of the former lease system, the tenant was also permitted to defer paying the rent until after the harvest, a periodic payment known as a 'gale.' This policy of farm the land now and pay later; quickly became known as the 'hanging gale,' as it hung like a sword over the head of the tenant. The saving grace of the former lease system however, was that because the lease was for a period of years, in the event of a poor crop one year, a good land owner would allow the payment to be postponed until the harvest of the next crop.

Under the new policy of conacre however, a tenant was offered a contract to grow a single crop; and the contract provided no deferment provision for the rent payment if the crop failed. To make the situation even worse; the tenant was only offered a fraction of the amount of land that had been provided under the old lease system. Depending on the quality of the land; a conacre contract for good land was typically a quarter-acre; and up to one-half acre for poor soil. In a good year, parcels this size could feed a typical family of seven, and make a small profit after paying the rent. However, if the weather turned bad, a blight, or anything else effected the harvest; not only would the tenant farmer lack enough food to feed his family, but he would be unable to pay the rent. In such cases, the landowner could evict the family from the land; and the tenant farmer himself became a debtor who could be sent to prison; leaving his wife and children to struggle on their own. Consequently, the poor were trapped in a ruthless land scheme that was guaranteed to keep them in perpetual bondage.

As the last days of October were ending, the members of Parliament; many of the near bankrupt English landowners, as well as the desperate tenant farmers; prayed and clung to their single remaining hope; that nature would grant them a mild winter and a good harvest next year.

Chapter 35

There is an old expression that when it rains it pours. Rather than the mild weather that everyone had hoped and prayed for; the winter was unusually wet and cold, adding untold misery to the people of Ireland. Hunger in Ireland was common place. The Irish had lived and dealt with it for untold generations, and it was accepted as a part of life. Being cold however, was not. Whether they had enough food to eat or went hungry changed from season to season, year to year. What they had never lacked was a small cottage or makeshift shelter for their families, however crude it might be; and an abundance of peat to burn and keep them warm and cozy. Now, even that consolation was about to change.

As the effects of the famine deepened; many of the English landowners with large estates saw in the growing crisis, the legal means by which they could permanently rid their land of the Irish, and create large grain and cattle farms. Non-payment of rent gave them full authority to evict the tenant and their family. During one heated debate in Parliament regarding what should the landowners be required to do for their tenants; a member of the House of Lords stated that, 'it was the landlords right to do as he pleased with his property. If he allowed the tenants to stay, it was as a favor, an act of kindness. However, he could also choose to exercise his legal right to evict them. The government must not interfere with property Rights, else the value of property itself would suffer. Without such government protections; no one would invest capital, and property would become valueless.'

Reports of these meetings in Parliament, complete with member comments such as the one above; were published in the English press, and within days the newspapers were being distributed in Ireland. As rumors quickly spread among the tenants that Parliament would not interfere with the land owner's legal right to evict them, a new panic set in. Whatever few possessions they had left were sold to help raise the money for the rent payment. But it was a futile hope born of desperation. The reality was that very few had anything left to sell. They had previously killed their pigs and family cow for lack of food to feed them. What little clothing and bed linens they had possessed, had been pawned or sold to buy food; with the result that hundreds of thousands were now reduced to wearing rags, and sleeping on bare straw mats. The tenants were now completely at the mercy of the landowners.

There were those who were fortunate enough to have a compassionate landlord. Rents were drastically reduced; deferred until a good harvest; or in some instances forgiven altogether because of the extreme circumstances. For the less fortunate however, if the landowner chose to evict them; it was almost tantamount to a death sentence.

Ruthless English landowners, wishing to be viewed by the public as abiding by the law; would first send a written notice to the tenant demanding full payment of rent within a few days, knowing full well they would be unable to pay it. When the allotted time was up; crowbar gangs; brutal, pitiless men hired by the landlords; would suddenly appear at the tenant's cottage, forcefully evict everyone, tear down the cottage and burn whatever was left. Nothing was left to insure that another family could move in. Further, strict orders were given to all of the other tenants, that no one else living on the land owner's property, including relatives; could shelter the now homeless family.

Now homeless, some of the destitute tenants dug holes in the culverts along side the roads in which to shelter their families.   Known as scalpes, or scalpeens, they were nothing more than shallow holes a few feet deep; and covered with whatever boards, branches, grass, or cloth that could be found to help keep out the rain.   Even these wretched quarters did not escape the landlord's crowbar gangs.   Whenever they were found, they were ripped apart; the boards, branches, twigs, and grass roof burned; and the impoverished starving inhabitants were driven away again.

Nor were these evictions isolated instances of an occasional family here and there. In many cases; a single English landowner would evict several hundred tenants from his property, and destroy their cottages to prevent their return. As the practice of eviction was adopted and accelerated by other English landowners; what started as a score of homeless families; soon became hundreds; then thousands; then tens of thousands.   Homeless starving families now filled the roads, wandering from village to village in search of food; or a place to get in out of the cold, wet, winter weather.   The numbers of dying, emaciated, half naked bodies found lying in the ditches along side the roads began increasing. Half frozen adults, even if they had possessed a shovel; were too exhausted to dig a grave for their parents, spouse, or children.   For many adults death would have been a welcome relief; and they struggled to survive only because of their children.

A week after he left for Arden, Father Grant returned to Saint Patrick's a new invigorated man. It was well that he had recovered because of what awaited him. With scores of families, old women and men arriving daily in Kilrush - all relating terrible stories of hardship - Father Grant had his staff remove all of the church's objects of worship, placed them in safe storage, and unlocked the doors of Saint Patrick's. Literally overnight it became a refuge for dozens of families who now crowded every inch of floor space. To make room for the elderly who were often alone, most of the men chose to stay outside rather than be with their wives and children. Those who were physically able helped the Sisters in the kitchen and in the soup lines, which now operated from dawn to dusk.

A few blocks down the street, Reverend Swagart had also opened the Methodist Church as a shelter; and he and Grant met almost daily to compare notes and keep track of available supplies. The Director of the Quakers, which initially ran their soup kitchen and kept to themselves; soon discovered that Father Grant and Reverend Swagart were quite different than many of the ministers they had met in other areas. It quickly became apparent that these men were totally dedicated to helping everyone; and not simply determined to protect their religious turf by only helping their own members. Within a couple of weeks, the three leaders had become friends and developed a plan that permitted one group to focus on a morning meal; and the other two to prepare a late afternoon meal, which always drew a much larger crowd. A week later, they would rotate, giving each group a chance to get some much needed rest.

At Arden, the situation was far less critical, and in some ways almost normal. A food rationing plan at been implemented due to the uncertainly of the viability of future crops; but it was relatively mild, and everyone had enough to eat everyday. Furthermore, all the Tenants wives had been required to take cooking classes, and learn how to prepare meals made from corn. While the cooking classes at Saint Patrick's had not been successful, Ruth Shea had great results with the women at Arden. In fact, after eating some of Ruth's corn custard and hot corn bread, several of the employees and farm families were over-heard saying that they would never go back to eating potatoes alone; even when they became plentiful again.

Lawrence and Neil hired more local men to help work the farm and run the dairy operation even though they did not really need them. It helped provide a small income to their families, and give them a sense of security, however modest. They also hired additional men to become roving guards, and prevent potential looting, or the slaughter of their livestock.

A couple of days after Father Grant left to return to Kilrush, Lawrence and Sally decided they should ride out to Holy Jim's Canyon and check to see if everything was alright. From the reports they continued to receive from Kilrush; no-one had seen any of the residents from the Canyon in several weeks. Sally was certain that if there had been a major problem, Jim would have come to Arden; or at least sent someone in his place. Never-the-less, the total lack of information was frightening in its implication.

When they arrived at the entrance to the Canyon about two miles off the road, the first thing they noticed were the large yellow signs,

QUARANTINED CHOLERA, KEEP OUT.

"I don't believe it," Sally said. "Doc Cain, or Jim would have notified us.

"I'm sure you're right, but we can't stop here. We need to know what the situation is," Lawrence replied, "let's go see."

Even though they doubted the truthfulness of the signs, they still approached the small cluster of cottages carefully looking for any signs of sickness. As they slowly rode up to one of the homes, a woman came out and waving her arms in the air, calling out "Cholera, cholera....go back." Suddenly, she recognized Sally.

"Mrs. Bligh, Mr.Bligh," she called dropping her arms and nodding toward Lawrence. "'Tis ok," she said walking up to their horses, "never ye mind about the cholera; everyone is fine. 'Tis been a long time since we seen ye."

"If everyone's fine, why the signs?" Lawrence asked.

"Ta keep strangers out, and keep 'em from stealing our crops. It was the old Hermits idea," she said pointing up the lake.

"Sounds like something he would do," Lawrence thought to himself. "Do you know him?" he asked.

"No. Only spoke ta him two, three times. Once when they were building the dam years ago; and a few weeks ago when they decided ta put up the signs. Strange man he is, live'n up there alone by his-self. And his cussin!...well ye know about that. Some say he don't pay no rent; lives there for free;" she said pointing again toward the lake, "fer keepin his eye on the lake for the landowner. Nobody knows who he is."

"Well we're glad that everyone's OK," Sally said. "We need to see if Jim's alright."

"Mind the cussin Mrs.Bligh, he'll burn yer ears off he will. 'Tis a wonder God doesn't strike the man dead."

As they rode through the cluster of cottages, they noticed no evidence of blighted fields, in fact everything appeared to be normal. They passed men and women who were busy working around their homes; children were running and playing; people were feeding their pigs, cows, and chickens. Here and there, someone would recognize them and wave hello. As they got closer to Jim's cabin on the lake, they passed two boys on their way back home carrying several trout.

"Sally, the blight never touched them. Everything here is normal."

At that moment, Jim stepped out of his cottage and saw them, "Well, bless me soul, royalty has come a callin; and me here in old patched breeches."

"So 'tis royalty we are now," Sally called back trying to mimic his brogue.

"Aye. Here no doubt to steal my last shilling for the Queen," he laughed walking toward them waving his walking stick.

They both dismounted, and Lawrence reached out and shook his hand. "Good to see you again."

"You old codger," Sally said giving him a little hug. "You gave us a real scare with those signs. We didn't know what we'd find up here."

"Well, well, if a couple of signs gets me a hug, I'll put up a dozen more tomorrow," he said with a big smile. Seriously, the idea was ta scare strangers away. Com'on up to the house where we can sit and talk."

Sitting around his table, Jim told them of how two months ago, one of the men had gone into Kilrush and learned of the terrible blight; that was the first we knew about it. Thank god that he kept his mouth shut. Didn't say nothin to anyone in town about the situation here in the Canyon."

"The blight didn't touch you?" Lawrence asked.

"Didn't lose a single plant, t'was a miracle."

"But why?" Sally asked. "How did this canyon escape the blight."

"Well, no doubt God spared us because of my pious holy living," Jim replied with a laugh. "Can't wait to tell Father Grant; how's he doin? These must be terrible times for him, for all of you. T'was good that the almighty took Carmichael before this happened."

"Yes, that was a blessing; though we all miss him...and Agnes too."

"Poor old Carmichael and Agnes. Always felt sorry for them; loving each other as they did."

"You knew about that?" Sally asked.

"Carmichael told me one day. Years of unfulfilled love all because of the damned Catholic Church and their idiotic doctrine of celibacy. Course the Popes and Cardinals had their mistresses and bastard children running all over

Rome." He stopped to regain his composure. "Sorry about that; now where were we? Oh yes, the blight."

"It's worse than you can imagine," Sally replied, and then she and Lawrence proceeded to tell him about all that had happened.

Jim was silent as he listened to them, and then spoke. "I've no idea of why we were spared. For reasons we'll never know, the blight passed over us. But when Tom came back from town and told us what was happening; I called a meeting with the folks down the hill. We decided to put up the signs, and if anyone did come up the canyon, some of the women would run out to warn them away. I know "tis selfish; but if the folks out there knew we had good crops, they'd strip us bare in a day or two, then we'd be starving."

"You did the right thing," Lawrence replied, "but what are you doing for supplies; you must need some things from town?"

"We've been lucky. There are very few things we really need from town – understand the difference between 'need and want.' Anyway, a month ago Doc Cain came up here – we go fishing now and then - and I told him about what was going on. He kept it to himself, and when ever he comes up, he brings the few things we need in his carriage."

"So Doc Cain, Lawrence, and I are the only ones that know?"

"Aye."

"Don't worry, we'll keep your secret," Lawrence said. "Jim," he continued with a serious tone in his voice, "for the moment you're fine here. But you need to start thinking about what happens months from now. There's a lot of us who are convinced this is going to get much worse; and so does Parliament."

"Speaking of Parliament," Jim interrupted, "the last time Doc was here he brought me a stack of newspapers. Sally,

I read about your meetings with Peel. Looks like you got through to him. Do you think they'll do much more?"

"They have little choice now; they've got to provide more help. They're sending tons of corn meal; opening clinics for the sick; and trying to create jobs…like the road building programs; but its hard for them. The public's attitude is beginning to change; but the politician's still cling to the notion government should not be spending tax dollars to help people. That's never been done before, and no one wants to be the first to change it. Sir Robert told me that they had hoped to raise money from the English Land Owners, but too many of them are broke. Even worse, many of the English landlords are using the crisis as a legal means of evicting their tenants."

"Greedy bastards…sorry for the language Sally."

"They're certainly that; but the law's on their side" she replied.

"As I was about to say Jim," Lawrence broke in, "many of us believe this crisis is going to get much worse. We need to be thinking of long range planning. What if some wandering starving families ignore your signs, and come up here? A lot of these folks are so hungry and desperate they won't hesitate risking cholera for something to eat. Going further, what if next years crop fails?"

"We figured sooner or later, somebody would come up here. What we've done is to hide most of our potatoes in small caches around the lake. The folks here only keep what they need for two or three days. But I understand what you're saying. Have you made any long range plans?"

"We have a planning meeting setup for the first of next week at Arden; will you come?"

"Sure. Who else will be there?"

"There will be about a dozen or so; just about everyone who's involved in trying to make the best of a terrible situation. We're going to need your help. Incidentally, since you had that meeting about the signs; do any of your tenants know who you really are?"

"Heavens no. They all think I'm just the old recluse that lives alone by the lake. Except for that meeting, they hardly ever speak to me."

"Are you still having your man collect the rents?"

"Sure. They had a good harvest, and paying the rent gives them a sense of pride and security. If the time comes they can't pay it, I'll work something out with them."

Sally started laughing, "Can you imagine the look on their faces if they found out who you really are, and that you own all this?"

"They'll not find out if I can help it. I enjoy my peace and quiet. Besides, its fun pretending to be a poor recluse. Sure keeps the busy-body widows away," he laughed.

"A scallywag is what you are," Sally replied. "When I think of how happy you could make some poor widow, why...."

Jim looked at Lawrence, "Peel never had a chance with your Sally after him - almost feel sorry for him. And just think, after she had a little talk with him; his own Party tossed him out. Ah, you're a dangerous Lass, you are."

"You have no idea. An 'exceptional pot stirrer' is what Peel called her," Lawrence replied grasping her hand, "Sweetheart, we need to get home."

Lawrence stepped through the door into the yard. Sally stopped in the doorway and turned to Jim. "Were you ever married?"

His countenance changed, and she saw a softness she had never noticed before.

He reached out his calloused hand and with a touch as gentle as a butterfly; his fingers brushed her cheek, "that's a long story. Another time perhaps," he whispered.

She was taken aback, by the sudden change in his demeanor; and normally crusty voice; even when not filled with profanity. She stared at him for a moment and walked through the door, "Another time then," she said turning and looking back with a smile.

He waved goodbye, quietly saying to himself, "Ah Sally; if only you knew the old memories you've awakened."

As they headed back down the canyon, Lawrence was busy talking about their meeting with Jim, and all the things that would need to be done. She was not hearing a word he was saying. Her thoughts were on Jim; this unusual and very wealthy man who chose to live as a poor recluse; and who they had also learned, anonymously gave large sums of money to the local churches; sent food and medicine to those in need; and paid Doc Cain's bills for those who could not.

What had happened in his past she wondered? Why had he left his ancestral family home up north? What prompted him to touch her cheek like that? Of one thing she was certain, she would meet with him again and do her best to find out. Suddenly she became aware of the fact that Lawrence had reined in his horse and was now behind her.

"Sally?" he called out, "I've been talking my head off, and I don't think you've heard anything I've said? Where are you?"

"I'm right here dear, now what were you saying?"

When the first shipments of Indian corn arrived in Kilrush, the Irish stubbornly refused to eat it. Prison inmates, and those in the public workhouses rioted; claiming it was poison and would not touch it. Time and increasing hunger however, finally drove the Irish to eat Peel's Brimstone, their contemptuous term for the corn-meal due to the yellow color.

Previous to the new government shipments, the meal had only been available from the hated gombeen man; a greedy Irish money-lender who also traded in meal and grain at exorbitant prices to the public. However, due to widespread famine and because it was available from the government Depots at cost; there was a tremendous rush to buy it. The result was shortages everywhere; especially in western Ireland where shipping was very hazardous due to the lack of good sea ports; and the high cost to transport it overland. Consequently, in some regions such as County Clare where Kilrush was situated; when the cost of shipping was added to the cost of the meal, the price rose to staggering amounts virtually overnight.

As a result, even the few that had a little money to purchase the meal were quickly priced out of the market. Thus despite the British governments attempt to help alleviate the dire straits of the Irish, the crisis continued to deepen.

Chapter 36

Despite the wonderful dinner, good wine, and the other efforts the Bligh's made to help lighten the mood; the meeting at Arden was very somber. Following dinner, the fifteen invited guests adjourned to the parlor to talk. After a few introductory words by Lawrence; Father Grant began by giving his assessment of the crisis.

"The reality is that the situation is continuing to deteriorate day-by-day as increasing numbers of people become homeless. Not just here in Kilrush and the surrounding area; but across most of Ireland. Had the blight been a local problem, we could have received help from neighboring towns or counties; but the problem is everywhere. Now added to hunger and homelessness, sickness is taking an increasing toll.

As most of you know; the government clinic in Kilrush quickly filled and overflowed unto the porch; and then to the yard surrounding the house. Doctor Cain put up quarantine signs around the property, but it was impossible to keep family members and friends from trying to comfort the sick and dying. Consequently, typhoid, cholera, and dysentery, is spreading rapidly; and new patients arrive everyday with no place to put them. Last week the Sister's cleared out the barn behind the church, and started caring for some of the sick there. We don't know how long we will have room."

"How's the food supply?" someone asked.

"Not good," Grant replied. "Between the Quaker's; the Methodist Church; and Saint Patrick's; we're feeding over three thousand people a day, and the number grows by the hour. The emergency stores we had originally set-aside, are long gone. The Bligh's have continued to supply us from here with potatoes; corn; some meat with which we make a thin stew; and dairy products, especially milk for the children; for which we'll be eternally grateful; but we all know this cannot continue indefinitely. The government sends corn meal whenever they can; but as you know the cost is beyond the reach of most people. Fortunately, the corn grown here at Arden has helped to make up the shortage."

The discussion about the present conditions continued for some time. Then Doctor Cain presented some grim statistics about the hundreds of sick people needing medicine they did not have; and the number of dead so far: over 1,200 just around Kilrush that they knew about. He estimated they would find many more bodies when they started searching the more remote areas.

"My real concern now is that these unburied corpses - the ones we don't know about - are being eaten by birds and wild animals. When they go to the creeks to drink, they'll spread more disease. We need to send out search parties to check the hollows and bogs... everywhere; and when a body is found, send out a wagon to bring it in for burial. There needs to be an accounting. I greatly fear that entire families are dying out there, and no one knows about it."

It was quiet for a few seconds as everyone considered the terrible, tragic implication of his last remark.

Finally Neil spoke up, "I'll get some men to organize search teams tomorrow Doc."

Jim then raised the critical question, "we know what we're facing now, today; but what about two, three, six, months from now?"

John spoke up first, "From all that I've heard and read, Ireland has never faced anything like this before. As Father Grant said earlier, this isn't just a local or regional problem; the crisis covers all of Ireland - and in case you are not aware of it - parts of England and several European countries as well. Food that would ordinarily be shipped to Ireland, is being sent to Europe because they'll pay higher prices. No point in kidding ourselves, by the time this is over, Ireland will be much different. It will never be as it was before. So whatever plans we make; I think we should begin by first understanding that a lot of folks, and I'm talking of thousands; tens of thousands; maybe hundreds of thousands; will no longer be living here."

It was a sobering thought, one that somehow had escaped most of those present. They knew that people were sick and many were dying; but that tens, or hundreds of thousands would be gone had not really reached their consciousness. Who would be left? What would be left? Arden would survive of course, it was self sufficient. Saint Patrick's and the Methodist church would survive even if only a few hundred people were left; but would Kilrush survive? They had all witnessed other towns die. Would there be enough people left to support the stores, the blacksmith shop, the fishing docks.

"Here's something else to consider, Neil said, "with tens of thousands of acres of land being pulled out of production, and turned into huge grain and cattle farms; I doubt there'll be enough land for growing food crops. Even if next years crops are good, we now have thousands of families who have been driven from their homes and land. Where can they go, how will they feed their families without land?"

"It hurts me to say this," Cassie spoke up, "but some of the English Land Owners may be right; Ireland will not be able to support the Irish people; some will have to leave."

Had this been a typical group of Irish people, there would have been howls of anger and threats to kill the English bastards. But these were thoughtful individuals who were willing to squarely face the facts as they were; not as they wished them to be.

Lord Baltimore, one of the English Land Owners who had become friends with the Bligh's, and had started to operate his estate as they did at Arden, spoke up, "We lost about ninety percent of our potato crop. I deferred the tenant's rent payments; but they have nothing left to support them financially. They're surviving on corn meal, Peel's Brimstone as they call it; but they won't have money for planting in the spring. What happens if I loan them the money to plant, and that crop should also fail?"

He was silent for a moment, and then continued softly, "I can't evict them; I couldn't live with myself. What I've decided; is to pay for the passage to Canada or America for anyone who wants to leave. I think it's their only real chance."

"Really?" Lawrence exclaimed, "Have you talked to anyone else about this?"

"Yes, Lord Blakeley, you remember him. He and I met about two weeks ago trying to figure out what was the best way to handle this situation. He's still not sure about the passage money idea, but I've made up my mind."

"It's drastic, but I understand that thousands who can afford the fare are leaving on their own," Doc Cain said.

"What's the cost?" Cassie asked.

"Anywhere from about 5£ and up, depending upon the ship and what's provided. I'm told that some of the ships are old derelicts; but with the growing demand, greedy ship owners will use anything that floats."

"Well I have to say your idea is something we need to seriously consider," Grant said. "All along I've been thinking of how we can take care of everyone here; but that's becoming almost impossible. In fact it is impossible."

"Lord Baltimore's idea may be the best solution," Sally added. "He's right that without the land; there's no place for these people to go, or be able to feed themselves. The government's helping now; but they'll not continue to ship food to Ireland indefinitely; let alone provide housing or land for hundreds of thousands of families."

"I haven't said anythin ta anyone before," Colin spoke up, "but Mary and I are takin our children and leavin for America." Because they were part of the small group of key leaders in Kilrush, his announcement hit everyone like a little shock wave.

"'Tis been a hard decision," he continued, "but in the past three months, my business has dropped over eighty percent. That's not enough business ta support one family, let alone two – countin Mary's folks and sisters. Most of the large landowners are changing ta raisin cattle, and the tenant farmers are bein driven off their land. Nobody needs tools or wagons repaired; an I can na see that changin fer along time. It's like Cassie - Lady Bligh - was sayin, some of us will have ta leave."

"It'll be a great loss to Kilrush and Saint Patrick's," Grant replied, "Mary has been such a wonderful help in our parish work; and it's hard to think of our town without you and your shop. I don't think there's anyone who doesn't know about how much you have given freely to the folks around here."

"We do na want ta leave," Colin replied slowly looking at the faces of his closest friends, "but Mary and I think 'tis the only chance fer us; especially our children."

"There's another family very close to us that's leaving," Father Grant said quietly. "Bridgit, Grace, and Peter. They came to see me last week, and their story is much the same as Colin and Mary's. The future's in America or Canada; not here."

Again, everyone was momentarily stunned.

"Who else is thinking of leaving?" Cassie asked. "Neil," she asked looking at him with a note of fear in her voice, "you're not going to take your family and leave us are you?"

"Cassie, you never need to worry about that. Arden's our home; you're our family. Besides, our children would never let us leave their adopted grandparents," he said with a laugh.

"Thank God," Cassie sighed. "for a moment; I felt a terrible sensation sweep over me."

For the next few minutes the talk turned to the heartbreak of those families that were being torn apart; grandparents staying here; their children, and grandchildren leaving Ireland. Perhaps worst of all, was the knowledge they would probably never see each other again. The simple and tragic fact was for a great many people; they had no choice if they wanted to survive, and hopefully have a chance at a new life.

"Colin's right, especially about the children," Jim spoke up, "there's no future for children here. The truth is, there hasn't been a future here for anyone in a long time. When each generation has less than the one before it; a nation can't survive. Perhaps the blight is a blessing in disguise, because it's forcing us to wake up from a foolish dream; 'Ireland for the Irish.' That dream died long ago, but the Irish are a stubborn lot; they kept the corpse propped up in the corner, hoping that somehow it would come back to life. I cannot blame you, I've done it myself."

"I've continued to look at this problem from the standpoint of trying to help everyone here," Neil said. "Maybe it's because I'm Irish; and subconsciously I rejected any thought of sending our people to Canada or America. Ireland for the Irish, as Jim just said. The hard reality is that it can't be done. Trying to keep them all here will only result in more death and unimaginable hardship. Given the choice between dying in Ireland; or the chance of a new life in Canada or America, Lord Baltimore's given us the answer. The question now is; who will go, and who will stay?"

Looking at Lord Baltimore Sally asked, "have you spoken to your tenants yet?"

"No, I wanted to meet everyone here tonight first, and see how you felt about the idea. I've already decided what I'm going to do; but if you see the value of this idea as I see it, and we all work together, perhaps we should consider chartering a ship."

"I like that idea," John replied, "it would give us a lot more control over the condition of the ship, and the onboard conditions these people will be facing."

"Absolutely," Lawrence added, "most of these people have never been more than twenty miles from their birthplace; let alone being knowledgeable about booking passage on a ship. They'd be sheep before wolves."

"Absolutely. Lambs for the slaughter," Jim remarked. "Every profiteer out there is gleefully rubbing his hands at how easy it will be to fleece these poor ignorant souls. I think those of us who've had some experience at traveling; should do a bit of checking around before anything's said to the tenants."

"That's fine, but we can't wait too long. Most of these folks are in a very desperate situation," Lord Baltimore replied. "At my estate, something must be done within a month at most. If I tell them about the free passage, it will do wonders for their spirits; even if it's a month or two away."

"He's right," Cassie said. "What these people need is hope for a future, something solid to look forward to."

"I suggest that Cassie and I leave for London within the next two or three days," John said. "I still have a lot of contacts in the shipping business; and Lawrence and Neil are doing a substantial amount of business with a couple of shipping companies now. Does anyone here know when the Mary Jane will be docking?"

"You're in luck Sir, she'll be in tamorra afternoon," Colin said, "and leavin the next afternoon on the outgoing tide."

"Excellent; that will give us just enough time to pack. With some luck, Cassie and I should be able to get some solid information on what's available, fare costs, etceteras, and be back here in a couple of weeks."

"That's settled then," Neil said, "we'll hold off making a final decision until after they return. Now there are some other problems we need to discuss, such as clothing. Most of the people coming into town are in rags. I see women whose clothing is so tattered they walk down the street with their arms wrapped around their breasts to avoid the shame."

"Cassie," Sally said, "while you're in London buy bolts of cloth, needles, thread, and bring them back with you. We can set up sewing areas at Saint Patrick's and the Methodist church."

"Great idea," Neil replied. "Next on my list is burying details. Earlier, you heard Doc Cain talking about the numbers of dead bodies along the roads, and back in the bogs and hollows. We need to set up regular crews..."

"And pick a place to bury them," Doc Cain interjected. "We need a large field, the town cemetery will never old all of them."

"I have a field that you can have," Jim said. "We should make it a proper cemetery. Someday folks might want to come back and place a memorial stone."

"Thank you Jim," several voices said in a chorus.

"On one condition," Jim added. "No one is to know that I gave it, agreed?"

"Jim," Father Grant said with a chuckle, "I don't think anyone around here believes you have enough money to buy a new shirt; let alone donate property for a cemetery."

That remark brought a hardy welcome laugh from everyone.

"Well just make sure it stays that way. I can't afford to have all those widows after me," he said with a big grin.

Then looking at his sleeves he asked, "do I need a new shirt?"

The meeting went on for another hour, until everyone felt they had covered all the critical issues. Cassie then invited everyone back to the dining room for some delicious fresh baked cake, pies, and hot coffee.

Many huge problems still lay before them; but they took comfort in the knowledge they had begun to find a way out of the terrible crisis.

Chapter 37

Two days later, not twenty miles from Arden, Lord Stuart was sitting proudly in the saddle of Satan, his coal black stallion. Had the sun been shining, the high polish on his black riding boots would have been visible a mile away, but it was not. It was a cold, rainy, windy, miserable day; and a shivering servant stood in the mud along side his horse holding an umbrella on a long pole to protect him from the rain. A cold arrogant smile spread across Stuart's face. He enjoyed watching others suffer; a trait he had discovered as a young boy when he deliberately killed his little sister's pet kitten.

"Stop shaking you ignorant fool," he yelled at the servant, "and hold that umbrella steady, I'm getting wet."

Not far away, he watched as his crowbar gangs were driving over two hundred and twenty families from their cottages. Almost fourteen hundred men, women, and children were being forced out into the cold rain; watching their homes being demolished; and their few possessions piled up for burning.

"He can na do this, 'tis agin the law," one tenant called to his neighbor.

"An who's ta stop him?" the man called back. "Do ye think the Constable would interfere? Nah, he would na lift a finger. These English bastards are the law."

One tenant, beside himself with grief and anger; bolted over to one of the crowbar men and grabbed the man's arm just as he was about to smash in the door to their cottage. The man spun around and struck the tenant across the face with an iron pole; splitting his check wide open; knocking him to the ground.

"Try that agin, an I'll kill ye," he yelled.

For about half an hour the tenants milled about, a few talking to each other; but most simply watching in stunned silence. Then slowly, the women keeping their children close to them, began walking toward the road weeping. The men, realizing that they were powerless to stop what was happening; clenched their fists, and quietly passed a vow among themselves that Stuart would pay for this. For most of the men, although they nodded an assent to the vow; knew they would never take part in any attempt at revenge. For a few however, that vow became a burning, gnawing feeling deep within them that would never be extinguished until something was done. The questions were; what was to be done, and when?

———————————

The following afternoon, Father Grant was standing on the steps of Saint Patrick's talking to Sean and Reverend Swagart, when they noticed the first of the evicted tenants slowly straggling into town. They were soaked to the skin, cold, dirty, and about to collapse from hunger and exhaustion. All three men ran down the steps toward them, asking where they were from. Within a few minutes, they learned of what Stuart had done.

"How many more are coming?" Grant asked.

"All of us, he evicted everybody," a women with four small children replied. "A thousand, maybe more."

"Closer to fourteen hundred," another woman said.

"My God," Swagart said with a touch of anger in his voice, "I knew Stuart was cold hearted, but I can see now he's utterly without mercy. The man's depraved."

"Whatever he may be," Grant replied, "we'd better get started taking care of these people. First, we need to get them inside. They'll all have pneumonia if we don't get them out of those wet clothes."

Grant reached down and picked up a little girl in a tattered dirty dress, "how would you like a bowl of hot porridge?" he asked brushing the hair away from her face. She nodded without speaking.

"Some of you follow me," he called out waving his arm, "the rest of you go with Reverend Swagart. Sean, would you run down and see if the Quakers can give us a hand; it's going to be a long day."

"What's your name?" he asked the little girl as they started up the steps.

"Molly," she answered in a timid voice.

"That's a wonderful name. Do you have any brothers and sisters?" Within a few moments, the little girl was chattering away and telling him about the bad men that had taken her dolly. "I think we have a little doll here at church that needs a new mother, could you take care of her for us?" Grant asked.

Her mother reached out and took hold of Grants sleeve, "God bless ye Father, we've nothin left an …." her voice faltered and stopped.

"You're here now and safe. We'll take care of you," he answered, silently asking God just how they were going to care for fourteen hundred more people.

Two weeks later, Lord Stuart accompanied by two young British solders, returned to the now empty fields where once all of his tenant's cottages had stood. The land had been scraped clean as he had ordered; here and there a few piles of tenant's belongings were still smoldering, but they too would soon be gone. He patted Satan's neck, "good riddance to rubbish," he whispered. As he rode slowly through the field, a man on horseback rode toward him.

"M'lord, I wanted ta let ye know we drove out the last of the tenants that had dug Scalps along the road. They're all gone now."

"Did you destroy the Scalps?"

"Yes m'lord, we filled 'em in. Anythin else for us ta do?"

"Keep patrolling the road, I don't want any of those people sneaking back here. And if you catch anyone, give them a beating they won't forget."

"Aye M'Lord, that we will," he replied with an expression indicating that he looked forward to the chance.

"Tomorrow, I'm sending you to Lord Clark's Estate. He's got a big job for you there."

As the man road away, Stuart called after him, "and don't forget to keep checking the roads."

Stuart turned to the two soldiers, "I want to check the area down by the stream so keep close. If we meet up with any of these filthy Irishmen, well…you know what to do."

They had gone about a mile when Stuart turned his horse on to an old wagon road that cut across his land. A mile further, an old cobblestone bridge crossed a small stream. At one time, happy Irish boys used to fish for trout here; but Stuart posted the land, and anyone caught fishing was fined and beaten.

Stuart was riding a few feet in front of the two soldiers as they crossed the bridge in single file. Suddenly, without any warning, a rope that had been carefully hidden in the dirt, leapt from the ground and snapped taught across the bridge just in front of Stuart's horse. As Satan reared back, six men who had been hiding under the bridge; jumped onto the bridge from both sides. Before the soldiers realized what was happening; four of the men quickly pulled them down off their horses and took their guns. Stuart swung around in his saddle to see what was happening; and was attacked by the other two men. One reached under his horse and cut the cinch in half, while the other man grabbed Stuart's arm and gave a violent pull. In one quick motion, the saddle and Stuart fell to the bridge. He had reached for his pistol, but the fall knocked it out of his hand and one of the men quickly picked it up.

"Best ye stay right where ye are," the man said pointing the pistol at him.

The soldiers were just starting to get to their feet when one of the men yelled, "stay down an take yer boots off." The young soldiers completely shaken by what had just happened, quickly sat down and pulled them off.

"We've no quarrel with ye lads, 'tis Stuart were after. Now if ye know what's good fer ye, you'll be heading back to yer barracks; very slow like. Ye won't be needin these anymore," he added as he threw their rifles into the stream, "and we'll be keeping the horses fer a spell. Now git!"

The soldiers gave a quick glance at Stuart who was still lying in the dirt, and then started walking back across the bridge.

"Get back here," Stuart yelled, "I'll have you shot for abandoning me."

"Keep movin lads," a man standing near them shouted, "his Royal Highness here isn't goin ta do anythin of the like."

Looking back and realizing that Stuart was as helpless as they were, they continued walking. Within a few steps however, they discovered that their tender feet were no match for the small stones that were scattered across the ground. As one of soldiers stopped to remove a small pebble from between his toes; they both realized it was going to be a very long, slow painful walk back to their barracks.

The six men watched the soldiers for a couple of minutes; then turned their attention to Stuart. Before pulling him to his feet, they removed his boots and bound his hands behind his back. Another man took down the rope that they had stretched across the bridge; tied a noose on one end, and placed it around Stuart's neck.

"You filthy Irish trash, you'll all hang for this," Stuart cursed.

"Seem's yer the one with a bit of rope around his neck," one answered giving a sharp tug on the rope.

"My men will be coming along at any minute; then we'll see who has a rope around their neck," Stuart replied with contempt.

"Yer men are long gone the other way; they'll not be comin back fer quite a spell. Now git ta yer feet, we're goin fer a walk." After hiding Stuart's saddle under the bridge; two of the men mounted the soldier's horses, and a third jumped up on Satan to ride him bareback. With Stuart walking in front, they started down the road.

Stuart, like the soldiers before him, soon found that it was impossible to avoid the small stones. If one foot managed to miss them, the other one did not. Before he had gone fifty yards, he was beginning to hobble.

"I can't walk on these stones," he complained, "they're cutting my feet, give me my boots."

"Ye didn't seem ta mind about the misery ye caused when ye drove all yer tenants offin yer land," one of the men replied.

Stuart looked back at the man who had spoken and noticed a fresh scar across his face. "My man should have killed you that day," he yelled back.

"Aye, if he had, maybe he'd still be alive his self."

Stuart stopped, "what did you mean by that?"

"Jes what he said," another man replied. "When we asked yer man if he believed in heaven or hell, he said he didn't rightly know. Now he does," he said giving him a sharp shove with his foot.

They continued on for perhaps half a mile. Stuart's feet were now bleeding; leaving little red tracks in the road.

"Tom, throw'em his boots, we need ta move faster."

While the boots helped protect his feet against the stones, they were badly cut and had started to swell. Even with the boots on, it was still very painful and he hobbled more than walked.

An agonizing mile further on, the man holding the end of the rope jerked it tight, pulling Stuart's head back so quickly that he almost fell. "Far as we go," he called.

The men on the horses dismounted and walked over to the edge of the road.

"Recognize this?" they said to Stuart, pointing to what had once been a Scalp. "A family lived in this 'til yer men drove 'em out."

Stuart looked down at the pile of dirt, rocks, and odd pieces of lumber and branches, now filling what had been a hole in the ground.

One of the men standing behind him untied his hands and pushed him forward, "Git down there and start cleanin it out."

"I'll do more than have you hung," Stuart replied, his voice seething with rage, "I'll have you all horse whipped until you're a bloody mess; then hang you."

One of the men doubled up his fist and gave Stuart a blow on the back of his head causing him to fall into the pile of rubble. "Start pickin up those boards."

Stuart began carefully pulling out the shattered boards, his tender hands soon pricked and bleeding by numerous splinters.

"Nice horse ye have," one of the men said. "Satan's a good name fer a devil's horse. I understand that ye have a stable hand that takes good care of him."

"What's it to you?"

"From what we hear, the Irish lad that lathers and brushes down Satan; lathers down yer pretty young wife too. Seems when yer gone, she likes ta spend her afternoons in the stable."

"Must be our young Irish boys can give her what ye can na give her," another said laughing. "As the lads tell it, she doesn't ride side saddle in the stable."

Stuart spun around with a piece of lumber in his hand, "you filthy bastards," he swore as he threw the board at them.

"Bastards? Na, we all know our mothers and fathers. It's the ungodly English like yerself that rapes the young servant girls and fathers the bastards; an trades one wife fer another. The way t'was told ta us, ye divorced yer first wife when she couldna give ye a son, and married the young filly; but she has na given ye one either. 'Tis a pity it is. If something should happen ta ye, ye have no sons to inherit yer estate. Yer young filly will git it all."

Stuart quietly cursed to himself. Not because of what they were saying about his wife; but because it only confirmed what he had long suspected. He had been a fool to marry a young flower whose fragrant scent attracted every pollinating bee in London and Ireland. He had been a cuckold, and he had little doubt that everyone knew it.

Half an hour later, the Scalp had been cleaned out and they pulled Stuart, now covered with scratches and grimy with dirt, out onto the road. Two of the men then jumped down into the hole.

"We're gonna let ye see what 'tis like ta live in a Scalp fer a few days. 'Course the family that lived here afore ye didn't have yer fine clothes and boots, ta help keep 'em warm at night. Two of the men grabbed Stuart by the arms and using a long rope; bound his hands together in front of him, tying the ends of the rope together around his boots; as another man wrapped a gag around his mouth tying it tightly behind his neck. Certain that the knots and gag were secure; they knocked him down, pushed him into the hole and stretched him out flat, face up.

About fifteen inches over Stuart's chest and face; they drove some boards into the dirt on the side of the hole, placing them so that they reached across to the other side: these boards would be used as supports. His legs and feet were pinned down with dirt and rocks so that he would be unable to kick and signal anyone passing by. Next, they placed more boards on top of and across the supports, and then covered everything with dirt, stones and branches, taking care to leave small gaps for air. When they were finished, the scalp appeared much like it had before; one that had been destroyed by Stuart's crowbar men.

For a few moments they listened carefully for any sounds coming from the Scalp. Hearing none, the six men carefully brushed away all their foot- prints and other signs of their work. Satisfied, they mounted the horses and headed across the fields back toward the main road. Two miles further they released the horses; separated into twos; and walked back to Kilrush.

For the next several hours, Stuart frantically tried to get his hands free and loosen the gag; but lying on his back and unable to roll over made it impossible. In the semi-darkness, he could barely discern the boards that were about fifteen inches above his face; all that separated him from the rocks and dirt above; and certain suffocation if they collapsed. At first, he stared at the boards, but after a little bit of dirt filtered through the boards and lightly fell on his face, he kept his eyes closed. With his back lying against the earth, his tailored clothing provided little insulation. Already he was beginning to feel the cold seep into his bones.

During the next day, several times he could hear some of his men as they came along the road checking the Scalps as he had ordered them. Twice, he could hear them talking only a few feet above him and he desperately tried to call-out and scream to them, but the gag was too tight. After a while, he could hear them riding away.

By the second day, he had given up on any chance to free himself and lay quietly. Certain that a search was underway to find him; his remaining hope was that he would be found and rescued. Bitterly cold; hunger, and now thirst, added to his torment. Except for the sound of his own breathing; there was deathly silence.

Memories of things long forgotten began creeping into his mind. Many years ago, he and John Bligh had once been business partners in London; and John had been just as ruthless as himself, caring for nothing but his own selfish interests. After Elizabeth's death however, John had completely changed; and without question was now one of the most honored and respected men in England and Ireland.

He recalled something John had told him privately at the meeting at Arden the year before, '...take care as to what you sow William, because that's what you'll reap.' At the time he thought John was a fool; now he realized that it was he who was the fool. "William Stuart," he said quietly to himself, "you sowed hatred; and hatred you've reaped."

He shook his head back and forth to shake away the dirt from his face, then very slowly opened his eyes fearful that dirt might get in them. Staring into the pitch black darkness, he reasoned it must be night, and drifted off into another fitful sleep.

When he awoke all sense of time was gone. He no longer had any idea of how long he had been buried here, but now thirst had become an agonizing torment; his tongue sticking to the roof of his mouth. He recalled the story he had heard as a child in Sunday School about the rich man in Hell begging for water. Strange he thought of how things believed long forgotten, remain hidden in your mind until some event recalls them.

On what he thought was day three; a rain-storm brought some welcome relief. Water trickled down through small cracks and crevices; and by sheer luck, one thin steady stream came close enough to his head that he was able to inch over and let the water soak through gag across his mouth. In a few seconds the water seeped into his mouth freeing his tongue. He continued to drink in this fashion until the little trickle stopped. He recalled the rain of two weeks ago, when his men were driving away the tenants. On that day, he would never have taken a drink of rain water; now he cherished every drop, dirt and all.

With his thirst quenched, he began considering how cleverly those men had ambushed him, and buried him in this scalp. Those men had not acted in haste; and theirs was not a willy-nilly plan carried out at the last moment; nor was this location chosen without very careful consideration. This was a fairly well traveled farm road; a place that searchers would quickly pass by looking for more obscure locations. He had been deliberately hidden in plain view.

Eight years ago, the son of Lord Higginbothom had viciously raped two young local village girls. Even though they identified him as their attacker, the Magistrate refused to prosecute him for lack of any physical evidence. Two months later, he went out riding one afternoon and was never seen again.

Five years ago, Lord Blackthorne, who had severely beaten a tenant and his wife with a horse whip; also vanished. No he thought to himself; the men who buried me here knew exactly what they were doing. They had done it before.

For the past ten, twenty, thirty hours, he could no longer tell, he had struggled to keep awake fearing that if he closed his eyes, they would never open again in this life. His thoughts returned to the day he had killed his sister's kitten for amusement. When his father had learned what he had done, he had thrashed him with a cane; warning him about this sadistic streak, 'A dance with the devil never ends,' he had warned. 'You better learn to change, or you'll come to a bad end.' He closed his eyes; his father had been right.

For the next month, the investigators sent up from London listened to the soldier's reports as to what had happened the day the men took Stuart; and questioned dozens of Irish tenants, all professing they knew nothing of the incident, or the whereabouts of Lord Stuart. Extensive searches were conducted for miles around; and except for finding the missing saddle, they found no trace of him.

Although there was no actual physical evidence of foul play beyond the abduction; the Authorities official report concluded that Lord Stuart, like several other English Landowners, had in all likelihood been murdered and his body secretly buried.

Following the lengthy investigation, and with no further reason to stay in Ireland; Stuart's very rich young widow - who had grudgingly worn black mourning dress for three days - gave instructions to the Manager to put the Estate up for sale, and happily left for England.

Three weeks later, two handsome young men from Ireland arrived at her London Country Estate, bringing with them Lord Stuart's horse Satan. To the consternation of the Estate Manager; she insisted on personally giving them a tour of the stables; and very detailed instructions as to their new duties.

Chapter 38

It was a day of great rejoicing, and a day of bitter sadness. For weeks, hundreds of people had been anticipating and preparing for boarding the ship that would take them on the first leg of their journey to a new world of life and hope. For thousands of others who were remaining in Ireland; it meant the loss of family, loved ones, and the death of an old Irish dream.

The dock in Kilrush was awash with a sea of people, so many that the Harbor Master feared the dock might collapse under the weight. Accordingly, he ordered the crowds back on the land, and had the Constable limit the dock only to those who were departing; goodbyes would have to take place on the land.

Tied up snug against the pilings, the Mary Jane's Captain watched as the crew lowered the gang plank. He thought of the thousands of times he had docked here in Kilrush, carrying passengers; residents; government officials; and supplies; but today was unlike any he had witnessed before. With very few exceptions, today's passengers would never be returning.

Standing near the dock, surrounded by scores of familiar faces, Father Grant hugged and shook the hands of the men and women who would soon be leaving. As family after family came up to him, he would lift each small child and hold them tenderly as he said goodbye. Many years before, by an act of cruel fate, he had lost his own wife and three children. Now because of another bitter twist of fate, he was losing hundreds of men, women, and children whom he had grown to love as dearly as he had loved his own family. Tears rolled down his cheeks, as he kissed the children one last time. Never again would he see them at Saint Patrick's, or playing in their yards at home. He would never get the chance to watch them grow up; be confirmed; offer them Holy Communion; or have the joy of joining some of them in marriage. Not far away, Reverend Swagart was experiencing the same emotions as he bid his final farewell to many of his congregation, as well as numerous friends from the community.

Scattered along the street, small clusters of people were gathered around Sean and Kathleen; Doctor Cain; Lawrence and Sally; John and Cassie. Some of the people were about to leave, while others were there to say goodbye and wish them luck. Even though almost everyone there had little more than the clothes on their back, somehow they had managed to bring a small gift for their departing loved one, or friend; even if it was nothing more than a crocheted lace hanky; a carved wooden toy for a child; or a carefully hand written card wishing them success in the new world.

There was one notable absence from the crowd near the dock; Jim sat alone on a hill overlooking the bustling activity. He was emotionally torn between wanting to personally say goodbye to many of the residents of the canyon; people he had known for many years, and for whom he had anonymously paid their passage; and his need to remain known only as Jim, the poor recluse. As he watched loved ones and friends clasp each other for the last time, his mind went back to another bitter farewell many, many years ago.

Shortly after the battle with the English in 1798 when his leg had been severely injured, he returned to his parent's estate, their ancestral home in Northern Ireland. Angry about the defeat of Ireland and becoming increasingly restless, his father suggested he take a two or three month tour of Europe to help settle his mind. 'When you're ready to return, we and Ireland will still be here,' his father had told him.

Starting in France, he wandered around Europe and then Asia as the months stretched into several years. In Germany he met a beautiful dark haired young woman named Gretchen; they fell in love, were married, and he took her home to meet his parents. The next year was the happiest time of his life, as he and Gretchen went everywhere and did everything together. When she told him that she was expecting a baby, he literally danced for joy to the great amusement of his mother, and embarrassment of his father.

A month before the baby was due to be born, he went on a business trip for his father who had not been feeling well. Two weeks later while still away, he received a letter from the family Butler, requesting that he return home as quickly as possible; cholera had struck the family. The letter went on to say that his parents and wife had gone to visit some friends, and unwittingly drank water from a contaminated well.

Immediately setting out for home and despite all haste, he arrived home the morning after his parents died; and learned that his beloved Gretchen was also dying. The family doctor told him that through sheer force of will alone, she had clung to life to see him one more time. When he asked about the baby, the doctor silently shook his head, the baby had already died, but he had not told Gretchen. Ignoring the doctors warning that cholera was highly infectious; he climbed into bed with her and held her in his arms until she died the following afternoon. Within the space of a few days, his life had plummeted from untold joy to utter despair.

Following the funeral, the terrible day in which he buried his parents, his wife, and their unborn child, a girl; he returned to the Manor and refused to leave Gretchen's bedroom. The servants would leave food at the door, and return hours later to find he had hardly eaten anything. For days on end, close friends, the doctor, even the family solicitor, would stand outside the bedroom door trying to reason with him, but to no avail. Finally, the doctor told everyone to leave him alone, there was nothing anyone could do. In time, he would come out on his own, or die.

Three weeks later he emerged gaunt and haggard. He had lost about fifteen pounds and his clothes hung loosely over his frame; his hair and beard were dirty, matted, and untrimmed; and his eyes had a glazed, sunken, lifeless quality. Walking slowly down the stairs and into the study, he asked the Butler to send for the family solicitor. The next afternoon with the solicitor present, he had the Butler assemble all the servants in the parlor, where he notified them he was going to sell the Estate. Sensing their anxiety, he then set their minds at ease by stating that it was very likely the new owner would keep them on. That had all happened almost forty years ago, but it was as vivid in his mind as if it had happened yesterday.

No one ever learned what had happened to him during the time he remained in the bedroom, but when he emerged, it was evident to all that a profound change had occurred; he was not the same person. After the estate was sold he left Ireland; returning a year later to the Kilrush area where he was unknown. Secretly, he bought over a thousand acres including what would later become known as Holy Jim's Canyon. There he built his little cottage and quietly assumed the character of a poor recluse.

Years later, following the disastrous flood; he had his close friend and confidant, Father Carmichael, organize building the dam, which created the lake. By directing the money through Saint Patrick's, no one ever discovered that he had paid for all the materials and labor. Now, once again his world was changing.

Looking down at the crowd in the street, he noticed Sally talking to Colin and Mary. It had been her striking resemblance to his lost Gretchen that he had noticed the first time Lawrence had brought her to his cottage. Had he and Gretchen's baby daughter lived, she would be about Sally's age now. Someday, next year perhaps when all of this was over, he would tell her. But that was the past and nothing could change it; what mattered now was the present, and the future. He continued watching until most of the passengers had boarded the ship. Then he got up, and started home.

It was the movement on the hill that caught Sally's eye, "Look," she said to Colin and Mary, that's Jim up there. I'll bet he's been watching from there for hours."

"Why would that old recluse come ta town and sit up there watchin what's goin on here?" Mary asked.

Sally thought for a moment, and decided that since they were leaving, it wouldn't hurt to tell Mary about Jim. "Will you promise to keep a secret?" she asked, "I mean really keep a secret?"

"Sure," Mary replied, "what is it?"

When she told her about Jim, who he really was, and that he had paid the passage for over fifty families, she stood there in stunned silence. "Many of these folks you see boarding the Mary Jane don't know it, but he paid their way to a new life; more families will follow on other ships because of his generosity."

"That foul mouthed, semi-hermit who lives up in the canyon?" Mary asked.

"One and the same," Sally answered.

"Colin," Mary said turning to him, "did you know who he was?"

"Yes, but like Sally and the others, I pledged to keep his secret."

"Mary," Sally asked, "when Colin did jobs for Saint Patrick's, who do you think paid for the work?"

"The church," she replied.

"And where do you suppose the money came from?" she didn't wait for an answer, "Jim; he's anonymously helped support both Saint Patrick's and the Methodist church for many years; as well as doing many other things for Kilrush."

"'Tis incredible," Mary said. "I would na have believed it, had ye not told me yerself."

"Now remember your promise to keep this a secret. Don't get tempted to tell anyone on the ship; because if word gets out someone will send a letter back here, and Jim never wants anyone to know."

They watched Jim disappear over the crest of the hill and turned back toward the dock. Since the crowd had thinned, the Constable was now allowing anyone unto the dock. The last few groups in the street were breaking up, and as they made their way to the dock, those who were leaving clung tightly to loved ones and friends. While almost everyone made promises of returning in a few years; and those who were staying behind smiled and said they would be waiting; in their heart and soul they never expected to see each other again in this life.

Besides Colin, Mary, and their children; one of the hardest farewells for many of the people in and around Kilrush, was saying goodbye to Bridgit, Grace, and Peter. Finally. The loss of these people would be a great loss to the town.

As they all stood in a circle holding hands with their dearest friends; Father Grant, Kathleen, Sean, Lawrence and Sally, John and Cassie, Colin and Mary, and Reverend Swagart; the emotion was so powerful that no one wanted to be the first to say goodbye. Finally, Grace broke the silence.

"I had a dream last night."

In an instant, everyone turned to look at Grace with apprehension.

"We're gonna live in a big white house," she said with a lilt in her voice, "and Mommy will have a beautiful flower garden."

A collective sigh of relief went up, and Father Grant reached down and lifted her into his arms. "Grace, there's nothing anyone could have said here more wonderful than what you just said."

"Well 'tis true, and all around are big mountains covered with trees."

"Why that's jes what Grace told me months ago," Bridgit replied, a note of surprise in her voice. "We had gone ta the cemetery ta see the family plots, and Grace said we would na be buried there because we were goin to a place where there was mountains and valleys."

"And what about our family?" Colin asked, "did ye see in yer dream where we'll be livin?

"Jes down the street from our house; that's where yer shop will be," she answered.

Colin and Mary looked at each other in amazement, there was no way that Grace could have known that they had talked with Peter and Bridgit, and they had decided to stay together in America.

"God knows all the secrets, and he seems to enjoy telling Grace about them," Father Grant said with a chuckle. "Grace, you don't know it, but you have given us all a wonderful sense of assurance. In every adversity there is a seed of greater benefit; one of our goals should be to try and discover it. Out of the great tragedy here - the famine - God has opened new doors for thousands of people, you among them."

As he was finishing speaking they heard the ships bell, it was the final boarding call.

"The tide's beginning to turn," Peter said, "and the Captain wants to go out with it."

"We have a little something we wish to give you," Cassie said, handing a small package to Peter and another to Colin. "You can open the packages later on board."

There was a flurry of handshakes, hugs, and kisses; and they all started walking out the dock. The rails of the Mary Jane were lined with men, women, and children, waving and calling goodbyes as the last few stragglers boarded, and the gang plank was pulled up.

"Cast off all lines," the first mate called. Several men scurried along the dock lifting the mooring lines off the hawsers and dropping them along side the dock, while men on board immediately pulled them on deck. "Back the jib," came the order, and the ship slowly began to ease away from the dock, and slip back toward the open river. As she began to swing into the current, the Mate shouted, "hoist the mains'l."

The men, women, and girls, were still lining the rail waving and trying to get one last look; a picture to burn in their memory of their family, a friend, someone they would not ever see again. The young boys however, totally captivated by the ship and everything about it, had left the rail to watch the crew. They listened to the men singing a sea chantey as they hauled on the sheets raising the mains'l up the mast. They heard the rustle of stiff canvas being unfolded, and the muffled crack of the sail as it caught the wind and filled out, slightly pushing the ship over. Their eyes were bright with sights they had never seen before, except perhaps at distance; and their ears heard new sounds like the whisper of the wind in the ships rigging. As more sails were raised the ship heeled a bit more, and for the first time they had that exciting sensation as the deck shifted under their feet.

Over the next few hours, something mysterious began to happen to some of the boys, the ancient lure of ships and the sea seeped into their bones and took root. From this point on, it made little difference where their parents might settle down; when the time came, they would return to the sea as surely as bright silvery salmon return to the stream where they were born.

For almost an hour, the crowd stood on the dock watching the Mary Jane grow smaller as she headed down river for the open sea until she was hull down, and only the sails could be seen, then they too disappeared. It was over, they were all gone.

In silence, the crowd slowly walked from the dock and down the street. Their lives and Kilrush would never again be the same. Ryan and his wife Mabel sat on the bench in front of their blacksmith shop. Mabel stared into space; Mary, Colin, and their grandchildren were gone. Ryan would be forced to return to work; but she wondered, how long would it be before there was any work to do? With their other daughters still unmarried and living at home, the future held little promise for any of them. "Why God, why did this happen to us?" she said quietly as she began to weep. But there was no reply from heaven.

Similar scenes were repeated throughout the town and country-side, as individuals, families, and business men, considered what the loss of so many people would do to the community. Some businesses would have to sharply reduce the number of workers; others would simply cease to exist. Shipping would be reduced; some of the fishing boats would relocate to another home port. In every area of life, major changes would take place, but those things could be adjusted to. What would be very difficult, almost impossible to deal with; was the loss of hundreds, even thousands of families, friends, and neighbors. The very social fabric of Kilrush, and Ireland, was being ripped and torn apart.

In one sense, those onboard the Mary Jane had it easier. Their minds were distracted by the constant activity on the ship; learning to walk on a rolling deck; checking their belongings again and again; trying to keep track of the children and making sure that one didn't fall overboard.

Beyond all these physical things, was the fact they were on their way to a new life in a new world; one far different from the one they were leaving. A place that didn't recognize class distinction; and from what they had heard, would not tolerate it. A place where everyone was free to live, and work, wherever they chose. Not everyone believed all the stories they had heard; but even if only half of them were true, America would be heaven compared to what they were leaving.

Peter, Bridgit, Colin, Mary, and their children, had remained standing at the stern rail watching and waving to their friends on the dock until they, and Kilrush faded into the distance. The ship was miles down the river now and as they drew closer to where it emptied into the sea, they could feel the ship begin to rise and fall as the incoming swells met the out going tide. Grace was especially interested, because she was experiencing what her Daddy had done hundreds of times.

"Is it always like this Daddy?" she asked, "going up and down on the waves?"

"No, sometimes the sea is as smooth as a piece of glass. At other times, it's so rough you have to hang on to keep from being washed overboard. It's nice today."

"Do ye know how ta put the sails up, and what all the ropes are fer?"

"Sure, come with me," he said leading her to the base of the main mast. "Now this is called a line– never call them ropes," he said placing it in her hand, "that's what landlubbers call them."

"A land lubber," she giggled, "what's a land lubber?"

"Someone that lives and works on land like you," he said pulling on her pigtails.

"Now as I was starting to say before a pretty little girl interrupted me, this piece of line is called a 'sheet' and this is the one the men use to raise and lower the mains'l."

By now, a small group of boys had begun to gather around Peter and Grace.

"What are those ropes for?" one boy asked, pointing to several lines secured at the base of the mast.

"He's a land lubber Daddy," she said giggling.

"I think you're right Grace," he chuckled. "Ok boys, come closer and I'll teach you something about ships and sailing."

With Grace standing next to him, he pointed to different parts of the ship; told them what it was called; and what it was for. "The front of the ship is the bow; the rear is called the stern; this big sails are called the mains'l - never call them main sails -; the tall skinny sails at the bow are called jibs; this line is called a halyard; this one's a stay." Grace held his hand tightly, the envy of every boy there.

Suddenly, the ship rose and fell sharply as a large swell flowed under her keel. Peter looked up, off the starboard side was Loop Head, they were at the mouth of the river.

"Hold on boys, we're leaving the river and going out into the ocean. It's usually kind of bouncy here."

"Bouncy?" a boy asked.

"Sure, up and down like bouncing a ball," he said just as another large swell rolled under the boat.

"Hey, this is fun," some of the boys called to each other, "while a couple of others moaned, "I don't feel good.""

"Sea sickness," Peter told them.

"You mean I'll have ta take medicine if I go out on the ocean?"

"No, it's a different kind of being sick," Peter answered. "It only lasts for a little while. Your body has to adjust to moving all the time because of the waves."

As the ship moved farther out away from land, he knew from long experience what was coming next, so he told Grace and the boys to pay attention. "The Captain is going to change course... turn the boat."

"Shush and listen," he said, and a moment later came the order.

"Bring her to 220 degrees," the Captain called.

At that instant, the helmsman began turning the ships wheel, as several of the crew started pulling in on some lines, while other men released others. The ship heeled sharply to port as it began to swing to the south; but just as quickly it straightened up as the men trimmed the sails for the new heading.

"Does it aways start ta tip over, when ye turn?" a boy asked.

"Not always. That's called 'heeling,' and it depends on where the wind is coming from."

He had just finished explaining how the wind made the ship move, when Bridgit, Colin, Mary, and their children walked over carrying the boxes Cassie had given them. Because of all the activity and commotion on board, they had forgotten to open them.

"What do ye think's in them?" Grace asked.

"Let's find out," Peter replied. Taking her by the hand, they all went below. Finding a table in the corner of the salon, Peter said, "Ok, let's see what's inside, you first Colin."

Colin unwrapped the paper covering revealing a wooden case, inside there was a collection of carefully folded papers, and a sealed envelope. Colin took out the papers and unfolded them, on top was a letter addressed to Mary and himself. He handed the letter to Mary to read aloud.

"Dear Colin and Mary:

When you read this you will be on your way to America. As you know, the Mary Jane will take you to

Liverpool. There you will board the 'Shamrock', the ship that John chartered to take you to Boston, in America. It's a very good ship, with a fine Captain who is well acquainted with the Port Authorities in America. You and your family will have a private cabin, and all of your food and other necessities have been paid for. Also on board will be several other families from the Kilrush area. Some were able to pay for their own passage, while others had their passage paid by various donors.

From what we were told while we were in London, Boston will soon be over-run with immigrants, making it difficult to start your new life there. Two days ago by chance, we received a letter from Percy and Ruth Shea, who said they have a cousin in Kane Pennsylvania, a town in the Allegany Mountains in western Pennsylvania. According to their cousin Robert, the town needs a blacksmith, and he thought it would be a good place for your family to settle down.

To help you get established, in the sealed envelope is £200 which you should convert to American money while you are in Boston. It should be enough to get you settled in Kane, and open your shop. Also enclosed is a letter of credit for an additional £100 drawn on the Bank of England, if you need it. This is our gift to you.

We shall all miss you dearly. Perhaps one day we will come to America and visit you in your new home.

Love and prayers,
John, Cassie, Lawrence, Sally.

As she finished reading the letter, Mary's hand dropped to her lap and tears began to flow. "T'was a terrible hard decision ta leave Kilrush, our families, and so many friends like Kathleen, Sean, and the Bligh's. The other thing was that," she choked back a sob; "we had just enough money ta pay fer our passage, but almost nothing left fer when we got there. Colin was hope'n he could get a job at a shop in Boston, an...." her voice gave way to sobs of joy. "An now," she continued regaining her composure; "everythin has been taken care of. We even have a place ta go an settle down."

"Where's Pennsa....what did you call it?" Bridgit asked. "Is it near Boston?"

They all looked at Peter who knew more about the world than they did.

"The letter said Kane, Pennsylvania. I don't know where it is," he replied, "but wait here and I'll ask the Captain."

A few moments later he returned. "He's not sure, but he thinks its west of Boston."

"West!" Mary exclaimed, "isn't that where the Indians are?"

"I don't think so. Pennsylvania was one of the original Colonies near the ocean. I think the Indians are much farther west. The Captain said to ask the Captain of the Shamrock when we get to Liverpool; he's been to America several times and would know more about it."

"I think we can all wait a few more days," Colin said. "Peter, I think you should open your box now."

Upon opening their box, Peter found a similar collection of papers, with a letter for Bridgit and himself.

The letter from the Bligh's was very similar to the one Mary had just read with a few exceptions. They too were encouraged to move to Kane, and there was an envelope with £200 to get settled, and the letter of credit for an additional £100. The significant difference was an additional letter addressed to Peter from Father Grant.

Dear Peter:
I believe that your intention was to continue fishing when you arrived in America. Now, having read Cassie's letter, you are wondering about what you would do in a town in the mountains of Pennsylvania, a very long way from the

ocean. However, after all the things that happened between you and Bridgit, you know that God's plans are always far ahead of our own.

Several weeks ago, when I first learned that you were going to America, I wrote to an old friend of mine in London, Reverend Leander Powers, a Lutheran minister. Leander is the Chairman of the committee to find pastors for churches in America. I told him that you had graduated from a Catholic Seminary, but had left the priesthood a number of years ago and become a fisherman; that you were now married, and had a daughter. I felt that there was no reason to tell him any of the circumstances that lead you leave the priesthood; many men before you left the church to get married. In any event, that's past history, behind you and forgotten.

Leander wrote back to me, and said they were actively looking for qualified ministers to pastor churches in many rural areas of America. He told me that they would welcome the opportunity to meet with you when you arrived in Boston. When you meet with Leander, I'm certain he will be aware of any church openings in that area.

In closing, let me say that God's ways are not our ways. I grew up in a protestant church; and as you know had a long career in the Army before becoming a priest. You grew up in a catholic family, became a priest and then left the church to become a fisherman. We have only to read the scriptures to see the varied lives the prophets and disciples lived; all the while God's hand was on them, waiting for the appointed time.

I believe your appointed time has come to return to the ministry. The past years have taught you a great deal about life, men, women, and families; that you would never have learned as a priest. Now, it's time to put that understanding and knowledge to work. As Father Carmichael would have said; help build the kingdom of God.

A final thought. Bridgit, more than Grace, may have a difficult time leaving the Catholic Church. You might tell her that unlike Ireland, there are very few Catholics in America. I do not know anything about Kane Pennsylvania, but I suspect there may not be a Catholic church there. Also, remind her that the Lutheran church is very close to Catholicism. Remember, Martin Luther had been a Catholic Priest.

I realize that all this has come as a complete surprise; but please carefully consider and pray about this wonderful opportunity. It may be the answer to what you and Bridgit have been praying for.

In His Service,
Gordon Grant

When Peter finished reading the letter aloud and looked up; it was evident from the expressions on the others faces that they were as surprised as he was.

"It's another miracle," Bridgit exclaimed. "If ye ever doubted that God has his hand on our lives, doubt no more. All the talks we had about what ta do when we got ta America; and hope'n that Colin and Peter would be able ta get work, so that we could stay together."

"And what about when Peter was gone fishin?" Mary asked. "One of the reasons we wanted ta stay together was so that me and Colin would be close by ta watch over ye. If he becomes a minister in Kane, everythin works out. But what about the Lutheran Church Bridgit, how do ye feel about that?"

Bridgit looked around at everyone and smiled. "We was all raised Catholic because our parents were Catholic; Ireland is catholic; an the church has been wonderful ta me and Grace. But in the past few years, I got ta know an respect Reverend Swagart, and Sean who left the church an became a protestant. Peter has told me many stories about the men he works with when he's fishin; men from many different churches. 'Tis not the church, but the folks that's in it matters most. Like I said before, it's a miracle."

"Colin, Mary, Bridgit; think of it," Peter said calling their names to emphasize his point, "every concern we had and prayed about has been answered. You're right Bridgit, it's all a miracle from God."

With their cares and anxieties gone, the next two and a half days voyage to Liverpool, England was like a pleasant holiday. Peter continued his sailing lessons for Grace and the boys; Colin began imagining how he would set up his shop in Kane; and Bridgit and Mary talked about what the town, church, houses, and the people would be like. The children like all children, thought nothing about the days or months ahead; they simply had as much fun as they could, and fell sound asleep every night tired and happy.

There was one exception; Grace; who was having more dreams.

Chapter 39

Liverpool, England. A teaming city of two hundred and fifty thousand residents, recently swollen to almost three hundred and fifty thousand, and growing by thousands of Irish refugees a day. Of the multitude arriving; less than half were waiting to board a ship that would take them to America or Canada. Because the Americans continued to have an anti-Catholic tradition, a lingering effect of the Puritan era; the American Port Authorities increased entry fees, and also required the ships Captain to post a Bond; making emigration to the United States more expensive.

The result was that fares were two to three times as high as fares to Canada. For the majority of individuals bound for Canada because of the cheaper fare; the immigrants considered it merely a transition point on their way to the United States. Possessed of a hatred of England centuries old; many of the Irish immigrants had no intention of remaining in a place they viewed as another English nation loyal to the Queen.

The majority of the refugees pouring into Liverpool however, had no money for passage to the new world, or anywhere else. These were the tens of thousands of desperate, wretched, starving, penniless, men, women, and children; many of whom made the voyage from Ireland to Liverpool as ballast in the black dirty hold of an empty returning coal ship. It was not the hope or dream of a new life in a new world that had brought them here. They came because they knew that once they were in England, the government would give them food to feed their families;

and somewhere they would be able to find shelter from the cold and rain.

As the Mary Jane sailed into the harbor, her deck was crowded with excited passengers anxious to catch their first glimpse of Liverpool. The first sight to greet their eyes, were scores of ships of every description filling the approach to the harbor. Within an hour they saw more ships than they had seen in all their previous life. Ships from all over the world carrying cargoes of every description were anchored in the harbor, and docked along the quay. Just a few years ago, before slavery had been abolished in England; there would have been slave ships bound for Africa, the United States, and South America.

Now the cargoes were silks, and tea, from China; spices from the islands of the Indian Ocean; great quantities of cotton and lumber from the United States; sugar from the West Indies; and hundreds of other items; an almost endless list of goods passed through the docks at Liverpool. Tilting their heads back to gaze up at a magnificent China Tea Clipper they realized that in comparison, the Mary Jane appeared insignificant.

As she sailed farther up the harbor, there was an audible gasp of amazement from the passengers as they caught sight of what they thought must be the largest building in the world; the newly built Albert Dock, named after Prince Albert, Queen Victoria's husband. Six stories high and city blocks long; it was built to house the cargoes of the hundreds of ships entering and leaving Liverpool. Faced with red brick, it was constructed of cast iron, masonry, and stone. Without any structural wood, it was the first building considered fireproof.

Beyond the docks; the excited passengers could see streets lined with thousands of buildings large and small; the steeples of great churches; crowds of people everywhere; elegant carriages; delivery wagons piled high with produce, dry goods, wine and beer; and in the distance something most had never seen before; railroad trains, their huge iron locomotives throwing great plumes of black smoke into the grey overcast sky.

As the Mary Jane tied up to the dock and the crew set the gang plank in place, the Captain gathered everyone on deck, and cautioned them about safety in Liverpool.

"This is one of the great cities of the world, but watch where you're going. Pay attention to the people around you, and keep your children next to you. It's a fine City, but the thousands of refugees have attracted thieves and pick-pockets from all over England. I suggest you leave your valuables on board; and take only enough money for what you plan to buy.

We'll be in port for four days; so those of you who are waiting for another ship are welcome to stay on board as long as we are here. You can check with the Harbor Master to find out when your ship will arrive. One final note of warning; if you go ashore, be certain to return to the ship before nightfall. The docks can be a very dangerous place; especially at night."

For Peter, the first order of business was finding out if the Shamrock was in port. Going ashore, he learned that she was scheduled to arrive the next morning. The Harbor Master informed him that after repairs had been completed and stores taken aboard, the Captain of the Shamrock would start boarding passengers, he estimated that would be in about three days.

Since they now had a few days free time; both families decided to take the opportunity to see something of Liverpool, a City almost a hundred times the size of Kilrush. Peter, who had been born in London, had also been to many other cities both large and small. Colin and Mary had spent their honeymoon in Bristol, a busy thriving city although much smaller than Liverpool. Bridgit and Grace however, had never been outside of Kilrush. Since

Peter was English and obviously the most experienced traveler, he was quickly appointed as their guide.

After stepping ashore, their senses were quickly overwhelmed by the sights, sounds, and smells coming from every direction. Deciding to first investigate the shopping and market area; they had only gone two blocks when Colin saw a blacksmith's supply store. A block farther, Bridgit and Mary were overjoyed to find shop, next to shop, next to shop, of clothing for women, and children. Then there were the toy stores; shoe stores; haberdashery and tobacco shops; furniture stores; music shops with windows filled with instruments; small bakeries, book stores; quaint curio shops; and restaurants of every size and description offering foods from India, China, Japan, plus dozens of countries they had never heard of. There were even a few Irish Pubs.

"Now remember," Peter said, "we agreed that today we would just explore. Tomorrow if you're interested, you can return to shop." One glance at Mary, Bridgit, and the children, told him a team of wild horses couldn't stop them from returning.

After wandering among the countless streets taking in the sights and making mental notes of places they wanted to return to; they unexpectedly found themselves in Prince's Park. A glorious city park filled with hundreds of magnificent old oak, chestnut, maple, and elm trees; manicured paths; and carefully tended flower gardens. Here and there they saw families stretched out on the grass under the trees having a picnic. But what startled them most, was the hot air balloon rides. Huge colorful balloons with large wicker baskets that carried excited passengers up and over the city.

"See it as the birds do," the Barker called out, "get your tickets here."

"I never coulda imagined such a place," Bridgit exclaimed in wonderment.

"'Tis what heaven must be like," Grace said, her eyes growing wider by the minute.

"Ireland will na have anythin like this in a hundred years," Mary replied. "I wonder what America will be like?"

"Well, it's a new country so it will not have three hundred year old churches," Peter laughed pointing across the street to a great old stone church.

"Think about that," Colin said, gazing up at a steeple that seemed to reach into the clouds, "folks were coming to this church for almost a hundred years before the first Colonists settled in the New World."

"I can na wait ta get there," Grace said. "I want ta see the mountains and the forests, I've never seen them before, except in my dreams."

"I'm hungry," one of Mary's children said, "me too," another added.

"Can we eat in a restaurant Daddy?" Grace asked.

Peter looked at Bridgit and the others, "why not. It will be nice to get away from the ships food. Lord knows we'll have plenty of it in the weeks ahead."

"I wonder what they eat in Kane?" Mary asked.

"Whatever it is, I'm sure its not just potatoes," Colin replied, "or Peel's Brimstone."

Early the following morning, Colin set out for the Blacksmith shop; while Bridgit and Mary gathered up the children and eagerly set out for the clothing stores. The evening before; they had decided that since the Bligh's had given them the money, this would be a good time to buy some things that might not be available in America. Peter told them to go on ahead, that he had some business to take care of; and that he would catch up with everyone later. He watched the women and children as they almost ran down the gang plank in anticipation of a full day of shopping; something they had never experienced before. After making certain that they were out of sight; he left the ship and headed for a Lutheran Church they had passed the day before.

"No time like the present to find out what my future might be like," he said to himself as he walked the five blocks to the church, up the stone steps and through the door. Noticing a woman sweeping the floor, he asked, "Is the Pastor here? I'd like to speak with him if I may."

The days in Liverpool went quickly; far too quickly for Bridgit and Mary who had quickly developed an addiction for shopping, and spent every daylight hour scurrying through scores of shops, both thoroughly convinced this must be what heaven would be like. By the end of the third day, Peter and Colin had to buy two large steamer trunks to hold all their purchases.

"Ladies," Peter said, "America is not a wilderness, "they do have stores there."

The Owner of the Blacksmith supply shop, upon learning that Colin was headed for America, had a large wooden shipping crate made to hold his purchases, and gave him a catalog to order from once he was settled in Kane.

"If you get tired of doing the work yourself, I'm looking for a good experienced man to represent my Company over there. You can make a lot of money selling Colin, and it's a lot easier on the arms," he laughed.

"I never thought of selling, but I'll keep it in mind," Colin answered. He whistled as he walked back to the ship remembering that just a few weeks ago, he and Mary had been so concerned about how they would survive in America. Now he had been given the money for a new shop, and a job offer as a salesman. The rumors he had heard were true; America was the land of opportunity.... and he wasn't even there yet.

Over twice the size of the Mary Jane, the Shamrock was a beautiful new ship rigged as a Bark, her three masts reaching high into the sky. Three days before, Peter had watched her glide up the harbor and anchor as she awaited a slip at the dock. An hour later, the Captain was rowed ashore, and as he stepped on the dock Peter introduced himself. Upon learning that Peter had spent many years at sea fishing, the Captain grasped his hand and confided that many years ago he had been a fisherman; and immediately there was a bond of comradeship.

As the two men headed down the street, the Captain told him that several months earlier; he had been seriously considering making a voyage to San Francisco, on the west coast of America. "Even had a poster designed to attract travelers," he added. But just as he was about to place advertisements in the newspapers, Lord Bligh approached him about chartering his ship to make several trips to America.

"To be honest Peter, while the trip to San Francisco would have made me a lot of money; I also knew that going around the Horn could cost me my ship; that's a very nasty piece of water. So when Lord Bligh made me an offer I couldn't refuse, that settled it. This next voyage will be the first trip to Boston; then two trips to New Orleans during the winter months; and another to Boston next spring."

"John's a remarkable man, in fact his entire family is," Peter replied.

"You know Lord Bligh?"....but before Peter could answer he continued, "obviously you must if you call him John. Come to think of it, he and his wife asked me to call them by their first names, but it seemed strange."

Peter laughed, "If you think that's strange, you should see them at a Friday night dance at the Catholic Church. They're both out there dancing with anyone that wants to dance and believe me, Cassie can wear you out. They may be titled aristocracy and one of the richest couples in

England, but you'd never know it in Kilrush. Their son
Lawrence and his wife Sally are just like them.

"Dancing? ....at a Catholic Church?" the Captain asked.

"Oh yes. In fact Father Grant, from Saint Patrick's and
Reverend Swagart from the Methodist Church, are among
the Bligh's closest friends."

"So Lord Bligh's chartering the Shamrock on behalf of
the two churches."

"Heavens, no. He and Cassie, plus a couple of other
wealthy friends, are paying for everything including the
passenger's fares, food...everything."

"Remarkable, very remarkable," the Captain replied. "I
don't know if you realize how fortunate you are to have
friends like the Bligh's. Out in that harbor right now, are
old floating derelicts that should never be allowed to sail
again, that are selling cheap tickets for Canada and
America.

Unscrupulous greedy Owners pack the people aboard at
double the ships capacity; and don't provide enough food
or water for the voyage. They even board passengers who
are seriously ill....I think it's criminal; but there are no
laws to stop them. If anyone dies at sea, they just dump the
body overboard. Coffin ships we call them, because that's
what they are, floating death traps."

Looking up he noticed that he had arrived at his
destination. "This is where I was headed, a meeting with
my Insurance Broker." As they shook hands, he added,
"it'll be a pleasure to have you aboard Peter. I'm looking
forward to meeting your wife and daughter....and many
more conversations."

Peter turned around and began walking back to the Mary
Jane. He had gone about three blocks when a gold lettered
sign hanging over the sidewalk caught his attention. He
stopped in front of the shop and walked in. Half an hour
later, he walked out with a rigid cardboard tube under his

arm and a smile on his face. "More questions answered," he said to himself as he headed for the docks.

That evening as everyone gathered around him, Peter unrolled the maps he had purchased. "Here's where we're going; this is Pennsylvania, and there's Kane," he said pointing to a dot on the map in western Pennsylvania. "It's about six hundred miles from Boston. Think of it, that's more than twice the length of Ireland."

Mary traced her fingers over the little marks that indicated the peaks of rugged mountains with long narrow valleys between them where their new homes would be; a place so very different from Ireland. In all their lives, none of them had ever seen a hill higher than a few hundred feet. In Pennsylvania, the mountains were thousands of feet high. Then they all stared at the sheer immense size of the United States, and the vast white empty space that covered two thirds of the map.

"We could put all of Ireland into the United States several times, and still have room left over," Colin said.

"That's good," Peter replied, "because before this is over, I have a feeling that thousands and thousands of our friends and neighbors will be joining us."

For the second time, departure day had arrived. This time however, it was not a day of sad tear filled goodbyes; but a day of eager anticipation and excitement. For the past several days, the few travelers who had some extra money roamed the streets of Liverpool; buying clothing here and there, or something to that would help them remember Liverpool in the years to come. For most of the passengers however, it was checking and rechecking the few possessions they had brought from home; and talking endlessly with others about what they thought America would be like, and how soon it would take them to find work and get settled.

Yesterday afternoon, many of the people from Kilrush had gathered along the dock to watch the Mary Jane depart; waving farewell to the Captain and crew, their last link to what had once been apart of their home. For a few brief moments, their thoughts returned to the only home they had ever known. It was in the green hills and valleys of Ireland that their parents, grandparents, and ancestors lived and died for generation after generation. Their minds told them they were going to a new world; a place that would offer them hope and a security they had before never possessed; and would never have if they returned home. But for many, their heart was on the Mary Jane. No matter how bright with opportunity America might be; or how prosperous and secure they might become; Ireland would always haunt their dreams. That fair green misty Isle that would be reborn again and again through songs, poetry, and literature written by future generations that had never been there. After all they would tell you; it had long been known that when God took a day off, he went to Ireland.

Their quiet thoughts were suddenly broken by a terrible scream, "Look, look," a woman on the dock yelled as she pointed, "that ship's sinking."

"She's right," a man exclaimed. "Those are Irish folk; I watched 'em boarding this mornin."

"'Tis one of the coffin ships we've been hearin about. They're not even out of the harbor an she's goin down. Com'on lads," he called, "there's a dory tied up by the dock. We need ta try ta save some of those folks."

While most of the people watched helplessly, horrified by what was happening; several seaman who had been working on the dock, and others from some of the nearby ships; quickly manned numerous small boats and rowed frantically toward the sinking ship, and the scores of screaming people already in the water. Mothers and fathers desperately trying to hang-on to their children; struggling to keep from being pulled under by their heavy water soaked clothing. Others were frantically trying to get away from being entangled and dragged down by the rigging of the sinking ship.

Heroic as the efforts of the rescuers were; over half the women and children, together with many of the men, drowned. For those who survived; most lost at least one member of their family; and everything they possessed went down with the ship.

The shrill high pitched sound of a boatswain's pipe interrupted the dock gazers fixation on the tragic scene unfolding before them. Today, the Shamrock was scheduled to depart in late-afternoon on the out-going tide. All their personal baggage had been brought aboard, and now it was just a matter of walking around the deck, or sitting and waiting.

An hour later, the clang of the ships bell signaled fifteen minutes until the gang plank was pulled aboard. Moments later, the First Mate informed the Captain that everyone was aboard, and final preparations had been made for departure. A tiny tug boat pulled along side and the dock lines were singled up. Satisfied that everything was ready; the Captain gave the First Mate the order to cast-off the remaining dock lines and get ready to make sail.

The tug boat eased the Shamrock away from the dock, and started pulling her toward the open water under bare poles. Half an hour later, free of the heavy harbor traffic and with open water ahead; the towing line was released and the order was given to hoist sail. Within minutes, over a dozen sails blossomed; crowning the Shamrock in a cloud of white; while a small wake began bubbling behind her.

Lining the rails, almost two hundred Irish immigrants watched as the harbor and Liverpool receded into the distance. From this point on, there was no turning back. The next time their feet touched land, it would be in America.

Colin, Mary, and their children stood at the stern rail next to Peter, Bridgit, and Grace. They thought of the letters and stories that had come back to Ireland from relatives and friends who had left years ago, never to return. Silently, they wondered if they would ever return; and how many more people would leave Ireland. Looking at their small children who were laughing as they watched the gulls following the ship; they were both sad and happy. Sad that their children would never really remember Kilrush; Arden; Saint Patrick's; Father Grant; the family and friends left behind. But happy that they would have a chance at a far better life.

Hours later under fair winds, the Shamrock entered the open waters of the Atlantic and England faded into the evening mist. Except for occasionally pointing to something on the ship that caught their attention; the passengers were mostly quiet; lost in their thoughts trying to imagine what America would be like.

For Peter, Bridgit, Colin and Mary, their thoughts were on Kane and living in the mountains. One thing was certain; everything would be new and very different from what they had known.

Grace turned around and faced forward; a gentle smile on her face. Ireland now belonged to her past. There had been another dream, one she had not told to anyone else yet. She knew what her new home would be like; and she also knew that in a few months she would have a little brother.

The End